NEVER
NEVER

LIZ BUTCHER

This is a work of fiction. Names, characters, places, and incidents are products of the author's imagination or are used fictitiously and are not to be construed as real. Any resemblance to actual events, locales, organizations, or persons, living or dead, is entirely coincidental.

Cover Design by Andrew Butcher
Editing by Heather Haunert

THIS BOOK IS FOR THE GREATEST MAN
I'VE EVER KNOWN.
MY POPPY.
MY BIGGEST FAN.
THERE AREN'T ANY WORDS TO
EXPRESS HOW MUCH YOU ARE MISSED.

CHAPTER ONE

Wendy blinked three times before opening her eyes as wide as she could. Despite her efforts to see, only blackness greeted her. The darkness was thick and inky, and she stretched her arms out as far as she could reach, only to encounter nothing. Wendy felt more curious than afraid, but as she questioned that, she was pulled from her thoughts; the laughter of children encircled her. She turned one way, then the other, hoping to catch a glimpse of them, but there was nothing.

The joy in their laughter brought a smile to her face, and she took a moment to simply enjoy it. As she did, the darkness faded away, revealing an oasis of green trees and blooming flowers in every imaginable colour. It almost overwhelmed her senses so that she forgot the children, as she adjusted to the amazing smells and increasing light.

Wendy jumped as a loud *whoop* came from beside her. She turned to see a boy of about thirteen. Noticing her startled expression, he gestured up to the large tree branch he'd jumped from and winked playfully at her before running through the trees ahead. With each tree he passed, another boy joined him, then another, and yet another. She tried to count them, but they were so busy ducking and weaving as they pretended to gallivant and sword fight that it was impossible. She could determine, however, that they ranged in age—the eldest appeared to be the teen boy that had startled her, whereas the youngest didn't look older than four or five.

Their joy was infectious and swept over her in waves of warmth, like rays from the sun. Feeling content, Wendy sat down amongst the flowers to watch the boys laugh and play.

Is there really any better sound in the world than children laughing?

As she watched them, a thought niggled at her, trying to push its way to the forefront of her mind. Although she tried to ignore it—preferring to stay in her joyful bubble—the thought persisted until she finally acknowledged it.

Where am I, and how did I get here?

As though the enchantment was broken, the boys stopped what they were doing, their laughter ceasing abruptly as they all turned to face her. Her own smile was replaced by a heavy frown. She wanted to tell the boys that everything was fine, to keep playing.

Placing her palms on the grass, she started to push herself up to her feet but then froze. Right before her eyes, the colour from the boys seemed to drain away—not just the rosiness in their cheeks but the very tone of their skin, the colour of their hair, and the brightness of their clothes. Gasping, she watched dark, black shadows spread around their eyes that now sunk into their tiny faces.

Wendy forced herself to look away, telling herself she was having a bad dream. She turned her attention instead to the flowers surrounding her. They, too, faded to grey and lay wilted and brittle around her. Gone were the beautiful floral scents she'd inhaled only moments before, replaced by repugnant smells of rotting fruit and something akin to rotten. The stench was an onslaught to her senses, and she gagged, her eyes watering.

Each breath took increasing effort. She clutched at her chest as though she could somehow ease the constriction. A hissing, deflating sound forced her to look up at the boys, and her eyes widened as a high-pitched whimper escaped her. The boys were mere shadows of their former selves—their eyes were dark, black pits, and their mouths hung slack in silent howls. Heart-wrenching sobs filled her ears, and she scanned the boys, trying to see which of them emitted the terrible sobbing before realising she was the source.

Movement beyond them caught her attention. She gripped at the brittle grass, oblivious to the way it disintegrated in her hands as she stared at a pair of bulbous, disembodied eyes. They were hovering a head or so above the tallest boy. The eyes were green, an unearthly hue, both vibrant and iridescent— and terrifying. She knew those eyes. She knew who they belonged to.

Wendy... My Wendy... You can't hide from me... I'm coming for you...

Scrambling backward, she tried to get to her feet so she could run away, but thick, thorny vines shot out from the dead flowers, binding her in place.

Wendy tumbled to the ground, banging her knee painfully on the cold, wooden floor. Swearing to herself, she tried to free her legs from the tangle of sheets. She could still see the unnatural glow of his eyes in their disembodied hover, watching her in the darkness.

Squeezing her eyes tightly, she clutched the sheets to her chest.

It's not real. He's not here. It's not real.

She repeated the mantra until her breathing slowed, and she felt less like a terrified child and more like the capable adult she was.

Opening her eyes, Wendy cautiously scanned the room. She knew it was just a nightmare—she'd had it more times than she cared to count. Yet, she struggled to shake off the horrible questions that always followed.

What if? What if he's still out there looking for me?

A fiery ball of panic welled within her chest, before spreading its prickling warmth throughout her body. She felt heat rise up her neck and into her cheeks and instinctively gasped as though the anxiety was trying to drag her under some imagined, watery depths. She fought against it, trying to focus on annoyance rather than fear—it'd been so long since he'd visited her in her sleep that a part of her might have actually believed the nightmares were over for good.

With the initial wave of paralysing fear subsiding, her rational mind surged ahead, and Wendy felt her helpless inner child slipping away. Reaching up, she fumbled for the bedside lamp, instantly relieved as the room flooded with light. Yet, the nightmare left a heavy veil of anxiety behind, making it impossible for her to discard the feeling that something—or someone—was coming.

Untangling herself from the sheets, Wendy got to her feet. She tossed the sheets on the bed before sitting on its edge. As tired as she was, she was hesitant to lie back down—the single bed was now a little uncomfortable for her adult form—instead, she scanned her childhood bedroom. It was little surprise the nightmare had returned. Here. Now. It was as though she'd dared it to, simply by sleeping in this room.

Nothing could have prepared her for seeing his eyes again. The thought alone was enough to make her heart start pounding like a drum. She focused on where the light was brightest, radiating out across the base of the tarnished lamp and illuminating the white bedside table. Like most of the objects in her room, both had seen better days.

Looking around the room, Wendy scanned the posters of Jonathan Brandis and NKOTB adorning the walls, feeling disconnected from the young girl who'd once put them there. There had been a time when this room had been her haven, a sanctuary just for her. He took that away from her. She hated that she still felt this way, in what had once been her favourite room in the whole house. The bedroom represented her—the old Wendy—the fifteen-year-old with rose-coloured glasses and a happy, uncomplicated life. It felt like someone else's life.

Wendy sighed; her sorrow overtaking her anxiety. The reason for her return hurtled to the forefront of her mind. Today was their mother's funeral.

For the past three weeks, Wendy had stayed in the guest room closest to her mother's. Her brother, Michael, had already made it up for her without needing to check her sleeping preference. Yet, on the eve of the funeral, Wendy decided it was high time she moved past fears and sleep in her childhood bedroom. She'd ignored the fact that everything was exactly the same as it was the last time she'd seen it— or that there wasn't a speck of dust or the musty smell you would expect in a room untouched for years. Instead, she told herself spending the night there would be a form of closure. It was easy during

5

the day to convince oneself nothing would happen, yet in the dark of the night—and on the back of the nightmare—that logic felt like a pipedream.

It wasn't that Wendy never visited, though she didn't as often as she should have. Her own place was only an hour away, in the hustle and bustle of the city. Wendy had often used the distance as an excuse not to visit more, but now that both of her parents were gone, it seemed like a ridiculous excuse. She knew her parents understood the real reason she kept away.

Taking a deep breath, Wendy rubbed her hands along the tops of her legs, not wanting to dredge up the memories of her fifteen-year-old self. When everything had changed. The three weeks she'd spent with her ailing mother was the longest she'd stayed under her parents' roof since. The long absences were easily justified by the knowledge her brothers were there, though they'd only been children themselves at the time. Now, they ran the family business— Darling Winery.

Even after their father passed away, Wendy convinced herself Michael and John were more than capable of looking after their mother. She was ashamed to admit that even after receiving her mother's diagnosis, she still chose not to increase her visits. Yet, when she received the call from Michael telling her she was almost out of time, Wendy forced herself to move home for the duration of their mother's last days.

Wendy was on leave for a mere twenty-four hours when a teenage girl was reported missing. A rather nasty argument ensued between her and Michael when she told him she wanted to work the case. It was a moral conundrum that tore her in half—of course she wanted to spend her mother's last days with her, but she also felt a responsibility to the missing girl.

NEVER, NEVER

It was a high-profile case—the teenage daughter of the newly elected Lord Mayor Malcolm Fryair. The news appeared to have a bias towards a disgruntled teen wanting to torment her parents, rather than something insidious. Watching it, she felt her instincts grind, and she knew she wanted to work the case. In the end, the choice wasn't hers. The inspector ordered her to take her leave as planned and shut her down when she questioned who he'd put on the case. The decision angered her, but there was nothing she could do aside from tracking the case via the news and deciphering what facts she could.

Lilly, her long-time girlfriend, had offered to come with her, but Wendy declined. As much as she loved Lilly, she needed this time alone with her family. Her daughter, Jane, came and went, happily juggling her work commitments as a busy, city-based journalist, and spending time at the family estate.

Together, with her two younger brothers, they fulfilled their mother's wishes to spend her final days in the family home—she wanted to pass there, in the same room where her husband had passed in his sleep ten years earlier, and not in some cold, sterile hospital room. They'd provided the best medical support money could buy and set their mother up comfortably in her own bed, surrounded by monitors and equipment, and with nursing staff and family waiting on her hand and foot. She'd wanted for nothing—except more time.

Rubbing her eyes with the heels of her hands to stop the tears that threatened to spill, Wendy conceded there was no hope of returning to sleep. Yet, she was beyond fatigued and reluctantly lay back against the pillows and stared up at the ceiling, hoping to at least give her body the chance to rest. Instead, it felt like the nightmare had triggered something within her, causing old wounds to crack open and ooze the virulent memories into the forefront of her mind. The lack of sleep rendered her all but helpless to stop them. Instead, she tried to focus on happier elements.

Recalling her early childhood, there was nothing but fond memories—they'd led a charmed life in their vineyard bubble, exactly how they all liked it. Wendy was close to her brothers and her parents and was the well-known favourite of Nanna—her father's beloved childhood nanny, who had become an ingrained member of the family and lived at the estate since her father was a boy.

The perfection of her world was not meant to last. Wendy sat up as another wave of anxiety swept over her. She reluctantly thought of those painful memories. Pushing her mind to skip forward to the aftermath, she thought about how her relationships with her family changed. Despite their best efforts and intentions, things were never the same— especially between Wendy and her parents. They'd all but smothered her with love and the illusion of protection that only thinly veiled the guilt she saw in their eyes when they looked at her.

Her brothers knew something bad happened but were just relieved their big sister was home again. It was Nanna she grew closer to and confided in. She knew it hurt her parents, especially her mother, yet Wendy never seemed to move beyond the feeling that they'd let her down. They were her parents— their job was to protect her, to keep her safe. They had failed.

During her last conversation with her mother, Wendy saw the intense desperation in her mother's eyes as she pleaded with Wendy to listen to her. She'd gripped her hand with remarkable strength, given her frail condition. Wendy couldn't explain why, but something about the look in her mother's eyes, the expression on her face, stunned and scared her.

Nothing her mother said made any sense. At the time, Wendy told herself it was a consequence of all the pain medication her mother was on, yet she felt the urgency behind her words. More importantly, her detective skills refused to allow her to ignore her gut feeling that there was a truth behind the final words her mother had desperately tried to impart—and she knew in her heart that her mother knew she was about to die.

Wendy gripped the side of the bed with both hands as she chastised herself for not being able to decipher the message her mother had left behind. In a huff, she got up from the bed and walked to the window, pushing it open. Met with a rush of cool night air, laced with the smell of her mother's beloved roses that lined the front of the house below, she inhaled deeply. It felt rejuvenating, and her anxiety began to subside. She made a mental note to gather some of the roses for the funeral and rubbed her arms, more for comfort than against the cool. Looking out over the vineyard that spanned across the land as far as she could see, she pictured the ghosts of their childhood, of three children running and hiding in the vines—one of their favourite pastimes.

Wendy tried to fix the image in her mind of her mother working among the roses, tenderly pruning and caring for them, always smiling—humming a tune to herself more often than not. She focused on the memory with everything she had until the last of the awful, exhausting emotions slipped away. She didn't feel safe—not completely. She never did—but she felt reassured, as though her mother had wrapped her arms around her.

Wendy yawned, calm enough for fatigue to set in. Leaving the window open, she returned to the bed and buried herself in a cocoon of blankets, the lamp still on. Just as she was about to fall into the comforting nothingness of sleep, her mother's smile was replaced by the ominous green eyes of her nightmares, and she hurled the blankets off and pressed her back up against the headboard.

As she again scanned the room, her eyes wide, hot tears spilled down her cheeks; her fear melded with anger and frustration—she felt violated that the horror of her nightmares encroached on such a precious memory. After a few moments, she launched herself away from the safety of the wall and off the bed and strode over to the closed bedroom door.

With shaking hands, she grabbed the dressing gown from its hook and wrapped it tightly around her. Stepping over to the antique dresser, she leaned down to inspect her reflection. There were dark circles under her hazel eyes, and her deep, chestnut hair—still pulled back in a braid—was wildly dishevelled, giving her a somewhat crazy appearance. She tugged at her face, trying to smooth out any imaginary lines, feeling much older than her thirty-five years. Her self-inspection was interrupted as she stifled a yawn and resigned to the fact there would be no more sleep for her tonight.

Leaving the room, she felt both agitated and relieved when she pulled the door closed behind her. Skilfully manoeuvring down the staircase—she knew the path of each creaky spot like the back of her hand—Wendy made it to the ground floor without a sound and walked into the kitchen. She gave a startled yelp. Her brothers were sitting at the kitchen island.

"Couldn't sleep?" John asked, pushing his glasses back up his nose. Wendy gave him a wry smile in answer and walked over to one of the kitchen cabinets to retrieve her favourite teacup.

"Wendy? Sleep? That would imply she'd stopped moving for more than ten minutes," joked her youngest brother, Michael, running his fingers through his already tousled blonde hair.

"Oh, shut up. I sleep—I just don't need a lot. What about you two? Clearly, the sandman hasn't been kind to you either." She stood opposite them at the bench, reached for the pot of tea sitting between them and poured herself a generous cup.

John sighed as he wrapped his hands around his cup. "I got pissed off with the tossing and turning."

"Same here," Michael added, stifling a yawn. "I couldn't sleep knowing we're burying Mum today. I still can't get my head around the idea."

"I know," Wendy agreed, running her finger around the rim of the cup, not having the words to say anything further. They sat silently for a few moments, each lost in their own thoughts.

"Does this make us orphans now?" Michael asked.

John sighed, rubbing his temples. "I guess it does—they're both gone now. But can you be considered an orphan when you're an adult?"

Michael shrugged, then was overcome with another yawn, and Wendy stared quietly into the cup of tea in front of her, as though it somehow held the answers to all of her questions. "What time is it?" she finally asked.

John tapped the screen of his phone, which lay on the bench, revealing the time atop a background image of their parents. "It's a quarter to five."

Michael queried, "Itching to catch the early morning news?" His smile said he was joking, but the sharp glint in his eye revealed his annoyance.

"No, I wanted to know the time. Since when was wanting to watch the news a crime anyway?" she asked, keeping her voice playful, not wanting a fight with her brother today of all days. It wasn't like them to fight, but he'd been sour since they'd argued over her wanting to take on the missing girl case. Since their mother passed, he seemed to be trying to start an argument, and she wondered how much longer he would stew on his grievances before finally snapping. She didn't have to wait long.

"Our mother's not even in the ground yet, and you can't wait to get back to work," he accused.

"That's not true, nor is it fair," Wendy replied, wishing her brother had opted to stew on it a little longer.

"You're kidding me, aren't you? Are the two of you really going to argue about this *today*?" John intervened. Wendy and Michael said nothing; both lowered sheepish gazes to their mugs.

"That's what I thought," John continued, "and Wendy, if you want to watch the news, then watch the bloody news."

Offering an olive branch, Michael cleared his throat and looked up at his sister. "What time is Lilly arriving?"

"Fairly early, as far as I know. She wanted to meet us here rather than at the cemetery."

"I'm surprised she didn't spend time here with you," John stated.

Wendy flicked her brother a quick look. "She would have jumped at the chance, but I asked her not to."

"Why on earth not?" Michael asked, and Wendy saw John's tactful look, which their brother chose to ignore.

Wendy shrugged. "I wanted this time together, just us. And Jane, of course. I mean, not saying Lilly isn't my family. Of course she is..."

John leaned forward and grasped his sister's hand with his own. "You don't have to explain. We understand."

"Thanks. I appreciate it," she replied and picked up her cup, taking a sip of tea.

"But out of curiosity, is Lilly allowed to keep a toothbrush at your place yet? I mean, you guys have been together for what, three or four years now?" John joked, in an attempt to lighten the mood.

"Ugh, seriously..." Wendy groaned, looking up at the ceiling to hide the blush on her cheeks. Her brothers chuckled.

"You realize most couples actually cohabitate after this long," Michael jumped on the bandwagon.

"I'm so glad my commitment issues are a source of amusement for you both." Wendy rolled her eyes but smiled at them both. She knew they didn't mean anything by their jibes.

"We're just messing around," John said with a smile, "though Lilly must have the patience of an angel."

Wendy shrugged. "She gets me. Honestly, I think she enjoys her own independence as much as I do, so it works for us."

"That's the main thing," John replied. Wendy, still feeling coy, turned her back to her brothers and took her time refilling the kettle for another round of tea.

"Are the two of you planning to continue working the vineyard?" she asked over her shoulder.

"Of course, why wouldn't we?" John asked. "I know you think we took on the family business out of obligation, but I, for one, actually love working here. I can't speak for Michael, but I can't imagine doing anything else."

"I can imagine doing other things," Michael stated with a smile, "but I'm with John. This is where I belong."

"What about you? Can you see yourself joining us here, or is that a stupid question?"

Wendy chuckled softly, "It is a little. I love my job—I don't think there's much detective work at a winery."

"Is there any tea left for me?" Came a voice from behind them. They all turned to see Jane leaning against the doorway, smiling at them.

"Of course there is," Michael replied. He got up from his stool, peering out the window as though surprised to find the sun had risen. He grabbed another cup from the overhead cupboard and placed it in front of his niece, and she joined them in the kitchen.

"Good morning, sweetheart," Wendy said. Her daughter walked over and kissed her mother on the cheek. "Did you get much sleep?"

"Funnily enough, I did," Jane replied, moving on to her uncles, greeting them both with a kiss and a hug before sitting on the spare stool next to Michael.

Wendy looked over at her daughter. It still surprised her how alike they looked—so much so they were often mistaken for sisters. Jane had the same thick, long chestnut hair that fell in natural waves around her heart-shaped face and the same hazel eyes. The soft, early morning sunlight came through the window at such an angle that it appeared to encircle Jane's head like an aura or a halo.

It made Wendy smile—but a sense of foreboding washed over her like a buzz of electricity, and a rushing noise filled her ears with such intensity that she feared she'd fall over, and the smile quickly fell from her face. She gripped the bench to stabilize herself. Forcing her gaze from her daughter, she told herself it was only the remnants of her nightmare coupled with the day ahead that had her senses on edge.

"Mum? What is it? Are you okay?" Jane asked, half rising from her chair.

Wendy gave her best reassuring smile and brushed off their concerned looks. "I'm fine, really. I'm just over-tired." She busied herself with refilling everyone's cups, knowing all of them would see the lie in her eyes given the chance.

Wendy always prided herself on her innate sixth sense—it had proven essential in more than one case. The downside was that she couldn't pick and choose when it reared its head, and a lot was going on in her head.

Something else was also niggling from the darkest recesses of her mind, trying to get her attention. She mentally cast it back into the shadows, refusing to acknowledge it. Today wasn't the day. Wendy cleared her throat, wanting to change the subject. "Has anyone checked in on Nanna?" she asked.

"I popped in before I went to bed last night, but she was already in bed," Michael answered, wrapping his hands around his newly warm cup.

"Was Carole still up?" John asked.

Michael nodded. "Yeah, but I didn't want to disturb her more than I did already. I'm sure she looks forward to her own time. I just said a quick goodnight and left."

"Why does she have a caretaker instead of just going into a home like normal people do?" Jane half-joked.

"Jane! What a horrible thing to say. It's not like you to be so cold. This has been her home for a lot longer than you or I have been around."

"I didn't mean it like that—exactly. I just mean that this house is enormous, and now it's just Nanna here with Uncle Mike and Uncle John spending most of their time out in the vineyard or working out in the warehouses. It sounds like the setting for a horror movie—the senile old woman and her caretaker, navigating the depths of an old house…"

John laughed aloud. "There's that fantastic imagination coming out, Jane. You were never going to be anything other than a writer."

Jane gave her uncle a rueful smile before looking to Michael for back-up.

"I hear the sentiment behind your creative delivery, and if she ever became a danger to herself, we might have to reconsider her living arrangements. But for now, she's not doing any harm, either to herself or anyone else, and Carole has proven more than adequate in her role. Both Dad and Mum wanted to see out their final days here, and so does Nanna. She's also somewhat beyond benefiting from any of the social aspects provided by residential care, and a change in scene at this point would likely do more harm than good."

"That's very diplomatic of you, Uncle," Jane replied.

"Look, sweetheart, I know you and Nanna have never been the best of friends—and that's not your fault. But she's still family. I'm sure she would love it if you went and said hello," Wendy said.

Jane stood up and walked over to the kitchen sink to rinse out her cup. "You know that's not true. She likely wouldn't know who I was or if I was even there—or she would pretend not to."

Wendy went to open her mouth in protest but was stopped as Jane placed a hand on her mother's shoulder. "Maybe later, Mum," she compromised. "For now, I'm going to freshen up and get ready. It's going to be a long day."

Wendy watched her daughter leave the room and sighed.

"It's not your fault they don't get along," Michael said.

"I just don't understand it. Nanna was always so kind to us, so loving. I can't help but feel that Jane has missed out on getting to know that side of her because of how... well... you know."

John reached over and clasped her hand in his. "We all adore Jane—Mum and Dad did too, you know that."

Wendy gave her brothers a small smile, knowing the day was going to be sad enough without adding to it. "I'd better go make sure Carole has Nanna up." She took a final swig from her cup of tea and left the kitchen.

CHAPTER TWO

Wendy took her time walking through the manor towards Nanna's quarters, Jane's queries echoing in her mind. Her own mother had voiced similar concerns, albeit more tactfully. She hadn't wanted to put Nanna into a nursing home, but she had wanted to move her from her wing—which seemed so far from the rest of the house these days—and settle her in a room closer to her own. The doctor had advised against it, stating familiarity was key. As a compromise, her parents had hired Carole, a home health nurse, who had turned out to be an invaluable companion.

Wendy wandered through one wide hallway to the next, pausing to look at the odd portrait or artwork that adorned the walls and had for as long as she could remember. Yet, she couldn't remember the last time she'd actually paid any attention to them—if she ever had. It felt like only yesterday that Nanna had chastised her and her brothers for running through these halls, far more fearful they'd break something than that they'd hurt themselves.

Nanna had always been kindly, yet stern—a perfect counterbalance to her carefree parents who, more often than not, were chastised alongside their children. Wendy smiled, recalling her mother's hand grasping her own, the skirts of their dresses billowing out around them as her mother spun them around to hide behind a nearby statue while Nanna called out to them.

She'd looked up at her mother as they crouched together, both of them stifling their giggles with their hands, her mother's eyes vibrant with laughter.

Wendy wiped tears from her eyes that she hadn't noticed forming and picked up the pace. She knew from their father's passing that any recollection of memories would be bittersweet and sad—more so now that both parents were gone.

The door to Nanna's quarters was slightly ajar. Wendy knocked twice before calling out. When there was no answer, she pushed it open and walked into the sitting room. The large television was on silent where it sat on a low wooden cabinet, a black lace crocheted runner buffering its stand from the wood. She saw the morning's news highlights flashing across the screen but forced herself to look away.

"Hello? Nanna? Carole?" She walked over to the lounge and took a seat, not wanting to venture any further without invitation, despite the numerous times she'd been there. It was a little strange, but even though Nanna's residence was in the same house, it always felt like she was visiting an entirely different place.

"Good morning, Wendy. How are you holding up?" Carole asked, stepping through a door to the left of the room, wiping her arms with a towel. She was a short, middle-aged woman with kindly brown eyes and olive skin and curly black hair that always fought to free itself, no matter how she tried to restrain it, resulting in her always seeming somewhat dishevelled.

"As well as can be expected, thank you. How is Nanna this morning?"

"About the same. We've just finished with her shower."

Wendy nodded. "Does she know what today is?"

Carole sighed and glanced over her shoulder. "It's hard to say, though she isn't having a very good morning, so I'm thinking so."

"Could I see her?"

"Of course. I'll just finish helping her dress, and I'll bring her out."

Wendy gave a nod of agreement—she knew how particular Nanna was about her appearance—or at least had been—and Carole was meticulous in upholding Nanna's expectations, regardless of whether Nanna was aware of it or not. Carole retreated to the sitting room, and Wendy tried to refrain from fidgeting with her hands while fighting to keep her memories at bay.

Ow!

Holding her hand up, she found she'd dug her nails into her cuticles so hard that she'd caused one to tear and bleed. Despite the pain, she was grateful for the distraction.

At the soft sound of wheels turning, Wendy looked up to see Carole pushing Nanna into the room. She watched Carole manoeuvre the wheelchair beside the lounge before helping Nanna out of the chair and onto the more comfortable couch. "No walker today?" Wendy asked, concerned by how frail Nanna looked.

"Not today. She's a little unsteady on her feet," Carole answered kindly, and with her hand on Nanna's shoulder, leaned down to eye level. "Wendy's here to see you. I'll leave you ladies alone while I go clean up." Flashing Wendy a quick smile, she turned and left the room.

"Hey, Nanna. You look so beautiful this morning," Wendy said as she walked over and kissed her on the cheek. She sat beside her. Picking up one of Nanna's hands from where it rested on her lap, Wendy held it with both of her own.

She convinced herself she felt the faintest of squeezes from Nanna and squeezed back while admiring her elegant outfit, which consisted of a long, black, pleated silk skirt and a black high-necked top decorated with a delicate spray of dark grey beads across the chest. Around her neck hung the heart-shaped pendant she always wore—Wendy knew it held images of her parents on one side and the three Darling children on the other. As a child, Wendy had often loved sitting on Nanna's lap asking her to show them to her again and again.

Wendy reached over and gently tucked a loose strand of pearly white hair behind Nanna's ear, admiring her trademark chignon that Carole had mastered.

"It's going to be a big day, Nanna, for all of us. I know you loved Mother like she was your own, just like you loved Father and all of us." Wendy waited patiently, but there was no answer as Nanna stared stoically at the television. Despite her best efforts, she was unable to work out if Nanna was lucid or not. Instead, she looked around the room, listening to the sounds of Carole bustling around unseen beyond the sitting room.

The walls were cluttered with framed photographs of the family, going back to when her father was a child, and Nanna first joined the household. It was a reminder that Nanna didn't share Darling blood. She was part of their family, regardless. Though for the first time, she wondered how Nanna had come to be employed by her grandparents—who was she beforehand? Where had she come from? Did she have a family of her own? Wendy didn't recall her ever mentioning any. To her knowledge, there'd been no one to contact as Nanna deteriorated. It saddened her to realise no one left could tell her—least of all Nanna herself.

Despite the lack of reference to her own family tree, Nanna had been well-schooled on the Darling family history and had beguiled Wendy and her brothers with embellished stories of their ancestors. As a result, Wendy was fascinated by old photographs and looking into the eyes of those long since passed. She wondered if one day, her descendants would feel the same way about photos of her.

Feeling a lump forming in her throat, she turned and looked over the sparsely decorated living room. It hadn't always been so, but once Nanna's mobility declined, changes were made. The only furniture in the room was a well-worn chaise, with an ugly quilted cushion Wendy made during her first year of high school, and a neatly folded blanket, crocheted in shades of blue. A small, wooden, rectangular coffee table sat in front of it, with stacks of books on the ledge beneath that may have once been read but had been left untouched for ages. She glanced at Carole's watch left behind on the coffee table, and seeing the time, reluctantly got up.

"Well, I'd better go and get ready myself. I'll come and check on you again when it's time to go, okay?" She leaned over and planted a soft kiss on Nanna's cheek, careful not to disrupt her carefully applied makeup. As Wendy stood, Carole walked back into the sitting room as though on cue.

Wendy gave her a quick wave as she walked around the couch. Reaching the door, she turned back, surprised to see Nanna clasping the locket in her hand. It was just for a moment, then she lowered her hand into her lap, the locket once again forgotten.

Wendy walked into her bedroom and over to the wardrobe where her black dress hung, ready for the funeral.

"There she is," came a voice from the window, and Wendy jumped. She turned to find Lilly sitting in the desk chair she'd dragged over, her feet resting upon the window ledge.

"Hey, love. I'm so sorry. I didn't realise you'd arrived." She took a moment, admiring the beauty of her girlfriend, which still took her breath away even after three - going on four - years. Lilly wore a black, long-sleeved dress with a wide, pointed collar and matching cuffs, over black opaque stockings, and a pair of black Doc Martin boots. Lilly's Native American heritage was evident with her beautiful almond-shaped chocolate eyes, her high cheekbones, and thick, flowing black hair that hung down over the back of the chair.

Relishing in the attention, Lilly lowered her feet and got up from the chair. "Don't worry about it. Michael said you were checking on Nanna, and I was happy to wait. Plus, I wanted to finally check out the mysterious bedroom from your misspent youth. It's insightful, to say the least."

Wendy laughed, "Don't judge me."

"Who's judging? NKOTB was the bomb." They laughed, and Lilly reached out and pulled Wendy in an embrace. Wendy hugged her tightly, realising she'd missed her girlfriend far more than she'd expected, and she wondered if she'd made the decision to distance herself. Pulling back, Lilly placed her hands on either side of Wendy's face and held her gaze. "How are you, really?"

"Tired...and sad. More deeply sad than I think I've ever been." Lilly was the one person Wendy could be one hundred percent honest with all the time. "Even when Dad died, it hurt like hell, and I miss him so much, but I knew we still had Mum, you know?"

Lilly nodded. "Of course. You don't need to explain. I'm here for you. Anything you need."

Wendy sighed and ran her hands down to Lilly's hips and leaned in for a kiss. She felt the stress of the past few weeks slip away like a discarded robe. "Actually, there is something I need," she said coyly. She grabbed Lilly's hands and led her to the bed.

"Now?" Lilly giggled, following without protest.

"Now," Wendy commanded, gently shoving her onto the bed.

Wendy stood, staring down at her mother's coffin, Jane tightly holding one hand and Lilly the other. She was aware that the reverend was speaking, but his words sounded far away, and she struggled to concentrate, to listen. Instead, Wendy's thoughts drifted to the tombstone beside her mother's freshly dug grave—her father's—and she wondered if they would truly be together again in their final resting place.

Inspecting her mother's coffin, she wondered if it was the one she'd selected, or if her brothers had made a change. The colour of the wood looked different from what she remembered—it had a honey-coloured warmth to it, which she admitted to herself was quite beautiful. She admired the way it complimented the deep pinks and stark whites of the bouquet of roses that rested atop it—from her mother's beloved rose garden, of course.

The rose garden. As the tear-inducing memory worked its way to the forefront of her mind, Wendy lifted her head and tried to distract herself by inspecting the large crowd in attendance. She recognised numerous faces—those who worked for the family, both past and present, distant relatives, and a large number of beloved friends of her parents that were as much family as anyone else. There were a great number of faces she didn't know, which wasn't surprising. The family name was a well-respected one.

It occurred to her that her mother—a social butterfly that had loved nothing more than surrounding herself with laughter and chatter—would have loved the turnout. The hot tears stung her eyes, more persistent than ever, and she blinked them away behind her oversized black sunglasses. Lilly squeezed her hand, and Wendy squeezed back. Once again, she tried to pay attention to the sermon, but she felt on edge, her senses suddenly on high alert.

An icy chill traced along the back of her neck, and her heart quickened as she felt herself being watched. Looking over her shoulder, she scanned the solemn faces before looking beyond them to the sparsely placed trees and the row of parked cars lining the narrow road beyond them. There was only the funeral party on the grounds, and yet, she couldn't shake the feeling that someone else was watching her.

Lilly squeezed her hand again, and Wendy turned around, ignoring her girlfriend's questioning expression. The sensation was persistent, like something was slowly crawling from the small of her back, along her spine, and up the back of her neck. It took all of her restraint not to reach up and swat away the imagined offender.

It felt like an eternity before the service finished. Wendy let herself be led away to the waiting cars; the loud bang of car doors closing was abrasive on her heightened nerves. Lilly opened the car door for her, but Wendy hesitated, turning back to where they'd all stood, half expecting to find a lone stranger looking back at her.

"Wendy?" Lilly prompted.

Wendy got into the car and slid into the middle of the back seat, and Lilly got in beside her, pulling the door closed. Jane was already seated to her right.

"I'm sorry," Wendy murmured.

"For what?" Jane asked.

"I zoned out back there."

"Don't apologise, Mum," Jane replied, removing a tissue from under the sleeve of her dress and wiping at her eyes with it. "I think Grandma would have loved the roses you picked."

Wendy nodded.

"Who were you looking for?" Jane asked.

"What do you mean?"

"You were looking over your shoulder at one point like you were looking for someone. Then again before we got in the car."

"Oh, that was nothing. I thought I saw someone, but I was mistaken." She stared straight out through the front windshield, not leaving room for further questions.

The house came alive as people filed in for the wake, as though relishing in the bustling noise of a social engagement. Wendy, however, felt her energy drain away with each commiseration and recalled memories their guests felt compelled to share. She watched with envy as Carole wheeled Nanna away for a rest, wanting nothing more than to go with her.

Instead, she found herself an empty chair in a corner and sat down. She leaned her head against the wall and folded her hands limply in her lap. There she stayed lost in her own grieving thoughts until she watched Michael say farewell to the last of the guests.

"I'm assuming you feel as exhausted as you look," Lilly stated as she approached and crouched down beside the chair. Wendy gave her a tired smile. "It's been a long day. Week. Month. What time is it?"

Lilly glanced at her watch. "It's just past five. I guess everyone stayed longer than we thought they would."

Wendy forced herself off the chair and looked around the room while stretching out her stiff arms and legs. "This place has that effect on people." She covered her mouth as a yawn took over. Lilly stood and held her hand out. Wendy took it without question, allowing Lilly to lead her to the stairs. "Where are we going? I need to start cleaning up."

"No, you don't. I'm going to run you a hot bath, and you are going to have some time to yourself. I don't care if you only stay in there fifteen minutes or a couple of hours, but you're going to do it."

"But..."

"No buts. The caterers have already started the clean-up, and I'll rally Jane and your brothers to help with whatever's left." Lilly placed her hand on Wendy's shoulder and turned her to face her. "I've given you the space you've needed this past month, but I can see you've spent so much energy on looking after everyone else that you haven't taken care of yourself. I know your love/hate relationship with this place and how you get when you spend any length of time here—and I'm not sure what possessed you to want to sleep in your old room—but I don't think it's good for you."

Wendy opened her mouth to protest, but Lilly held up her hand to stop her. "I promised I would never question you about your past, but that doesn't mean I'm blind. Between your mother, your memories, and your guilt over not working that missing girl case, I don't imagine you've slept more than a couple of hours at a time in weeks."

Wendy smiled sheepishly, looking down at her feet. "You're far too perceptive."

Lilly chuckled. "No, I just know you better than you know yourself sometimes. Does it still intimidate you?"

Wendy shrugged. "A little. But it's also nice."

"Good. On that note, let's get your cute butt upstairs."

Wendy admitted the hot water felt amazing against her exhausted body, encapsulating her like a warm blanket on a cold winter's evening. She didn't know if it was her fatigue, or the effects of the oils Lilly had poured into the bath, or both, but the combination was intoxicating. Wendy felt herself relaxing against her will, and as she found herself starting to nod off, she reluctantly pulled the plug and stood, watching the water circle down the drain, taking what it could of her stress with it.

Naked, she strolled into the bedroom and found her favourite pair of comfy leggings and a t-shirt laid out on the bed for her.

"Feeling better?" Lilly asked, back in the chair by the window with her feet up on the windowsill, a book in her hand.

Wendy gave a small smile, pulling on her clothes. "Absolutely. Thanks so much for taking care of everything downstairs. I hope it wasn't too much work."

"Are you kidding me? We hardly got a look in—the staff your brother hired was crazy-efficient. In fact, he seemed pretty keen to hire them on a permanent basis."

Wendy chuckled, pulling her wet hair up into a messy bun. "That probably isn't a bad idea. My brothers will be so busy with work, and this place needs some attention."

She walked over and gave Lilly a long, thankful kiss. As she straightened, she reached her arms up above her head and stretched, smiling to herself as Lilly watched in appreciation. Wendy's smile fell away as she noticed Lilly's overnight bag beneath her legs.

"You're not staying?"

Lilly lowered her feet and sat up straight. "Of course I can if you want me to, but I know you too well. You need to be alone. Well, as alone as you can be here with your family…"

"You are my family, too…"

"I know, sweetheart. You know what I mean. If you would like me to stay, I will—but don't ask me to stay because you think it will make me happy. You need to do what you need to do—I'll wait."

Wendy picked up Lilly's hands in her own, admiring her girlfriend's smooth olive skin. "It's ridiculous how well you know me—it's even more ridiculous you're still with me."

Lilly laughed. "It's true—you're incredibly lucky to have me, but I'm glad you acknowledge it." She squeezed Wendy's hands, and Wendy leaned in to kiss her, suddenly overwhelmed with gratitude.

Lilly pulled away. "I'd better leave before I end up in your bed again, and you're stuck with me for the evening."

"Would that be so bad?" Wendy smiled.

"Not at all. But having something to look forward to when you come home sure won't hurt." She gave Wendy a quick kiss and released her hands before picking up her bag off the floor.

"I'll walk you out," Wendy offered, and with her arm around Lilly's waist, she left the room.

CHAPTER THREE

Sitting on the back veranda, Wendy watched the remnants of the sunset, admiring the changing colours of the sky over the sprawling vineyard and reflected on what was one of the hardest days of her life. Like she periodically did, Wendy pondered the possibility of asking Lilly to finally move in with her, knowing that she wouldn't. It amazed her that Lilly understood her need for her own space when Wendy found it hard to explain, even to herself. Yet losing her mother made her reconsider the prospect, at least to some extent—she wondered if she would regret it in the future, should something happen to either of them if she hadn't taken the next step.

As she took a sip of wine, she tried to recapture the relaxing calm she'd experienced in the bath, willing the sunset to take the heaviness of the day with it as it traversed towards the horizon. Wendy had no idea where her brothers were but had no desire to seek them out. It was one of the benefits of her family home—there was more than enough room should anyone want their own space, which she did, more often than not.

Forcing all thoughts from her mind, she focused on the changing colours of the sky—the peach and tangerine weaving in amongst the amethyst, and she tried to recall the last time she'd actually stopped and appreciated a sunset—at least one not punctured by a skyline of high-rise buildings.

"Mind if I join you?"

Wendy looked up as Jane stepped out onto the porch.

"Of course not." Wendy smiled at her daughter and gestured to the spare seat on the other side of the round glass table between them.

"I'm having a chocolate fix if you want some," Jane offered, placing a bag of M & M's on the table. Wendy glanced at them quickly before looking away. Unable to convince herself of a good enough reason not to indulge, she turned back to the packet and gave it a shake, emptying half the contents onto the glass. She sifted through the colours casting the green ones aside before scooping up the remaining chocolates and nursing them in her hand.

"I'd totally forgotten you do that. Why is it always the green ones?" Jane asked.

"You know I hate the colour green," Wendy replied, enjoying the crunch of the candy shell in her mouth.

"You're a weirdo, Mum. Has Lilly left?"

"Yeah, she left about half an hour ago."

Jane nodded, needing no further explanation. "How are you after today?"

"Okay, I think. It's strange. I feel both guilty and relieved. I feel guilty because I should have made more of an effort to spend time with Mum and Dad. Especially with Mum, once Dad passed away. Instead,

I let myself get caught up in my work, and time just sped by. It feels shit knowing they're both gone, yet I feel relieved that it's done with. The weeks of waiting, not knowing how much longer Mum had, watching that vibrancy she was always known for seeping out of her. It was so emotionally stressful. Wanting her to stay with us, not wanting her to linger on in pain... does that sound cold? Selfish?"

She turned to Jane, the frown heavy across her brow.

"Of course it doesn't, Mum. It sounds perfectly human."

Wendy sighed and turned back towards the depleting sunset and sipped on her wine. She could hear the soft clatter of the candy-coated chocolates as Jane tossed them about in her hand.

"You've never really told me why you hated being here so much..."

"I don't hate being here..." Wendy replied in defence.

"Well, hate might be too strong a word. You have a complicated relationship with this place, yet I know you loved Grandma and Grandpa, and you love Uncle Mike and Uncle John... and Nanna."

Wendy took another sip of wine before answering, "It's just complicated." She could feel her daughter's sideways glances. "One day, Jane. One day I will tell you everything, but..."

"It's fine, Mum, really. I just want you to be happy."

"Thank you, sweetheart. I appreciate it."

"I'm finding myself really enjoying staying here, despite the circumstances. It's so beautiful. I mean, I already knew that, but it's like every time I leave here, I seem to forget."

Wendy nodded, wondering where Jane was heading. Still, Jane said nothing further, and the two continued to nibble on their chocolates in silence as they looked out over the peaceful estate, each lost in their own thoughts while being content in each other's company.

"Have you caught any of the news today?" Jane asked.

Wendy snuck a side-long glance at her daughter, trying to get a read on her before answering, but she got nothing, "Honestly, I haven't had the chance, but I think I'll head in and see if I can catch some now. Do you mind?"

Jane turned to her. "Of course not, Mum. You forget—news is a journalist's bread and butter." Wendy smiled at her daughter, and they got up and walked inside.

Wendy and Jane walked into the lounge room, and John greeted them from where he already sat on the couch with his feet up on the coffee table.

"You know Mum always hated it when you put your feet up on the table," Wendy joked, and John sheepishly lowered them to the floor as she sat beside him.

"I'm guessing it's news o'clock?" John chuckled as he grabbed the remote, flicking through the channels as Michael walked in from the other side of the room.

"Hey." Was all he said as he joined them.

"Do we want local or national news?" John asked.

"National, please," Wendy replied. She knew her mother's funeral would feature in the local news, and it was enough for her to replay the day in her mind, let alone having to see it on the news. Besides, it was the national news she longed to see.

Breaking news this evening on the Rosalie Fryair case after Allison Fryair, mother of missing teen and wife of Lord Mayor Donald Fryair, collapsed outside the Melbourne Central Police Station this afternoon. Mrs.

Fryair has frequented the station since the disappearance of her daughter three weeks ago, despite little progress on the case. Mrs. Fryair was taken to St. Vincent's Hospital and is presently being treated for exhaustion. The office of Mayor Fryair declined to comment.

When asked for an update on the investigation, Detective Chief Inspector Jared Helfer stated they were actively pursuing all avenues. Despite the efforts of local law enforcement canvassing the neighbourhood and conducting interviews with the Fryer's friends and family, they remain tight-lipped on significant leads.

Fifteen-year-old Rosalie Fryair was last seen by her parents around nine-thirty pm on the night of the 20th of February. Little information has been released surrounding the circumstances of her disappearance, though sources close to the family have advised the girl's bed appeared to have been slept in. The bedroom door remained closed, yet the bedroom window was found open, despite the cold night temperatures. We also have reason to believe that Rosalie's phone and identification were left behind.

It would be irresponsible not to consider the likelihood that an abduction has taken place—and if that is the case, with the rapid rise and controversial election of Lord Mayor Fryer just a few short months ago, a political motive needs consideration.

If anyone has seen Rosalie Fryair or knows of her whereabouts, please contact the police department via the Rosalie Fryer hotline...

"For shit's sake, do reporters even report the actual news anymore?" Michael scowled. "No offence, Jane."

"None taken." She winked.

"But seriously, why do they always have to go for sensationalism? And why are they pretending like it's not an abduction? It doesn't make any sense."

"I'm sure they're investigating all avenues, regardless of what they're telling the media," said Wendy, quickly defending her profession.

"My guess is they're being dictated to by the Lord Mayor. I would put money on that everything has to go through him first," Jane stated.

"I wouldn't be surprised. He seems like a piece of work," Michael scoffed.

"But why would the Lord Mayor prefer people to think his daughter ran away, rather than abducted? Shouldn't it be the other way around?" Wendy said.

"Unless he knows what happened..." Jane said, only half-jokingly.

"The plot thickens..." Michael replied.

"Or maybe there's a third possibility," Jane said.

"What would that be?" John asked.

"Perhaps she simply vanished into thin air, right from her very own bedroom." Jane laughed, not noticing the sudden stillness that fell over her family.

"I'm sure the police are on top of it," Wendy stated, her voice coming out in a long croak, and she swallowed thickly, feeling as though she would choke on the very air she breathed.

Without turning away from the television screen, John slid his hand across the couch and grasped his sister's hand.

"Mum? What is it?" Jane asked, "You've gone pale." Wendy half-turned, a terse smile on her face, wishing she had a better poker face.

"I'm fine, sweetheart. I just feel awful for the girl's family; it's a horrifying time for them."

"I know. It was a huge opportunity to land the coverage for the newspaper, but I'll admit it's hard not to get emotionally invested. Her family is just so distraught—and understandably so. I get why you want to be on the case so badly."

Wendy shot her daughter a look of surprise. "You do?"

Jane nodded. "Of course. You want to find Rosalie—alive—and end this nightmare for all of them."

Wendy recovered quickly, squeezing John's hand, which still held hers. "Absolutely..." She snuck a look at Michael and found him scowling at the television, avoiding looking at her. Wendy shot him sideways glances, chewing on her lower lip as the others became engrossed in the next news story. She hated it when there was any tension between her and her brothers. They'd always been so close. Yet, she wasn't a pushover either, and while Michael had no issue making his discontent known on occasion, it wasn't a given that either she or John would stop what they wanted to do in order to appease him. She'd made no secret about her interest in the case and had done her best to keep up-to-date with any developments—she had to return to work at some point. She understood Michael was pissed off because he felt her attention hadn't been one hundred percent on their mother—and he was partly right. Yet, Wendy knew it was more than that too. While the disappearance of Rosalie Fryair had unleashed years of repressed emotions in Wendy, she knew it was the same—at least in part—for her brothers. They were only young at the time of her abduction, but not young enough to escape the impact it'd had on their family.

Wendy suddenly felt claustrophobic and restless and longed to see Nanna. At times like these, she truly missed the wisdom Nanna always had readily available to bestow upon them. It never mattered what the situation was, she'd always known exactly what to say to ease their minds. Unable to sit still any longer, Wendy got up from the lounge and, excusing herself, ignored the watchful stares of her brothers as she walked out of the room. She walked briskly through the manor towards Nanna's rooms, not paying attention to anything except the sound of her rapid footsteps echoing around her. The sitting-room door was open, and Wendy walked in to see Nanna perched on the couch, dressed in lilac satin pyjamas buttoned up to her neck. Her white hair was freshly washed and freed from its tight chignon, draped in a loose braid over her shoulder. Her hands sat clasped atop the crochet blanket that was draped over her lap, and she faced the television, an old rerun of M*A*S*H on its screen. Wendy wondered if she was actually watching it or simply staring.

Carole looked up from where she sat in the armchair, a cup of tea in her hand. "Hello, Wendy. Come and join us."

"Thanks, Carole."

"Would you like a cup of tea?" Carole asked, moving to get up.

Wendy stepped forward and waved her hand for her to sit back down. "No, thanks, Carole. I'm fine. I just wanted to spend some time with Nanna before she was off to bed."

"Of course. I'll give you some privacy."

"That's not necessary—I don't want to disrupt you."

"Honestly, it will give me the chance to have a hot shower and get things organised for tomorrow."

Wendy gave a quick nod and a small smile as she watched Carole leave the room. She sat on the couch next to Nanna, who made no acknowledgement of her presence. Wendy didn't mind; she was used to it now—as used to it as one could be, watching a loved one slowly leave them. Regardless, Wendy felt better just to be near Nanna, instantly feeling soothed just being there. Wendy snuck glances at Nanna, trying to gauge from her near-blank expression if she had any comprehension that they'd buried our mother today. Stifling the urge to sigh, Wendy turned back to the television, trying not to think of how Nanna had become a mere shell of the woman she once was, or how much it truly pained her. Her heart already brimmed with enough sadness for one day. Wendy reached over to Nanna's hands and slipped her own under them, wanting to be close to her, and suddenly overwhelmed with the inevitable reality that she would lose Nanna, too.

Wendy quickly blinked back the tears before they had the chance to spill over. Instead, she forced herself to focus on the show. After a few minutes, she even found herself smiling at Hawkeye's shenanigans, just as Carole discreetly popped her head into the sitting room under the guise of seeing if Wendy needed anything. Wendy knew it was time to leave them to it. She stood up and bent over Nanna, placing a kiss on her forehead. As she pulled back, she could have sworn Nanna had looked her in the eyes, just for a millisecond, before staring up at the television once more. "That's okay, Nanna. I'll forgive you— Hawkeye's a hunk." As she stood up, Nanna's hand shot out and gripped her arm, causing her to yelp in surprise.

"Are you okay? What happened?" Carole asked as she hurried over. Wendy couldn't reply, staring open-mouthed as Nanna slowly turned her head and looked up at her.

"Don't follow the unicorn," she whispered. Wendy was speechless, mystified by the sudden intensity in Nanna's gaze.

"Don't follow the unicorn!" Nanna whispered again, with an urgency apparent in the way her fingers dug into Wendy's arm.

"It's been an exhausting day for both of you," Carole said quietly as she placed her hand on Nanna's shoulder. Instantly, Wendy's arm was released, and she tentatively rubbed it. "I should get Nanna to bed."

"Yes, of course," Wendy replied. "Love you, Nanna," Wendy said, to no response. "Goodnight, Carole."

As Wendy reached the door, she turned back and watched Carole lift the blanket from Nanna's lap, folding it neatly. With a frown, she stepped out into the hall, Nanna's warning echoing on a loop. She tried to tell herself it was just a random, nonsensical utterance that was nothing more than a consequence of Nanna's condition, yet she couldn't shake the look on Nanna's face. Despite *what* she said, there seemed to be intent behind it. A desperation. A warning.

Why a unicorn?

Wendy rubbed her aching temples, trying to make sense of the nonsensical statement, but exhaustion from the past few weeks caught up with her all at once, and with the hope that she may actually get some sleep, she headed off to her own room.

After three hours of tossing and turning, watching the bedroom walls close in on her, Wendy finally gave up and got up. Wanting to escape the claustrophobia of the room, she silently made her way downstairs to the kitchen and put the kettle on. She sat at the bench for a moment, the warmth of the tea only just starting to seep through the china and into her hands, when the claustrophobia crept over her once more. Picking up her cup, she walked through the back door and onto the veranda. Despite the crisp, cold air, Wendy let her dressing gown hang open, not wanting to feel restrained, and she relished in its rejuvenating freshness. Taking a seat, she placed her cup on the glass table and withdrew her phone from the pocket of her dressing gown and opened a text from Lilly. It simply let her know that she was home safe and for Wendy to give her a call when she wanted to talk. Wendy sighed and rested her head back against the wall behind her, her thoughts cycling through her mind over and over—Rosalie Fryair, Nanna, the unicorn reference, her mother, Lilly—over and over. The sound of creaking wood made her jump, and she looked up to see John hovering in the doorway.

"You scared me!" she exclaimed in a loud whisper.

"Sorry, I didn't mean to. I heard you come downstairs earlier, and when I saw you weren't in the kitchen, I figured you would come out here."

"I didn't mean to wake you."

"Nah," John replied, walking over and taking the seat on the other side of the table. "I wasn't sleeping much myself anyway." He picked up Wendy's cup and took a swig. "I'm not surprised you're not sleeping in that bloody bedroom."

Wendy attempted a grin, but it came across as a grimace. "What can I say? I'm on a mission." She retrieved her cup and took a sip.

"You're stubborn is what you are. What do you hope to gain from sleeping in there? Why now, after all this time? Why not stay in one of the numerous guest rooms like you usually do?"

Wendy shrugged. "I can't hide from the past forever." She could feel John's eyes on her, but she refused to meet them.

"Does this have anything to do with Lilly?" he finally asked.

Wendy gripped her cup tightly, fighting against the sudden urge to fidget. "Maybe. In part. I've always just cruised along in our relationship. I wouldn't say I've taken her for granted; I know how lucky I am to have her. I guess with everything that's happened I'm questioning why we haven't taken the next steps."

"Has Lilly said something?"

"No, not at all. I think she would like to live together, and it would likely work. We both value our own space, so we're on the same page that way. I just don't know if it's something I can do. I don't want to enter into such a big change only to want to back out a month in. That wouldn't be fair to Lilly. There's just something wrong with me..."

"No. There's not. It's normal to feel trepidation in relationships."

"But there is. You know there is. I think that's why I need to sleep in my old room—like I'm trying to get some kind of closure for what happened to me. When I...came home...the focus quickly shifted from my own trauma to preparing for the fact I was going to become a mother at the age of sixteen. I had to just kind of push away all thoughts of what happened—I couldn't deal with both the memories and motherhood at the same time. Pursuing any kind of relationship had never crossed my mind, especially not one with a woman. So when I met Lilly, I think I unconsciously made the decision not to question anything, to just go along with it. But I guess you can only do that for so long, right?"

"You're a good person. You know that, don't you? Despite everything you've been through, you've never let it hold you back. I mean, look at Jane—you have an amazing daughter who adores you, a career that you kick ass at, and a partner who supports you, no matter what. Not to mention two exceptionally handsome brothers…"

Wendy reached over the table and swatted him. "I know, I'm incredibly fortunate. But I just feel…I don't know…that something's changing… I don't know how to explain it."

John cleared his throat. "Of course it's changing. We just lost our mother, and for the first time in our lives, we're without our parents. I think we're all feeling a little lost right now. I also know how much this Rosalie Fryair case has been on your mind—no matter how much you try and downplay it. It doesn't take a genius to see how badly you want to be working the case—or why. I mean, there are enough similarities between her case and what happened to you, even I can see them. Do you resent having to be here instead of working?"

Wendy gave a little shrug. "Resent isn't the right word. I'm grateful for the time we got to spend with Mum before she passed. We didn't have that luxury with Dad. In saying that, it's also frustrating observing the case from the outside, watching the days and the weeks pass by with seemingly no change in the case and wondering if I could somehow make a difference—needing to make a difference."

She sensed her brother's stare, and she turned to him. "You think I'm obsessive."

"Well, yes," he chuckled, "but that's what makes you a good detective. I'm…we're…me and Michael…are worried what working this case could mean for you. It's brought up enough for us; I can't imagine what it must do to you."

Wendy didn't say anything, and after a few pensive moments, John continued, "Have you considered it might be different? That it's not an abduction, and she's just run off like the news seems to suggest?"

Wendy scoffed at him. "Please. No teenage girl has the means to disappear without a trace, especially not one with a face as well-known as Rosalie's. I mean, all through her father's campaign, there she was, by his side, like a punctuation mark against his family-inspired policies. Not to mention, no teenage girl would go anywhere without their mobile and bank cards in this day and age."

"I agree it's strange, but I just worry that regardless of what has or hasn't happened to her, the case is still too close to home for you. You've had more than your fair share of shit, and I don't want to see you putting yourself through unnecessary torment. This case is too personal for you."

"I have worked missing person cases before—I'm a detective, remember?"

"Of course. But have you worked one previously with as many parallels to your own?"

"That's irrelevant. The reality is there is no escaping it, regardless of whether I'm working it or not—it's all over the news, it's all anyone's talking about. So of course, it's going to bring up the past, and all that came with it—but I think that's why I would be good for the case. I'm an asset, not a liability, damn it." Wendy scowled, crossing her arms across her chest. Her brother remained silent; John let her be, knowing when to stop pushing.

Wendy took a few moments to calm herself, not wanting to prove her brother right. "It's been twenty years since I was abducted. Some days it feels like a lifetime ago, and other days it still feels raw, like it was only yesterday. I still have nightmares, rather frequently at the moment. It's always with me, no matter how well I hide it. But I've learnt to live with it—in spite of it—in spite of *him*. I know Rosalie is not me, but she's still a teenage girl, and she's missing. Casting aside all the bullshit, it's my job to find her, and I should be able to do my job without anyone doubting my ability to do so."

John drummed the fingers of his left hand on the table, and Wendy counted the reiterations: *one, two, three, four, five...*

"So, call your boss in the morning...later in the morning...and don't let him off the phone until you're on the case."

"Are you sure?" She turned to face him, wanting to see his expression for herself.

John massaged his forehead between his eyebrows. "Of course, I'm sure. Michael won't be happy. In fact, I think he will be down-right pissed off. Not for the reasons you think..." he said, holding up his free hand to stop Wendy before she could counter-argue. "He's always been proud of you, and he knows how driven you are. He's just worried, we both are, but I think his agitation stems from his grief—he just wants us all close right now. He's never understood that when he wants to hold everyone tight, that's usually the time you need to be on your own."

Wendy only nodded, not meeting her brother's gaze, both stunned and touched that he knew her so well. John sighed again and got up from the chair. "Well, I've said my piece. You know what you're doing." Yawning, he stretched his arms. "I'm going to go in and try to get another hour or two of shut-eye."

"Okay," Wendy replied and gave him a small smile.

John walked to the doorway. "And Wendy?" he paused, looking back at her.

"Yeah?"

"Do what you need to do. Just know that we're here if you need us."

"Thanks, John."

Once she was sure he was well within the house, she let out a long rush of air, feeling as though a first hurdle was overcome. Wendy played with her empty cup, running her finger around the rim over and over as she watched the sky lighten across the horizon, her thoughts with a teenage girl who was out there, somewhere, waiting—needing—to be found.

CHAPTER FOUR

W endy sat on the edge of her bed staring down at her phone, waiting for the clock on the screen to click over to 6 am. Her boss was a pre-dawn riser, one of those people who liked an early morning run, but she'd still felt she needed to wait for a semi-decent time to call him—the anticipation had turned her into a jittery mess. Yet, as her thumb hovered over the screen, she hesitated to unlock it as the spiralling nerves in her stomach cranked it up a notch. Wendy knew she was being ridiculous; it was a phone call. It wasn't even like she had to speak to him in person. Taking a deep breath, she reminded herself what it meant to her to get assigned to the Fryair case. She refused to consider the possibility that he'd tell her no again.

Finally, Wendy took a deep breath and unlocked her phone, selecting her boss's number from her phonebook with her thumb before raising the phone to her ear. After the fifth ring, her boss finally answered. "Detective Darling, aren't you supposed to be on leave? I wouldn't have answered if I didn't think you would keep calling me until I did."

Wendy smiled to herself—persistence was one of her 'double-edged' traits—an asset to her job, and annoyance to those around her. When she didn't respond, he continued, "I truly am sorry to hear of your mother's passing," he said, his voice solemn.

"Thank you, I appreciate it. That being said, I need to come back to work."

"Look, Darling, it's only been..."

"I know what you're going to say, and please don't. I need to be busy—I need to work, and without it, I feel like I'm going stir crazy." She could almost

47

hear her boss's brain ticking over through the silence on the other end of the phone. Just as she was about to check that he was still on the line, he finally answered, "Well, perhaps come back onto some light duties and just see how..."

"I want to work the Fryair case." Her demand was met with more silence.

"Hello?" she finally said.

He cleared his throat. "We already have a team assigned to the case..."

"I know you do, and with all due respect, they haven't found her yet. Let me help. I need this."

"Detective Darling," he replied, his gruff voice indicating his annoyance at repeatedly being cut off, "the significance of this case isn't lost on me. A case like this needs officers who can keep an open mind— it's imperative—and I'm not confident that you can. At least not on this case—and that's not even taking your recent loss into consideration."

Hearing the doubt from her boss stung like a slap in the face, and it was Wendy's turn for pensive silence. Collecting herself, she took a deep breath before answering, "I understand your concerns, sir, but with all due respect, I honestly feel they're unwarranted. What happened to me was twenty years ago, and not once in all the time since have I let it define me in any way. I've certainly never given you, or anyone else cause to think it impacts my ability to do my job. On the contrary, I've proven myself time and again that I'm an excellent detective, and I know I would be an asset to the case. My own experience and a fresh set of eyes could be just what's needed."

When there was no immediate answer, Wendy strained her ears as she thought she could hear him drumming his fingers on his desk.

"Evidently, you're going to be a thorn in my side until I agree—and with pressure from both the media and the Lord Mayor's office, we could use all the help we can get."

"Thank you, b…"

"Hold on, Darling. Before you get too excited, I have three conditions."

"Of course, anything…" Wendy found herself holding her breath as she waited for further instruction.

"Firstly, I want you to be honest with yourself. It's been a terrible time for you and your family, and if you need more time to grieve, then I think you should take it."

"I appreciate that boss," Wendy cut in impatiently, "but as I explained, busying myself with work is what I need right now…"

"Just think about it," he cut her off. "Secondly, you won't be running lead on the case. Detective Roberts is heading the operation, and you can partner him. I still feel this case is a little too close to home for you to run point, and Roberts has proven to be an effective lead." He paused, waiting for Wendy to argue the point, and she clenched her jaw, ignoring the sharp pain it caused to shoot up into her forehead. When an argument didn't come, he continued, "Thirdly, before you step back in the station, I want you to have a session with the psychologist. I know you're dismissive about the potential impact this case may have on you, but I have a duty of care to ensure you are fit to work it. The pressure of the case and what it represents for you, coinciding with the loss of another parent, would be a huge strain on anyone—including myself."

"How soon can I make an appointment?" Wendy asked through clenched teeth.

"I'll have the details sent through to you. Once I have a report on my desk clearing you for duty—or not, I will call you. Do you hear me, Darling?" he prompted sternly. "I will call you. Now go and spend time with your family."

Wendy mumbled her thanks before terminating the call and hurtling the phone across the carpet. Resting her head in her hands, she closed her eyes. She felt a strange combination of relief that she could potentially work the case and dismay at the conditions attached. Wendy hated jumping through hoops, and the absolute last thing she wanted to do was talk to a shrink, but she'd backed herself into a corner. If she went, she risked being deemed unfit to work the case, and if she didn't go, she definitely wouldn't work the case while also planting a rather large seed in her boss's mind that she wasn't as together and capable as she'd wanted him to believe.

Wendy flopped backwards onto the bed, her hands over her eyes.

Shit!

Pacing the length of the kitchen, Wendy eyed her handiwork; it was a breakfast spread to beat all breakfast spreads. There were sausages, bacon, croissants, eggs, fruit, mushrooms, spinach, steaming coffee, and brewing tea. She paused; her arms folded across her chest as she eyed all the food. She conceded she might have gone slightly overboard—a combination of insomnia and guilt. Wendy hoped the breakfast would serve as an olive branch, a way to appease her family—specifically Michael—when she told them she was—hopefully—returning to work.

"Please don't tell me my senses deceive me..." Michael's voice wafted into the kitchen as he approached. He popped his head through the doorway. "This looks amazing. I could smell it as soon as I woke up." He walked over and gave his big sister a kiss on the cheek before taking a seat. Without another word, he began to load up his plate.

Wendy anxiously chewed on her thumbnail as she forced herself to take a seat opposite her brother, busying herself by pouring a generous cup of coffee, closing her eyes, and inhaling the heady aroma.

"Nice of you to wait for the rest of us," John joked as he entered the kitchen.

"Have to eat it while it's hot," Michael replied without turning around, too busy shovelling more food into his mouth.

"Is that coffee I can smell?" Jane asked a few steps behind her uncle. Wendy smiled as her daughter walked over, and standing behind her mother, wrapped her arms around her shoulders. Wendy patted her daughter's hand, instantly feeling comforted. Without asking, she knew she would have Jane's full support in taking the case. Despite being the one most affected by her mother's career and the demands it placed on her life, she never complained, never made Wendy feel guilty for doing what she loved. And Wendy adored her for it. Though that knowledge never made it any easier when she had to disappoint her.

It wasn't until they were half-way through their breakfast that her brothers realised she wasn't eating.

"Not hungry?" John queried, his cutlery held mid-air as he looked at her questioningly.

Wendy gave him a small smile. "Not this morning. I'm happy with coffee for now."

John lowered his coffee and nudged Michael, who reluctantly did the same. Jane continued nibbling at her food, looking from her uncles to her mother, and back again as though anticipating a sparring match.

"You have an announcement, I take it?" Michael stated.

Wendy glanced quickly at Jane, who gave her a nod of encouragement. "I do."

"So, you didn't cook us this amazing breakfast out of the goodness of your heart?" John asked, his eyes twinkling with amusement, and Wendy appreciated his attempt to try to diffuse the increasing tension that surrounded them.

"I spoke to my boss..."

"When?" Michael interrupted, "This morning? It's barely half seven."

Wendy nodded. Michael responded by muttering under his breath. "Don't mutter at me, Michael. Say what you think," Wendy said firmly. She watched as her brothers looked at each other, not missing the warning shot John gave their brother.

Michael sighed and took a gulp of his coffee. "Fine then. Come on, let's have it. What's happening?" he asked, picking his cutlery back up and busying himself with his plate of food.

Wendy cleared her throat and looked down at her own coffee, suddenly feeling nervous. "I'm on the Fryair case. Well, I have a couple of hoops to jump through first, but then I'm on the case."

Michael let his cutlery clatter onto his plate but remained silent.

John cleared his throat, flicking a quick sideways glance at Jane, not wanting to say too much. "You know my concerns—which essentially are also Michael's..."

"What's there to be concerned about, Uncles? Mum is good at her job, and I honestly believe she's the best shot that the family has at finding their daughter. Why wouldn't you support her wanting to help someone?" Jane asked.

"It's complicated..." Michael stated.

"Then explain it to me. We're all adults here, aren't we?" she asked, pushing her plate aside and with her elbows on the table, rested her head in her hands.

"Well..." Michael started, and Wendy sucked in a sharp breath.

"It's just the timing, is all," John cut in. Wendy tried to hide her relief as John smoothly steered the conversation to safer ground. "We've only just said goodbye to Mum, Nanna isn't doing so well, and there's a lot of fine print we need to go through regarding the estate and all that. It's just something we would have liked to go through as a family, but in saying that," he turned and held his sister's gaze, "we both understand the importance of your mother's work, don't we Michael?"

Michael nodded. "Do what you have to do. You know how we feel about it."

Wendy turned to Jane. "Of course you have my support, Mum. Always. Just make sure you give me the inside scoop," she joked, and Wendy smiled. "I'm happy to stay on here a little longer and help out with any estate stuff and sorting through Grandmother's wing like we'd originally planned."

"Are you sure?" Wendy asked.

Jane nodded and flashed her mother a reassuring smile. "Of course. I've arranged to work from here indefinitely. I'll have to go into the city once a week for the staff meetings, but thanks to modern technology, I can do most of what I need to do from here."

Wendy reached out and squeezed her daughter's extended hand. "Love you, kiddo."

"Right back at you, Mum."

"My only request, Wendy, is that you come back here when you can. I think it's more important than ever to spend time together," Michael stated quietly.

"Of course," Wendy replied, hoping to break the ice with a smile, but he wouldn't meet her gaze.

"Now that's all sorted, can we enjoy the rest of this delicious breakfast in peace?" Jane held her cup up as though toasting, before taking a sip and putting it back on the table in exchange for a slice of rockmelon.

Wendy watched on as they all ate, knowing she would need to clear the air with Michael before she went back to work. She needed to get to the bottom of his concerns.

CHAPTER FIVE

Wendy stared out the enormous window, mesmerised by the immaculate glass which spanned almost the whole length of the wall, not quite floor-to-ceiling, but close. On the other side, dozens of tree branches danced and weaved in the wind, like they were beckoning her outside—she would have happily obeyed. They were three stories up, and the branches were so close together it was near impossible to determine which branches belonged to which tree. Now and then, a branch would tap against the glass, making Wendy think of a small child, tapping at the window to get her attention.

"Wendy?"

She jumped and turned back to face the psychologist. "I'm sorry. What were you saying?"

The doctor smiled kindly, discreetly looking at her watch. "Why do you think you're here this morning?"

"Well, my mother just passed away..."

"I'm sorry to hear that..."

"Thank you; I appreciate that," she replied, subtly shifting in her seat, trying to hide her discomfort. "I want to return to work, and my boss wants to make sure I'm emotionally stable enough not to hinder the investigation," Wendy replied, trying to keep the sarcasm from her voice.

"And how long is it since your mother passed?"

"About a week. Her funeral was yesterday."

The psychologist paused momentarily, her hand hovering the pen above her notepad as she looked at Wendy.

"You don't feel that it's too soon to return to work?" she finally asked.

"No, I don't. I need to be busy—to work."

The psychologist nodded slowly and made a quick note. "Do you often find yourself restless? Fidgety?"

Wendy shrugged. "No more than anyone else, I wouldn't think." She unclenched her hands as slowly as she could, not wanting to draw attention to them in case the doctor misinterpreted her impatience for anything else.

The doctor looked at her for a moment, her expression unreadable as Wendy stared back, trying her best to appear as relaxed and nonchalant as possible. The doctor was the first to look away, flicking a glance down at her notepad before speaking, "Aside from the passing of your mother, is there any other reason your boss may be concerned about your emotional capabilities at the moment?"

Wendy fought the urge to sigh. It irritated her that she was being asked questions she was sure the psychologist already knew the answer to. "Look, I just want to get back to work."

The doctor stared at her again, for longer this time, but Wendy was stubborn, and she feigned scratching her nose to hide the small smile of satisfaction that crept across her face as once again, the psychologist was the first to look away. "You have an interest in working the Rosalie Fryair case, I'm told."

Wendy responded with a nod.

"You said you just want to return to work, yet you have specifically requested to return to work in order to work this case. Why is that?"

"The victim's been missing for almost four weeks now. Why wouldn't I want to help find her?"

The psychologist paused, jotting something on her notepad, leaving Wendy wondering what on earth she could be writing.

"Have you worked on this type of case before?"

"I've worked on missing persons cases before, yes, but not exactly like this one, no."

"Have you worked cases with significant media attention?"

"How is that relevant?"

"It's not the appeal of the high-profile case that drives you?"

"Absolutely not." Wendy scowled at the suggestion.

"I'm assuming there are a number of active cases of one kind or another currently handled by your precinct."

"Of course."

"Why not return to work on one of those? Perhaps something a little less demanding?"

Wendy closed her eyes as she answered, "Because I feel a missing person, regardless of their age or social standing, should be the priority—but most especially when it's a young person."

"Is there another reason, perhaps, that's driving you to pursue this case?"

Wendy was becoming annoyed and impatient, and she dropped the pretence, massaging her temples.

"You obviously have my file. My past is right there in front of you."

"I do. However, I would like to hear it from you, in your own words."

Wendy tried to force her jaw to unclench. "I had a traumatic experience as a teenager, and the chief is unnecessarily concerned that this case will trigger dormant memories that could potentially render me incapable of doing my job. Perhaps even make me a liability."

"That's quite a detached analysis you've concluded there."

Wendy shrugged, reminding herself that she didn't want to give away any reason to be kept off the case.

"Do you think your boss's concerns are justified?"

"No. I don't. It was a long time ago. A very long time ago, and not once has it had any bearing on my ability to do my job—a job which I happen to be exceptional at, I might add. So, if we're done here, I'd really like to get back to it..." Wendy rose from her seat, but the psychologist raised her hand, and like a reprimanded school girl, Wendy found herself sitting back down before she had the chance to register what she was doing.

The psychologist shifted in her own seat, uncrossing her ankles and lifting up her foot to rest on the opposite knee. Her attempt to achieve a more relaxed look to entice Wendy to open up didn't escape Wendy's attention, but she let it slide as the next question was asked. "So, how old were you?"

Wendy inhaled deeply. "I was fifteen when I was abducted and sixteen when I was found. Yes, it was a nightmare and not an experience I would wish on anyone—but it's an experience I have sufficiently dealt with—and put behind me, and as far as I can tell. It's not the Fryair case dredging it up; it's my boss and yourself." Wendy was unable to keep the anger from her voice, and she could feel the scowl deepen across her brow.

"Take me back to what happened," the psychologist instructed; her head was tilted slightly to the side as she waited to gauge her client's reaction.

Turning to the trees, she scanned the swaying branches, as though they held some kind of answer for her. "I told you it was a long time ago. I went through my years of counselling."

"I appreciate that, Wendy; however, my job is to assess whether you're fit to work this case due to your personal history. So, if you want the clearance, then I need you to tell me what you remember."

Wendy kept her face turned away, the steely poker face she'd perfected as a detective now elusive, leaving her feeling vulnerable, and worse still, potentially incapable of continuing to portray herself as an emotionally stable officer. Slipping her clenched hand down the gap between her leg and the arm of the chair, she squeezed hard until her fingernails dug sharply into her palm. The pain, however minor, acted like a windscreen-wiper, pushing away her doubts so she could regain her composure long enough to turn back to the doctor. "There isn't a lot to tell. I'm not being difficult; I've just never had much recollection of the time. All I can tell you is when I was fifteen, I was abducted from my bedroom in the middle of the night. I was gone for roughly six months before I was found wandering the streets on the dawn of my sixteenth birthday. I had no memory of how long I'd been walking before I was found."

Silence followed for a few seconds, her admission hanging heavy in the air.

"What do you remember about the time you were missing?"

"I just answered that. I don't have any recollections aside from a few nonsensical images that I'm fairly certain are just the remnants of a warped coping mechanism..."

"So, you do have some memories?"

Wendy stared at the doctor, wondering if she was purposefully trying to goad her. "No, how many times do I have to tell you..."

"You just said you recalled a few nonsensical images." She sat there with an annoyingly patient expression; her pen poised over her pad. Wendy wanted to reach over and slap her. "Give me an example—I know you said your memories are nonsensical," the doctor stated, holding her hands up in defence before Wendy had the chance to rebuff, "but I would like to hear them anyway."

Wendy looked down at her lap, feeling at a loss. All she wanted to do was to get out of there, yet it was apparent that until she gave the psychologist something—anything—she wasn't going anywhere. Reluctantly, she conceded defeat and raised her head. "My abductor's eyes. I don't know that I'd call it a recollection, but I still have nightmares about his eyes." Wendy caught the slightest flicker of a frown dash across the doctor's face so quickly that she couldn't guarantee she'd even seen it.

"What was so notable about his eyes?"

Once again, Wendy turned towards the trees, feeling less exposed in her explanation that way, "They were like nothing I'd ever seen before or since. They were very large. Abnormally so and rounded towards his nose before tapering out to points at their outer edge. They were an eerie emerald green that had an iridescent sheen to them. It was often pitch black where I was held, and I'd regularly wake up or just turn around and see his eyes across the room, watching me. You couldn't see the rest of him, just his eyes, hovering there like two spectral lights. Staring. Unblinking."

"How did that make you feel?"

"That's a bit of a stupid question," Wendy blurted out before she could stop herself, and the psychologist responded with a sharply raised eyebrow.

"I was terrified. It was intimidating and creepy. Even as I grew to expect it, the way his stare made me feel never diminished. When he became angry, they would expand outwards, and the green would intensely glow, the eyes themselves rimmed in red, like blood—they looked so bizarre they'd almost be comical if it wasn't so terrifying." Wendy paused, looking down at her hands and suddenly became engrossed with pushing the quick down into the nail bed of one finger with the nail of another.

"Did that happen often?" the psychologist prompted when Wendy didn't continue.

Wendy released her hands and shrugged. "I don't remember. More than a few times, but beyond that, I can't be more specific." She watched as the psychologist jotted a few points down on her pad. "I wouldn't put too much stead in it, I mean, I used to think I had a little friend that was a green fairy too," Wendy said with an attempt at a laugh that instead fell flat.

The psychologist's hand paused half-way across the page as she looked up at her client. "A green fairy?"

Shit.

"Obviously, I'm aware fairies are imaginary," Wendy said quickly, furious at herself for revealing anything that could result in her sanity being questioned. "It's not like I saw a green fairy per se, that's just how I remember relating to it at the time. I don't know. It made me feel less alone or something."

The doctor nodded. "Can you tell me anything more about this green fairy?" she asked, looking down at her notepad.

Wendy frowned. "Not really. It's not like I saw a miniature woman in a green dress with wings on her back, fluttering about."

"Well, what did you see?"

Wendy looked up at the wall above the doctor's head, trying to find the right words to try to explain what she saw.

"Flashes of green light. Sometimes quick bursts, other times they were longer, pulsating flashes, and both were always just on my peripheral vision—I never got to look straight at the source—and it didn't happen all the time either. I think it might have happened more after eating or drinking, but again I couldn't be certain."

"Were there any sounds accompanying these flashes?"

Wendy's face scrunched as she tried to recall the memories, and it felt as though the very act of trying to remember made it easier to do so—and the thought terrified her. Yet she knew she had to continue.

"I'd hear a ringing sound in my ears—no, more like a tinkling, almost like tiny chimes or bells. At first it scared me because I didn't know where the sound was coming from or what caused it, and it was always so close to my ears. Like having tinnitus, but it was coming from outside of my ear—or at least that was what I thought. At the time, I told myself it was this little fairy trying to communicate with me, like having a little friend in the darkness. I even had a name for her."

"What was that?"

NEVER, NEVER

"Tinkerbell." Wendy looked up and watched the doctor scrawl across her notepad. "I was a young girl at the time, remember."

"Our minds are masters of deceit. You were gone for many months, and it's not a stretch to consider that your mind created this entity, this Tinkerbell, as company. A means of self-preservation to help you endure your captivity. Likewise, your memories of your captor are ones of a monster, and again, this isn't a reflection of his true self, but a manifestation your mind has created, essentially turning him into a monster in appearance, instead of just in nature."

Wendy nodded slowly, appreciating how rational she made it sound, but cautious that it might somehow be a trap—that she was being led into a false sense of security in the hopes she'd reveal some pivotal piece of information. The doctor took her silence as a cue to continue with her questions. "Do you remember anything about where you were held? What did you do to occupy your time? Were you the only one there? Aside from Tinkerbell, that is."

Wendy's eyes darted across the carpet as she tried to recall something. "I slept a lot—I always felt so tired, and I had no concept of time—there was no way of knowing if it was day or night. Yet, I remember a clock—or clocks. Sometimes there'd be ticking..."

Wendy clenched her fists again as the mere thought of the sound put her on edge. Banishing the thought from her mind, she did her best to appear calm. She pushed herself back into her chair, as an image slowly spread across her mind's eye, coming into focus as though she was moving towards it through a veil of fog.

"Wendy?" the psychologist prompted, and Wendy shifted under the increasing intensity of the psychologist's stare. "What is it?"

Clearing her throat, Wendy spoke softly, not entirely confident in the memory, "I think there was another man there. I don't think I was scared of him, though; he was just strange…"

"Tell me about him. Did he hurt you?"

"No, not at all—at least, not that I recall. I feel like he might have been… incredibly cheerful and friendly. In an over-the-top kind of way—like a clown but without a costume. He was only my height at the time, if not a little shorter, with a rotund physique," Wendy's voice increased from its whisper as she gained confidence in the memory unfolding before her.

"He'd bring me food, but it was always a big song and dance like he was serving up an extravagant tea party when it was really a sandwich and some water. I never knew what to make of him, but it was like we were both there in the same room, but not in the same place. Perhaps in hindsight, he wasn't quite right himself."

Wendy stopped talking, listening to the rapid scratching of the pen against the doctor's notepad, "How often do you think you saw him? Multiple times a day? Every couple of days? Sporadically?"

Wendy frowned as she struggled to recollect the specifics. "I honestly can't say. Like I told you, I don't recall having any concept of time. I don't think I was ever actually hungry or thirsty, so I must have been fed regularly enough."

"Would it be fair to say you saw this man more than the man with the green eyes?"

"Yeah, that would be fair."

"Did he ever give you a name or mention anything about the other man?" the doctor asked, gently tapping the tip of her pen on the paper.

"Um, no. I don't think so. He babbled a lot, but rarely said much about anything other than the food he was bringing me. Eventually, I stopped listening to him. Smee! I think his name was Smee," Wendy all but shouted as the name popped into her head.

"Were you able to provide a description of him to the police?"

"No. Anytime I tried to recall his face, it was like a blank canvas—there was nothing there. It sounds impossible, I know, but I couldn't describe him beyond height and shape, nothing about his features at all."

Again, the doctor was silent as she made further notes. Wendy rubbed her forehead, aching with the strain of unlocking memories she'd kept buried for over twenty years.

"Let's talk about the man that abducted you. What do you recall about him aside from his eyes?"

Wendy resumed picking the edges of her fingernails, the stinging pain as the skin split and bled. A welcome distraction.

"Nothing of any great consequence. It was mainly his eyes, which I've already told you about."

"I'd like you to try to tell me more about him."

Wendy took a deep breath, "I can't tell you what I don't know. His eyes are what I remember most."

"So, you never saw him in full—just his eyes?"

Wendy shifted in her seat again, crossing and uncrossing her legs. "Well, no. I saw him in person plenty of times. I just don't remember much about it."

"I think you do; you just don't want to remember."

"Can you really blame me?" Wendy scoffed, with an edge to her voice, but before she could argue the point further, her mind decided to unveil another image. Wendy closed her mouth as she tried to focus on it, but it felt like she was looking at it through an unfocused microscope.

"He...he was very androgynous in appearance. I remember feeling uncertain if he was a male or female initially. He was tall and thin, and he looked young, like he was in his early twenties or younger— certainly not a great deal older than I was at the time. Yet he always talked like he was much older. His features were delicate, with a long, slim nose, high cheekbones... incredibly beautiful in a strange kind of way..." Wendy trailed off, surprising herself with the revelation. She looked over at the psychologist and noted her look of curiosity, and she hastened her description. "His hair was a sandy blonde and cropped short, except for a long fringe that would constantly fall across one eye." Wendy fell silent, stumbling on another detail that her mind suddenly tried to block her from seeing.

"Go on," the doctor prompted again.

"I... I remember his hands."

"Why his hands?"

"His fingers were long, freakishly so. At least, that's how I remember them." She tried to ignore the scratching on the notepad.

"Did he speak to you during his visits?"

"Yeah, I think he did. He seemed to like to talk, but like Smee, it was never about anything real. He liked to tell stories, mostly about adventures with pirates and Indians and mermaids. I thought he was crazy, but I learned early on not to question it and just to let him talk. He got angry if I didn't." A shudder coursed through her at the memory, and she was grateful the psychologist's attention was on her pen and paper.

"Did he have a name?"

Wendy turned once more to the trees. The wind outside had picked up, and the branches whipped back and forward in a frenzy. She stared at them, as though expecting them to reveal the name of the captor. Wendy's eyebrows raised in surprise as a name slipped into her head like someone had soundlessly whispered it into her ear.

"Pan. He told me to call him Pan."

Wendy bounced the name around in her mind, wondering why she'd recalled it now after all this time when she never could in the past. Her mind suddenly felt as though it was buzzing as all the buried memories rushed forward.

"When you were found," the doctor continued, "you were three months pregnant. Did the abuse commence from the time you were abducted, or did it begin later on?"

Wendy sucked in a sharp breath at the question. "Pan never touched me, at least not in that manner." The psychologist raised her eyebrows, her disbelief evident, but Wendy continued, "He liked to stroke my hair—sometimes he'd even ask to brush it with this old, antique-looking silver brush. Other times he'd insist on holding my hand while we talked—but it was more like his long fingers wrapped around my wrist. I always felt repulsed, but I never dared let it show. The only other physical contact was when I questioned him or did something to anger him. He would get in a rage, and he would backhand me across the face."

"So, he was violent towards you."

"No. Well, yes. But it wasn't all the time…"

"It's common for victims of abuse to bury the memories…"

"I understand that I've seen it happen myself, but that's not what's happening here. I wasn't raped. The medical examination I underwent afterwards confirmed I was still a virgin. The doctors were just as stumped by my pregnancy as I was."

Wendy watched as the doctor referred to a file that rested on her lap beneath her notepad, her expression neutral. "Can you tell me about your escape?"

Wendy opened her mouth and closed it again. It felt like the memory was right there, on the edges of her consciousness, but she couldn't quite grasp it. Wendy looked over to the psychologist's large wooden desk, distracted by a ticking noise she hadn't noticed before. Her mouth fell open as she saw a large clock facing her; it's ticking slowly quickening. She shot a look at the doctor, who was watching her intently. Wendy swallowed thickly, certain the clock wasn't really there, and as she watched the second hand move spasmodically from one marker to the next, the ticking grew louder. With wide eyes, she stole a glance at the psychologist, incredulous that she continued to sit there like nothing was happening. A sense of déjà vu swept over her, and she closed her eyes, willing the ticking to stop.

"Wendy? Are you okay?" The doctor leaned forward but made no effort to get up from her chair.

Wendy nodded, not trusting herself to speak. She didn't understand why, but the loud ticking set every fibre of her being on edge, and a knot of anxiety started spiralling within her stomach, growing in size with each tick.

Another image flashed before her, this time of a man, tall and burly with long hair that hung in thick curls just below his shoulders. He had a perfectly manicured handlebar moustache that twitched when he spoke. Then came the sound of something heavy, like it was dragging along concrete, and she instinctively froze.

Wendy shoved her hands beneath her legs and leaned forward, worrying she was losing control of the direction her session was taking.

Stop it! You're going to blow it!

"Wendy? Do you remember how you escaped?"

Wendy opened her mouth to answer but was overcome with a dizziness that rendered her mute. The light from the room faded away as though she was falling backwards into a tunnel until all she could see was darkness. She squeezed her eyes tightly as

Pan's evil green eyes lit up like two small lanterns hovering before her. Though she couldn't see him, Wendy could feel his smirk penetrate the blackness. She knew it was a threat—she'd said too much. The doctor's voice wafted over to her, sounding far away, and Wendy forced herself to focus on it, feeling like a child being woken up from a dream they didn't want to leave behind.

"Wendy? Are you alright? Can I get you a glass of water?" the doctor asked, placing the file and her notepad on the side table and getting up from her couch.

Wendy held up her hand. "No, thank you. I'm fine." She felt her heart sink as she watched the doctor sit back down, not looking convinced.

"Look, let's cut to the chase. I need to be on this case, and with all due respect, I don't need you or my boss reminding me that I've been through some shit. The only impact my experience will have on my ability to work the case is that I will be completely driven and dedicated to finding her. I want to be on this case because I believe my experiences will give me an insight and an edge that can only be of benefit. Rosalie's been missing for three weeks, and we all know what the stats look like on survival rates versus the duration of a disappearance. Yet, I'm proof that there might still be hope."

"You're aware that you can be too driven, too focused, and that can be detrimental, both to you and the investigation?"

Wendy nodded. "I'm a detective. It's part of the job description. I know how to maintain the balance." Wendy held the doctor's gaze, unblinking, not allowing herself to become distracted as the doctor watched her, her head tilted to the side again while she lightly tapped her pen on the notepad.

"I'll issue my report to your boss before noon. I'm sure he will be in touch."

CHAPTER SIX

Wendy walked briskly to her car without a single look back at the psychologist's office. Sliding into the driver's seat, she pulled the door shut behind her and, with a sigh of both frustration and relief, rested her head against the headrest. With her eyes squeezed shut, Wendy tried to repel the memories that were clawing their way back to the forefront of her mind. She felt angry and annoyed that the doctor had continued to push. Wendy understood that it was her job, yet at the same time, she couldn't see the point of dredging up the darkness of her past if it wasn't an issue for her in the present. There was only one thing to do when she felt this agitated. Reaching into her jacket pocket, Wendy withdrew her phone and called Lilly.

The call was answered on the second ring, and Wendy knew her girlfriend eagerly awaited her update.

"Hey, love. How are you?" Lilly asked. "Have you had your appointment yet?"

Wendy felt her body relax into the car seat at the sound of her voice. "Yeah, I just finished up."

"How did it go?"

Wendy sighed, "Honestly, I have no idea. I don't feel confident about it. I think I may have given her more reason to doubt my capabilities than support my decision to return to work."

"How so?"

"Well, she just kept asking irrelevant questions about my past... I'd rather just leave it there."

"I'm sorry, I know how you hate talking about it. Though if you've never told me about it, I don't know what makes her think she can get it out of you." Lilly laughed, and while Wendy laughed along with her, it sounded hollow and superficial in her ears.

"Exactly. Her incessant persistence just pissed me off. I mean, I was trying my best to at least look like I was calm and collected, but the longer the questioning went on, the angrier and more agitated I felt. It didn't seem important that I repeatedly told her none of it had any bearing on my ability to do a bloody good job."

Lilly was silent for a moment. "Well, there is no point worrying about it for now. I'm sure it's just part of the process to cover themselves, but your track record speaks for itself. They'd be crazy. No, negligent, if they didn't put you on the case."

Wendy smiled to herself at the heated tone in Lilly's voice. "I guess what's done is done. All I can do now is wait and see what they say."

"Did they say how long it would take them to deliberate or whatever?"

"Yeah, she said she would have her report to him by noon."

"Well, that's something, at least. I don't imagine your boss will keep you waiting unnecessarily. What are you going to do while you wait?"

Wendy looked out the car window, realising she hadn't actually thought that far ahead. "Not sure yet. Maybe I'll go grab a coffee or something."

"That's a great idea. Well, I had better get back to work, but keep me posted, okay?"

"Will do. Love you."

"Love you, too."

Wendy ended the call and absently slipped the phone back into her jacket pocket. Inserting the key into the ignition, she let the engine run while she turned on the radio, quickly lowering the volume as the hourly news blasted from the speakers.

...Rosalie is an intelligent, gregarious young woman with a bright future ahead of her. We're a close-knit family, and if there was something wrong, we firmly believe she would have come to us. We fear for her safety and want nothing more than for her to come home to us. We beg of you, if anyone knows anything, or has seen Rosalie, or has any information that can help us find her, please come forward...

Wendy turned the radio off, chewing her bottom lip as she drummed her fingers on the steering wheel. Without thinking about it, she found herself driving around town. Images of Pan, of Smee, of her abduction, circled around in her mind, causing her insides to twist into knots. For the first time, she questioned if perhaps her boss *was* justified in his concerns. Could she be in denial about just how much the past still affected her? With a scowl, she shook her head, both to rid herself of the self-doubt and of the images themselves. Yet driving down the street, with every child she saw comforted by their parent's presence, joyful in their bubble of safety, Wendy felt acutely aware of how unsafe they all were. At how easily—how swiftly—that could change. In an instant, any one of those children could find themselves wrenched from their families and everything they'd ever known and loved. For the first time in many years, Wendy wondered if Pan had taken other children. Or was she the only one? And if so, why her? She'd always known he hadn't selected her by chance. It wasn't like they lived in a populated neighbourhood where he could have stood in the middle of a street and taken his pick of any number of houses to approach. That thought had terrified her years after the fact, a reason why she'd refused to let herself think on it again—until today. Wendy wondered if Pan was still out there today, this very second, watching a child innocently playing, waiting for the perfect time to take them. Or watching her. Either thought was horrifying, and as a wave of nausea threatened to overcome her, she quickly pulled over to the side of the road, oblivious to the sounding of neighbouring cars honking and angry drivers swearing as they manoeuvred around her.

Folding her arms across the steering wheel, she rested her head against them, taking deep breaths while trying to clear her mind of all thoughts of the past, of evil lurking around every corner. Gradually, the anxiety and panic subsided, and Wendy let out a long, shaky exhalation and raised her head. As she watched the bustling hive of activity from both traffic and pedestrians alike, Wendy was in two minds about how to kill time while she waited. She didn't really feel like being around people, but the last thing she wanted to do was hover outside the station, waiting for her boss to call—or, worse still, go home to be alone with her own thoughts. She eyed a coffee shop slightly up the road and decided it was the least conspicuous location to pass the time and likely cooler than sitting in her car.

NEVER, NEVER

Stepping into the cafe, the smell of freshly brewed coffee almost bowled her over, and she instantly craved a mug of her own. Having placed her order, Wendy scanned the room for a place to sit and honed in on an empty seat at the bench that ran the length of the window. Knowing there was nothing to pass the time like a little people-watching, she agilely ducked and weaved her way through the busy shop to the chair.

With a huff, she settled into the seat and gazed out the window at the people walking past. Instantly, her mind wandered back to her psych session, and Wendy tried to convince herself that despite her mini freak-out and her near-constant fidgeting, it hadn't gone as badly as she'd thought. It didn't matter whether she believed it or not. She just hoped by thinking her session had gone well would make it so. Wendy smiled gratefully as the waitress placed the steaming cappuccino in front of her, marvelling at how she'd navigated the crowded café without spilling a drop. Wendy wrapped her hands around the warm mug and returned to people-watching. Flicking a quick glance down the street to where her car was parked across the road, Wendy took a sip of her coffee. She froze, cup in mid-air, as she noticed a girl standing beside the car. She stood so still as to appear completely out of place when everyone was moving so quickly around her. Her hair was short, framing her face in delicate layers that accentuated her pixie-like appearance. Her brown eyes were firmly fixed on Wendy, open wide in a frozen stare of fear. Wendy slowly rose from her seat, absently taking in the long white nightgown the girl wore, and she forced herself to blink, certain she must be seeing things. Yet, when she opened her eyes, the girl was still there—and there was no mistaking who it was. Wendy had seen her photo more times than she could count.

It was Rosalie Fryair.

Rosalie's mouth opened and closed, as though she was trying to speak. The effect made her look like a fish out of water, gasping madly for air. Wendy tried to move, but her body felt weighted down like she was draped in invisible chains, and she grasped hopelessly for a logical explanation for what she saw. She could only look on as Rosalie placed her hand on the hood of Wendy's car while she took a shaky step forward like she was unsure of her ability to do so. She took another step forward and then, lifting her hand from the hood, another. With her movements more deliberate, she stepped from the footpath and off the curb until she was standing on the street in front of the car, all the while, her eyes never leaving Wendy's, her mouth still moving in silent pleas.

Wendy willed herself to move as she watched Rosalie take small, sideways steps towards the road itself. It was then that Wendy noticed the truck moving down the road, oblivious to the girl about to step out in front of him. "No!" Wendy cried, knocking over her cup of coffee, her immobility forgotten. Ignorant to the annoyed mutterings of the surrounding patrons, Wendy leaned forward and pounded on the glass, desperate to stop Rosalie from moving any further. Despite her efforts, Rosalie took another step, almost clear from the protection of the parked cars, and Wendy sent her chair tumbling backwards as she surged through the crowded café and out the door. She hit the pavement just as the truck passed by her, unhindered, throwing up a gust of wind that threw her hair back off her face. Watching it pass, her mouth fell open when there was no screech of brakes, no impact, or horrified cries of passers-by. Her relief was short-lived as she looked over to her car, only to find Rosalie was no longer there. Despite scanning the people walking up and down either side of the street, she was unable to spot the girl. Turning around, she saw the throng of onlookers from the coffee shop staring out the window at her, but she ignored their bewildered expressions and jogged along the footpath, peering through the storefronts for any sign of Rosalie. Yet with each shop she passed, her uncertainty grew, and she stopped to lean breathlessly against the brick wall, her hands braced on her thighs as she scanned the street again. With a shake of her head, she pushed herself off the wall and crossed the street, wanting to avoid the stares of anyone in the café. She strode over to her car, keeping her head down, and when she reached it, inspected the hood for any sign that the girl had touched it—a handprint, anything—but there was nothing. Wendy kicked the front tire and swore as pain radiated through her toe. She got in the car and gripped the steering wheel, pushing herself back against the seat.

Get it together, Darling. One visit with the psych and you're ready to lose the plot.

She wished she'd never agreed to the appointment. As far as she could tell, it had done more harm than good.

The end justifies the means if you find Rosalie. You just have to get assigned to the damn case.

On cue, her phone rang, and she fumbled as she tried to grab it out of her jacket pocket. "Detective Darling speaking."

"Detective," her boss greeted her, with no need to introduce himself. "I'm calling to discuss the outcome of your evaluation."

Wendy felt her hand shake, and she struggled to keep the phone to her ear, swallowing thickly as the nervous flurry of butterflies tormented her stomach. "Yes, I'm listening, Sir."

"I'm satisfied with the report I received on your review, and you'll be pleased to know I'm assigning you to the Fryair case."

Wendy's mouth fell open in surprise. "That... that's fantastic news, Sir. Thank you, I'll get on it straight away, I'm sure there's a lot to catch up on and..."

"You didn't let me finish," her boss cut in. "I have one condition."

"Sir?"

"You take the rest of the day off."

"Sir, that's not necessary ... "

"It's not a request, Darling—it's an order. I appreciate that this morning's session would have been difficult for you, and I want you clear-headed and focused. So, take the rest of the day off—deal with whatever you need to deal with—and make whatever arrangements you need to with your family. Then come in fresh tomorrow. You'll be working around the clock from that point on, so make the most of the downtime. Detective Roberts will be ready to brief you on the case first thing in the morning."

"Yes, Sir. Thank you, Sir." Wendy ended the call and tossed her phone onto the passenger seat. She was grateful to be on the case, and after seeing Rosalie's ghostly apparition, she was all the more eager to get to work. She couldn't explain it, but she felt like she was meant to be on the case, that only she could find Rosalie. Perhaps it was just the memories the case triggered, maybe it was more than that. Either way, she knew there was only one way to find out. Starting the engine, Wendy hesitantly looked in the rear-view mirror, half expecting to see Rosalie again, standing by the car. Once convinced she was alone, she pulled out into the street without looking back again.

Wendy looked up at the townhouse she called home and smiled. After three weeks away, she looked forward to sleeping in her own bed. Sure, it was a dwarf of a place in comparison to the Darling estate, but it was hers. It was tall and narrow, spanning three floors and an attic. A small set of stairs led from the pavement down to the ground floor, which was an independent and generous sized flat that belonged to a little old lady by the name of Mertha, who Wendy only ever saw if she happened to be home on a Sunday morning when Mertha was either picked up or dropped off by her granddaughter for their weekly shopping and catch up.

Steep, dark grey concrete stairs lined either side with wrought-iron rails, which led from the pavement up to Wendy's teal green front door. She loved the splash of colour against the dreary dark brick of the building. Large rectangular windows framed either side of the door, with heavy drapes pulled firmly closed across them—Wendy didn't like the thought that anyone walking past might be able to see in, so they almost always stayed closed.

Letting herself in, she dumped her bags just inside the door, making sure to close it firmly behind her, double-checking the lock. Gathering her bags back up, she climbed the stairs, her phone already nestled between her shoulder and her ear as she called Lilly. She answered on the first ring.

"How did it go?"

"I'm on the case."

"Oh, sweetheart. I'm happy for you. I know what this case means to you. I take it you start straight away?"

"Actually, no. I've been ordered to take the rest of the day off, sort myself out, and start fresh in the morning. It's annoying."

"I think it sounds like a smart idea. Get some rest— I know you barely slept after insisting on staying in that old room of yours."

"I don't know. I think I feel too wired."

"Do you want me to come over after work? We can just get some takeout and watch a movie?"

Wendy considered the offer for a moment, torn. "Actually, I think I might just stay alone tonight if that's okay."

Lilly chuckled. "Of course. I'll text you after work and see how you're doing."

Wendy again reminded herself how fortunate she was to have such an amazing partner as she hoisted her bags onto the bed and contently looked up. The master room was beyond generous, but what she loved about it was the wall of glass along the far wall that extended up on an angle and made up part of the roof. Looking straight out, all she could see were the trees from the heritage-listed parklands that halted at her rear fence. But looking straight up, she had a perfect view of the sky. It was a view Wendy adored, especially when it was raining, or on a clear night when she couldn't sleep and only had the stars and the moon to keep her company.

Kicking her shoes off, she sprawled across what little section of her bed wasn't obstructed with bags. Nothing felt so good as returning to your own bed after a time away. With a yawn, she closed her eyes, telling herself she would have just a quick power nap before she unpacked.

Wendy awoke with a start, bolting up into a seated position, her eyes darting around the room. She tried to catch her breath—she felt like she'd been holding it underwater for too long. It took her a few moments to realise she was back in her own room—her adult room—and no longer at the manor. With a groan, Wendy realised her quick nap had lasted far longer than she'd planned. Not only was it now dark out, the faint lightening of the horizon told her it would soon be morning.

I can't remember the last time I slept for that long.

Leaning back against her elbows, she tried to shake the feeling that something had woken her, telling herself it was just another bad dream. Not bothering to check the time, Wendy pushed herself off the bed and went and sat in a well-worn armchair beside the window to gaze up at the clear night sky. She felt on edge and regretted not asking Lilly to stay.

There was very little light from the moon, but that only meant there were more stars to admire. However, with the inner-city light pollution, there weren't as many to see as there were back at the manor—but there were enough to keep her mind entertained during the long nights when her insomnia was at its worst.

Her eyelids felt heavy, and they kept dropping shut before her brain took over and forced them back open again. They'd finally closed completely, her body relaxing into the seat when an odd sound sent them flying back open again. Alert and on edge, she sat up straight, leaning forward as she looked towards the open bedroom door, listening intently. Hearing it again, she quietly rose to her feet and tip-toed across the room, the plush carpet muting her movements. Standing just inside the doorway, she willed her breathing to quiet—it sounded so loud, echoing in her ears as she strained to determine where the sound was coming from. It came a third time, a soft clatter from downstairs. Wendy felt her heartbeat speed up, certain the sound came from the kitchen—where her back door was located.

Hugging the wall, she crept down the stairs, keeping her eyes fixed firmly on the lounge room below her. She gasped as a light turned on from the kitchen, and she quickly covered her mouth and tried to press herself against the wall. A shadow crossed the light that flooded out across the adjacent lounge room carpet, and Wendy felt frozen in fear as she scanned the room for something, anything she could use to defend herself.

Toughen up, for crying out loud. You're supposed to be a damn detective!

She silently cursed herself for leaving her phone upstairs, but she saw her gym gear shoved in the corner, gathering dust, and hurried over to it. As quietly as she could, she moved aside the rolled-up yoga mat and retrieved a dumbbell. At best, she'd be able to get a decent blow in if it came to that. Wendy moved across the carpet, careful to keep to the edges of the light until she reached the entrance to the kitchen.

"You scared the shit out of me!" she exclaimed as she saw Jane arranging crockery and cutlery on the small, square dining table.

Jane looked up and smiled. "I wanted to surprise you," she declared, walking over and giving her mother an affectionate hug and a kiss on the cheek.

"You do realise you were seconds away from being clobbered by a 5kg hand weight," Wendy replied.

Jane laughed. "Well, at least you would have finally found a use for it."

Wendy smiled. "What on earth are you doing here so early? Actually, what time is it? Not that I'm not happy to see you."

"It's about five, five-thirty, I think. I couldn't sleep, and I felt bad that I'd missed your call yesterday. I could tell from your voicemail how relieved you were, and I thought it would be nice to surprise you with a breakfast that consisted of something more than coffee. Besides, it's not like you would have been sleeping. Oh, shit." Jane paused and looked up at her mother. "You weren't asleep, were you?"

Wendy chuckled. "No, I wasn't. And thank you for this. Have I told you that you're my favourite daughter?"

"Not lately," Jane replied, grinning, "Now sit down, and I'll pour you coffee."

Wendy pulled out a chair and sat down, admiring her daughter's handiwork, surprised that she'd managed to find anything matching to lay out on the table.

"Will Lilly be joining us?" Jane asked.

Wendy shook her head. "She didn't stay last night."

Jane simply nodded in reply as she turned back to the stove. Wendy supposed she was used to her mother's unconventional, long-term-strangely-committed-but-non-committal-relationship.

"I know it's a lot to ask," Wendy started, "but with this case, I won't have a lot of time to help your uncles with everything. You said you still have a couple of weeks leave, and I was wondering..."

"It's fine, Mum," Jane said with a laugh. "Despite the circumstances, I'm actually enjoying spending time with them. It's nice at the estate—like I said, I'm not sure why we haven't spent more time there."

Wendy avoided the comment and took a sip of her coffee. "Would you also mind checking in on Nanna for me while you're there?"

She peered at her daughter over the rim of her mug.

"Yes, mum..." Jane replied drolly, and even though her back was turned, Wendy knew she was rolling her eyes.

"I'm just worried about her, is all," Wendy explained.

"You know I'll check in on her, Mum. I'll let you know if anything is going on." Jane turned back to the stove and hummed quietly to herself while she cooked. Wendy watched on, only half paying attention as she thought about the day ahead.

CHAPTER SEVEN

Despite her eagerness to start working the case, Wendy found herself sitting in her car, staring up at the bland and fairly inconspicuous building before her. An unexpected bout of nerves kept her from opening the car door, and she allowed herself a few minutes to get composed. Wendy knew she was being ridiculous, not wanting to enter the station at any less than one hundred percent. The last thing she needed was anyone else doubting her ability to do her job— especially her new partner.

Decisively, she pushed the door open and stepped out of the car, slinging her bag over her shoulder. Wendy strode across the carpark, counting the steps as she walked along the side of the station and around to the front. Usually, she came and went from the rear, but today it felt right to go through the front door. She took the stairs two and at a time, only hesitating for a moment with her hand braced against the wall, before taking a deep breath and pushing it open.

"Good morning, Kath," she said to the officer sitting behind the front desk.

"Welcome back, Wendy. I was so sorry to hear of your mother's passing."

"Thank you. I appreciate it," Wendy replied, with a tight smile, looking over the familiar walls to help keep her emotions in check. Despite the peaceful quiet of the foyer, she knew all too well the hustle and bustle that awaited on the other side of the wall.

"Before you go in, Jared has left a message asking to see you in his office as soon as you get in."

Wendy gave a nod of thanks and walked past the front desk, through the door, and into the heart of the station, suddenly nervous to see her boss, Senior Detective Jared Helfer. She did her best attempt at a warm smile as she was greeted by fellow officers, humbly accepting their condolences—she was never comfortable when the attention was directed her way. Except when she was briefing others on a case— then she was in her element.

The length of the station suddenly felt endless as she made her way across it, stopped by everyone that she passed. Eventually, she started dismissing her colleagues, albeit kindly, by telling them she had to hurry as the boss was waiting for her.

Wendy knocked twice on his office door. She wasn't kept waiting as he called her in. "Good morning, Sir," Wendy stated as she closed the door behind her, trying to keep the nerves from her voice.

"Detective Darling. Welcome back to work."

"Thank you, Sir."

"First of all, I truly am sorry for your loss. How are you feeling?" His face flushed slightly, well-known for his discomfort in personal conversations.

"Thank you, Sir. I'm doing as well as can be expected, and I'm eager to work."

"Good." His shoulders seemed to lower at not having to have a heart to heart. "I expect you to hit the ground running—this Fryair case has gone on too long as it is, and I'm getting heat from above. I want that girl found yesterday. Am I right in assuming this won't be a problem?"

"Correct, Sir."

Her boss stared at her intently, his expression unreadable. She stared back, unflinching, refusing to show any signs of weakness.

"Excellent. Now, Detective Rupert Roberts is new to our station, so I know you haven't worked with him yet—but let me assure you, he has strong credentials, and despite the lack of leads on the case, he's not leaving a single stone unturned."

"I don't doubt it, Sir."

"Very good. In that case, he's waiting for you in the briefing room".

"Thank you, Sir," she replied, and left the office, unable to hold back a hint of a smile as she wove her way through the station to the briefing room. While she'd heard the news of Detective Roberts' appointment, she hadn't given it a second thought until now. He had a reputation as a highly competent detective with one of the best close percentages in the country—but he also had a reputation as a ladies' man. Said to be handsome, very, in fact—it was said he was more than aware of it and known to play on his charm when the occasion called for it—and Wendy suspected even when there wasn't. It occurred to Wendy that may well be the reason they'd been partnered up—she made no secret of her relationship with Lilly. As she reached the briefing room, Wendy reminded herself not to judge Detective Roberts despite the fact everything she'd heard about him made him sound like the kind of person she would usually avoid.

The door was open, and she peered in to find three officers were talking inside—one sitting on a table with the other two facing him, their backs to the door. Wendy knocked on the wall, not wanting to barge in.

"Detective Dah-ling! Glad to see you could finally join us," Detective Rupert Roberts stated, clearly amused at his pronunciation of her surname. He made no move to get up from the table, obviously expecting Wendy to go to him. He gave a nod to the other two officers, and they turned and walked out of the room, greeting Wendy in passing.

"Roberts." Wendy greeted her fellow detective, trying to hide her distaste as he flashed his perfect smile at her. She held out her hand, forcing herself to hold his gaze as they shook. The handshake went on a few seconds too long, and she wondered if he was intentionally trying to make her feel uncomfortable, to assert his dominance in their partnership. Either way, she had no intention of letting him win. Wendy reminded herself that Roberts was known to be an excellent detective, but beyond that, she couldn't see what the hype was all about. Sure, he was handsome in a clean-cut Boy Scout kind of way, with his dark blonde hair and deep green eyes. She could see how his Scottish accent made the females—and even some of the male contingent of the staff—swoon somewhat, but beyond that, she hoped his work proved more impressive than his smug disposition. Regardless, she was stuck with him.

"So, you're ready to get started?" he asked, crossing his arms over his chest as he leaned against the table again. Wendy refused to look at him further, instead scanning the evidence that spanned across the room. She could feel the intensity of his gaze and was annoyed as a warm flush ran up from her neck and into her cheeks.

"Let's get started, shall we?"

Roberts cleared his throat, making no effort to move. "I'll tell you what, how about you grab us both a coffee, and I'll tell you everything you need to know."

Wendy looked over her shoulder, her first instinct to tell him to shove it. But one look at his smug expression told her he was baiting her, and she didn't want to give him the satisfaction of taking the bait. "Sure." Wendy smiled through clenched teeth and left the room.

"Bloody hell, Darling. You could stand a spoon up in that coffee," Roberts exclaimed as she placed her mug on the table before her.

"Fortunately, I'm not asking you to drink it," she replied innocently.

"Touché…" he replied, taking a swig from his own mug. He scrunched his face, indicating it was passable, and Wendy rolled her eyes before she could stop herself. He caught the look, and instead of annoyance, he grinned at her. "Right," Roberts replied, placing his mug on the table and turned to face the evidence boards.

Finally.

Wendy thought to herself as she moved in closer for a better look.

Roberts pointed to a photo at the top of the board. "Rosalie Fryair. Fifteen years old and last seen in the family home, in her bedroom at approximately 9 PM, 9th of November, believed to be going to bed."

"Who made that assumption?" Wendy asked.

"Her mother. She said when she ducked into Rosalie's room to say goodnight, she was already dressed in her pyjamas and sitting on her bed chatting to one of her school friends via her laptop."

Wendy nodded, but Roberts continued before she could say anything, "Before you ask, the 'pyjamas' consisted of a nightgown, more like a long t-shirt with a picture of a lightning strike on the front. Wendy kept her eyes on the image of Rosalie as she recalled seeing her in the street, and she pictured the nightie exactly as Roberts described it. She swallowed thickly, feeling like she was going to gag, and it took all her concentration to make sure she didn't, causing her to zone out momentarily.

"Sorry, what was that?" she asked.

Roberts flashed her a sideways look of annoyance, his eyebrow raised at her as though questioning her dedication to the case. "I said, the nightgown wasn't found in her room, and there was no evidence that she'd changed clothes prior to her disappearance. According to her parents, nothing seemed to be missing from the room at all." He pointed to a series of photos taken from inside the bedroom.

"Here you can see the laptop was left closed at the foot of her bed, and her mobile phone was on the bedside table, plugged into the charger. Her train pass and bank cards were all in the phone cover. To her parent's best knowledge, all of her shoes were still there, and her school bag was on her desk chair with her house keys inside it." He made a point of turning back to look at Wendy to ensure she was following, and she gave him a nod, clenching her jaw as she struggled to hold back the barb that threatened to blurt out. He pointed to another photo as he moved past it. "The double windows on the left side of the bedroom were found wide open, and Mrs. Fryair is certain they were closed when she'd said goodnight to her daughter."

"So? Rosalie could have just opened them."

"True. This was found snagged on the edge of the bottom right corner of the window." He pointed at the photo, and Wendy stepped closer for a better look. She inspected the close-up shot of the broken necklace hanging from a slim splintered piece of the window frame and felt her heart pound. She blinked, trying to process what she was seeing. Hanging from the delicate silver chain was an oval locket with a unicorn adorning the front. Bordering the locket looked like tiny pieces of hematite.

Roberts shoved his hands in his pockets and rocked slowly back and forward on the balls of his feet. Wendy ignored his annoyance as Nanna's words repeated in her mind, *don't follow the unicorn...*

Roberts cleared his throat, and Wendy stepped back, nodding for him to continue his brief. Wendy forced herself to listen, but her gaze wandered back to the necklace at every opportunity. As much as she tried to tell herself it was a coincidence, she couldn't discredit the possibility that what she thought were random words plucked from the fog of Nanna's mind was actually a moment of lucidity. A warning.

But how?

Roberts tapped at another photograph, drawing her attention to Rosalie's bedroom. The photo was of the window at the rear of the room, which started about a metre from the carpet and was made of two large panes of glass, framed in white wood. They were open outwards, and Wendy shuddered as a sense of déjà vu washed over her. She shook it off and leaned in for a closer look. There was nothing special about their design, yet as she looked at them, the déjà vu intensified.

I can see my hands; I'm holding them out in front of me. I'm reaching out and pushing open my bedroom window. I put my foot up on the ledge, but my legs feel funny, and my foot slips off. I stumble and hit my elbow on the window ledge. I know it should hurt, but it doesn't. I put my foot up again, this time making sure I hold on to the window frame for balance. I'm standing on the ledge. I can see the moon shining up above, not quite full, yet lighting up the garden below. The flowers look so tiny from up here. There is a slight wind blowing around me, but I'm not cold. I see a flurry of green sparks out of the corner of my eyes, but I'm not bothered by them. I nod, as though spoken to and step off the ledge.

She shook her head, forcing the image away. Wendy couldn't tell if it was a memory or just her imagination. Either way, she knew it had no business being in her forethoughts right now.

"Look, do you want to go over this another time?" Roberts paused, his finger hovering before a photo of the undisturbed garden bed below the window, his handsome features marred by the scowl that darkened them.

"I'm paying attention. I'm just taking everything in if that's alright with you," she replied huffily and made a point of inspecting the image he was pointing at, chastising herself for her unprofessionalism. She pointed to the flower bed. "There doesn't look to be any signs of disturbance. Is this the flowerbed directly beneath the bedroom window?"

Roberts nodded. "Correct. No signs of an impact either amongst the flowers or in the grass on the other side of it. Admittedly, it's harder to see impact damage in the grass than the flowers, but from that height, we would expect to see something."

They never found any disturbance below my bedroom, either.

Wendy rubbed her forehead, wishing the past to stay locked away. The last thing she wanted to do was review the case with any bias. She tried to focus on all the evidence before her, to take it all in with fresh eyes and try to find anything that was overlooked, even if she had to remind herself every thirty seconds that there was no connection between her past and this case.

"As you're aware, the powers that be have advised the press and the public that we're treating it as a missing persons case. We've been told to stay clear of any implications of an abduction."

"Is that wise? Why wouldn't they pursue all avenues?" she asked.

Roberts massaged his forehead. "Honestly, no. I don't think it is. But our hands are tied. There seems to be more concern around how the word 'abduction' will affect the new Lord Mayor's status with the public."

"Are you serious? How can his political standing be more important than his missing daughter?"

"Nothing is more important than his daughter, you would think. I don't know if the directive is coming directly from him or his PR people. Either way, we have to abide by it."

"Bloody bullshit," Wendy said, more to herself than to Roberts.

"At the end of the day, we have no evidence, no suspects, and no leads—not a damn one."

He leaned back against the table again, his arms crossed against his chest while he frowned up at the photos. Wendy shot him a side-long glance and could see from the clenching of his jaw that he was frustrated by the lack of progress on the case. She leaned on the table beside him. "So who's been interviewed so far?"

Roberts reached behind him and picked up a thick folder, handing it to her. "Her parents were both home the evening Rosalie disappeared. We briefly questioned her sister, Jessica, who's a year younger, but she was staying at a friend's house to work on an assignment."

"And that was confirmed?"

"Of course," Roberts continued. "We also interviewed her two closest friends, Nicole Winter and Jasmine Archer. As we know, friends tend to know more about each other's lives than their families, despite how close the parents may think their relationship is."

"Did that garner anything?"

"Nada. They weren't overly helpful. We also obtained the parents' permission to review both Rosalie's phone and her laptop, but the last update from the IT crew was they'd found nothing helpful there either."

"Who was Rosalie chatting with on her laptop when her mother checked in on her?"

"That was Nicole. They were chatting via Facebook Messenger, and we've already reviewed the chat thread. Mostly talking about their weekend plans and some music festival they were hoping to go to in a couple of months. Nothing remotely sinister and nothing to even indicate Rosalie was on edge. Or fearful. Certainly nothing alluding to what was about to happen." He leaned over, glancing over her shoulder as she flicked through the sheets of paper.

"So, if Rosalie planned to run away, shouldn't there be some mention of it in the transcript? Even if they used some kind of code word for her plans, it should be evident in hindsight. But there really is nothing. It's just the ramblings of two teenage girls without a care in the world."

"Exactly. I mean, just because she came from a privileged family doesn't mean her home life was perfect, but we've found no evidence to suggest that—so why would she want to run away?"

"What about a boyfriend? Someone older maybe or someone her parents didn't approve of?"

"We went down that line of questioning with her friends, and they said Rosalie wasn't even 'crushing' on anyone right now—their choice of word, not mine. Her social media accounts seemed to support that. Yet we're expected to treat it like a runaway case. It just doesn't fly."

"This case feels really off," Wendy said quietly.

Roberts sighed, "You can say that again. Honestly, it's nice to be able to share the load. The case has been doing my head in, between the dead-ends and politics…"

"Well, hopefully, a fresh set of eyes will help. Are we thinking her father has something to do with this?"

Roberts rubbed his chin, and Wendy thought he seemed hesitant to answer. "There's a tonne of politics going on behind the scenes, and there's a good chance someone knows something and isn't telling us. But do I think he's directly responsible for his daughter's disappearance? I don't. Really the only thing I do know is, despite our best efforts, we've gotten nowhere in three weeks."

Wendy flicked over the interview transcripts with Rosalie's parents but wanted to hear Roberts' impression first hand. "What was her father like when you spoke to him?"

His face twisted in thought like he was trying to find a diplomatic way to word it. "He's a politician, tough to get a read on. All fake smiles and firm handshakes. A friendly voice with a demanding stare. I wouldn't want to get on the wrong side of him. His answers were vague, to say the least—he definitely has that skill of talking without really saying anything. The timing feels suspicious between his rapid rise to position and his daughter's disappearance, but I still can't understand the need to keep an abduction off the table."

"What about the mother?"

"She was a bloody open book compared to her husband. Absolutely distraught—the exact reaction you would expect from a parent whose child has been abducted."

Wendy turned and faced him, frowning. "You said abducted..."

Roberts nodded. "I think if their daughter were simply missing, we would expect concern, panic, tears, but there'd be hope that she'd show up. Her reaction was intense—literally inconsolable..."

"Like she doesn't expect her daughter to come home," Wendy said softly, her eyebrows raised.

"Strictly between you and me, of course. But there's more to this case than meets the eye."

Wendy walked the length of the evidence boards, trying to find something, anything, that would give them a clue as to what happened.

"And the friends said nothing had bothered Rosalie in the lead up to her disappearance?"

"Nothing that's panned out. They both mentioned that Rosalie had become a bit of an insomniac in recent months. There was apparently a repetitive nightmare behind it—or so they said. But again, that's not really anything to go on. Who sleeps well these days?"

"By repetitive, how often did she have it? Weekly? Nightly? Every other night?" Wendy asked.

Roberts shrugged. "They couldn't say."

"Did they know what the nightmare consisted of?

Roberts shook his head. "They both thought it was a bit weird that Rosalie knew the nightmare was always the same, yet the only thing she could recall from it was 'creepy floating green eyes' quote-unquote."

Wendy all but fell against the table, her legs threatening to give way beneath her as she gripped the edge. Despite her light weight, the table creaked under the sudden pressure, and the sound grated on her nerves that suddenly felt raw and exposed. Suddenly mindful of her erratic breathing, Wendy hoped Roberts couldn't hear the sudden thundering of her heart against her chest. Hot, acidic bile rose up in her throat, and she forced herself to swallow it, using all her will power to cast aside the urge to vomit. Fortunately, Roberts got up and began pacing, oblivious to Wendy's reaction.

No, no, no, no, no, no... it can't be... it's not possible...

With a shaky hand, Wendy picked up one of the files and made a show of flicking through the pages until she felt semi-confident that she could speak. "Who else knew about the nightmare?" she finally asked.

"Her family said they'd heard her call out in her sleep more than once, but I don't think Rosalie confided in them the specifics."

Keeping her head down, Wendy squeezed her eyes shut as the eyes from her own nightmares tried to push their way to the forefront of her mind. "You don't mind if I hold on to these? I want to go through them further," Wendy asked.

Roberts nodded. "I'd expect nothing less."

"And I want to take a look at the Fryair's house. I know you've already gone through the place with a fine-tooth comb, but I need to see it for myself. Photos are one thing..." Wendy trailed off, cautious not to offend him on her first day on the case.

Roberts pulled his keys from his back pocket and waved them at her. "Let's go."

CHAPTER EIGHT

The drive felt like it took longer than it actually did as Wendy played over the case details. Staring out the window, she chewed on her fingernails while trying to keep the anxiety from gnawing at her insides. The random sideways glances Roberts cast in her direction didn't go unnoticed, though she didn't acknowledge them. The fact that she could feel his gaze on her, however brief, made her shift in her seat.

She was relieved when they pulled alongside the curb. As Wendy got out of the car, she looked up at the house, trying to take in as much detail as she could. Two large trees stood on either side of the front yard like a frame, revealing the setback house in the middle. It looked like all the other houses in the neighbourhood—two stories with an attic marked by small windows and larger, rectangular windows decorating the other two floors. The window frames were painted white, offsetting the dark grey bricks. The front door was nothing special, also white, with two narrow panes of glass decorating the top half. There was a narrow bed of flowers running along the front of the house, which Wendy knew from the crime photos ran the whole way around the house.

"It seems a fairly modest house, given Fryair's recent appointment," Wendy mentioned, more to herself than Roberts, but he replied anyway.

"The house apparently dates back through the Fryair family to when it was first built in the 1850s." He seemed proud of this piece of knowledge, and Wendy gave an absent nod as she stepped onto the path that led to the front door, inspecting the pristinely manicured, perfectly trimmed lawn as she walked. Roberts, two steps behind her, caught her inspecting the grass.

"What is it?" he asked.

"Nothing really, it just feels odd that with everything going on, the yard is well looked after. Do the Fryair's have a gardener?"

"They don't. Mr. Fryair, however, is the proud owner of a green thumb and finds working in the garden relaxing. It appears the hobby has become somewhat of an obsession in recent weeks."

"Over the disappearance of his daughter or guilt over his involvement," Wendy said quietly, ensuring only Roberts would hear her.

"That's the million-dollar question. According to Mrs. Fryair, he'll work in the garden until well into the night."

"How does he see? The nearest street lamp is over there, and the light at the front door wouldn't illuminate much."

"Apparently, he wears one of those lights that will strap to your head." Wendy and Roberts exchanged a look and tried to stifle their chuckles as they reached the porch.

"I'm sure you have seen on the news that Cynthia Wilson is acting Lord Mayor while Malcolm Fryair is taking an extended leave of absence. Though the word on the street is, it wasn't voluntary, despite what he says. Apparently, Fryair was starting to create a bit of a political buzz, and not in a good way, coming to work dishevelled, hanging up on foreign diplomats, and behaving erratically... some even say drunk."

"Which I'd say is understandable, given the circumstances," Wendy cut in.

"I don't disagree with you. But not the best look for a man in his newly elected position. At least they had the sense to realise that sacking a man whose daughter was missing would also create unwanted media uproar, and so he's on an indefinite leave of absence. Hence the gardening."

"What about Mrs. Fryair?" Wendy asked, lowering her voice as they approached the front door.

"Mrs. Fryair—Anne—seems to be indifferent to her husband's obsession. She seems to alternate between annoyance with him spending so much time out here and stressed that he's not spending more time with his family. In between that, she focuses on her own obsession—baking."

"What about work?" Wendy asked.

"Nothing official, though she's always been heavily involved in local charity and community projects, and she sits on a number of boards for prominent firms here in Melbourne. Oh, and I warn you now, it's not worth declining Mrs. Fryair's attempts to feed you. It will only upset her. The silver lining is her baking is amazing," he instructed.

Wendy didn't answer as Roberts knocked on the door. When there was no answer, he knocked again. The sound of footsteps neared, and the door was flung open.

"Hi, Jessica. I didn't expect to find you home today," Roberts stated as Wendy found herself looking at a pretty teenage girl. She tucked her hair behind her ear and gave a half-smile that didn't reach her eyes.

"Pupil free day. But of course, I'm not allowed to leave the house, so it's even more boring than if I'd gone to school."

"Well, luckily for you, school's back on tomorrow," Roberts replied, prompting a shy smile from the girl. Roberts gave a quick nod and gestured to Wendy beside him. "This is my friend, Detective Darling. She's joining me on the case, and I just wanted to show her around."

"Hi, Jessica. You can call me Wendy."

"Hey." The girl only gave her a quick look of acknowledgement before she looked back at Roberts, her cheeks slightly flushed with youthful infatuation, and it was all Wendy could do not to roll her eyes.

"Jessica! What did I tell you about opening the front door? Only your father or I can open the front door. You never know who will be on the other side!" exclaimed Anne Fryair as she stormed down the hall, frantically wiping her hands on her apron.

"There's glass in the front door, Mum. Pretty sure I can see who's on the other side of it," Jessica replied, pulling a face that her mother couldn't see as she folded her arms across her chest.

"Sorry to bother you, Anne. I called Malcolm this morning, and he said it would be okay to swing by."

"Of course. Mal has just gone to the nursery; he's decided to expand the flower bed from around the house and line the path to the front door."

NEVER, NEVER

"I'm sure he'll do a wonderful job. Anne, the reason I'm here is I wanted to introduce you to another detective who is joining me on your daughter's case."

"I'm Detective Wendy Darling. Nice to meet you, Mrs. Fryair." Wendy stepped forward and held out her hand.

"Nice to meet you, Detective. Please, call me Anne," she replied as she shook hands. "I'm thrilled to hear the police are increasing resources to help find our daughter."

Wendy shot a quick glance at Roberts before looking back at Anne. "I was hoping to have a look around for myself. Is that okay with you?"

Anne nodded and stepped back from the door, bumping into Jessica, who hovered behind her. "Of course, please come in."

Wendy and Roberts stepped into the house, their shoes sounding heavy atop the immaculately polished wooden floors. The entry was small but uncluttered. There was a stunning staircase running up the wall to the right and a narrow side table along the opposite wall. Hanging above it was a large, round mirror. To the left, the entryway spread into a wide hallway, which Wendy assumed led into the rest of the house. The wall was lined with framed photos of the Fryair family, both ancestral and recent.

"I can walk around with you, in case you have any questions," Jessica offered, twirling her hair around her fingers as she gazed up at Roberts.

"Don't bother the detectives, Jessica. They know where they're going. You can keep out of their way and come and help me in the kitchen. Thank you." With a groan, the teen turned and skulked down the hall.

"When you're done, please come into the kitchen. I'll put the kettle on, and I've just pulled a sultana cake from the oven," Anne announced, her smile too wide, as though overcompensating for the sadness in her eyes.

"Of course," Roberts replied and started up the stairway, flicking Wendy a quick look to follow him. "Nice to meet you," Wendy said softly, as she ascended the stairway. Thirteen steps later, they

stepped up onto the landing, walking past two bedrooms before Roberts opened the third door, stepping back to allow Wendy inside. She instantly started piecing together what she'd reviewed in the photos with what she saw before her. Aside from the seized mobile phone and laptop, Rosalie's room had remained untouched since her disappearance.

Roberts remained silent as he stood in the doorway, allowing Wendy to lose herself in her observations. She looked down at the bed, with its wooden frame and black duvet cover with silver stars. She reached down and ran her fingers along the matching pillowcase, where the slight indentation from Rosalie's resting head was still present. She looked at the phone charger cord lying across the bedside table, following it down to where it plugged into the wall down beside the bed leg. Opening the top drawer of the dresser, she rummaged through the contents, consisting of little more than an array of wild-coloured nail polishes, two pairs of sunglasses, some bits and pieces of decorative jewellery, a couple of pens, and band pins. The second drawer contained underwear and the third socks. Once they were closed again, Wendy stood back, noticing something wasn't quite right, and she stepped around to the side of the drawers for a better look.

"Looking for something?" Roberts asked.

"Hmm," Wendy replied as she crouched down. The middle and bottom drawers weren't quite flush, which was easier to spot from the side. With both hands, she pulled the middle drawer completely out and reached her hand into the back of the chest. Her fingers brushed against something, and she grabbed hold of it, pulling it out for a better look. In her hands, she held an A4 exercise book.

"Well, shit!" Roberts exclaimed as he stepped into the room as she got to her feet and opened it up.

Flicking through the pages, Wendy felt as though the floor was opening up beneath her, that she was already falling through it with nothing to stop her fall. The notebook was half-filled, mostly with drawings of large green eyes staring back at them. There were no other features, just the eyes. In some versions, the eyes were encapsulated by thick, angry black charcoal, bringing their luminosity to life. In others, the eyes were rimmed with red, giving them an even more sinister appearance. As she felt her hands tremble, she closed the notebook before Roberts had the chance to notice.

"Hey! I was still looking at those," he complained. Wendy swallowed thickly and handed him the notebook, choosing to distract herself by walking around the rest of the room and inspecting it. She struggled to remain objective as her mind instinctively drew similarities between Rosalie's bedroom and her own childhood bedroom, where she had disappeared from all those years ago. Obviously, the décor was a little more modern, and the posters on the walls were of bands Wendy had never heard of, but the general layout was very similar. The bed and bedside table were situated against the far wall, in the opposite direction of the window. Wendy stood in the middle of the room and looked from one end to the other and back again.

"What is it? Roberts asked as he tucked the notebook under his arm and walked over to her.

"I'm not sure yet. Mrs. Fryair reported the window was shut when she came in to say goodnight to Rosalie, but then it was open the following morning..."

"Which in itself doesn't mean anything," Roberts replied. "She could have gotten up, opened the window, and climbed out."

Wendy nodded. "True, but how? We're two stories up, and there isn't anything she could use to shimmy down. If she'd used something from within the room to get down, or propped a ladder up beforehand, then we'd expect to see some evidence of that. Yet the evidence photos show no sign of any disruption."

"And yet, the same can be said in reverse. If someone abducted her, we would expect to see evidence of those things, too. Hence the dilemma," Roberts replied.

Wendy walked over to the window and pushed it open. Looking down, there was just a sheer, two-story drop of brick wall, ending in the flowers of the garden bed below, bordered with more perfectly manicured grass. As she leaned on the window ledge and stared out, she felt an overwhelming surge of déjà vu return. Blinking, Wendy watched as the day turned to night before her, the backyard illuminated by an engorged full moon. A wide, goofy smile spread across her face as she felt a strange, sluggish joy wash over her—like a combination of being drunk and sleepwalking. A faint haze appeared out of nowhere, slowly covering everything until it felt as though she was looking inside a cloud. With a quick flash of green in the corners of her eyes, she heard a faint musical tingling in her ears, and Wendy felt the sudden urge to climb up onto the window ledge...

"Whoa, Dah-ling!" Roberts exclaimed as he pulled her away from the window. "What the hell are you doing?" Wendy spun around, feeling disorientated as she suddenly found herself back in the daylight—and in Rosalie's room. Unsure of what had just happened, she shrugged Roberts grip away, embarrassed that he'd witnessed it. "What the hell am I doing? What the hell are you doing?" she hissed.

"You almost fell out the damn window!" he exclaimed, his eyebrows raised in alarm.

"No, I didn't. I knew what I was doing. I was just trying to gain some perspective. Now, I want to inspect the yard."

Without meeting his questioning stare, she stormed past him and out of the room. She hurried past Jessica, who was lurking in the hallway, and took the stairs two at a time. From there, she followed the smells of baking into the kitchen to find Anne Fryair. The woman looked up with her façade of a smile. "Finished already, detective?"

"Not quite. I was hoping to look around outside."

"Of course." Mrs. Fryair hurried from around the kitchen bench and led Wendy past the dining table and into the laundry. "Just through there, then around to your right to get to the backyard."

Wendy thanked her, waiting for her to head back to the kitchen before she opened the door and stepped outside. The yard was spacious with fruit trees lining the rear fence, all perfectly manicured. Along the far side of the fence to her right, there looked to be an extensive herb garden; however, it was the flower bed lining the rear of the house that she was most interested in inspecting. She walked over and stood a couple of metres in front of it and looked up at Rosalie's bedroom window. Roberts was standing at Rosalie's window, frowning down at her. She held his gaze for a few moments before scanning the brick wall downwards to the flower bed below.

There didn't appear to be any scuff marks or scratches, no indication of anything having leaned against it or dragged up or down it—she moved closer, knowing it wasn't always obvious with brick walls. She made a mental note to check over the forensic notes when she got back to the station to see if there was something in their samples that had been overlooked. Kneeling down, she ran her hands gently through the flowers adorning the bed along the wall, not wanting to damage them as she tried to reveal the dirt beneath them. The flowers themselves were undamaged—no crushed petals, no snapped or bent stems. As far as she could tell, no damaged flowers had been removed from the bed either. There didn't appear to be any imprints or indentations in the soil— not that she really expected to find anything after so long. She sighed, not sure whether she was disappointed or relieved at finding no further evidence. Yet she had hoped she would miraculously find something—anything to quieten her instincts which had gnawed at her incessantly from the moment they'd set foot in Rosalie's room, the feeling that Rosalie's disappearance was just like hers. She couldn't explain why now, after twenty years, Pan would choose to strike again, but it all felt like too much of a coincidence not to be connected somehow. Either that, or she was delusional.

Massaging the middle of her forehead with her thumb, Wendy reminded herself angrily that she needed to remain objective, and it annoyed her that she kept looking for reasons to link Rosalie's case to her own experience.

Maybe I'm not as competent for this case as I wanted to believe.

She stood up and stepped back slowly, scanning the grass as she moved—she wondered how many times the Lord Mayor had mowed the lawn since his daughter's disappearance, considering the possibility that his gardening obsession wasn't so much about keeping busy, and more about ensuring no evidence was left behind. Wendy couldn't say why—she'd only seen the man on television—but her gut told her he knew something.

Staring at the grass around her feet, she wondered if there was any point asking Mrs. Fryair when her husband's love of gardening started—but her experience told her there was little information lurking behind Mrs. Fryair's vacant eyes. Glancing back up at the window, Wendy was relieved to find Roberts was no longer peering out at her, and she withdrew her phone from her pocket. Dialling the direct number for Nanna's rooms, she held the phone to her ear, her gaze now focusing on the back door. After what felt like an eternity, Carole answered the phone. "Hello, Carole speaking."

"Hi, Carole, it's just me, Wendy. I was wondering if you could do me a favour. Is Nanna free?"

"I'm sorry, Wendy. She's having a nap at the moment. She's only been asleep for about half an hour, so it may be a little while before she wakes up."

Wendy thought for a moment.

"Wendy?" Carole prompted.

"Sorry, Carole. Don't worry; I'll just come out to the house and see her in person."

"Not a problem. I'm sure she'd love the visit." Wendy hung up the phone, slipping it back into her pocket as she headed back into the house. She could hear Roberts in the kitchen, charming Mrs. Fryair with his inane babbling over her baking.

"There she is," Roberts announced, turning to face her from where he sat perched on the stool at the kitchen bench, Jessica sitting next to him, her head resting on her hand as she stared at him with her doe-like eyes. Wendy felt a distaste in the back of her mouth at how relaxed he looked with them, but she forced a small smile as she stepped into the kitchen.

"Please, take a seat," Anne Fryair offered, gesturing to the empty seat on the other side of Roberts. "Do you prefer coffee or tea?"

Wendy opened her mouth to decline, but Roberts flashed her a quick look, reminding her of his earlier warning. "Uh, tea is perfect. Thank you, Mrs. Fryair."

"Anne."

"Thank you, Anne." Wendy slid onto the stool. She looked past Roberts and gave Jessica what she hoped was a friendly smile, but it didn't take a genius to see the girl was less than impressed with someone taking Roberts' attention from her. It was all she could do to keep up her end of the mindless banter as they sipped their tea and ate their slices of fresh-baked cake— making sure they ate quick enough to be efficient, without looking like they were rushing to get out of there, though Wendy had to concede to herself. The cake was amazing. Roberts had already discreetly kicked her once for tapping her foot incessantly on the stool's footrest.

As they finally climbed back into the car, Wendy checked the time on the dashboard, mentally calculating how long it would take her to get out to the house to see Nanna and back again.

"So, are you going to tell me what's going on?" Roberts asked her, checking for traffic behind him as he pulled the car out onto the street.

"What are you talking about?"

"Dah-ling, please. I'm a detective—I can tell you're sitting on something."

"If I had something concrete, I would tell you."

"I don't care if it's concrete or not. If you have something—anything—I need to hear about it."

She stared out the window, tapping her mouth with her fingers, trying to work out the best way to inform him without receiving an onslaught of questions in response.

"I think I might have a lead on something—but I'm not sure enough to share just yet. Give me until the end of the day, and if it turns out to be something, you'll be the first to know."

She turned to look at him and could see his jaw clench and unclench before he spoke. "Whatever you say," he replied quietly, refusing to look at her. She frowned, his response confusing her. It felt like he took her rebuttal personally. It certainly wasn't the smart-ass quip she'd expected from him. Yet she was stubborn in her resolve—the last thing she wanted was her partner accusing her of bias—or thinking she was crazy for fixating on the senile ramblings of an old woman.

The rest of the drive felt tense and uncomfortable, and Wendy was relieved when Roberts pulled the car into the station and reversed into a parking spot.

"I'll give you a call when I get back. I might be a few hours."

"Sure," he replied, still refusing to look at her as he got out of the car and closed the door behind him. Without a backwards glance, he stormed off towards the station, leaving Wendy in the car, bewildered. Once he was inside, she opened the car door and got out, unable to keep from looking back at the closed station door as she walked over to her own car.

CHAPTER NINE

Wendy drove along the rocky driveway that spanned several kilometres from the main road to the house, lined on either side by the family's prized grapevines. She could see Jane ahead, strolling through them, her back to the road. Wendy watched as she drove past, hand ready to wave, but her daughter didn't seem to hear the car. She pulled up at the front of the house. Getting out, she started for the vineyard to weave her way over to Jane. Despite Wendy calling her daughter's name, Jane didn't turn around. It wasn't until Wendy was close enough to reach out and touch her that she realised her daughter wore wireless earbuds. Jane jumped and turned to her mother. "Oh! Mum, you scared me!" she exclaimed, pulling the earbuds from her ears before the two embraced.

"Sorry, sweetheart. I didn't mean to startle you. How loud do you have those things anyway?"

Jane chuckled. "Obviously too loud. I couldn't decide between reading a book and taking a walk. It's such a nice day, so I figured why not do both?"

Wendy looked down at her daughter's hands, devoid of any book, frowning slightly.

"An audiobook, Mum," Jane replied and smiled as she shook the earbuds in the palm of her hand.

"Ah. Whatever happened to people just reading good old-fashioned books?" she asked, half-joking.

"Because it's the modern world, and this way, we can multitask."

"Yes. Well, multitasking isn't exactly my forte." They both laughed, and Wendy threw her arm across her daughter's shoulder as they continued to stroll through the rows of grapevines. Wendy admired the way the vines weaved their way across the trellises, laden with grapes not yet ripe.

"So, do you feel better now that you're on the case?" Jane asked.

"Better probably isn't the right word. It feels good to be on the case; I feel like I can contribute now—hopefully. But no miraculous findings so far."

"Well, don't take it too personally, Mum. You've only been on the case a few hours." Jane laughed, causing Wendy to smile—she'd always had exceedingly high expectations for herself. Wendy decided to cast aside the case for the moment and enjoy spending time with Jane, even if it was brief. They walked in silence for a little while, both enjoying the fresh, clean air, and as Wendy looked up at the near-cloudless sky, she marvelled at how easily they fell in step together, how being with her daughter made Wendy feel like she was her whole self.

"Mum, can I ask you something?"

"Of course you can."

Jane didn't say anything straight away, as though she was trying to think of the best way to word her question. Wendy remained silent, not wanting to push.

"The other night, when we were watching the news, you seemed to be really affected by it. I mean, beyond the nature of the case itself—and it wasn't just you. Uncle Mike and Uncle John seemed on edge, too."

"Well, it's an awful thing to happen to a family. Who wouldn't feel for them?"

"Of course. But I'm a journalist, Mum. I'm used to reading people, and there's something more going on—and I want to know what it is. If it was just you, I could probably justify the reaction as concern for the girl and your dedication as a detective in wanting to help find her. But it was all three of you reacting at the same time. There is clearly more to it—I can't work out what, but we aren't supposed to have any secrets, remember?"

Now it was Wendy's turn to be silent as she lowered her arm from Jane's shoulder and grasped her hand instead. As much as she prided herself on their honest relationship, she felt guilty that there was one secret she'd always kept from her daughter. She didn't know which would be worse, telling her the truth or the realisation she'd been lied to all these years. Yet Wendy knew Jane was right. She wasn't stupid, and it wasn't fair to make her doubt her instincts when she knew there was something going on.

Wendy squeezed Jane's hand, trying to find the words. She'd always told Jane that she didn't know who her father was, that she was the result of a one-night stand with a handsome stranger during her rebellious youth—and that she'd been too young and naïve. As shitty as it made her feel, it was the only story she could come up with that wouldn't lead to any pursuit of his identity, and she'd worked hard to be the best mother AND father she could be in the hopes Jane would never think less of her for her misgivings.

"Look, Jane. You know I love you more than anything, right?"

Jane squeezed her hand. "Of course I do, Mum."

Wendy took a deep breath. "You're going to think I'm a hypocrite." She rubbed her forehead with her free hand, wishing she could back-peddle and restart the whole conversation.

"Just tell me," Jane replied, and Wendy could hear the sudden concern in her daughter's voice, and she knew she had no choice but to tell her everything.

"The reason your uncles and I seemed so affected by the disappearance of Rosalie Fryair, a teenage girl, is because I was abducted when I was fifteen."

"What?" Jane gasped, spinning around to face her mother as she pulled them both to a stop, her mouth agape. "How did I never know this?"

"There's more," Wendy stated as she reached out and grabbed her daughter's other hand in hers. "I was gone for six months, and on my sixteenth birthday, I escaped. I don't remember how. I just remember one morning I was just walking down a street in the fog...free."

"Oh, Mum. I'm so sorry. I don't even know what to say..."

"Jane," Wendy said, forcing her daughter to look her in her eyes. "When the police took me to the hospital, I found out I was three months pregnant. With you."

Jane stared at her, blinking, her mouth opening and closing as she struggled to process the information. All the while, Wendy squeezed her hands tight, trying to convey as much reassurance and love as she could. She could see the realisation in Jane's face, the way her eyes widened as the timeline made sense, already knowing how young her mother was when she'd had her. Wendy felt hot tears sting her eyes as they welled in her daughters. Jane opened her mouth, but then closed it again, giving a quick shake of her head.

"I know what you're thinking, but I wasn't raped. You were not conceived in rape. My abductor never touched me. Not like that."

"Huh? But how? That's not possible. Is it just that you don't remember? I mean, no one could blame you for blocking out something like that..."

Wendy looked over her daughter's head. "It shouldn't be possible, but it's true. If it's any consolation, the doctors confirmed I was still a virgin. In fact, they were just as dumbfounded as the rest of us."

Jane whimpered as she shuffled on the spot. Wendy was certain if she wasn't holding onto her so tightly, Jane would flee across the vineyard.

"I honestly don't know how else to explain it, which is why I—we—never told you the truth. I think it was easier, especially for the family, to accept the lie as the truth because what really happened just seemed so unfathomable."

They stood in silence for a few moments, staring at each other through their tears. Wendy braced herself for the hurt and the anger she knew Jane was more than entitled to feel. Her mouth fell open when Jane released her hands and threw her arms around her. "Oh, Mum. I am so sorry you went through that. I can't even imagine what that must have been like for you. Abducted? You must have been so scared, and then to find out you were pregnant." She pulled back. "But why? Why did you keep me? After everything you went through, and you were so young. I mean, didn't

Grandma and Grandpa want you to...to get rid of me?"

Wendy shrugged. "I can't explain it, to be honest. When I found out about you, I wasn't surprised. I mean, I was in shock, but when I let it sink in, I realised a part of me already knew. From that moment on, I never questioned the how or the why—I believed I was meant to have you, that you were mine. Obviously, Mum and Dad found my 'immaculate conception' much harder to swallow, and even the doctors were baffled despite their medical examination. I suppose it's human nature to be sceptical. So yes, both your grandparents and a doctor recommended, or should I say offered, the route of termination. You have to know, though; it was never a consideration for me. Not for one second. You and I were meant to be, and the how and the why just weren't relevant—and I've never looked back— not once."

Jane released one of her mother's hands and wiped her face with the back of her hand. "Is that why things have always been strained between Nanna and me? I've always felt like she didn't want me around, and you've always made me feel that it was a figment of my imagination."

Wendy squeezed her daughter's hand. "I'm so sorry. Honestly, I've never really discussed it with her—not for lack of trying. Any time I tried to raise it with her, she always shot me down. I think in many ways, Nanna felt responsible...like she should have protected me or prevented it from happening somehow. Even though she was already an old lady when I was a teen, she'd been the family nanny since your grandfather was a child. Her...attitude towards you isn't personal exactly, though I know it's always felt that way."

Jane turned and looked down the row of winding vines, nodding her head slowly, and it broke Wendy's heart to see Jane struggling as though she was trying not to choke on all the new information. Wendy wanted to tell her that everything would be okay, but she knew it wasn't her place to say—she had to let Jane process the news in her own way; it was the very least she owed her.

"Why didn't Grandma and Grandpa feel the same way as Nanna? They were always so good to me. In fact, they spoiled me rotten." Jane kept her head turned away as she spoke.

"Naturally, they didn't understand my insistence on becoming a mother at sixteen, regardless of the circumstances. Yet the minute you were born, they fell completely in love with you—we all did. It was then I knew they felt the same way I did. The how or the why was no longer important—you were a Darling, and that was all that mattered."

"What about Uncle John and Uncle Michael?"

"They were both too young to grasp what had happened. They just knew they had a niece to play with, which they both thought was the most amazing thing ever. It wasn't until they were both much older that they put two and two together, but by then, it didn't matter. We were a family."

Wendy watched the myriad of expressions flash across her daughter's face. Her heart panged at the knowledge she was responsible for. Wendy felt helpless, unsure whether to give her space or reach out and embrace her. So, she just stood there... waiting, chewing on her bottom lip until she could taste the metallic blood in her mouth. After what felt like an eternity, Jane stepped forward and wrapped her arms around her mother, squeezing tightly. Wendy could feel the faint tremble coursing through her body as she hugged back. "I am so sorry I didn't tell you sooner. I promise it was the only secret

I've ever kept from you. I just wanted to protect you from the darkness of my past, and I didn't want you ever to question my love for you."

Jane stepped back and grasped her mother's hand. "I understand. I do. Honestly, if I'd known sooner, I don't think I would've been able to handle it—especially not as a teen when I was going through the whole adolescent identity crisis thing. It's shit, I won't lie, but I think I'm more upset about what it must have been like for you, all those months hidden away."

Wendy didn't say anything but gave her daughter's hand a gentle squeeze in response. Jane was quiet for a moment, looking around the vineyard, her expression unreadable.

"Am I anything like him?" Jane whispered.

Wendy felt a jolt at the unexpected question, but she quickly recovered, not wanting to hesitate in her response. "Not in the slightest. Not in any way, shape, or form. You're one hundred percent Darling. I mean that."

Jane met her mother's gaze and gave a small nod. "Well, that's a silver lining, I suppose."

"Jane, honey…"

"It's okay, Mum. I mean, I'll be okay. It will take a while for it all to sink in…but look around. I had a great upbringing. I was surrounded by so much warmth and love. I'm not sure I understand how you could have gone through with having me, after what you went through, but I suppose I'm selfish in feeling grateful that you did. I'm sure I'll have questions for you, but for now, I just want to enjoy the rest of my walk with my Mum."

Wendy nodded, and arm in arm, they continued through the vineyard.

"So that explains why the Fryair case means so much to you," Jane finally said.

"I've worked on numerous cases since I became a detective, some of the missing persons cases. But not one that's felt so..." Wendy trailed off, unable to find the words.

"Close to home?" Jane offered.

"Yeah, something like that."

"So you think she's been abducted. She's not just missing, as in a runaway?" Jane asked.

"Off the record?" Wendy asked, testing the waters with an attempt at humour as she gave her daughter a tentative smile.

"Off the record," Jane replied, smiling back, and Wendy felt as though a weight was lifting off her shoulders, at least in part.

"It's hard to say. We honestly don't think the runaway theory has any credence..."

"We?"

"Oh, I'm partnering on the case with a new detective at the precinct, Rupert Roberts." Wendy felt her face flush and made a show of inspecting the vines until it subsided.

What the fuck...

Clearing her throat, she continued, "There's just so much that doesn't add up, and while my gut says she's been abducted, there's just nothing. No evidence, no leads, no witnesses. Nothing. For the first time in my career, I'm actually questioning..." she let the question hang, forcing herself to take a deep breath.

"You're worried, despite your best intentions, your past might be clouding your judgement?"

Wendy nodded. "I've never doubted my instinct— it's never been wrong. Yet, with this case, I can't help second-guess it."

"Your gut is telling you she's been abducted, right?"

Wendy nodded.

"So go with it. You said it yourself; your instinct has never been wrong. You're a bloody good detective,

Mum. You have one of the highest success rates in the country."

"How on earth would you know something like that?" Wendy asked, flabbergasted the information new to her.

Jane chuckled. "I also happen to be good at my job. I think you're looking at it the wrong way.

"How do you mean?"

"Well, maybe because of your boss's initial concerns, you're assuming your gut instincts must be clouded with bias. But did you consider it the other way? Maybe it's *because* of your own experience, your instincts are actually *heightened,* and you're picking up on something that can't be seen—or necessarily proven just yet."

Wendy nodded thoughtfully. "You never cease to amaze me, kiddo."

"I aim to please."

"You could be onto something. It's certainly worth considering."

"Can I offer some more advice?" Jane asked, causing her mother to laugh.

"Of course you can."

"You've only officially been on the case a few hours. Cut yourself some slack."

"Point taken. Now enough about me. How's work? It's good that you're able to work remotely for the interim."

"Actually, I was going to talk to you about that." Wendy caught the sideways glance her daughter shot in her direction but kept looking ahead as Jane continued, "I've come to enjoy being here. I love the old house, and walking through the vineyards, and seeing more of Uncle Mike and Uncle John."

"And all the wine you could want... "

"There's that, too. I haven't spoken to work yet, but if they're okay with me continuing to work remotely, I was thinking of perhaps making the move out here."

Wendy stopped walking and faced her daughter, whose shoulders were suddenly hunched up, her eyebrows pinched together.

"I know you've never felt comfortable being here for any length of time—which I absolutely understand now that I know the truth, but…"

"You don't have to explain. It is beautiful here, and I think it's wonderful that you love it—that you want to make it your home. I'm sure your uncles will be thrilled, too—and there's ample room."

Wendy watched as Jane relaxed again. "Thanks, Mum. It just really feels like home here, and I love the history, the family connection. And I'm a journalist. I can work anywhere, so hopefully, my boss and I can come to some kind of arrangement. But you know what, I think I would even be happy to make the commute on a daily basis if it came down to it."

Wendy laughed. "You say that now…"

Jane smiled. "True. Oh well, I'm sure it will work out."

"It will."

When they reached the house, mother and daughter parted ways, and Wendy walked briskly towards Nanna's residence. Nerves danced around her stomach, like sharp little needles of dread, intensifying the closer she got. Wendy realised it wasn't a lack of answers she was afraid of; it was that she would get one. She wanted more than anything to be wrong about the connection between her past and Rosalie's abduction.

Reaching the door, Wendy gave herself a mental shake, and with a quick huff, she knocked. "Come in,"

Carole's voice came muffled through the door. Wendy opened it, stepping into the sitting room to find Carole tucking a crocheted rug over Nanna's legs. She sat on the couch, once again facing the television.

"Well, look who has a visitor," Carole announced as she stood up, giving her back a slight stretch.

"Hi, Carole. How's Nanna today?"

"She's doing great. Not long up from her nap," Carole replied cheerfully and walked over to where Wendy stood. "Honestly," she said, her voice barely above a whisper, "she seems to have deteriorated somewhat since your mother passed. I could be wrong, but it's almost like she's taken her death harder than when your father died. It's strange, she often spoke of your father as though he was her own son, and I know she adored him. Though I suppose she was very close to your mother, too."

Wendy frowned, watching the back of Nanna's head as Jane's concerns echoed through her mind. "Deteriorating. How? Is she still safe living here?"

"Don't worry, she's not in harm's way, either to herself or to anyone else. I take good care of her."

"Oh, of course you do, Carole—I didn't mean it like that." She placed a reassuring hand on the woman's shoulder. "I'm just worried. I don't want to lose her, too."

"I understand. It could be grief, but she's retreated further into herself. I used to get a few conversations out of her a day—albeit short conversations, but they were glimpses of lucidity. But I honestly don't think she's said a word since we told her of your mother's passing.

At least she hasn't to me. A few times now, I've thought I've heard her whispering to herself, but as soon as I get close enough to hear for myself, it stops."

"Hmm." Wendy folded her arms across her chest, unsure why she felt obliged to withhold the brief, but intense warning Nanna had issued her. "Do you think it's worth getting her checked out by the doctor?"

"He's coming next week, but I can see if we can make it sooner."

"No, that'll be fine. Like you said, it's probably the grief, but we should just keep an extra eye on her until then, and if anything worries you, or she deteriorates further, we'll get the doctor over."

"Sounds like a plan. But for now, I thought I'd make a pot of tea for your visit. I'm sure she'd love for you to stay awhile. It might be just what she needs."

"Yes, that would be lovely. Thank you, Carole."

Carole rubbed Wendy's arm and walked out of the room, leaving Wendy watching Nanna, who'd not given any indication she knew Wendy was there. She walked around to the other side of the couch and sat down beside Nanna, resting her arm across the back of the seat behind Nanna's head. Looking up at the television, she saw an old black and white movie with Grace Kelly and Fred Astaire. She smiled to herself, recalling the many times growing up that she and her brothers had watched the old Hollywood classics with her. After a few minutes, Wendy touched Nanna on the arm.

"Hey, Nanna. I wanted to talk to you. Just the two of us if you're feeling up to it."

There was no reply, but she saw the slight twitch at the corner of Nanna's mouth and knew she was listening. Reaching down, she grabbed Nanna's hand in both of hers.

"Do you remember telling me not to follow the unicorn? I was wondering why you said that. Why a unicorn?" Wendy watched intently, looking for any kind of response, and she could have sworn she'd heard just the faintest of sighs, and it was enough to encourage Wendy to continue. "I only ask, because there's a case I'm working on, and you may have seen it on the news—the Rosalie Fryair case? Anyway, I came across a unicorn. Well, a piece of evidence that has a unicorn on it. That seemed like too much of a coincidence to me, despite... well despite... you know," she trailed off, feeling Nanna's hand tense slightly in hers. With a frown of concentration and concern, Wendy reassuringly squeezed Nanna's hand. "Don't worry, though. Everything's fine. I'm perfectly safe. I was just hoping you could tell me what made you say that." With a sigh, she leaned back against the couch and looked back up at the movie. After a few seconds, she felt a tug and looked down to see Nanna weakly trying to free her hand from Wendy's grasp. Quickly letting go, she watched as Nanna reached up to the necklace around her neck, her hands shaking as she tried to reach around to its clasp.

"You want to take it off?" Wendy asked. Nanna nodded slightly, and Wendy stood up and quickly walked around behind the couch, gently moving aside stray strands of Nanna's white hair as she unclasped the necklace. Sitting down again, Wendy held the necklace up for both of them to see. On a delicate silver chain hung a round locket. It was bordered by delicate, silver looped filigree; its face decorated with delicate, curling vines weaving in and out of each other.

"You must wear it," Nanna's voice came out hoarse, and Wendy dropped the necklace before quickly bending over to scoop it up off the carpet, trying to hide her surprise at the unexpected sound of Nanna's voice. She felt her heart ache upon realising how much she'd missed the sound.

"Nanna?" Wendy prompted, not wanting to lose the moment, "You want me to wear it?"

"You must wear it—it will keep you safe. Please, before it's too late," Nanna begged and gripped Wendy's arm with surprising strength. Wendy found herself flinching from the sudden pain.

"Okay," Wendy replied, gently unclasping Nanna's hand from her arm, and making a point of putting the necklace on, holding Nanna's lucid stare as she reached up and fastened the clasp behind her neck. "If it's what you want." She ran her fingers over the locket, holding it up, as she ran a nail between the joins, down to the tiny clasp that held the two sides closed.

"You mustn't open it!" Nanna hissed, and Wendy let it fall from her hand as she gaped at Nanna, wide-eyed.

"Why on earth not?" she asked.

"Hot tea coming right up," Carole announced as she walked back into the room, carrying a tray of clinking china. Wendy looked up, trying to mask her frustration at the interruption with a tight-lipped smile. Carole was oblivious, her eyes keenly watching the tray in her hands as she lowered it carefully onto the coffee table. When Wendy turned back to Nanna, the moment was lost, and Nanna's blank stare was back on the television screen.

Wendy went through the motions of drinking her tea and listening to Carole chatter away for the three of them, but her mind was on the necklace and the torrent of new questions tumbling through it vying for attention in her head. Once or twice, she could have sworn she'd seen Nanna flick a discrete sideways glance in her direction, but she couldn't be certain. Despite its delicateness, the locket felt heavy hanging from her neck, like a weighty reminder of why she was there. Wendy longed to open it—all the more because Nanna forbade it, and she wondered if she would have the will power to restrain herself once she was on her own. She caught Carole looking at her toying with it, her friendly expression darkening to a puzzled frown as she glanced from Nanna to Wendy and back again. Wendy dropped her hand and reached over to put her teacup back on the tray beside Nanna's untouched one. "Thank you so much for the cup of tea, Carole, but I should be heading back to work."

"Of course. I'm sure Nanna appreciates you visiting," Carole replied, standing up as she put her own cup on the tray. Wendy got to her feet and leaned over, placing a gentle kiss on Nanna's head.

"I'll see you soon, I promise." Pulling back, she hoped for a glimmer of recognition, but Nanna just stared past her, seeing into another time and place.

CHAPTER TEN

Wendy drove back to the station on autopilot, trying to make sense of her thoughts and feeling like she was trying to untangle a bunch of knotted yarn. Her usually logical and clear mind was failing her as she tried to sift through her emotions long enough to determine if there was anything tangible to connect Nanna's ramblings to Rosalie Fryair. Her mind told her it was a stretch; it was almost impossible, but her instinct was screaming at her that it was possible. What's more, since donning the locket, she felt on edge, like she was running out of time. Her frustration was growing exponentially the longer she failed to make sense of everything, and she wondered if Roberts had fared any better in her absence.

As she pulled into the police station car park, she saw Roberts come rushing out of the rear of the station; his phone pressed to his ear. Instantly, her mobile rang, and his name flashed across the screen.

Before she could answer it, he saw her and hung up. She lowered the window and stuck her head out. "What's going on?" she called out. Roberts reached the car with lengthy strides and let himself into the passenger side.

"Impeccable timing, Dah-ling. You can drive," he instructed, placing his hand on the back of her seat while looking over his shoulder at the road behind them, while absently latching his seatbelt with his free hand.

Closing the window, Wendy shot him a look as she reversed. "Are you going to tell me what's going on? Or, at the very least, where we are going?"

"Firstly, we're going to the hospital. Secondly, you won't believe who's just shown up," he replied without looking at her. Wendy stared at him agape, waiting for more information, as she got them back on the road. Roberts remained silent, which would normally piss Wendy off, but she was distracted by the prickling stir of nerves in the pit of her stomach. She didn't need him to respond. She knew the answer in her gut. Biting her lip, Wendy flicked him rapid, sideways glances while navigating her way through the heavy traffic, wanting to know more but not trusting that her voice wouldn't give away her apprehension.

Roberts turned and flashed her a grin. "You're stubborn. You know that?"

His smile caused an unfamiliar fluttering in her chest, and she quickly turned away, pulling a face. "What are you talking about?" She swallowed thickly, scowling as she made a show of watching the traffic, not wanting him to see the blush creep along her cheeks.

This is ridiculous. It's a damn smile, for crying out loud.

"You're obviously dying to know more, but you don't want to give me the satisfaction of asking," he stated with a smug chuckle that had the reverse effect on Wendy than his smile, and her blush faded away.

"If you say so, Detective."

He chuckled. "Come on, Dah-ling, don't be so defensive."

"Can we just focus on the case at hand?" she asked sternly, risking another look in his direction, wanting him to see she meant business.

Roberts' smile disappeared as he pursed his lips and nodded tersely. "Sure thing, detective, whatever you say." He turned from her, opting to stare out the window.

For fuck's sake... why is he so difficult to get along with...

Wendy cleared her throat. "So, Rosalie was found. Where was she found? Who found her? Is she okay? I'm assuming her parents have been notified..."

"Whoa, Dah-ling, one question at a time." He held his hands up as though stemming an onslaught, the smile back on his face, their disagreement forgotten. Wendy rolled her eyes and turned a corner.

"She wasn't found, exactly. She just turned up," he admitted.

"What?" She turned to him.

"Careful!" he exclaimed, and Wendy turned her attention back to the traffic that had suddenly slowed in front of her, and she hit the brakes, causing them to both strain against their seatbelts at the sudden halt. Roberts continued like nothing had happened. "Dispatch received a call a couple of hours ago from a truck driver reporting a Jane Doe he almost ran over. He claimed she just appeared in the middle of the highway—clearly not possible."

Wendy didn't respond right away as her nerves kicked up a notch.

"Earth to Dah-ling?"

"Sorry, I was just watching the traffic. Why are we just hearing about it now if dispatch received the call two hours ago?"

"I'm only getting the details second hand, but the driver had reported he thought the girl might be Rosalie Fryair, but the girl was in pretty rough shape, so he couldn't be sure—plus she'd also provided an entirely different name when asked."

"What about the officers attending the scene? Surely despite her appearance they would recognise the girl?" Wendy asked.

"They noted a resemblance, but the fact she provided another name threw them off."

"She must have been in pretty rough shape by the sound of it," Wendy stated, her mouth feeling as dry as sandpaper.

"Sounds like it. What I have so far is she's suffering from dehydration, and her clothes were torn, and her face scratched up. On top of that, the girl is fatigued and disoriented, so neither the officers nor the paramedics that took her to the hospital have gotten much sense out of her."

"Well, obviously, the first priority was to get her to the hospital," Wendy added, her knuckles turning white as she gripped the steering wheel, pressing her back against the seat.

"Absolutely. The drip they put her on hydrated her enough that she could confirm she was Rosalie Fryair. That's when we finally got the intel."

Wendy closed her eyes, wanting to feel relieved, yet she didn't. Turning the car off the main road and into the hospital parking entry, she frowned, a dark cloud of dread suspended above her, and it unnerved her.

"Where was she found?" she asked quietly, navigating the rows of cars for a free spot to park.

"Barrie Bridge, just over the Maribyrnong River coming out of Footscray—You know, where there's that statue of the children playing on the other side of the bridge?"

Wendy nodded semi-absently as she navigated the tight parking space between a large SUV and a concrete pole. "Did no other drivers see her? That's not a quiet road, no matter what the time of day. I don't imagine a dishevelled teen standing in the middle of the highway is something that you see everyday."

"I know. None of it makes sense, but all I have so far is one minute she wasn't there, and then then next she was, and the truck driver was the only one to see it happen."

"That's not possible. How long had he been driving for? Could fatigue be a factor? Has he been drug tested?"

"He was taken to the station, so we'll get a copy of the report when we get back, but right now, I'm more interested in seeing Rosalie." They got out of the car, and Wendy scanned the parking lot for the lift.

"So, aside from obtaining her name, what else have we got so far?" she asked, leading the way.

"Her family was notified, and I imagine they're also on their way here if they aren't here already."

As she led them to the lift, she flicked a quick glance over her shoulder at Roberts. "You said she gave a wrong name to the driver. That in itself seems odd—do you know what name she gave?"

"That, I don't know. We can get the details from the officers—they're still here. Is it important?"

"I have a feeling it could be."

"Ahh...the famous Dah-ling gut instinct. I've heard about this."

"Glad to see my reputation precedes me," Wendy replied, rolling her eyes as they stepped into the lift. She let Roberts press the button, and they stood in silence as the lift took them to ground level. They walked across the road and through the emergency entrance. They identified themselves at the desk and were directed around to the left to a smaller waiting room. They saw two uniformed officers standing in front of a closed door, one talking on their phone and the other looking around as patients and medical staff came and went. He nodded in acknowledgement when he saw them approach and tapped his partner on the shoulder. She spoke quickly into the phone and ended the call as they stepped towards them.

"Detective Darling. Welcome back. I was sorry to hear of your mother's passing." Officer Moretti said.

"Thank you, Judy, I appreciate that. This is Detective Rupert Roberts; he's recently joined our precinct." Roberts reached out and shook both of their hands.

"I'm Senior Constable Dale Evans," the second officer said.

"Pleasure," Roberts replied, before getting back to business, "So, where are we?"

"The medical staff is attending Miss Fryair. So far, there doesn't seem to be anything significantly wrong with her, not physically, anyway. Just a lot of scratches up both arms and across her chest and face. She's certainly looking a lot brighter with the drip, but they're running a battery of tests just to be sure. Her father has been fairly... vocal... in his insistence that she receive the very best of care," Moretti replied, nodding towards the closed door behind him.

"I can imagine," Wendy replied as she too looked at the door. "I take it that her parents are in there with her?"

"Yes," Evans replied. "They confirmed her identity, and they've been here for about half an hour."

"Feels longer," Moretti added dryly.

"Anything else we need to know before we head in?" Roberts asked.

Evans shook his head. "The doctors said they'll provide a further update once the test results come back. Rosalie hasn't been forthcoming about where she's been or what happened, but the poor girl's been through a lot."

"That she has. We'll take it from here. Keep us updated if anything of interest comes up in the driver's statement," Roberts requested as he gave them a nod. He led Wendy past them towards Rosalie's room.

"Oh, there was one more thing," Wendy stated, turning back, causing the officers to do the same, "She provided a false I.D. to the driver—do we know what name she used?"

Evans and Moretti exchanged a quick look before Moretti cleared her throat to answer. "She only gave a first name. It was Wendy."

Wendy struggled to swallow the thick knot of acidic bile that had formed in the back of her throat. The officers walked away, leaving her staring after them.

Roberts let out a low whistle beside her. "Well, shit. That's one hell of a coincidence, isn't it, Dah-ling?" Turning around, he reached for the door, but Wendy made a beeline towards the water cooler beside the nurses' station, suddenly overcome with the urge to vomit. With shaking hands, she filled the plastic cup to the brim and guzzled the water down like her life depended on it. The cold water was like a shock to her system, eradicating the nausea. Wendy disposed of the cup in the small bin beside the cooler and turned around to see Roberts staring at her.

"Sorry," she mumbled as she hurried back.

"If you're not up to this, detective, I can go in on my own."

"Not at all," she replied. As much as she hated the way he intentionally pronounced her surname, suddenly being called detective instead seemed like a less desirable option, given his disapproving tone.

Roberts knocked twice and slowly opened the door. Inside lay Rosalie Fryair propped up by pillows on the inclined bed. The first thing Wendy noticed was the girl looked far younger than her fifteen years. The hospital gown she wore did little to hide the angry red scratches that marked the pale skin along her arms and across her face. There were dark circles around her eyes, yet—outwardly at least—Rosalie seemed calm, and Wendy wondered if she'd been sedated. Her hair was wet and pulled back from her face, and Wendy knew the sting of the shower on so many cuts would be awful. On either side of Rosalie, suffocatingly close, sat Malcolm and Anne Fryair.

Senator Fryair stood as they entered. "Detective Roberts. I was wondering when you would get here. You wouldn't believe the saga we've had to endure here…" he trailed off as he saw Wendy enter the room. "I don't believe we've met."

Wendy stepped forward and held out her hand. "I'm Detective Darling, pleased to meet you, Senator." She struggled not to flinch as he intentionally squeezed her hand as they shook, looking her up and down. Her dislike for the man was instantaneous, and she turned her attention instead to Anne and Rosalie.

"Nice to see you again under better circumstances, Mrs. Fryair." Anne gave her a small smile, both her hands wrapped around her daughter's. "Hi, Rosalie. I'm Detective Darling, but you can call me Wendy if you like." She was about to take a seat on the edge of the bed but reconsidered when she heard Roberts not-so-discreetly clear his throat. She flashed him an apologetic look as she moved to the foot of the bed and allowed him to stand in her place.

"I'm Detective Roberts, Rosalie. How are you feeling?"

Rosalie gave a shrug and looked directly at him. Wendy watched Rosalie draw her knees up to her chest. Her mother reached over to readjust the blankets before the pair clasped hands again.

"How do you think she's feeling? She's been poked and prodded from the moment she got here. They didn't even have her in a private room initially. She was on a bed with a curtain wrapped around her for Christ's sake. I mean, do they not know who she is?"

"Malcolm," Anne said quietly.

"What?" he snapped, but Anne stayed silent.

"Actually, Sir, they didn't know who she was," Roberts said in defence.

"I find that hard to believe. We've only had her image flashed across every news station, every telegraph pole, and across social media since she disappeared." His voice increased in volume with each word.

"Unfortunately, the condition your daughter was in when she was found made it difficult to identify her—all the more so, when she gave a false name," Roberts advised. There was a slight coldness edging into his tone, but Wendy gathered she was the only one to notice it. She continued to observe the interaction between Roberts and the senator—each man vying for their dominance, and Anne, who's over-the-top friendliness they'd witnessed at the family home, was nowhere to be seen as she nestled alongside her daughter. Anne freed one of her hands and wrapped it protectively around Rosalie's shoulders, and the two leaned their heads together, lost in their own world. Wendy felt a pang of grief as she thought of her own mother, and she forced her attention back to the men instead.

"Yes, well..." Malcolm Fryair conceded, "clearly, my daughter has been through an ordeal."

"Which is why we are here," Roberts confirmed. "Rosalie, we would really like to talk to you about where you've been for the past few weeks. Do you think you feel up to talking about it?" The girl didn't answer, instead picking at the threads of the blanket with her free hand.

"I know you must be feeling overwhelmed right now, but it's important we hear your story as soon as we can—it will give us the best chance at finding who did this to you." Roberts' words appeared to fall on deaf ears as he failed to connect with the girl. He subtly glanced over his shoulder, giving Wendy the go-ahead to continue.

"Rosalie, I know it's a lot to process," she started.

"How could you possibly know?" whispered Rosalie.

"I know because when I was fifteen, I was also abducted." Wendy felt her face flush as Roberts, and Mr. and Mrs. Fryair all stared at her in varying expressions of surprise, but Wendy ignored them as Rosalie looked up at her with wide eyes. She had her attention, and she wasn't about to let it go.

"You're not just saying that?" Rosalie whispered, her idle hand now resting flat on the blanket beside her.

"It's not something I would ever joke about," Wendy replied solemnly, and Rosalie gave her the smallest of nods. "It really is important that you tell us what you recall about your abduction—as much as you can, anyway. Now because you're fifteen, we can't discuss this with you unless you have a parent or guardian with you. It's entirely your choice who you want with you. It can be both of your parents or one of them, or we can even get a social worker in if that would make you feel more comfortable."

"Excuse me? We're her parents. We have every right to be here. You can't just come in here and tell us what to do," Malcolm interjected, but Wendy ignored him.

They were all quiet for a moment, the anticipation growing thick and heavy as it swept around the room. Wendy gave Rosalie what she hoped was a reassuring smile, understanding the position she was in.

"This is ridiculous, we're both staying, and that's the end of it," Malcolm announced, his chest shoved out as though daring them to deny him.

"My mum," Rosalie whispered.

"Sorry, Rosalie, what did you say?" Wendy asked, leaning forward.

"Mum. Just my Mum." Neither Anne nor Rosalie looked at Malcolm as he swore and made threats to have the detectives' badges revoked as Roberts escorted him out of the room.

"You can sit in the waiting room, or there's a café on the first floor if you want to go and get yourself a coffee—we may be a little while," Roberts said firmly, closing the door against another barrage of ego-induced threats. He took the lead, pulling a chair up alongside the bed and sat down, leaving Wendy hovering at the foot of the bed. It didn't escape her attention that the girl slowly stretched her legs out again and no longer looked quite so anxious and tense now that her father had left. She watched while Rosalie stared down at her blanketed feet, hyper-aware of the deeper trauma Wendy knew now simmered beneath the surface. As though sensing her stare, Rosalie looked up, and Wendy instantly recognised the detachment in the girl's gaze—the haunted look of someone who wasn't really here. Someone who had one foot back in reality and the other still planted firmly in their nightmare, too afraid to believe in their freedom lest it be wrenched from them again. It was a look Wendy knew all too well—a look she still witnessed in her own reflection from time to time.

"So, Rosalie, do you think you feel up to answering a few questions for us?" Roberts asked.

"Yes," Rosalie replied, her voice barely a whisper, still not looking at the detective.

"Firstly, how are you feeling?"

The girl shrugged. "Okay, I guess. It all feels kind of weird."

"Why's that?" he prompted.

"That I'm here. Like, actually free. I dreamt about it so many times that now I keep expecting to wake up and find myself back in that awful place." She quickly wiped her eyes with the back of her hand. Wendy reached out and clasped her hand around Rosalie's blanketed foot and gave it a squeeze.

"You're safe now, and we're going to make sure you stay that way. You can help us do that by telling us whatever you remember, okay?" Roberts was leaning forward, somehow managing to look both eager and concerned.

Rosalie nodded and took a deep, shaky breath.

"Good girl. Now, if it gets too much, just let us know, and we can take a break if you really need to."

"I just want to get it over and done with," she replied.

Roberts gave a quick look over his shoulder at Wendy, as though checking she was paying attention, and she tried to withhold her annoyance as he began his questioning. "It was pretty chilly out this morning, but when you were found, you were wearing your nightie however, the paramedics reported your body temperature was normal. Do you know how long you'd been walking around?"

Rosalie frowned. "No. But I don't remember feeling cold either. I don't really recall feeling anything."

"Well, the fact that you weren't at the very least shivering makes me think that you must have been close by—only there isn't anywhere exactly 'close' to where you were walking, being that it was the middle of a highway. So, the next conclusion would be that perhaps you were driven there."

"Huh?" Rosalie looked up at him, frowning.

"Yes. As in someone drove you to that spot, or near enough, and left you there."

Rosalie shook her head. "No, I don't remember a car at all."

"What do you remember, honey?" Anne asked.

"Please, Mrs. Fryair. I know you're eager to help, but let us ask the questions, okay?" Roberts interrupted.

"Yes, of course, sorry," Anne replied, lowering her eyes to the bedding, mirroring her daughter's expression. Wendy frowned, wondering about the stark change in Anne Fryair's personality. It could be the shock and relief at Rosalie's return, but Wendy felt that there was something more to it. She made a mental note to discuss it with Roberts later as she focused on the questioning.

"All I remember is walking. Though at first, I didn't realise I was. Like for real. I couldn't see anything. There was just fog. I just thought I was having another dream, or maybe I was sleep-walking. When the fog started to clear, I saw I wasn't in my room anymore, but I told myself no matter how real it felt, it was just my mind playing tricks on me. Yet, the further I walked, the more the fog cleared, and that's when I realised I was walking along a road. A big road. There were buildings in the distance, and when I looked up, I saw the sky! I think I may have started crying, and I told myself I didn't care if it was just a dream; I was happy just to see the sky again. Then I heard a loud horn and screeching brakes, and it was like this massive truck just came out of nowhere."

"So, you didn't see or hear any traffic prior to the truck?"

Rosalie shook her head. "I didn't hear anything. Just my breathing. Like I said, I thought I was dreaming."

"You mentioned a room. Is that where you were?"

Rosalie opened her mouth momentarily before closing it, lowering her eyes to her lap as she started picking at the blanket again. Wendy watched the girl intently, yet with discretion, noting the small flickers of emotion that flashed across the girl's face. There was confusion, fear, anxiety, one after the other, darkening her pretty features and making her look small and vulnerable. Wendy wanted to reach out to embrace the girl to take her trauma away, but she knew she couldn't.

"I don't remember," Rosalie's voice was barely audible.

Wendy watched the muscles in the side of Roberts' face tense as he clenched his jaw, his frustration evident despite his attempts to hide it. She took it as an opportunity to change track. "What is the last thing you remember clearly, Rosalie?"

"Going to sleep, I guess."

"In the room you mentioned?" Roberts asked.

Rosalie briefly looked up at him before lowering her eyes once more. "No. In my own bed, at home. I remember Mum came in and said good night, Dad brought me in a cup of tea, and I talked to my friend on the laptop for about another five or ten minutes.

Then I went to sleep. Then I was walking in the middle of the road."

Wendy felt herself take on some of Roberts' frustration, yet mentally reminded herself of her own inability to recall that period of her life.

"Rosalie," Roberts said gently, reaching out and grabbing her hand. She stiffened at the sudden contact, but slowly relaxed as he sat still, waiting for her to meet his gaze. "How long do you think you were missing?"

She gave another little shrug. "A few days?"

"Rosalie, I'm sorry, but it's been four weeks," he replied gently.

"Huh?" The girl frowned.

"Four weeks ago, your parents said goodnight, and you hadn't been seen until today."

"What?" It was all the girl could muster as she flicked frantic glances from Wendy to her mother, to Roberts, and back to her mother. Tears began welling in her eyes as she sat up straighter, her legs moving back and forward as though she were treading water under the blankets. She seemed genuinely alarmed at how long she was gone.

Rosalie had freed both her hands and now wrung them anxiously against her chest. "I don't even know what to say. It can't be...it's not possible...it was only...it was only..." She started breathing too quickly, and Wendy recognised the all-too-familiar onset of a panic attack.

"You're okay, Rosalie, you're safe now. Just take a deep breath for me and hold it." Wendy watched as the girl complied, her damp, wide-eyed stare focused on Wendy as though she was her only tie to reality. "Now count to three and then slowly release it over three counts." They all listened intently to Rosalie's shaky exhalation.

"Good. Now do it again."

Rosalie did as she was told, and though the panic attack subsided, she looked visibly paler, and Wendy knew they wouldn't get anything more out of her tonight. Roberts seemed to have concluded the same.

"It's okay, Rosalie. We can pick this up after you've had the chance to get some rest. These things can take time. It's a lot to process, and while it may feel scary not to recall anything, you might find as you start to feel better, that some of the memories come back to you. We just want to get to the bottom of this and find the person that did this to you so we can make sure it doesn't happen again," Roberts stated.

"Just know that no matter what you remember, or how strange it might seem, you can tell us anything, and we won't judge you in any way," Wendy added. Rosalie lifted her head and stared at Wendy. Her eyebrows raised slightly with a mix of disbelief and hope—a look Wendy recalled well—the hope that someone would believe her but the knowledge they wouldn't, despite their best intentions. Wendy was determined to ensure Rosalie wouldn't ever see disbelief in her eyes.

Roberts was half out of the chair when Rosalie surprised them all. "There is something. I mean, it was weird, but it seemed real at the time, but now it just doesn't seem to make any sense…"

"It's okay, Rosalie," Roberts replied softly as he slowly lowered himself back into the chair. "Tell us anyway. Whatever you can recall will help us, no matter how strange or seemingly insignificant you think it is. Just describe the memories as they come to you and try not to focus too much on whether it makes sense or not."

Rosalie took a deep breath and fixed her gaze firmly on Wendy, as though she was waiting. Wendy walked around from the end of the bed to the side

143

with Roberts and perched on the edge of the bed. She reached out, squeezed Rosalie's leg, trying to convey as much reassurance in her expression as she could. The girl seemed to have forgotten all about Roberts, but Wendy knew that while it might bruise his ego, it didn't matter who she felt a connection to, just so long as they got some answers.

"It wasn't *exactly* true when I said that the last thing I remember was falling asleep in my own bed." She turned to her mother. "I'm sorry. I didn't mean to lie."

"It's okay, sweetheart. Just tell the detectives whatever you remember," Anne replied, lifting her hand from where it still rested on her daughter's shoulder and gently stroked Rosalie's hair. Wendy homed in on the subtle way her hand shook, and the nervous way Anne seemed to avoid looking at either Roberts or herself.

Rosalie leaned back against the pile of pillows stacked up behind her and gazed up at the ceiling. "Firstly, I just want to say I don't do drugs. I mean, there was one time, at Sandy Newman's 16th birthday earlier this year where some of the guys were passing around a joint, and I tried some weed." Anne's head snapped up as she stared at her daughter in shock. "It was just the one time, and I didn't even like it, Mum. It felt harsh on my throat and made me cough." She turned back to Wendy, "I know it's illegal and everything, but I..."

"Don't worry about that now," Roberts cut in, his shoulders hunched up as he did a lousy impression of leaning back to relax in the chair. "You're not going to get in trouble for that. How is it relevant?"

"Well, because I think I might have been drugged. I absolutely didn't take anything, but it's the only thing that makes sense. I went to bed like I said I did—and I'm pretty sure I fell asleep. I woke up feeling cold, and my window was wide open, and my blankets pushed back. I got up to go and close it, but I felt really groggy, like, my head felt super heavy and fuzzy, and I couldn't walk straight. I had to go really slowly 'cause I felt like I was going to fall over, and I didn't want to wake up Mum and Dad." She paused, putting her hand to her mouth and chewing on her thumbnail.

"Had you had anything to eat or drink before you went to bed? Had you brought anything from outside the house?"

"We all ate the same thing for dinner,'" Anne offered.

"Okay," Roberts said slowly. "Did you have anything between dinner and when you went to bed?"

Rosalie frowned. "No. Well, only the cup of tea Dad brought in. I had felt a bit yuck in the guts after dinner, and Dad thought some green tea might help.

Wendy saw Roberts straighten out of the corner of her eye, and she knew exactly what he was thinking—they had some questions for Senator Fryair, and he wasn't going to like them.

"So, you were walking towards the window..." Wendy prompted.

"There was this buzzing sound. Kinda high-pitched. I thought it was coming from in my actual ears, but it faded in and out like an annoying mosquito. Only it got worse the closer to the window I got." She paused, and after a quick glance at Roberts, she turned back to Wendy. "I was so dizzy, but not in an 'I'm-going-to-vomit' kind of way. More like each step made me feel like the ground was moving beneath my feet, and I started to see a green glow just out of the corners of my eyes—like tiny starbursts of green. I think I tried to turn my head to try to get a better look at what it was or where it came from, but it just left me all turned around, and I had to navigate my way back towards the window. I remember reaching my hand towards the window ledge. It felt like I was so close, but when I tried to grab it, I was still too far away. The buzzing started to sound more like bells, like tiny wind chimes or something. Thinking back, it reminded me of a pair of dangling silver earrings that made a tinkling sound when I moved. It sounds crazy, but it was like the tinkling was a voice, and though I couldn't understand the words, I knew what I was supposed to do." Rosalie paused as she looked at each of them. Wendy gave her a reassuring nod.

"I don't understand how or why, but I just knew the window was open for a reason. I climbed up on the windowsill and then…"

Rosalie paused, her breathing quickening as she closed her eyes.

"You're safe, Rosalie. Nothing can happen to you here. Just tell us what happened next," Wendy gently urged.

"I just…stepped off."

The three adults looked at her, trying to avoid directing their questioning expressions at each other.

Roberts once again leaned forward, resting his arms on the edge of the bed. "Rosalie, your bedroom is on the second floor, is that right?" She turned to him but hardly met his eyes as she nodded.

"We thoroughly inspected the garden, in particular, the area directly beneath your bedroom window. There was no sign of disturbance, nothing to suggest you'd jumped or fallen."

"Because that's not what happened," she replied matter-of-factly.

"Okay…" Roberts said slowly, his frown bordering on a scowl. Rosalie's explanation triggered something deep in the back of Wendy's mind, like a part of her knew what Rosalie was going to say. She dug her fingernails into the palm of her hand as she tried to determine which she feared more, hearing Rosalie say it or not.

"Well, tell us what did happen," Roberts finished, and Wendy could hear the slightest hint of annoyance in his voice, hoping Rosalie didn't catch it.

"I... I.." she faltered and turned to her mother for reassurance.

"Go ahead, honey. Just tell them the truth so we can get to the bottom of this."

Rosalie took a deep breath and leaned back against the pillow, looking up at the ceiling. "I flew."

"Out the window?" Roberts reiterated. "You flew out the window?"

Rosalie nodded, avoiding looking at any of them. Wendy kept perfectly still, trying to keep her face as expressionless as possible while ignoring the sidelong glances Roberts cast in her direction.

Rosalie didn't answer any further, as though feeling the waves of doubt rolling towards her, and a pang of guilt prompted Wendy to speak up. "So, Rosalie, you flew out the window—what enabled you to fly, and what stopped you from falling?"

The girl shook her head. "I don't know."

Wendy tried another track. "Did you see anything during this time, or do you recall how long you felt like you were flying?"

This time Rosalie just shook her head.

Wendy risked a glance at Roberts to find him looking at her, his eyebrow raised at her line of questioning, but she chose to ignore him. "Rosalie, do you recall what happened or where you were once the flying was over?"

"I don't want to talk any more. I'm tired." She rolled over so that her back was to Roberts, tucking her head under her mother's arm.

Silence engulfed them, and Wendy was uncertain if Roberts planned to push the issue or leave the girl be for now. He cleared his throat as he rose from his chair. "Just one more thing, Rosalie, and we'll leave. We would like to follow up with the doctor to see if there is anything in the test results that might assist us in the investigation. As a minor, we need permission from a guardian to discuss the results of your tests with the doctor—but I'd like to do you the courtesy of asking your permission first."

"Okay," Rosalie whispered.

"Mrs. Fryair, do we have your permission?"

"Absolutely." She paused to kiss the top of her daughter's head. "Anything we can do to help. I just want to make sure my baby is safe."

"Thank you. You get some rest, Rosalie. We'll talk again soon." He gave a nod of farewell to Anne and walked out of the room. Wendy followed him, pulling the door closed behind them.

CHAPTER ELEVEN

Roberts swore under his breath, and Wendy looked up to see Lord Mayor Fryair striding towards them. Wendy and Roberts stopped, and Roberts muttered something Wendy didn't catch. Malcolm had a smile plastered across his face, ever mindful of the potential voters and supporters around them, but his eyes flashed with rage. Leaning in close, he whispered through his clenched, immaculate teeth, "Don't think your boss won't hear about this. God only knows what nonsense you've filled my daughters head with."

"With all due respect, Sir, your daughter has the right to decide who her guardian is during questioning," Roberts replied, not smiling, and certainly not whispering.

Malcolm Fryair glanced around the room, giving a friendly smile and nod to anyone that happened to make eye contact. "You lower your voice if you know what's good for you, son."

Wendy felt Roberts tense beside her, and she discreetly placed a hand on his arm as she leaned forward. "We have finished with our questions, for now. You're welcome to see your daughter, though she's exhausted. She's been through an ordeal and needs her rest."

"And just what are you implying?" He looked her up and down, his smile faltering into a sneer for just a second before he remembered himself and smiled again.

"I'm not implying anything," she stated, her distaste for the man growing with his attempt to belittle her. "I'm telling you. She needs to rest. Going in there angry and upsetting her isn't going to help anyone."

Malcolm stared at her a moment before leaning in close until his mouth was beside her ear. It was all she could do to hold back the urge to shudder. "You even think to tell me how to speak to my daughter again, and I will have your badge. Don't think I can't do it."

Wendy didn't flinch as he stood back. "Excellent work, detectives, keep it up," he stated loudly, slapping Roberts on the back as he walked past them towards his daughter's room.

"What a mother..." Roberts started before Wendy nudged him.

"Ears." Roberts looked around the ever-bustling area and conceded it wasn't the best place to discuss their opinions of the Lord Mayor.

"Before we go, I want to speak to the doctor looking after Rosalie, see if there are any test results back—I want to see what's in her system. Something has to account for her colourful account of what happened. People don't go flying out of bedroom windows," Robert's stated. Wendy remained silent on the matter as she followed him to the nurses' station.

Once the doctor was paged, the detectives leaned against the counter, neither one really watching the scene before them as they each ran through the facts and theories swarming their minds.

"Detectives." They looked up as a man far younger than they expected walked around the corner, his white lab coat flapping out along-side him. His smile was pleasant, yet the slight frown on his face gave him a serious air. The way he held himself, with his shoulders back and his head held high, confident, but not arrogant, instantly elicited trust in his abilities. Wendy found herself forgetting about his youthful appearance. Roberts held out his hand as the doctor approached. "Detective Roberts and this is Detective Darling. We're investigating the Rosalie Fryair case."

"Yes, of course. Doctor March," he stated, shaking each of their hands. "I take it you're after the test results." He placed a manila folder on the bench, opening it to reveal a chart and a handful of papers. Wendy leaned in for a better look, appreciative of his efficient, no-nonsense nature.

"An interesting case, I'll give you that much."

"How so?" Roberts asked, withdrawing his notepad from his back pocket.

"Well, for starters, despite her outward appearance on arrival, she wasn't in too bad a shape. Dehydrated, but again, not as bad as first thought. All her vitals are excellent, there's no sign of malnutrition, and there's no evidence of rape or abuse..."

"But she's covered in scratches," Wendy cut in.

"That's where it gets interesting. They're self-inflicted."

"You can't be serious?" Wendy said before she could stop herself, her eyes wide.

"I'm afraid so. Skin embedded under her fingernails turned out to be her own, and the direction and nature of the scratch marks are indicative of self-infliction. Also, the marks only appear on her chest, face, arms, and abdomen—not on areas she wouldn't be able to reach herself." Dr. March paused, looking up at them as though daring them to question him further. Wendy opened her mouth before closing it again—it took a lot to surprise her, and she struggled to grasp what the doctor was telling them.

"Next, we have the toxicology report, which *may* illuminate the self-harm." Dr. March pulled another piece of paper from the file and placed it on top.

"So, there were drugs in her system?" Roberts jumped the gun, earning him a polite smile from the doctor, the corners of his mouth twitching in agitation. Roberts cleared his throat and shifted his feet. "My apologies, doctor. You were saying?"

"Yes, there were drugs in her system, or should I say *a* drug," he paused, as though expecting another interruption, his eyes still on the paperwork, but when none came, he continued. "The best I can figure is it's some form of hallucinogen, but we're still running some tests on the sample."

Wendy and Roberts looked sideways at each other, both wanting to ask the question. Doctor March gave a slight chuckle. "Yes, you can ask a question." Roberts opened his mouth to speak, but the doctor was already answering. "The lab is just as baffled as I am. Whatever this toxin is found in her blood, it's not like anything we've ever seen before. Obviously, we'll keep looking into it, but we will certainly be interested to see what information is revealed as part of your investigation." Doctor March closed the manila folder and scooped it off the desk.

"Hold on, what is it? You just said it was some form of hallucinogen?" Roberts asked, frowning.

"That's all I can tell you. Aside from that, we honestly don't know what it is at this stage—we haven't seen it before."

"How is that possible?" Wendy asked.

"Is it some kind of new street drug we don't know about?" Roberts added.

"It's definitely not synthetic—it's organic," the doctor replied, lowering his voice, so they had to lean in to hear him. Roberts shot Wendy a frown, and she jumped in.

"So, it's not man made. Forgive me, doctor, but what are the odds of an organic compound of this nature being unknown?"

The doctor stared at her, and at first, she thought he was thinking of a response, but his expression was so blank that it started to unnerve her. Before she could break the silence, he finally spoke. "That's probably a little beyond my scope. I suppose there could be undiscovered compounds and elements out there in nature, though with the modern world as it is, I wouldn't think it likely. Even less likely would be to find the said compound in the blood of a teenage girl in Melbourne, Australia. Yet, here we are."

"How long until we can find out exactly what it is?" Roberts asked.

"I can't give you a time frame, but I can ask the lab to contact you if they uncover any further information that might be of use."

"Thank you, doctor," Roberts replied.

"If that is all, I have to get to my rounds." He gave them a smile and whisking up the folder, he turned and walked back the way he came before the detectives could say anything further.

"He's not half odd," Roberts mentioned, as he stood up from where he leaned on the bench.

"I think he's the least odd thing about today," Wendy replied, suddenly feeling the overwhelming urge to yawn, but held it back.

"Yeah, well, that's true as well." He turned and stared at the closed door of Rosalie Fryair's room.

Through the slatted blinds of the small viewing window they could see Rosalie, seemingly asleep, still curled towards her mother. Anne was shaking her head, her hands covering her eyes as she turned away.

"What is it?" Wendy asked.

Roberts didn't say anything as Malcolm Fryair appeared in front of the window, his steely eyes briefly finding them across the room before he reached out and closed the blinds.

Roberts gave her a quick glance before placing his hand on her back, leading her out of the room and towards the exit. Wendy tried to ignore the tingling thrill that radiated outwards from his unexpected touch and unable to stop the shiver that ran up her back. She could only hope he hadn't felt it.

"There's something about Malcolm Fryair that's not sitting right with me."

"You mean, aside from his thinly-veiled threats and attempts at intimidation?"

Roberts tilted his head to the side as they walked, as though he was trying to think of how to explain it. "Obviously there's that. But there's something else. I can't put my finger on it, but there's just something about his whole attitude. Sure, I expected he might be a bit of a dick and try to pull the "I'm the Lord Mayor" card, but it's more than that. It's hard to explain."

"Give it a go," Wendy prompted as they exited the hospital and briskly walked towards her car.

"Well, for example, when he was threatening us— I believed him. Or at least I believed *he* thought he'd have our jobs and whatever crap he was spouting. My point is, he was sincere in his threats. I didn't feel any of that sincerity in his relief over Rosalie's return. None. Especially not when Mrs. Fryair's relief was so evident. It's like he was...I don't know..."

"Annoyed?"

Roberts turned, his eyebrows raised. "Yeah, that's it! Annoyance. Like Rosalie's return is an inconvenience rather than a blessing." They remained silent as they reached Wendy's car and simultaneously got in. Wendy shot Roberts a sideways glance as he pulled on his seatbelt. She felt guilty for her initial judgement about him. He was turning out to be every bit the quality detective she'd heard about, and she made a mental affirmation that she'd give him the respect he deserved from here on out. If they had any chance of finding out what the hell was going on, Wendy had to trust his instincts as much as she trusted her own.

"Had you seen the Fryair's together prior to now?"

"Of course. In answer to your next question, yes, the relationship between them in that room was strained at best."

"I don't think she looked directly at him once. Is that how they were together whenever you saw them at the house?"

Roberts took a moment, his mouth pursing tensely as he thought back. "Honestly, they were never in the same room for more than a minute or two. Mrs. Fryair was always dashing off to the kitchen to provide tea, or to get something out of the oven, or to check on Jessica for the tenth time. She was all smiles, of course, but you've seen that—the forced smile plastered on her face the whole time you're there."

Wendy nodded as she looked over her shoulder and backed the car out of the car park. "There definitely wasn't any of that. She was obviously relieved to be with her daughter—the way she clung to her made that evident enough. I'm just trying to figure out if the Anne Fryair we witnessed in there is the normal Anne Fryair—when she's not pretending to be a Stepford wife—or if there's something else going on."

"She certainly looked like someone with the weight of the world on her shoulders rather than someone who's missing daughter has just returned," Wendy stated, steering them out of the carpark and back onto the main road.

"The Malcolm Fryair I met in there—was that how he was in your previous interactions with him?"

"Yes and no. He had that whole politician thing about him."

Wendy made a sound of distaste but let him continue.

"He was solemn, but I wouldn't say he was sad. I assumed at the time he was putting on a brave front, though it didn't escape me that he was concerned with the impact of her disappearance on his recent election. Everything is smoke and mirrors with politics. It's all just appearances... oh, fuck."

"What? What is it?" Wendy darted furtive glances at Roberts while also trying to keep her eyes on the surrounding traffic.

"One second," he instructed as he pulled his phone out of his pocket and opened the browser. Wendy chewed on her lip as she tried to be patient.

"What do you think of this? So, Malcolm Fryair was a relative unknown up until the election campaign. He went from the outskirts of the outskirts of his party to the frontrunner seemingly overnight. Then a week after his surprise landslide win in the election, his eldest daughter disappears. During the investigation, we're repeatedly encouraged to dance around the abduction label, even when it seemed to be the most likely occurrence—a decision that impeded our ability to search for the girl."

"What are you saying? Do you think he was involved somehow? That he was behind it?"

Roberts rubbed at his chin as Wendy looked out the window, as though trying to measure his words carefully. "Yeah, I think that's what I'm saying. There was some serious hostility coming from him at the hospital, and I find myself wondering how much of it was due to concern for his daughter's wellbeing, and how much was due to his resentment of Rosalie being questioned without him."

"So, you think his power play was less to do with his political ego and more to do with his concern we might have something on him?"

"Exactly."

Wendy leaned her head back against the headrest as they pulled up at a set of lights. "I'd have to say that's exactly where I'm sitting. You would think Anne Fryair would have to be in on it, yet my gut feeling is that she wasn't—or at least not at the time."

Roberts turned to her. "Not at the time?"

"Yeah, her body language was so different today—she was so withdrawn, not looking at anyone other than Rosalie unless she had to. Despite the obvious relief to be at her daughter's side, there was something else going on there."

"You think it was guilt?" Roberts asked.

"Hmm…" Wendy postulated as she took off again. "Guilt doesn't feel right. I just keep seeing the look on her face, and to me it felt heavy, like something weighed heavily on her mind."

"If the Lord Mayor is behind the abduction—or in any way knew about it—there may be something in his response to the news of her reappearance. They were together when the call was put through, so Anne would have seen his reaction. If it wasn't what she expected, surely she would have questioned him."

"We have a lot of possibilities and nothing to back any of it up," Wendy sighed. "What concerns me are his connections. How far do they spread?"

"You mean within the police force?"

Wendy nodded. "He seemed pretty confident he could make our professional lives difficult. I bet the decision to skirt around calling it an abduction was his call, too."

"Surely Fryair hasn't been influential long enough to make those kinds of connections?"

Wendy gave a shrug. "I think it warrants further investigation—but if there is a connection, we might need to keep it between you and me for now."

"One hundred percent," Roberts agreed, resting an elbow on the window edge as he rubbed his forehead. "This is fucked up."

"Here you go. Black and hot," Roberts interrupted her thoughts as he handed her a cup of coffee.

"Thanks."

He leaned against the desk beside her, and they both stared at the investigation boards, quietly sipping their coffee.

"It's a hell of a thing," he said quietly, and Wendy was unsure if he'd spoken to her or to himself.

"What is?"

"What she's been through—still going through. Admittedly we don't know exactly what that is just yet, but to be abducted? To fear you'll never see your family and friends again? I can't imagine how it must feel to wonder if someone is coming to save you."

"I can," Wendy whispered.

"So what you said to Rosalie in there, that was true?"

"Yeah. It was a long time ago, though."

He turned and looked at her, his eyes wide. "Shit. I'm sorry. That was bloody insensitive. I feel like a bit of an asshole now."

"Don't. You didn't know. The important thing is that we help Rosalie."

"We'll get to the bottom of it," Roberts stated, his voice brimming with confidence as he set his shoulders. "The important thing is that she's back, and she's safe."

Wendy nodded, lost in thought as she looked at the photos of the Fryair's house—specifically Rosalie's bedroom window. She thought back to the investigation of her own abduction, the endless questions about how she was removed from the house. The police were stumped by the lack of evidence. No sign of forced entry, of no sign of movement or struggle in or around the perimeter of the house. Wendy had shared their frustration at her inability to provide them with the answers they were desperately seeking. Up until now, she'd never recalled how she'd left the house, but as she listened to Rosalie's testament, she'd had the strange sensation of déjà vu—and she thought back to the incident at the Fryair house when Roberts pulled her back from the window ledge.

Is it a memory? Or am I trying to create a connection where there isn't one?

"If only her story didn't sound like a bad acid trip," Roberts stated as he placed his cup on the desk and started pacing alongside the rows of images.

"What does your instinct tell you?" Wendy asked.

Roberts sighed, "My instinct says she's telling the truth, but that doesn't mean her perception of the truth is accurate. Sure, we can investigate the case based on instinct, but we can't arrest anyone on that alone."

"No, of course not, but following our instincts will lead us to the evidence."

"That's all well and good, but there's just so much…strangeness…in this case. I'm having trouble working out what my instincts are telling me. Except for Malcolm Fryair. He has something to do with it; I guarantee it." He stepped up to the middle board and removed a photo of the senator from the bottom corner and stuck it to the top centre. "Rosalie said her father brought her a cup of tea. Yet there was no teacup found in her room."

"So, he removed it before the police got there."

"Obviously. We could go through the kitchen and inspect every cup for possible residue, but I've seen Anne in that kitchen, there's not a single dirty mark to be found."

"Great, so another theory without any evidence."

"After speaking to the doctor, I think we can confidently say that the tea was spiked, and that's what caused her to see the strange green sparks. I'm completely thrown that the hospital doesn't know what the substance was in Rosalie's system."

Wendy rubbed her eyes with the heels of her hands, thinking back to her own recollections of the green sparks. She felt stupid that she'd let herself believe they were guidance from a magical green fairy.

"The trick now is to try and wade through her story and work out what recollections are caused by the drugs and what's the truth," Roberts continued, unaware of her lapse in concentration.

"Is it worth interviewing Anne again? Given her state at the hospital, perhaps she might be more forthcoming with information now."

"Anything is worth a shot at this point. I'm wondering if it's also worth interviewing Jessica again. I know she was only briefly questioned at the time of her sister's disappearance, given that she wasn't there at the time. But she might be able to shine some light on what the relationship is really like between Malcolm and the members of his family."

"We'd have to arrange it for a time when we know the senator won't be there. She'll need a guardian, but I think Anne will be amenable."

"I couldn't agree more." Roberts looked at Wendy. "It's something to go on at least. Looks like we make a good team, Dah-ling." He turned his back to her as he scanned the evidence, and Wendy couldn't stop the smile at his compliment.

They worked together in silence, adding what little information they'd gathered from Rosalie to their evidence wall before they were interrupted by a knock at the door. They both turned to see a uniformed officer standing there with a handful of papers.

"The hospital just emailed the medical report for Rosalie Fryair. I took the liberty of printing out a copy for you."

"Thanks," Roberts said, his charming smile plastered across his face as he stepped forward and collected the documents. Wendy rolled her eyes as the officer all but swooned, and she turned her back to them. Roberts slowly strolled over, skimming the pages in his hand.

"Anything new to report?" she asked without turning around.

"No, doesn't look like it. It will probably be days before we get any word on what the drug is, but once we do, that will give us another angle to pursue. For now, we focus on Malcolm Fryair."

"Is there a possibility he didn't know what was in the tea he gave his daughter?" Wendy postulated.

"Seriously?" Roberts scoffed.

"Putting aside your dislike of the man, we need to consider all angles. It's still a question that needs to be asked. I guarantee if accused of drugging his daughter, that's going to be his defence."

"You're right. So not only do we have to prove that the drug was in the tea, we have to prove that he knowingly drugged her." Roberts picked up a marker and drew a diagonal line under Malcolm's photo and wrote tea/drug underneath it.

"The big question," Roberts stated, "and probably the most fucked up, is what does a newly elected Mayor have to gain by participating in the abduction of his daughter?"

"That's the million-dollar question," Wendy replied quietly, feeling sick to her stomach. For the first time in her life, she wondered if her own father had played a role in her abduction. The thought alone was enough to make her want to run out of the office and keep running, but she forced herself to stare at the photograph of Rosalie until her focus shifted. She knew she had to get to the bottom of it—for both of them.

CHAPTER TWELVE

Wendy stood on the pavement, looking up at her front door with relief. She had no idea what time it was, only that it had been a long day, and she couldn't wait for a long, hot shower and the comfort of her bed that awaited her on the other side. It felt arduous, placing one foot in front of the other as she ascended the stairs, feeling like she needed to grip the railing just to support her weight, overcome with exhaustion.

Opening her front door, she was instantly hit with the aroma of cooking food, and she followed it towards the kitchen, her stomach growling loudly in gratitude—she couldn't recall when she'd last eaten.

"Hey, there she is!" Jane exclaimed, from where she stood at the kitchen island, dicing tomatoes. Lilly looked up from the stove and blew Wendy a kiss.

"What a nice surprise—again!" Wendy laughed.

"Lilly called and said she was planning on cooking dinner in the hopes you'd get a chance to eat at some point—and you know I can't resist her cooking. So I high-tailed it over here. I have to check-in at the office tomorrow anyway, so I figured I'd just crash here if that's okay. It would save me from driving back to the house late at night."

"Of course it is," Wendy replied, walking over and planting a kiss on her daughter's cheek, before moving on to where Lilly stood, stirring a wooden spoon through some heavenly concoction in a deep pot. Wrapping her hands around her partner's waist, she rested her head on Lilly's shoulder, peering into the pot for a closer look. "That smells amazing."

"It will taste amazing too, in about fifteen minutes. In the meantime, sit down and pour us all a glass of wine."

"You two are a pair of goddesses," Wendy stated, grabbing a bottle of Shiraz from the wine rack in the corner.

"Of course we are," Lilly replied, pausing her stirring to reach up and grab three wine glasses from the cupboard above her and handing them to Wendy.

"So, if the news is anything to go by, you've had a big day," Jane stated as she scooped up the diced tomato and tossed it into the salad bowl beside her.

"Yeah, you could say that."

"Her family must be so relieved. I can't believe she just showed up like that! I mean, obviously we all wanted her found, but after this long, who really expected she'd be found alive?"

"I thought you said if anyone could find her, it would be me," Wendy said, smiling as she slid a glass of wine across the benchtop towards her daughter.

"Of course. I just didn't necessarily think you'd find her alive." Jane picked up a piece of cucumber and ate it, smiling at her mother. Wendy returned the smile and took a seat.

"So, how is she?" Lilly asked.

"As well as can be expected. They'll keep her in the hospital for a few days for observation, but then she should be able to go home."

Wendy faded off as her thoughts retreated back to her own return home, post-abduction, and the mixed feelings that had come with it. Most notable was the way her room still looked exactly the same as she'd left it, yet no longer felt like her own. She recalled insisting on keeping her window closed at all times, regardless of the weather. The repetitive way she would find herself staring out of it, wondering if he was out there, somewhere, watching her, waiting for another opportunity to come for her.

"Earth to mum," Jane joked playfully.

"I'm sorry. It's just been a long day."

"Well, to be fair, it's been a long month. You're entitled to a little zoning out," Lilly replied, stepping over to the kitchen island to collect her glass of wine, delicately sipping it as she returned to stirring the pot.

"What is it?" Jane asked.

Wendy looked up, realising she was frowning heavily.

"It's nothing. Just thinking about the case."

"Everyone must be relieved she's back. What were the odds of you finding her on your first day on the case?" Lilly said, the pride evident in the smile she shot in Wendy's direction.

"Technically, I didn't find her. She just showed up out of nowhere."

"So, why do you look so troubled?" Jane asked.

"Well, just because she's back doesn't mean the case is closed. We still have to find the person who took her in the first place."

"It's probably a little anticlimactic—you had to jump through hoops to get on the case, and then she's back before you've really gotten started. Maybe a good night's sleep will help you get some renewed perspective," Lilly suggested.

"You make it sound like I wish she were still missing," Wendy half-joked, picking up her glass of wine for a gulp.

"No, of course not—you know what I mean," Lilly stated.

Wendy sighed. "Yeah, I do. If today was anything to go by, there's a hell of a lot of work to do if we're to get to the bottom of it."

"You will, Mum. If anyone can find out what happened, it's you. Though you have a partner on the case, right?"

Wendy coughed and sputtered on her wine.

"Are you okay?" Jane asked as Wendy tried to catch her breath. The wooden spoon clattered against the metal saucepan as Lilly rushed over to the sink to get Wendy a glass of water.

"I'm fine," Wendy said once she could speak. "The wine just went down the wrong pipe."

"Death by wine. There could be worse ways to go," Lilly joked as she returned to the stove, turning it off before removing the saucepan from the heat, the aroma of dinner causing Wendy's stomach to growl again in anticipation.

"So?" Jane asked once Wendy recovered. "Are you going to tell us about your partner?"

"Uh, there's not much to tell. I only met him today. He transferred to the station while I was on leave." Wendy kept her eyes on her wine glass, not trusting that either Jane or Lilly wouldn't see in her eyes the impact he'd had on her.

"Come on," teased Lilly. "You're a detective. You would have had him sussed out in the first few minutes."

Wendy chuckled. "He's proving to be an excellent detective, which is a relief. He's a little too cocky for my taste, and he plays on the whole annoying accent thing. But other than that, I think we'll work well together."

"Ohhhh, an accent! What is it?" Jane asked.

"Scottish, I think," Wendy replied, rolling her eyes as Jane feigned a swoon.

"Oh, I almost forgot!" Jane disappeared as she bent down behind the bench, lifting an old and decrepit cardboard box up onto the counter. "I was sorting through Grandma's belongings today, and I found this hidden on the top shelf of her wardrobe. That in itself was enough to pique my interest, but then I saw your name written on it and decided I probably shouldn't open it. Though I warn you, my resolve is weakening."

Wendy laughed. "You know curiosity killed the cat, right?"

"So? Cats also have nine lives," Jane retorted.

Wendy stood up to look at her name, scrawled across the top of the box in a semi-faded black marker. "Well, I'm ninety percent certain this is Dad's handwriting."

"So why was it in Grandma's room? Why didn't she give it to you when Grandpa died?" Lilly asked.

"I don't know," Wendy said slowly, running her fingers over the writing. "Maybe she forgot? Or maybe she didn't even know it was there. Dad could have put it there without telling her."

"Okay, well, now I'm intrigued too," Lilly stated while placing plates of steaming risotto in front of each of them. "You're just going to have to open it and put us out of our misery."

"Let's eat first. This smells amazing," Wendy replied, hunger trumping curiosity, and she moved the box onto a spare stool and returned to the home-cooked meal before her. Self-care wasn't her strong point, and when home alone, she usually didn't bother eating anything more complex than a piece of toast or some fruit. After a month of living back at the family home, she'd become spoiled with an endless array of delicious food, and she admitted to herself it was nice to share a meal with others. She tended to be hermit-like in her introversion when not prompted by others to socialise.

They ate in silence, Lilly's cooking too good to let go cold. Wendy smiled to herself as she watched Jane's subtle glances at the box, aware her daughter's journalistic nature was getting the better of her.

Jane and Wendy cleared the plates and stacked the dishwasher in record time while Lilly topped up their drinks.

"Alright," Wendy announced as she walked over to the box. "Let's check this out." There was a moment's hesitation as her hands hovered over the flaps. She held her breath, overwhelmed by the sudden urge to shove the box into the darkest shadows she could find and forget she'd ever seen it.

"Come on, Mum! The suspense is killing me!" Jane groaned, and Wendy shook off the sensation and grabbed the edge of the aging tape that half-heartedly attempted to keep the box sealed, yanking it off without any resistance. Folding the flaps outwards, the three of them leaned in for a closer look.

At first glance, the box appeared to be filled with family mementos and keepsakes, and Wendy felt herself marginally relax, chastising herself for getting worked up over nothing. But as she lifted a framed family photograph from the top of the pile, she realised the contents weren't entirely what they seemed.

"What's wrong?" Lilly asked as Wendy stood frozen, staring at the frame.

"Uh, I'm not exactly sure," she replied, trying to process what she was seeing while simultaneously wondering what it meant. She could feel Jane and Lilly's impatience growing as they hovered and shifted on either side of her, and Wendy reached over the box to set the frame on the bench so they could all see it.

"I don't get it," Lilly stated, as she squinted at the image. "It just looks like an old family portrait—taken in front of the vineyard if I'm not mistaken."

"You're not. But it's not the *where* that is the problem. It's the *who*."

"Well, that's a no-brainer," Jane piped up. "It's clearly not you and Uncle Mike and Uncle John, but I do recognise Great Grandma and Great Grandpa from photos of them from around the manor, so that's obviously Grandad standing there in front of them—he looks so cute with his shorts pulled up so high," Jane laughed. "And look at that hairstyle!"

Wendy didn't laugh with her. Instead, she tapped the person standing beside him. Jane's smile fell away and was replaced by a frown as she stared at the girl standing beside Wendy's father, half a head shorter and in a short, white frilly dress.

"Uh, Mum, I thought Grandpa was an only child?" Jane asked.

"So did I," Wendy replied.

"I don't understand. Who is that girl? Could she be a cousin?" Jane asked.

"I don't know. I don't think so. To my knowledge, there weren't any cousins, either in Dad's generation or mine."

"Oh, what the hell," Lilly stated as she leaned back, her glass of wine all but forgotten on the counter.

Jane picked the frame up for a closer look, and Wendy reached back into the box, withdrawing a bundle of old photographs bound together with a blue satin ribbon. Giving it a gentle tug, the bow released, and the ribbon fell to the floor, ignored. Wendy flicked through the photos. "What the actual fuck?!" she exclaimed.

"What? What is it?" Jane asked as she and Lilly leaned in for a better look.

"I don't believe it—the girl—she's in all of these photos!" Wendy shuffled through them faster and faster, watching her father and the girl become younger the further down the stack she moved until she reached the last image. It was a photo of a young boy, likely no older than two or three, his arm supported by pillows as he nursed a tiny, sleeping baby. With a trembling hand, she turned the photo over and read aloud,

James & Dawn, 18th March 1972.

(Ages 3 years & 5 days)

"It's his sister. I have an aunt."

"Holy shit," Jane replied. The three of them sat in silence, staring at each other as unspoken questions hovered around them.

"So, I'm probably stating the obvious here, but I'm assuming you didn't know about her before now?" Lilly asked.

Wendy shook her head. "No, and I'm pretty certain John and Michael don't know either."

"Do you think your mother knew about her?"

"Honestly, I can't say. Though Mum and Dad were always so close, I'd find it hard to believe she didn't."

"This is crazy," Jane added, rubbing her temples. "Where is she? Did something happen to her? Why was her existence hidden from the family? That seems like a pretty awful step to take if you ask me…" Jane rambled with rapid-fire questions.

"It doesn't make any sense," Wendy concurred as she fanned the photos out across the bench. "Judging by the later photos, my guess is Dawn was about fifteen or sixteen."

"So what happened when she was a teenager?" Lilly asked, but Wendy could only shake her head in response.

"Maybe there's something else in the box that will tell us," Lilly suggested, and Wendy pulled out the remaining items without inspection, spreading them out across the bench. There was a jewellery box, white with pink flowers and green leaves decorating the base and bordering the lid. Its tiny brass latch was missing a screw on the left side, causing it to hang slightly to the side. There was a greyish-brown teddy bear that had seen better days, with small patches where the fur had worn off and a round black nose that appeared to have been resewn more than once. A journal threatening to burst at the seams was bound with a wide rubber band, with hints of photographs and folded pieces of paper peeking out through the pages. A delicate and tarnished silver bracelet had Dawn's name engraved on it with a dainty bluebird dangling on a single ring from the name band. It sat alongside a series of silver baby keepsakes Wendy assumed were gifted to Dawn when she was born—a spoon with a duckling on the handle, a tiny mug with her name and date of birth engraved on it, and a rattle engraved with mice playfully spiralling up the handle. But it was the long, brittle-looking, ivory lace dress that Wendy picked up and held out before them.

"That looks like a Christening dress," Lilly murmured, reaching out to gently touch the ivory satin ribbon threaded through the midsection of the dress before cascading in two crinkled pieces down the front. "I thought your parents weren't religious?"

"They weren't—but that's not to say my grandparents weren't, at least to some extent. I couldn't say. I never knew them." She carefully laid the dress over the edge of the box and noticed she'd missed something. At the bottom of the box lay an A3 sized folder with a black ribbon binding it closed, making it look like a gift waiting to be unwrapped. Lifting it out and onto the bench, Wendy untied the ribbon, letting it fall away as she carefully lifted the front of the folder, listening to it crack as she opened it. Inside was a stack of artwork, and the three of them stared in appreciation as she gently went through them one by one.

"Oh, wow. These are amazing," Jane exclaimed as she leaned over for a better look. "She was clearly a talented artist."

Wendy traced Dawn's signature where it was placed in black cursive in the bottom right-hand corner of the page. She felt a strange pull as her fingers moved over the letters, as though a part of her recognised the familiar connection, even though they'd never met. She could feel Lilly and Jane eagerly waiting for her to move on to the next picture, and with a promise to herself that she would spend more time looking at them once she was alone, she turned the picture over and shuffled through the rest of the pile. Most of the images were done in charcoal, some watercolours, and some combining the two mediums thrown in for good measure—and all of them were amazing—still lifes, drawings of the estate, and portraits. There seemed to be no end to what she could paint or draw.

"Do you think it would be weird to frame some of these? Maybe hang them up at the manor? It seems such a shame they've been hidden away all this time," Jane commented.

"Not at all. I'm not sure how your uncles will react to this news, but I can't see them protesting—she's still family after all." Wendy's appreciation became concern the further into the pile they went. The images became darker in that they were almost all just charcoal but done in heavy, thick strokes, and the subject matter changed from realism to subject matter better suited to someone's nightmares. Wendy turned over page after page with increasing speed until she stopped on a drawing, her hand frozen at its edge as her breath caught in her throat so suddenly, she almost choked on it.

"Mum? What is it?" Jane asked, her voice high-pitched in her alarm as she placed her hand on her mother's shoulder.

Wendy couldn't reply as she stared down at the horrific portrait before her. The page was almost all negative space made up of angry streaks of thick charcoal, leaving the outline of what looked to be a young man; the only feature was his piercing green eyes—a stark contrast to all the black. The unnatural shade was captured so perfectly; it caused Wendy to shake at the recognition.

"Hey. Hey, hon. What is it? What's wrong?" Lilly asked, pushing the folder across the bench and out of Wendy's reach. Wendy blinked rapidly as she turned her back to them, trying to clear the vision from her eyes.

"Nothing, I'm fine."

"Like hell you are. What's going on?" Lilly pressed.

"Nothing. Seriously. It's just a lot to take in is all." Wendy reached behind her and retrieved her glass of wine, taking a generous sip while ignoring the concerned looks Jane and Lilly shot both at her and each other. The wine had its desired effect, and Wendy felt the warmth of the full-bodied red begin to lower the intensity of her anxiety enough that she trusted herself to speak. "I just need answers. I need to find out what happened to her and why she's been hidden from the rest of us for all these years. It doesn't make sense to do something like that. I mean, in all my life, I never once heard Dad mention anything about a sister."

"I know she's not in a good way, but would Nanna be of any help?" Lilly asked.

Wendy thought about it for a moment. "If I caught her in a lucid moment, she could be, but sadly they're becoming few and far between. She would have known her, though—I don't know exactly when she started working for our family, but I know Dad was only a boy."

"Could be worth a shot though," Jane prompted. "Is there anyone else in the family still alive that would know of her?"

Wendy shook her head. "No. Up until now, I thought Dad was an only child."

"I'm heading back to the manor after my meeting in the morning. If it's okay, I'll snoop around and see if I can find anything," Jane offered.

Wendy nodded absently. "I think I'll see if there's anything in the police records or anything about her online."

"Which can wait," Lilly stated firmly. "The last thing you need right now is something else to worry about on top of your case. I want you to take the night just to relax—have a time out."

"But," Wendy cut in.

"No. I'm not taking no for an answer. Jane will pour you another glass of wine, and I'll run you a hot bath, and you can bloody well relax and do as you're told," Lilly said kindly, but firmly, kissing her partner on the cheek. Wendy let herself be led off the chair and out of the kitchen. She turned and pulled a face at her daughter as she heard her laugh behind her, though she conceded a hot bath sounded like heaven.

CHAPTER THIRTEEN

Wendy let the bubbles engulf her, closing her eyes as she inhaled the scents of patchouli, ylang-ylang, lavender, and geranium and found herself relaxing in spite of herself. She attempted to overhear the not-so-discrete whisperings of Lilly and Jane on the other side of the bathroom door but found herself unable to focus—or care—as she slipped deeper into the bath. Keeping her eyes closed, she felt like she was wrapped in a cocoon of warmth and had to admit to herself, this was exactly what she needed. Despite the small fortune the custom bath had cost her, she was grateful to be able to stretch out her legs, straining her pointed toes to just brush against the other end of the tub. As beads of sweat formed along her forehead and ran down her face and neck, Wendy lifted a foot out of the water and rested it on the tap, the cold of the metal a pleasant contrast against her warm skin. She reluctantly opened her eyes as she reached up for the glass of wine that sat on the edge of the bath beside her head, not trusting her coordination with her eyes closed not to smash it on the tiles. As she sipped on the wine, her eyes drifted up to the book she'd placed on the vanity, but she was too relaxed to read. The pendant of the necklace Nanna gave her dangled off the edge—she knew she'd been told not to take it off, but surely Nanna hadn't wanted her to ruin it either. Closing her eyes again, her mind started running over everything the day had held, and she felt exhausted just thinking about it. The day felt endless like she'd somehow crammed extra hours into it. Images of Dawn's darker art worked their way to the forefront of her mind, and she wondered how her aunt knew about Pan. The thought was persistent, despite Wendy's best efforts to hold it back.

Was she abducted also? By Pan? How could he take both of us? That's not possible. What if the box was hidden because he took her, and she never came back?

Wendy sat up as a fresh wave of anxiety took over, like a dark and ominous cloud threatening to engulf her if she couldn't work out how to keep ahead of it. Knowing she'd find no further solace in the bath, she reluctantly pulled the plug and got out. With only a towel wrapped around her, she sauntered into her room, leaving the bathroom door open in the hopes the lingering smells of the oils would waft into the bedroom. Her mouth fell open as she was met by at least a dozen candles, their flickering light dancing along the walls and across the ceiling, enticing her to come closer.

Wendy jumped as she heard the click of the bedroom door close to her right, and she turned to see Lilly leaning against it, wearing a sheer, black negligee that draped elegantly over her ample curves.

"Wow, you look amazing." Wendy eyed her up and down in appreciation. "Is that new?"

"It is." Lilly smiled and moved slowly towards her, making sure Wendy had every opportunity to appreciate the view.

"Where's Jane?" Wendy asked softly as Lilly stopped in front of her.

"She went to bed. She said she has an early start tomorrow for work, then the long drive back to the estate. I think she's eager to get back to see what else she can dig up on the Darling family tree."

Wendy nodded distractedly. She opened her mouth to comment but found her mind failing her as Lilly ran her hands across Wendy's bare shoulders. Wendy let her towel fall to her feet as Lilly's fingertips continued down her arms before clasping her hands. Wendy ran her thumb across the small tattoo of a tiger that adorned the inside of Lilly's right wrist and gasped as Lilly leaned in and pressed her warm lips against Wendy's neck.

"I thought we were overdue for some lengthy quality time together," Lilly whispered as she moved her lips slowly up Wendy's neck and gently ran her teeth over her ear lobe. Wendy could only moan in response. Her eyes closed as she enjoyed the sensations that coursed through her. She shivered—a combination of the sudden cool air caressing her exposed skin and Lilly's warm hands running over her breasts. Wendy moaned again, feeling incapable of anything else, and Lilly kissed her in response, gently squeezing her breasts with her hands as she wedged her thigh between Wendy's.

Without protest, Wendy let her hips rock back and forward as though they had a life of their own as she slid her hands under Lilly's negligee and around to her arse, squeezing hard as she ground herself against her. The image of Roberts' intense gaze flashed before her, and Wendy jumped, instinctively pulling back, her eyes wide, and she raised her hand to the side of her face as though she'd been slapped.

"What? What is it?" Lilly asked, pulling Wendy's hand away from her face and holding it in both of her own as she planted a kiss on her palm.

Wendy frowned, shaking her head in an attempt to rid herself of the unwanted image. She gave Lilly a reassuring smile, placing her hands on her girlfriend's hips and pulled her back towards her. "Nothing, I'm fine. Sorry."

"Are you sure? We don't have to…"

"I said I'm fine," Wendy replied, cutting off any further queries with a kiss as she focused on keeping her mind blank until she once again felt that she was present in the moment. Just her and Lilly. Their embrace tightened as their kisses deepened, and Wendy no longer felt the need to guard her thoughts as her body took over, moving against Lilly's as their passion intensified.

"That's more like it," Lilly said as they came up for air, and with a wicked grin, Wendy led them to the bed. Lilly pushed her back onto it, and Wendy stretched out luxuriously as Lilly leaned over her, pushing her thighs apart. Gazing up at the stars above, she gasped with pleasure as she felt Lilly's mouth on her, and she let all thoughts of the day and recent weeks fade away into oblivion until there was nothing left but undulating pleasure.

Wendy opened her eyes, surprised to see the faint glow of dawn pushing up against the night. With a yawn, she realised she couldn't recall the last time she'd slept through the whole night. Frowning, she turned from the windows to the annoying buzz coming from her bedside table, where she suspiciously eyed the culprit that had awoken her. She reached over and snagged her mobile, ignoring the strange flutter in her chest as she saw Roberts' name flashed across the screen.

Holding it against her chest, she quickly looked down at where Lilly still peacefully slept, the faintest hint of a snore as she inhaled. Not wanting to wake her, she swung her legs over the side of the bed and tiptoed over to the chair by the window. "Roberts," she answered the phone.

"Good morning to you too, Dah-ling."

Wendy bit her lip to prevent the smile that threatened to break and reminded herself it was only a day ago his ridiculous pronunciation of her surname infuriated her. "Sorry, good morning. Wait, it's barely even dawn—has there been a development?"

"Good work, detective," Roberts replied, and Wendy could hear the smile in his voice. "I got a call from the hospital. Apparently, Rosalie Fryair had some kind of panic attack, or a psychotic break, or something. They wouldn't tell me much over the phone."

"I wouldn't think that's all that surprising, given what she's been through. So why is the hospital calling you? I'm assuming her parents were contacted."

"Well, no. For whatever reason, Rosalie specifically requested her parents weren't contacted, but requested that she see you—and only you."

"Can we do that? She's still a minor. We can't question her without a guardian."

"Well, technically, you aren't questioning her. She requested to see you."

NEVER, NEVER

Wendy didn't answer right away, instead running the legalities through her head as she tucked her phone between her cheek and her shoulder and got to her feet, quickly picking up a pair of leggings and a half-dirty sweater dress that sat bunched on the trunk at the foot of her bed.

"I'll be out front in about fifteen," Roberts stated.

Wendy fumbled with the phone, almost dropping it on the wooden trunk. "I thought you said she wanted to talk to me?"

"She does—but don't think for a second I'm not coming with you. I'll see what updates I can get out of the medical staff while you speak to her. It's called teamwork, detective." He terminated the call before she had the chance to protest, and just like that, her easy annoyance with her partner returned.

Quietly placing the phone on the trunk, she tiptoed towards the bathroom. She swallowed a yelp as she stood on some hard and randomly discarded item on the floor and half-hopped, half-stumbled until she accidentally banged her shoulder into the doorframe, cursing as she slipped into the bathroom, closing the door behind her. Turning the light on, she dumped her clothes on the bench and turned on the water. She shivered in the cold of the bathroom, impatiently shoving her hand in and out of the running water as she waited for it to warm. It had only reached lukewarm when she became too impatient and jumped in anyway. Wendy attempted to wash in record speed, cursing to herself as she dropped the soap and then knocked the conditioner off the rack, sending both clattering to the shower base. Exiting the shower, she quickly towelled herself dry before yanking her clothes on. Turning off the light, she opened the door and stepped as quietly as she could back to the trunk, extra careful not to tread on anything. Sitting on the edge, Wendy tapped the screen on the phone, realising Roberts would arrive any second, and the last thing she wanted was to give him the satisfaction of having him wait for her. She reached down and pulled on a pair of socks that lay discarded on the carpet before grabbing a boot. When she couldn't see its mate, she knelt down with a huff. She fished it out from where it lay, half-wedged under the trunk, and sat back to put it on.

"Ah-hem..."

Wendy looked up, her foot half in the boot, to find Lilly looking down at her, face flushed with sleep and framed by her wild and tangled black hair. She absently held the bedsheet to her chest with one hand, but the sheet fell low on one side, revealing her breast, and it was all Wendy could do to finish pulling on her boot.

"Is this an 'I can't sleep' thing, or a work thing?" she asked, stifling a yawn.

"It's a work thing. I was trying not to wake you."

"Mmm-hmm," Lilly replied, climbing off the bed before soundlessly walking across the carpet towards the bathroom. Wendy sighed as she looked after her, admiring her partner's effortless, soundless grace— unlike Wendy's bumbling curse of making increasing noise the more she tried to be quiet. She got to her feet and looked around the room for her handbag, certain she'd brought it up.

"Hey, babe. Have you seen my handbag?" she whispered loudly against the semi-closed bathroom door.

"Yeah, it's down in the kitchen where you left it."

Wendy rolled her eyes at the sudden recollection. "Okay, well, I'm going to go meet Roberts out front. Go back to bed if you like."

"Absolutely," Lilly replied through another yawn. "Unlike some people, I actually need more than a couple of hours of sleep."

"There are twenty-four perfectly usable hours in the day," she joked, but the smile fell quickly from her face as she felt the sudden urge to push open the door and throw herself into Lilly's arms. Instead, she gripped the doorframe, resting her head against it as an inexplicable wave of anxiety washed over her, spreading through her body like a wildfire. She squeezed her eyes shut and could see only red, like two bright warning lights trying to stop her going any further. Wendy forced herself to take three slow, deep breaths as she pushed it aside. It had only been a matter of seconds, yet it left a mark, and she couldn't shake the nonsensical feeling that she wasn't going to see Lilly again.

"I'll try to get back for a coffee before your day kicks off if you want to hang around," Wendy offered through the door.

"Sounds good. Be safe, text me when you're on your way home, and I'll have it ready when you get here."

"Will do." Wendy forced herself to leave the room and head down the stairs toward the kitchen to retrieve her handbag. At the front door, she grabbed her jacket and a scarf before stepping out into the frigid morning air, quietly closing the door behind her. Pleased to see she'd beaten Roberts, she considered ducking back inside to retrieve some gloves as her fingers quickly started to sting in the cold—but she knew the minute she stepped back inside, her partner would arrive. Instead, she shoved her hands into her jacket pockets and pondered Rosalie's request. Wendy didn't feel overly concerned by the news that Rosalie had some kind of episode or that she'd requested to speak to her over Roberts or even her own parents—it certainly wasn't unusual given what she'd been through. If anything, it was a positive development that she'd garnered the girl's trust. It could only lead to Rosalie opening up and hopefully giving them something they could use. Before she could dwell on it further, she saw Roberts' car approach, slowing as he pulled up to the curb. She wound the scarf around her neck and took the steps two at a time, ignoring the way Roberts peered at her through the window. Once she was in the car, he pulled away from the curb as she reached for her seatbelt, casting subtle, sideways glances in his direction.

Roberts cleared his throat, his attention fixed firmly on the road ahead. "There's a surprising amount of traffic on the road already, but we should still have a fairly quick run to the hospital."

"Thanks for the traffic report, partner," Wendy laughed despite herself. Roberts finally looked over at her, a sheepish grin lighting up his face.

"There's coffee beside you, smartarse," he said.

She looked down at the two cup holders between their seats. "You're amazing, thank you." She grabbed the one from the front and took a swig before scrunching up her face in distaste.

"Oh, sorry. Yours is the other one," Roberts' chuckled as Wendy replaced the cup and picked up the second one, relieved to taste nothing but strong, black coffee.

"Wow—how much sugar do you have in your coffee? That was crazy sweet."

"Don't be judging my coffee, Dah-ling," he replied, navigating a roundabout. As they fell into silence, Wendy felt acutely aware of their proximity, and the previous night's incident popped into her head, causing her to almost choke on a mouthful of coffee.

"You alright there?" Roberts asked, alternating rapid glances between her and the road.

"Yeah, yeah. I'm fine. It just went down the wrong way," she reassured him, hoping he'd attribute the rosy flush in her cheeks to the cold.

Instead, she stared out the window as the sunrise took hold of the morning, quietly sipping on her coffee, enjoying the sensation of the warmth seeping from the cup into her cold fingers. It confused her the way Roberts popped into her head unexpectedly. Everything she'd heard about him prior to meeting him only elicited dislike. Yet, overlooking his easy charm and quick wit, she had to admit he was impressive to work with, and she tried to convince herself that was where the attraction lay—nothing more than a professional admiration. To think anything further caused Wendy to shift in her seat, making her feel sick to her stomach that she'd somehow dishonoured Lilly simply by thinking it. Struggling to swallow a mouthful of coffee, it sickened her further that she was just another colleague caught up in the charms of Rupert Roberts. Wendy forced her thoughts back to her girlfriend. They'd been together for years and loved each other dearly. Wendy had never had a boyfriend—neither before nor after her abduction—and had remained single and completely disinterested in dating while Jane was a child. Friends and family tried to gently nudge her into the dating scene from time to time. Wendy always declined. After her experience, she preferred an uncomplicated, relatively quiet existence, and she knew she was never alone—not when she had Jane and her family. She was content with life that way, at least, until she met Lilly in a bookstore on her 30th birthday.

Wendy continued to watch the sunrise through the passenger window as she recalled that birthday—one that had seen her start the day amped up on caffeine after a particularly persistent run of insomnia. Her brothers had gifted her a voucher for her favourite independent bookstore, and she'd made sure she was there before opening.

It was a totally cliché meeting—Wendy reached for a book, and just as she'd grabbed it, so did someone else. The unexpected touch had startled Wendy, and in her highly caffeinated state, she'd stumbled backwards and knocked over a book display. As she bent down, frantically fumbling with the books as she tried to re-stack them, she'd looked up to find the most beautiful woman helping her. And that was how she'd met Lilly. The book they'd both reached for was then gifted to Wendy from Lilly, and they'd been inseparable ever since. Despite all Wendy's quirks and her inability to commit to them living under the one roof, Lilly still stood by her and the birthday book, a first edition of James Barrie's Margaret Ogilvy, still held a prized spot on her bookshelf. Wendy was proud to admit she'd only had eyes for Lilly since that day, at least until now. Frowning, she refused to entertain what it could mean. Since starting her relationship with Lilly, she'd just assumed she wasn't interested in men—it made sense considering what she'd been through and so she'd never questioned it, until now. Massaging the bridge of her nose, she quietly chastised herself for allowing her mind to wander and forced herself to focus on work. Rosalie needed them and deserved her absolute focus and attention.

"You alright there, Dah-ling?" Roberts asked as he pulled the car into the hospital car park.

"Yeah, of course. I'm just thinking about the case and wondering if Rosalie might have recalled some new information for us."

"We can only hope." He replied, bringing the car to a stop and pulling the keys out of the ignition. She

186

watched as he opened the car door and got out, pocketing his keys as he did so.

"Today, Dah-ling," he stated, closing the door behind him before weaving his way through the cars. Swearing under her breath, she hurried after him, keeping half a step behind as they entered the hospital and navigated their way to Rosalie's room. Roberts knocked gently on the door, and when they heard a muffled reply, he opened the door and stood back so Wendy could enter. Rosalie lay semi-reclined, her hands lying listlessly by her sides as a nurse stood at her side, taking her blood pressure. The girl was gazing up at the small television mounted on the wall, the only other source of light aside from the dim glow of the light above the bedhead.

"Not quite the chaotic scene I'd anticipated," Roberts whispered so only Wendy could hear him, but she didn't respond. "I'll go and hunt down the doctor and find out exactly what happened; then I'll grab us a couple more coffees. That should give you enough time," he whispered again, this time close enough that Wendy could feel his breath against her ear, and she fought against the shiver that threatened to course through her.

Wendy looked over her shoulder, watching him walk away, equally annoyed with herself for enjoying his proximity and infuriated that he'd felt the need to etch out a time frame for her when she was more than capable of doing her job. Giving herself a mental shake, she walked over to the end of the bed, giving a nod and a smile at the nurse as she watched her record her readings.

"She's had a bit of a rough night, but Rosalie's nice and relaxed now." The girl didn't move as they spoke but continued to watch the television in silence as the nurse held her wrist with one hand and watched her wristwatch on the other. "I wanted to give her something to help her sleep, but she was adamant she had to speak to you first." The nurse smiled, but her eyes sternly conveyed her point.

"I'll try not to keep her too long."

"Good. Just let the nurses' station know when you're finished, and one of us will give her something then." Wendy nodded once and watched Rosalie as she waited for the nurse to leave the room.

"Hey, Rosalie," she finally said. "How are you feeling?" she asked. Rosalie blinked and with an electrical buzz, the television turned off. Wendy looked over her shoulder in surprise at the now black screen and tried to keep her expression neutral as she turned back to Rosalie, who now sat upright, her hands still lying idly by her sides. Wendy cleared her throat as her senses started to wind up, like someone had taken a crank to a generator, leaving her hyper-alert. She felt an unease present now that wasn't there when she'd seen the girl previously.

"I was told you wanted to see me," she stated, distracting herself by grabbing the chair from the corner and dragging it beside the bed where she sat.

"Yeah, I guess I did."

Rosalie's erect posture seemed unnatural and only triggered Wendy's senses further, and she fought against them, reminding herself the girl was the victim.

When the girl failed to elaborate further, Wendy tried another track. "So I hear you've had a rough night. Do you want to tell me about it?"

Rosalie stared past Wendy to the television, as though it was still on. She sat there, unblinking, and as much as Wendy wanted to turn around, she refused to. Forcing herself to keep her expression neutral, Wendy's instinct was on high alert. There was something off about Rosalie. She seemed completely different from the girl she'd spoken to earlier. Gone was the sad and withdrawn victim. She wondered if this was the result of a 'come down' from the substance found in her system, but her gut told her that wasn't so. This was something else.

"Rosalie? What did you want to talk to me about?" Wendy kept her voice soft, friendly, but there was a sternness now, an impatience.

Rosalie gave a slight nod, so slight it would have gone unnoticed if Wendy hadn't been watching her so intently, but she remained silent.

"There must be a reason you asked for me in the middle of the night. I'm here if you want to talk, but I'll go if you would prefer to rest." Wendy stepped back from the bed, feigning a departure. Rosalie's head slowly drooped forward, her hair falling forward across her face.

"Rosalie?"

The girl looked up at the detective through her hair, though all Wendy could see was the eerie smile that crept across the girl's face. Wendy was unable to stop the icy shiver running up her back at her expression—Rosalie looked like the cat that got the canary, and there was something familiar about the smile that made Wendy want to get as far from Rosalie as possible. Instead, she cleared her throat and forced herself to question the girl a final time.

"So, do you want to tell me what happened?"

Rosalie shrugged, but her movements seemed slow, almost exaggerated, like she was a puppet controlled by strings. "I wanted to leave. They wouldn't let me."

"I understand that you must be eager to get home, you've been through a terrible ordeal, and the doctors just want to make sure you're recovered before you leave. If you do everything asked of you, I'm sure you'll be home in no time. I heard you were quite upset, and I ..."

"Who said I was upset?" Rosalie cut in, and Wendy's eyes widened in surprise at the change in Rosalie's voice. It sounded off—a little too high, as though she was hysterical and on the verge of screeching. Yet to look at, the girl looked calm and in control.

Rosalie sighed loudly, the creepy smile still pinned to her face. "Perhaps I was having a moment of inner turmoil."

"Inner turmoil..." Wendy repeated slowly, unsure of what to make of it. "Why don't you tell me about it?"

Rosalie remained quiet for a moment, the forefingers on each hand slowly drawing circles on the bedding in hypnotic rotations. "You won't understand..."

"Try me."

Rosalie continued drawing circles on the blanket, the smile set on her face. Wendy stood up, her desire to flee intensifying with each passing second, no matter how much she tried to convince herself she was being ridiculous—her instincts would have none of it. Wendy opened her mouth to speak but was silenced as Rosalie's head shot up.

"You shouldn't have run from me." The girl's voice remained high-pitched, but another slightly deeper voice paired with it, as though someone else was there speaking with her.

Wendy gripped the edge of the bed as the air rushed from her lungs so violently, she felt like she'd been punched. It was a voice she knew well, and despite the fact she hadn't heard it in years, it was embedded deep within her. It took all of her focus to keep her expression blank as her mind raced, trying to come up with a logical explanation as her memories strained against their barricade, already weakened by the recent prodding.

"I didn't run from you, Rosalie. I don't know what you're talking about." She finally replied, trying to keep her voice light and tremor-free.

"Yes, you do."

The girl continued to stare from beneath her hair, the smirk holding steady except for the slightest twitch that tugged at the left corner of her mouth. Wendy refused to look away, not wanting the girl to see how shaken she was. "No, I don't. Why don't you tell me about it?"

Wendy knew Rosalie was listening to her. She was still tracing circles on the blanket, but there was no answer. Wendy suddenly became aware of the quiet surrounding them—except for the steady tick-tock of the clock on the wall. She couldn't hear the hushed hustle and bustle of the hospital world beyond the bedroom door. There was nothing to drown away the sound of the ticking. She felt her teeth grate against each other as the sound became louder, tick-tock, TICK-TOCK. No longer interested in Rosalie, Wendy fought against her every instinct to look up at the clock, but as the ticking continued to taunt her, she caved and glanced up to where the clock hung above Rosalie's bed. TICK-TOCK... TICK... TOCK... The ticking stopped, and the sudden silence felt oppressive before it was rapidly filled with the thundering sound of her heartbeat in her ears. The old panic rushed through her like an electrical current.

"Roberts..." She'd intended to call out his name, but her voice came out a barely audible squeak. Forcing her eyes from the clock, Wendy looked over her shoulder, willing Roberts to walk through the door and for reality to return. The door to the room slowly creaked open, and Wendy's mouth fell open as she saw that the hospital had come to a standstill. All the hospital staff seemed frozen in place. Two nurses side by side, half a step out of sync, their mouths open mid-sentence; a doctor flicking over the page of the chart he was reading, the page still half-curled, paused midway through turning over; another nurse behind the nurses' station, leaning over as though reading something on the computer screen, her hand hovering over the mouse. Before she could inspect the scene any further, she spun around as the dual voice taunted her.

"Now, look what you've gone and done…"

"I didn't do this," she whispered, staring at Rosalie. Wendy held her breath as she watched Rosalie slowly rise off the bed, the blanket that covered her legs falling away. Wendy blinked rapidly, welcoming the thought that she was hallucinating. However, within a matter of seconds, Rosalie hovered a good half a meter above the bed, still cross-legged, her hands hanging by her sides and her face still partially obscured by her hair.

"Oh, but you did, Detective. You did this when you left… when you ran away… you were never supposed to leave. You could have ruined everything."

The ticking started again, but when Wendy looked back up at the clock, she found the clock hands moving in the opposite direction. She barrelled backwards, her back slamming against the wall heavily, and Rosalie chuckled with a deep and throaty amusement that sounded surreal coming out of the body of a teenage girl.

She groped along the wall, keeping her back to it until her hand gripped the edge of the doorway. She hurtled herself out of the room, but the dark laughter followed her. Wendy pulled up short as she almost ran into one of the frozen nurses, and she fell

192

backwards onto the ground, her wrist taking the bulk of the impact. She looked up, breathing heavily. The nurse stood before her, unseeing as she peered down at the fob watch she held in her left hand. Behind them stood five nurses huddled together, one with her arm reaching over them, pointing to a room further down the hall.

Then she saw Roberts. He, too, was frozen in place half-way around the corner, his eyes firmly fixed on the two cups of coffee he held in his hands.

"Roberts!" she called and picked herself up off the ground and hurried towards him, careful to make sure she gave any of the staff a wide berth. Reaching out, she gently touched his hands and was surprised to find the cups within them still hot. "Roberts!" she yelled, but there was no response. Wendy tried to shake him, but he was rock solid, like a statue. She allowed herself a single sob, a single moment of fear and helplessness before she forced back the tears and willed her rational thinking to stay ahead of her emotions.

Still holding onto her hands, she scanned the scene before her, trying to work out what had happened— and what to do next. Lowering her hands, she cautiously tiptoed towards Rosalie's room as it hit her that the laughing had stopped. Wendy pressed herself up against the wall beside the door and carefully leaned in, peering over her shoulder. When she saw the room was empty, she stepped the whole way in, dashing over to the other side of the room in case the girl had fallen—or was hiding—down beside the bed. Wendy couldn't ignore the goosebumps that spread like wildfire across her skin, and she quickly scanned the frozen faces surrounding her, fearful she'd see Rosalie peering out at her. Instead of locating the girl, the ticking started again. The sound surrounded her, as though it came from every clock, every watch or fob, all in sync, taunting her. Wendy shuddered as the panic crept up her spine, reaching around the back of her neck, causing her to cringe. The old memories pushed against their wall, and Wendy knew something was coming for her—it was like déjà vu yet not of the place. It felt as though she was a child about to look under the bed, hoping not to find a monster, but knowing it was there. Turning her attention back to Roberts, she reached inside his jacket and pulled out the notebook and pen he kept in the pocket. Wendy quickly scribbled him a note, hoping he'd be able to read her frantic scrawl before returning the pad back to his pocket.

The ticking not only grew louder but faster, and Wendy knew she was running out of time. She stepped back from Roberts, taking a final look at his down-turned face. "I'm counting on you." The tingling along her spine intensified as all of her senses tried to pull her in different directions. Shuffling across the floor, Wendy found a moment of relief as she felt the firm security of a wall at her back, and she pressed her hands against it. The old memory finally broke free from its shackles, and Wendy recalled the cause of the ticking. Closing her eyes, she told herself she was mistaken, that it was all in her mind—her memories were distorted by both trauma and time.

It's not real.

You know it's not real.

Surely, it's not real?

A high-pitched hum now sounded alongside the ticking, and Wendy raised her hands over her ears, cringing in agony. The wall behind the nurses' station and slightly to the right appeared to glisten and glean, and Wendy struggled to keep her eyes focused on the spot. Suddenly, the ticking stopped, and she slowly lowered her hands, both mesmerised and terrified by the growing patch of distortion on the wall. Her breath caught in her throat as a long snout protruded, slowly opening a couple of inches to reveal its razor-sharp teeth. Wendy whimpered as it seemed to sniff the air. Apparently satisfied, the crocodile moved further into the room, its seemingly endless snout finally giving way to a wide head with two bulbous yellow eyes on either side with narrow black slits darkening the centres. First, one enormous webbed foot entered the room, its long, curved claws clattering on the linoleum, shortly followed by a second clawed foot from the other side of the crocodile's broad body. Wendy slipped down the wall and curled up into a ball on the floor, all pretences of sanity escaping her as she gaped at the apparition before her. The crocodile opened its jaws a little wider, and a low, guttural growl thundered as though from some primordial depths, and Wendy could feel every part of her trembling. The creature dragged itself across the floor causing a scratching, scraping sound that complimented its growls and horror-inducing effect. It moved through the frozen scene of people as though they weren't even there, and it was so large that it couldn't enter the foyer completely, leaving its rear and tail hidden. The growling ceased as it closed its jaws and lowered its head to the floor. Wendy held her breath, and the only sound was the sweeping of the crocodile's body as it neared her. She squeezed her eyes shut, trying to stifle her whimpering as the edge of its snout touched her shoe. Turning her head to the side, she willed it all to go away, knowing that it wouldn't. Wendy felt a blast of hot, putrid reptilian breath hit her squarely in the face as the crocodile suddenly opened its jaws.

"It's time." Wendy's eyes flew open, and she screamed as Rosalie sat crouched beside her, the girl's grinning face barely an inch from her own. Before she could make an effort to move, the girl gripped both of Wendy's wrists tightly, and Wendy gagged on the fetid air as she was suddenly engulfed in darkness.

CHAPTER FOURTEEN

R oberts stumbled forward as though tripping over his own feet and fumbled to keep from dropping the cups of coffee in his hand. He knew he'd never hear the end of it from Darling if he returned empty-handed. Discreetly looking around as he tried to regain his composure, he was concerned to see that everyone else seemed to be doing the same thing. With a frown, he quickly looked down, ensuring there wasn't anything to trip over. Two nurses hurried across his path. He looked up, his ears keening as they talked in hushed voices.

"Did something just happen?"

"I don't know. I feel kind of strange."

"What time is it?" one asked.

The other lifted the fob watch that hung from her shirt. "That can't be right..."

Roberts watched them as they turned down the hall and out of earshot. He told himself he was being paranoid, but he couldn't shake the feeling that something was wrong. Looking over at Rosalie's room, he was surprised to see the shutters closed and the bedroom door open. He strode over, his gut already telling him what his eyes confirmed once he peered inside. Rosalie lay on the bed, slightly propped up with pillows. Her face was turned away from him, but he could see her eyes closed—and Wendy was nowhere to be seen. His frown deepened, and he felt the tension tighten across his forehead as he slowly turned on his heel and inspected the foyer, which suddenly seemed to be bustling with activity. But as he peered one way then the other, he couldn't see any sign of her, and he hurried over to the nurses' station and placed the coffees on the bench with such force coffee flew out of the small holes in the lids and onto the counter.

"Excuse me, but have you seen my partner? She was in there with Rosalie Fryair." He gestured towards the room. The nurse looked up from her chair, her eyes fixed firmly on the spilled coffee before she looked at the detective with a single eyebrow raised. Roberts made no move to wipe up his mess, instead pointing again towards the room. The nurse got to her feet and peered over towards Rosalie's room.

"No, sorry. I haven't seen her since the two of you first went in there, but it's not like we don't have other rooms, other patients. Perhaps she popped down to the toilets. They're just down the hall to your left." She sat back down and turned her attention back to the computer, and Roberts raised his eyebrows at the dismissal but said nothing. With the coffees forgotten, he walked towards the corridor. He peered down to where he could see the toilet signs protruding from the wall about half-way down, but he had no intention of hovering outside the toilets to wait for her. Instead, he moved over to a small row of five seats that lined the narrow wall opposite the nurses' station, the end two providing a view down the corridor. Leaning his head back against the wall, he crossed his arms across his chest and stifled a yawn. After a few seconds, his impatience kicked in, and he tapped the floor with this shoe, drumming along to whichever random tune popped into his head first while he waited for his partner to return. Recalling something his mother used to say about watched clocks, he turned his scowl to the hustle and bustle around him. He fidgeted as his unease grew, like mist creeping across the grass on a cold morning, and he unfolded his arms, running his hands down his leg to tap at his knees instead. Something wasn't right. He was starting to garner both questioning looks and flickering glances of annoyance, and he decisively got to his feet and stormed down towards the toilet with long strides. He hesitated as he stood before the lady's restroom door and looked both up and down the corridor before biting the bullet and rapping loudly.

"Hello? Anyone in there?" There was no response, and he took another look around before knocking again. "This is the police—come out now." He could see Wendy rolling her eyes at the request, and he almost believed she would throw open the door at any second. Yet there was still nothing. No longer caring if anyone saw him, he pushed open the door and walked in, calling loudly, "Hello?"

The only response was his own voice as it echoed off the tiles. Before him stood four stalls, each with the doors slightly opened, but he needed to be certain his partner wasn't there. In rapid succession, he walked over and pushed open each door, revealing empty stall after empty stall.

Where the fuck is she?

Roberts fished his phone from his pocket and dialled her number, his other hand clenching his hip as he turned and saw his reflection in the mirror. He felt surprised by the concern that reflected back at him as Wendy's phone went straight to voicemail, and he hung up without leaving a message. Swearing under his breath, he pulled the door open and almost bowled over a startled woman as he fled the female restroom. Tossing an apology over his shoulder, he jogged towards the waiting area, concerned by his own growing fear that something had happened to Detective Darling, and the clock was ticking. He'd stopped trying to tell himself he was being ridiculous, instead of trusting in his appraisal of his partner's commitment to her work and the knowledge that she wouldn't have wandered far without letting him know. Hell, he was certain even if she had to rush off for some kind of family emergency, she would have at least called or texted him if she couldn't wait to tell him in person. He walked back through the foyer and the seats where he'd sat but found he was no longer able to do anything other than pace. Roberts grabbed his phone out of his pocket once more and dialled Wendy's number.

Wendy opened her eyes, but there was nothing but darkness. She rubbed them, but the darkness was so encapsulating that she couldn't see her hands in front of her face. As the pounding in her head distracted her, she closed her eyes fiercely against the pain. Massaging her temples, she tried to remember where she was. She felt disorientated—not just where she was, but *how* she got there. Without the ability to see, she wasn't certain if she was standing or lying. There was no sensation, nothing to make her feel as though she was touching anything. Her heart skipped a beat as a flurry of green sparks erupted from the edge of her peripheral vision, leaving a bright afterglow in the intense blackness. She squeezed her eyes shut.

No, no, no, no!

Wendy told herself she imagined it, that there would be a perfectly logical explanation for what was happening. But then her recollection flooded back to her as images of Roberts, the hospital, and Rosalie flashed before her eyes before the final terrifying image scorched her mind as the crocodile opened its enormous jaws before her.

Wendy felt tears well in her eyes as she heard a faint, bell-like ringing in her ears.

Tink?

She shook her head as soon as she'd said it, knowing it was nothing more than a misremembered aspect of her past—and she was an adult now. Yet another bright flash of green sprung outwards, blinding her, and she was overcome with dizziness. Wendy felt herself fall backward, landing heavily on her back. Nursing her pounding head in her hands, she was grateful that she'd at least landed on something soft.

It's okay. You're okay. You're not back. You're not back. You're not...

Wendy whimpered as fear threatened to take hold of her, and she curled up into a tight ball. She counted to ten before forcing herself to stretch back out and focus on the tangible. Rolling onto her back, she spread her hands out on either side of her and noted

201

what felt like a blanket—thick, yet slightly scratchy against the skin. She raised her hands up and felt the flat pillow beneath her head. Unable to fend off the sobs, Wendy rolled to the edge of the bed and slid off onto the cold cement floor she knew was waiting for her. Burying her head in her hands, she felt them trembling against her face, her body already knowing what she was refusing to admit. She was back.

The green sparks came again, and Wendy braced herself against the cold, hard floor in anticipation of another wave of nausea, yet the sparks didn't seem as intense as they were. She wondered if that was the case, or if she was just getting used to them. When she felt certain enough that she wasn't going to be sick, Wendy leaned her head back against the edge of the bed and tried her best to regain some rationality and perspective.

Okay. So what do we know? I was at the hospital with Roberts. Rosalie—Pan spoke to me. Then the crocodile came. And now?

Wendy rubbed the spot on her forehead between her brows with her thumbs. Her mind battled against the knowledge that it was Pan who'd come for her, and the rejection of the notion as a figment of a deluded and traumatised mind.

Could it be a hallucination? Maybe a gas leak? Or a psychotic break?

No matter what theories she tried to run through her mind, nothing made any sense, no matter how she tried to convince herself. Yet the thought her childhood tormentor and abductor baiting her before threatening her through the body of another girl was too much. Then the ferocious crocodile had returned for her—well, that was the stuff of nightmares and something she never thought she'd face. Yet, it was her reality.

Wendy didn't know how long she sat there on the cold, concrete floor battling between her thoughts and her fears, only to find herself without solace. Her exhaustion led her into a brief sleep before her mind thrust the images of the crocodile before her once more. Finally, she forced herself to her feet, swaying dangerously as the sparks and the ringing kicked back in and intensified. Giggles filled her ears and echoed around the room so that it sounded like a group of people laughing. Realising she was the one laughing, Wendy covered her mouth trying to stifle the sound, yet she couldn't get past the sudden hilarious fact that for all these years, she'd thought her only comfort during her captivity had come from a green fairy. As though in response, the green sparks angrily pulsated, causing Wendy to laugh harder. She could hear the slight hint of hysteria on the edge of the laughter echoed back to her, and somewhere in the depths of her mind, a rational thought pushed its way forward. Wendy held her breath until she was almost certain that she had the giggling under control. Once the echoes subsided into whispers, Wendy listened intently for any indication that her captor approached. She feared she'd made more noise than she'd realised, and the sudden threat of a confrontation was the sobering up she needed. An attempt to walk resulted in a stumble and Wendy clutched her head, feeling like it was the only way to keep herself upright. She turned so that she could feel the outer edge of her right leg pressed against the bed, and she dragged it along until she could no longer feel it. Wendy reached her right hand out and felt the cold, rough cement wall. Staggering against it, she rested there for a moment and took slow, deep breaths as another wave of nausea took hold of her. Her eyes fluttered closed, then open, then closed again. When she opened them, Wendy groaned. She was fearful she'd again lost time, but in the endless darkness, she had no way of knowing. Pushing herself off the wall, she kept one hand firmly pressed against it, using it as a guide as she concentrated, placing one foot in front of the other. It didn't feel as complicated as it had when she'd first attempted it, and she conceded her little nap—regardless of the length—may have done her some good and alleviated the effects of whatever was affecting her.

Feeling a renewed sense of purpose, her fears were slowly reduced to a simmer as her persistence took over. Wendy felt as though her sight was adjusting to the pervasive darkness, though she still didn't trust her senses completely. Not that there appeared to be much to see. After walking a few metres, she realised the wall felt curved rather than flat, and before she could question her senses, a memory rushed back to her—of walking around the room just like this, when she was fifteen. Only in her memory, she could see the room in its circular entirety, and she squeezed her eyes shut as she tried to retrieve the details while simultaneously taking deep breaths to combat the rising panic at the thought of having returned to her original place of captivity.

Pan.

The recognition hit her with full force that knocked the air from her lungs, and Wendy was grateful for the wall at her back as it served to prop her up. Swallowing thickly, Wendy was oblivious to the tears that ran down her cheeks as the deepest part of her being recognised the eyes that had haunted her nightmares for the past twenty years. She didn't know if she was relieved by the confirmation that her memories weren't an embellishment on the truth or all the more terrified by it. His eyes were as ugly, freakish, and horrifying as she remembered—and with a heart so heavy it pulled her down to her knees, Wendy accepted she was once again Pan's prisoner.

NEVER, NEVER

With his phone pressed to his ear, Roberts listened to the ringing as he waited for the call to be answered, yet instinctively knowing it wouldn't pick up. He spun in circles, scanning the room for any signs of Wendy and the faces of those around him for any clues. The call went through to Wendy's voicemail for the fifth time, and he swore aloud, causing those nearest him to stare. Roberts hardly noticed as he terminated the call and immediately redialled. While he knew it was a waste of time, it gave him a purpose while he tried to figure out what the hell had happened. Roberts rubbed the back of his neck with his free hand. He felt conflicted, knowing he could easily call the station and have Darling's phone traced. Yet he was smart enough to know there was tension between Darling and their boss, and while he didn't know what it was over, he felt a strange loyalty to his new partner.

Just give her a chance. She'll show up with some flippant reason for her absence that will piss you off, and things will go on as they were.

Roberts angrily ended the call before deciding to try one final time as he changed direction. A faint burst of light caught his attention a few metres away from under one of the waiting room chairs. Lowering the still-ringing phone, he peered at the light as it slowly moved on the floor, and with a realisation, he hurried over to it. "Excuse me," he said to an elderly woman sitting on the chair above it, not waiting for her acknowledgement before he dropped to his knees and reached around her legs to grab the phone from under her chair. Ignorant to her indignant outcry, Roberts sat back on his heels, a ringing second mobile vibrating in his hands. Staring at his own name on the screen, he knew it was Wendy's mobile, and he hung up the call. His name vanished, replaced by a photo of Wendy and who he assumed from the likeness to be her daughter.

Fuck.

Clenching his phone in one hand and Wendy's in the other, he strode over to the nurses' station, fear gripping him tightly. Roberts didn't know what unnerved him more, the fact he felt afraid, or the realisation he didn't know what to be afraid of.

Time seemed to stop as Wendy and Pan stared at each other, and the room felt swollen by the torrent of memories that now revealed themselves in distorted and broken fragments. As the eyes appeared to move closer, an involuntary whimper escaped her, and Wendy tried to push herself into the wall itself, willing it to be just another nightmare. Pan moved closer still, and as he did, he revealed himself—the glow from his eyes seemed to spread throughout him until he appeared illuminated from within. Wendy's eyes widened with the realisation he looked exactly the same as he had the last time she had seen him—twenty years ago. He sported the same short-cropped black hair with the long fringe that hung down across his forehead, the same boyish features punctuated by his sharp cheekbones and rosebud lips. Pan still had the slim, boyish figure of a youth not yet bridging the gap between boyhood and manhood. He was tall, emphasised by his scrawniness, and he wore long, grey pants that hung from his narrow hips before giving way to frayed hems that fell to his bare feet, not quite reaching the floor. Wendy couldn't tell if the colour was the material or layers of dirt and grime. His shirt was green and patched with various pieces of material used to repair tears over the years.

"Not possible…" she breathed.

"That's the problem with growing up, Wendy. You constrict your world view with the impossible rather than what is."

Wendy said nothing as he continued his agonising approach, finally stopping a couple of metres in front of her.

"The years have been kind to you, Wendy—more than kind." He observed her in silence, his head tilted to the side, and Wendy forced herself not to fidget under the intensity of his stare.

"Why am I back here?" she growled, surprised to hear no trace of fear in her voice, only anger.

A small smile swept fleetingly across his face. "The same thing I've always wanted, Wendy, since the first day I laid eyes on you. We're destined to be together, you and I."

"You're insane!" Wendy spat, acknowledging for the first time that he was just a youth—and she was now an adult who was more than equipped to take him down should he try to come any closer. "In case you haven't noticed, I'm not a child anymore. You no longer have any power over me," she declared, sounding more convincing than she felt—her scars of terror ran too deep for such a shallow fix.

An angry redness swelled around his engorged eyes as the corner of his mouth turned up in a sneer, and Wendy felt like a fraud as her body trembled at the sight, giving away her false bravado. It intensified with every step he took, and she tried to find something else to focus on until she could recover her wits. Pan stepped close enough she could see the bottom of his jaw twitching as he clenched and unclenched it.

"Well," he said, his voice so low she could feel its bass reverberate through the concrete and up through the soles of her feet. "That's disappointing. Perhaps you need more time to think about it." He backed away into the shadows as he spoke, the light that illuminated him receded inwards with each step he took until once again all she could see were his eyes. They seemed to hover there for a moment like they were disembodied. Wendy felt frozen in place, not wanting to give Pan any reason to venture back out of the shadows, but also not wanting to be left alone in the endless darkness. As Pan's eyes faded to nothing, Wendy could feel the repressive energy of her surroundings relinquish its grip.

I have to find a way out of here. I have to find my way home.

CHAPTER FIFTEEN

"Excuse me." Roberts cleared his throat as he confronted the same nurse he'd spoken to earlier, only semi-aware that the two cups of coffee he'd placed on the counter were still there. The nurse appeared to ignore him as she typed away on the computer.

"Excuse me, urgent police business," he said dryly, and the nurse sighed before grudgingly looking up at him. For the first time, Roberts noticed the fatigue that marked her face, and he realised her hours were probably as seemingly endless as his own. He felt like a bit of a dick. "Look, I'm sorry. I appreciate you're busy." He absently drummed his fingers on the counter before catching the scowl on the nurse's face. He withdrew his hand and cleared his throat, not wanting to get her further offside.

"Can I help you?"

He took a quick look at her name tag. "Yes, Tara, I don't think I actually introduced myself before. I'm Senior Detective Rupert Roberts." He held up his identification. "I've been working the Rosalie Fryair case with my partner, Senior Detective Wendy Darling. Somehow within the past half hour, she's disappeared. Last time I saw her, she was in the room with your patient. When I returned, she was gone— and yes, I checked the bathrooms already."

"Maybe she got called away?" the nurse suggested, doing her best to stifle a yawn as she stood up from the chair.

"I found her phone on the floor over there." He turned and gestured to the row of seats against the opposite wall. "There's no way she would have left without it. The fact that it was found out here and not in Rosalie's room leads me to believe that she came out here."

"Well, I'm sorry, detective, but I already told you I didn't see her," Tara replied, her voice defensive.

Roberts was quick to appease her as she held up her hands. "I know, and I'm not questioning that. I need to see the surveillance footage of this area for the past hour. Can you point me in the right direction?"

The scowl fell away from Tara's face as her eyes widened. "Do you think something's happened to her?"

"That's what I'm trying to find out," he replied.

It seemed to be the boost the nurse needed, and she picked up the phone, quickly punching in some numbers. Tara held a brief conversation. Her face turned away from Roberts, so he was unable to hear what she was saying. Once she hung up, she turned and walked around to the front of the counter.

"Please, come with me." Tara started off down the corridor, not needing to check if the detective followed. They walked down to the lifts, Roberts not paying any attention to where they were going, too busy mentally tracing back his steps since they'd arrived, scanning his memory for any sign or suggestion that something wasn't quite right. He frowned when he couldn't find anything, feeling as though he was letting his partner down.

They stepped out of the lift and walked a short distance along another corridor, completely identical to the one they'd just left. He almost ran into the nurse as she stopped and knocked on a door, and he quickly glanced around them, noticing there was no one else around, and he wondered where the hell they were. The door was yanked open, revealing a burly security guard so tall and broad he seemed to fill up the entire entryway.

"Hey, Frank," Tara greeted him.

"Thanks, Tara. Sorry I couldn't come down myself. Two of my staff called in sick, so it's only the monitors and me this morning."

"Not a problem—I needed a little walk anyway," Tara replied, stepping aside to make way for Roberts. "This is Senior Detective Roberts."

Roberts reached out and offered his hand, which Frank grasped firmly. "I understand you need to see some footage?"

Roberts nodded.

"I'll leave you both to it." Tara started back down the hall.

"Thanks for your help, Tara—I appreciate it," Roberts called out, and she gave a small wave of acknowledgement over her shoulder as she headed back to the lifts, her rubber Crocs squeaking across the linoleum floor.

"Come in and take a seat," Frank offered as he took his place before the multiple screens set out before him. "Are you looking for something in particular? Or just a general overview?"

"I'm looking for my partner. You should be fine to narrow the footage to the one area, and if we can take it back to an hour, that should be more than enough." He sat down beside Frank, ignoring the sideways glance he shot at him.

"Can you give me a little more to go on?"

Roberts kept his eyes on the screens. "I left my partner in a room with a patient. When I came back, she was gone." He expected to be asked the obvious questions and was grateful when they didn't come.

"Going back an hour..." Frank said quietly as he turned knobs and pressed buttons. "Do you recall from which direction you entered that area?"

Roberts thought back. "We came in through the emergency entrance, then around through to the observation wards and the small foyer there. So we entered from the left of the room."

"Do you want the footage from when you both entered the hospital or just when you entered the foyer?"

"Just the foyer for now. If need be, we can track back further later."

Frank nodded as he expertly pulled the footage up on the main screen before them and guided it to where they needed. Together they intently watched the screen and the flurry of activity, looking all the busier for the quickened movements.

"There, slow it down..." Roberts instructed, pointing to the monitor as he spotted himself and Wendy enter from the left. They both walked toward the camera and Rosalie's room off-screen.

"Pause it," Roberts instructed while he scanned the frozen footage looking for any sign that they were being watched or followed. But as far as he could tell, everyone else in the room was a patient or a staff member. Given the hour, there didn't appear to be many, if any, family members. He took a second look, frustrated that he couldn't see any indication of what was to come.

"Is there another camera so we can see the entrance to the room?" he asked, and Frank nodded as he typed in a few instructions and pulled up a different angle of the room. This time they were looking at the area from behind the nurses' station, the camera angled to the left, giving a slightly off perspective. However, Roberts could see what he needed, and as Frank pressed the play button, he watched as he opened the door to Rosalie's room before leaving shortly after and striding back across the foyer.

"Do you need me to track your movements from here?" Frank asked.

"No, thanks. I need to see what happens when my partner leaves the room—stay on this camera," he instructed as they watched him walk out of view. Roberts silently cursed himself for having closed the girl's door behind him and wishing he could see in.

"Can we zoom in at all?"

"Only a little bit before the footage becomes distorted. But what am I focusing on when the door's shut?" Frank asked as he fiddled with the controls.

"Not the door—the observation window." Roberts inwardly groaned as the picture distorted the more Frank tried to zoom in, but there was enough focus that he could make out Wendy in the room.

"It looks like they were just talking," Frank observed.

"How could you tell what they were doing? We can barely make them out," Roberts scowled.

"Years and years of practise," Frank replied dryly, and Roberts shot him a look, eyebrows raised.

"I apologise, Frank. I didn't mean to criticise..."

"All good. Look." Frank dismissed him as he slowed the footage down again and pointed to the bottom right corner of the screen where Roberts had just re-entered, a cup of coffee in each hand. A thick, black line waved through the footage like a pulse, and the footage waivered momentarily before righting itself.

"What was that?" Roberts asked.

"I don't know." Frank rewound ten seconds and pressed play. They watched as the same thing happened again. "Well, that rules out a system error. Obviously, something has created an interference."

"What, like something electrical?" Roberts asked.

Frank shrugged. "Electrical, electro-magnetic even. But these systems are pretty sturdy. I can't say I've seen any issues like this before." Frank pressed play, and once the footage righted itself. They watched Roberts cross the floor in front of the camera towards Rosalie's room, only now the blinds over the observation window were closed and the door wide open.

"Shit," Frank exhaled. "We missed her coming out of the room."

"Go back to the spot where the footage glitches," Roberts instructed, and Frank complied, equally intrigued. As the screen distorted, Roberts pointed to the time stamp in the corner.

"What the fuck? Frank looked at Roberts with a frown, his mouth slightly agape.

"Seven minutes," Frank interceded. "Somehow, during the interference, we've lost seven minutes of surveillance."

"That's not possible. It's just not. At best, the footage would freeze, or the camera would blank for seven minutes, but you can't just lose seven minutes of camera time. The only way that would happen would be if someone edited the footage, which obviously isn't the case since I'm the only one here." Frank suddenly leaned back, eyebrows raised.

"It's alright, Frank," Roberts assured him. "I know you haven't doctored the footage. But there is something weird going on."

"You've got that right," Frank replied, looking back to the screen.

"So the facts at hand are before the glitch we could see Wendy... uh, Detective Darling... in the room with Rosalie. After the glitch, we can only see Rosalie, and the door to the room is open. Despite losing seven minutes of time, no one on screen has moved position."

"You're right!" Frank exclaimed, as though it hadn't occurred to him prior. "So, what? Everyone was frozen? That's even less likely, isn't it?"

"Up until today, I would have agreed, but I'm not prepared to rule anything out at the moment, no matter how crazy it seems. Can we view the footage of the surrounding cameras? See if we can track where she went?" Roberts asked, leaning back into his chair and releasing a deep breath as he undid the top button of his shirt, trying to relieve the growing tightness in his chest.

Frank centralised footage after footage, and they intently scrutinised frame after frame for any sign of Darling. Roberts groaned with frustration, stretching his hands behind his head as they realised the search was useless. There was no sign of her.

"Sorry, Detective. I don't know how we didn't catch her on camera." Frank massaged his forehead with his thumbs.

"I appreciate the help, Frank. Any chance you can make me copies of these? Maybe some fresh eyes back at the station will pick up on something we're missing."

"Yeah, of course. It will take me a few minutes."

Roberts stood and clamped his hand on Frank's shoulder in thanks before stepping out into the hall. Pulling his phone out of his pocket, he took a deep breath, bracing himself as he called the boss. Just as he was about to hang up the call, it was answered.

"This had better be important, Roberts. Do you have any idea what time it is?" the chief barked down the phone, his voice gruff with sleep.

"Actually, Sir, I don't," Roberts admitted without apology. "But we have a situation here at the hospital."

"The girl—what's happened?" the chief asked, suddenly sounding far more alert and interested.

"Rosalie is doing fine—it's Darling. She's missing."

There was a brief silence on the other end of the phone, and Roberts wondered if he'd heard him.

"What do you mean, missing?"

"As in one minute she was here, and literally the next minute she was gone. I've spent the past thirty minutes tracking surveillance footage and haven't found a damned thing."

"Start at the beginning and tell me everything." His boss's voice was stern and alert.

Roberts took a deep breath and filled his boss in with the little information he knew. "What I can't work out is where the hell she went. There's no sign of her on any of the other cameras, and what's more, the issue with the time lost on the surveillance camera wasn't replicated on any of the other cameras. Whatever happened seems to have focused solely on that one area."

"Well, she can't have vanished into thin air. What did Rosalie have to say? I take it you questioned her?"

"No, not yet—she was asleep."

"Well, bloody hell. Wake her up! She was the last one to see her for Christ's sake. I'll send some backup—our new priority is finding Detective Darling."

"Boss? Is there something I need to know?" Roberts asked, sensing something behind the urgency in his boss's voice.

"Just find her, Roberts. Now."

Roberts withdrew the phone from his ear and stared at the blank screen, a fresh layer of unease now added to his current level of worry. Shoving it back into his pocket, he poked his head back into the surveillance room. "Frank, I'm just going to head back downstairs. I'll check back later for those copies." Frank gave him a two-fingered salute without taking his eyes off the monitors. Roberts turned on his heel and hurried back down the hall.

Wendy had no concept of time. She had no idea how long she stood there, bound in place by fear with her back pressed up against the wall, not wanting to move, fearful Pan was still lurking in the darkness watching her. She straightened as a moment of clarity pierced through her mind.

Pan entered the room—and he left—there has to be a way out.

With newfound courage, she spread her hands out across the surface of the wall and scurried along it in the hopes of finding the door Pan used. But her hands felt nothing except smooth, curved concrete as she dragged them across it. Before she knew it, Wendy ran straight into the edge of the bed, and pain radiated outwards from her shins. Collapsing onto the bed, she clutched at her legs in agony.

What the hell is going on?

Rolling up to a sitting position, Wendy pulled her knees to her chest, embracing her aching shins and groaning in pain and frustration. The room was circular, that much was clear. That in itself concerned her—it could only mean one thing. Yet she forced the thought and the line of questions it evoked out of her mind to focus on the task at hand. Her hands hadn't left the wall once, the whole way back to the bed, but she hadn't found any indication of a door. Wendy told herself that was ridiculous—Pan had come and gone, so she should be able to as well. He still thought of her as the timid and fearful child that she once was—not the trained and skilled detective she was now. Sure, she was still fearful, but she planned to use that to her advantage. There was a way out, and she was going to find it. Wendy got to her feet, assuming that in her frantic search she had overlooked the exit, which was likely more subtle than a simple door with a handle. She had to retrace her steps again—this time slowly and with care.

Ignoring the pain in her shins, Wendy moved carefully around the bed until she was in contact with the wall again. This time she moved her hands around the cool cement, feeling for any sign of a crack or handle as she walked around, making sure she left no part unexamined. It felt strange relying on her hands to investigate something her eyes couldn't, but then her fingertips slipped over a narrow slit. Wendy paused, afraid to move her hands in case she lost the spot. With a deep breath, she ran her fingers up and down, sensing the slit ran vertically for most, if not the entire length of the wall. Lowering her fingers so that they were in front of her, Wendy applied pressure, and with an excited gasp, she felt a shift. The wall parted just slightly, and she forced her fingers further in. There was a scratching sound as the bottom of the wall scraped along the concrete underfoot. It sounded so loud in the silence, but she didn't stop. Wendy felt her heart quicken in excitement as it gave way, creating an opening before her. There was only more darkness. Wendy stood there for a moment, trying to get a hold of the disappointment of not finding a more obvious indication that she was on her way to freedom. Stepping forward, she strained her ears for any sound, fearful the noise of the door opening had alerted Pan to her movements. Reaching out to the inside of the wall, she ran her hands up and down in the hopes of finding a light switch. She paused as she felt a raised notch, and without letting herself consider any consequences, she turned it on. A light flickered once, twice, before emitting a steady flow of dim yellow light, so dull the illumination was more like that of a nightlight and didn't extend past the doorway.

Wendy felt her heart sink as she found herself standing in a small bathroom. There was a toilet against the wall to her left with a modest basin beside it, and rolls of toilet paper stacked beneath it. To her right stood a narrow shower with two towels, a bathmat, and a face washer hanging from racks alongside it. Frowning to herself, Wendy stepped further into the bathroom, examining the clean white tiles that lined the walls and floor. Lifting the toilet seat, she was surprised to find it, too, was clean. In fact, the whole room was immaculate, like she'd walked into the bathroom of a hotel. The supply of toilet paper and towels was unnerving, and she felt confused by the cleanliness and preparation. Her disappointment was all-consuming after the anti-climactic find, and Wendy stared at the rolls of toilet paper, disheartened at the concept of being prisoner long enough to need to use them.

Walking backwards out of the room, Wendy's fear bubbled back to the surface, and anxiety and fear spread through her with a prickly warmth, making her want to crawl out of her very skin. Gasping for air as the panic attack took full force, she gripped at her chest with one hand as though she could somehow slow the thundering of her heart. With her other hand, she used the wall to guide her back to the bed. Collapsing awkwardly onto the mattress, Wendy curled up in the foetal position, briefly observing the oddness of the way the bathroom light stopped short at the entrance before she lost all control and sobbed.

Please, not again. Please...

CHAPTER SIXTEEN

Wendy groaned sluggishly as a ringing buzzed in her ears. She swatted at the air as though trying to rid herself of an annoying mosquito. When the sound didn't move on, Wendy opened her eyes and was startled to see a flurry of green sparks from the edges of her vision, albeit fainter than before. An overwhelming urge to vomit overcame her, and she launched herself off the bed and stumbled towards the bathroom. Wendy fell to her knees and gripped the toilet seat, forcing herself to take slow, deep breaths. Just as she hoped the sparks and ringing had stopped of their own accord, an acidic rush pushed up from her stomach, burning her throat as she opened her mouth and vomited into the toilet. She heaved repeatedly until there was nothing left, before letting go of the toilet and falling against the wall to her right. Wendy felt as though the last of her energy had been spent, and she would fall asleep right there on the bathroom floor—she didn't care. Her eyes felt dry and sore as she gently rubbed at them. She wondered how long she'd cried before she fell asleep. Too tired to fend them off, the invasive and debilitating thoughts filtered through.

Where am I?

How long have I been here already?

Is Roberts looking for me?

Can he find me?

Is Jane safe?

Will I see any of them again?

How can I survive this a second time?

Why me?

Why me?

A sound came from back in the room, and Wendy raised her head from where it rested against the wall, wondering if it was her imagination or if Pan was back waiting to terrify and taunt her. She cursed the bathroom light for not piercing the darkness beyond the door as she longed to see what was lurking out there waiting for her. Straining her ears, she thought she could hear the soft tap and scrap of shoes on the concrete floor, and her fear of Pan's return faltered. She didn't think it likely Pan had left barefoot only to return with shoes on. Wondering if perhaps there was another prisoner, Wendy pushed herself up off the wall, feeling sapped of all energy as she rolled forward onto her hands and knees. Not confident she could make it to her feet, Wendy crawled to the doorway, mindful to try and keep close to the wall as much as possible, not wanting to be visible in case whoever it was approaching was a threat—she didn't want to alert anyone to her presence if they didn't know she was here.

The sound came again, and this time Wendy was certain they were footsteps—slow and purposeful, and Wendy frowned as it occurred to her that whoever was in there *wanted* to be heard.

"Wendy?"

She jumped as a man's deep, baritone voice spoke in the darkness, much closer to her than she'd thought. Wendy didn't answer as she froze in place.

"Wendy," the voice came again, and Wendy whimpered as she saw a pair of leather boots appear before her in the doorway.

"Don't be afraid," the voice softened and sounded pleading as a large, calloused hand reached down, outstretched towards her. There was something familiar about his voice, like an old memory she couldn't quite recall. Yet her senses told her he wasn't a threat. Despite her logic telling her to back up and close the bathroom door, she tried to force herself to calm down as she shakily reached her hand up. She could hardly raise it above her head, but the man stepped forward and grabbed her hand in a powerful grip and lifted her effortlessly to her feet. She saw a quick flash of his face as the room swayed around her.

"I know you," she whispered, and she felt her fear slide away like a sheet being pulled from over her eyes.

"Yes, you do," the man replied as he half led, half carried her from the bathroom. Wendy let herself be guided, distracted by the sheer height of this man she hoped was her rescuer. She was tall, and her head barely reached his shoulders.

"Despite the dire circumstances, it is nice to see you again, Mistress Wendy." He lowered her to the bed and took a step back. Wendy felt a slight movement of air and realised he was actually bowing to her in the darkness.

223

"I... I'm sorry... I feel like I know you... I just need to rest, then maybe I'll remem..." her eyelids felt weighted, too heavy to keep open any longer, and she let them close as she trailed off. Her eyes flew back open as a light flashed on the other side of them.

A light radiated outward from the man as though he, himself, was a candle flame puncturing the darkness. Wendy gasped as the recognition hit her, and the recollections of her past rushed back to her.

"Cap... Captain?" she stuttered.

How is this possible?

Wendy's eyes ran over the knee-high black leather boots that folded down at the top like a cuff, and the black pants tucked neatly into them. The man's long, red double-breasted jacket had large brass buttons, and the flowing white bit of his shirt spilled out from the top before coming together in the lace at his neck. The man she'd known during her captivity as Captain stood before her, unaged, just as Pan had been. His stance was authoritative, but without arrogance, and his hands were clasped behind his back. His thick, black curly hair cascaded past his shoulders, immaculately styled, as was his perfectly manicured handlebar moustache that twitched slightly. His bushy eyebrows scrunched together in observation.

"You don't look at all well, Mistress Wendy."

Wendy felt faint, as though any little piece of help or self-delusion now eluded her, leaving her with nothing but the most surreal of realities. "It's really happened, hasn't it?" she breathed, barely audible in her horror. "After all these years..."

Captain remained silently observing her; the only movement was the twitching of his moustache as though he was deliberating on one thought then another until he appeared to settle on the best course of action. "Yes, that would appear to be the correct observation. In fact, it would seem Pan has exceeded both our assessments of his capabilities, I'm afraid, and for that, I am sincerely apologetic. I'll admit I had to come and see for myself—I honestly never thought he could do it, despite his incessant pursuit of you. When his endless endeavour to find you seemed fruitless as the years passed, I suppose I became too lax in my concerns for your safety. I mean, so much time had passed, and he still hadn't gotten to you..." he trailed off with a slight shake of his head, as though mentally chastising himself.

Wendy could only sit and stare as her well-hidden memories flooded back, one after the other, like a maniacal slideshow of images from days she preferred to keep buried. Through her fear, though, the memories that came forward of Captain were ones of a semi-gruff kindness during her abduction, an apologetic guardianship of sorts. However, if her recollections were correct, his time with her had been limited and always brief. There was no specific reason she could pinpoint as yet as to why she could trust him, but instincts were all she had now, and they told her she could count on him.

"You're remembering me," he stated, raising his head high while peering at her down his nose, as though curious as to what her recollections of him were, but he was too polite to ask.

"I...I think so...I mean, there's a lot to take in. I don't know that I can really tell what's real and what isn't."

He lowered his head, looking at his out-turned feet and sighed. "No, I don't imagine you could. Reality is hardly a tangible thing, especially here. I've never really understood people's desire to grip so tightly to something so variable. But I digress..." Despite his attempt to speak quietly, the deepness of his voice seemed to still bounce off the surrounding walls, like a low vibration.

"Can you get me out of here?" she asked, her eyebrows raised in sudden hope, wondering why she hadn't thought to ask that straight away. She gripped the mattress with both hands, not feeling strong enough to either hope or deal with the blow of disappointment. Captain's gaze remained lowered to the floor, his hands still behind his back as he dragged the heel of one of his boots in a small circle on the concrete.

"Now that's a question without a simple answer."

"Why?" Wendy asked, swallowing thickly as she felt the decline coming, but not understanding why.

"Wendy, what do you remember about your escape from Pan?"

"Nothing, really. I was just surrounded by whiteness like I was in the fog, and then I was found. I was never able to recall how I got there or how long I'd been on my own before someone found me..." Wendy trailed off as she was struck by the uncanny similarities between her own reappearance and Rosalie's.

Captain seemed perplexed, his bushy eyebrows ramming together as he stared past her. Wendy looked up at him, uncertain whether to keep talking or not. Opting for silence, she didn't have to wait long before Captain spoke, "So you didn't return willingly?"

"What? No! Of course I bloody didn't. What kind of question is that?" Wendy scoffed in disbelief.

Captain let out a deep sigh, his expression unchanging, still weighted by his thoughts.

"Honestly, it's a question I never thought I'd ask. You see, one of the unique aspects of Pan's power is the ability to get into the minds of his victims—they always come willingly, though they never realise what they're doing until it's too late. He then uses their memories to keep them trapped here. It was your memories of him, of your time here, that he's spent years trying to access, hoping to coax you back within his grasp again. But if your memories were gone, then there was nothing tethering you to him. So, what changed?"

"There was another girl. A case that parallels my own experiences; it's eerily similar."

Hook nodded slowly, the knot between his brows loosening slightly at the revelation. "I suppose that's quite clever. When he couldn't get to you directly, he found another way. Yet there's still something missing. It was like you were somehow cloaked from him, and then suddenly, you weren't."

Wendy's eyes widened as she thought back to Nanna, to the necklace she'd given her, and pleaded with Wendy to heed her warning.

That can't be it—she gave me the necklace after Rosalie had already disappeared. If I was hidden from Pan's view, there has to be more to it...

She shook her head. "I don't know what to tell you. I don't remember anything about how I escaped the last time, and I recall very little about my captivity—but if you can help me escape..."

"I can't."

Wendy felt her eyes well as helplessness embedded itself deep within her chest.

"I'm sorry if I could..."

Wendy turned away from him, resting her head on her knees as she pulled them to her chest.

"We grew quite close, you and I. You were here for months, and it was like having a daughter in a sense. One day, you were particularly upset—inconsolable, really—overcome with a wave of homesickness, and it dawned on me how selfish I'd been. I had so enjoyed your companionship that I think I'd subconsciously avoided trying to find some way to help free you. It was selfish, but I didn't want you to leave. The guilt from that realisation fuelled me to find a way, and while it wasn't overnight, I found an opportunity and helped you escape…"

Wendy slowly raised her head. Piece by piece, the memories of her escape came together as the Captain's words swept over her.

I was sleeping, and someone was gently shaking me by the arm. I opened my eyes, surprised to find Captain kneeling beside the bed, his voice low and urgent, telling me to hurry. 'It's now or never!' I felt groggy, but the Captain's grasp was firm on my arm as he led me through an endless maze of tunnels. The cool on my face moved by quickly, and it felt like we were running, yet my feet never seemed to touch the floor. Just when my body couldn't go any further, the tunnel opened outwards, revealing a haze that only increased my disorientation and confusion.

"You have to keep running. Just keep going in that direction, and you will be free." He shoved me gently in the back and not caring whether I could see or not, I ran.

"Thank you…" I whispered.

"I would do it again if I could, but I need you to know the first escape wasn't without consequences." Wendy watched as Captain lowered one hand from behind his back, letting it fall at his side before he lowered the other.

Wendy gasped, her hands flying over her mouth as she saw the enormous silver hook that replaced his hand. "What happened?"

The Captain raised it, turning it one way, then the other, as though inspecting it for the first time. "This is what happened once Pan worked out that you were gone—and that I'd helped you escape."

"Holy shit… I am so sorry…"

He held up his good hand and silenced her. "It was my decision. Like I said, I had come to think of you as a

228

daughter, and this was a small price to pay—despite the new name of "Hook" that's come with it."

"Hook? That's just cruel…"

"It was intended to be, but I wear the name with pride. It's not often these days that I get to do some good. So from here on out, it's what I want you to call me as well. However, the more dire consequence to your previous escape is that Pan has taken extra measures this time around to ensure I don't betray him again—especially since he's waited so long to get you back."

Wendy was unable to stop the sudden sobs that wracked her body at the realisation. Her worst nightmare had finally come true.

"I'm sorry. The last thing I want to do is upset you. Without any need for manners over the decades, I'm afraid my manner must be less than comforting to you." He pulled a lace handkerchief from within his jacket and held it out to her. Wendy took it, wiping her eyes as she tried to find a silver lining in the fact that at least she had an ally of sorts. Closing the gap between them, Hook sat on the edge of the bed beside her, waiting for her to calm.

Wiping her eyes, Wendy took a deep breath. "I need to know everything. If you can't help me, then I need to find a way to help myself—and knowledge is power."

"Perhaps you should get some rest first…"

"Now. Please. Starting with how you know Pan, and how you came to be here."

Hook stared at her, but she remained unflinching, and finally, he let out a reluctant sigh. "What do you want to know?"

"Everything. How did you meet Pan? How did you come to be here with him? What power does he hold over you?"

Hook gave a wry smile. "I imagine you're quite the detective." When Wendy didn't answer, Hook gave a slight shake of his head and began. "It seems like another lifetime—and I suppose in many ways, it was. I was the captain of a British trade ship—I spent ninety percent of my time on the water, and I loved every second of it..."

"Wait—a British trade ship? You mean like one of those old ones?" Wendy cut in.

"Do you want to know the story or not?" Hook replied kindly, but there was an edge of pain to his voice that tugged at Wendy's heartstrings as it occurred to her Hook's memories might be as painful as her own.

"I'm sorry, I won't interrupt again."

"I'd had a blessed naval career really and was well respected everywhere I went. I'd never lost any cargo and often made voyages in record time, thanks to constant good fortune on the water. However, during one particularly tumultuous storm—an enigma in itself, we were thrown off course, and my ship ran aground in shallow waters, tearing the hull to shreds on a coral bed. We found ourselves on a small and seemingly desolate island. There was no trace of it on our maps, and I'd never come across it before in all my journeys. We assumed that the storm had thrown us off course much further than we'd first calculated. We had no choice but to salvage what we could from the waters and set up camp on the beach until we could either repair the damage to the ship's hull or help arrived—neither of which seemed likely.

On our third night there, I was asleep in my tent when I was awoken by the most beautiful song. It was a woman's voice, soft and melodic, and at first, I thought it was coming to me along with the evening breeze. Yet, it steadily grew both louder and softer, if that makes sense, and before I knew what was happening, my tent opened and in stepped the most beautiful young woman I had ever seen. Her hair was blonde, the colour of the sand lined beach around us, and it fell in waves to her hips. She was as naked as the day she was born, but all I could focus on was her song. It seemed to encircle me, wrapping around me, binding me to my partial dream state so that I felt like I couldn't wake up properly. I don't remember either of us moving, but the next thing I knew, my pants were down around my ankles. Her song filled my ears, and I closed my eyes, unable to understand the words, yet feeling myself respond to them. When I opened my eyes, she was straddling me, still singing as she rocked back and forward. I experienced the most intense pleasure—after which I think I passed out." He cleared his throat, as though embarrassed for getting caught up in the memory. "The next morning, I was awoken by a baby's cries, and when I sat up, there was Pan, swaddled, and cranky at my feet."

"So the woman...was she? Did she?" Wendy tried to find logic in his story, but her head was swimming.

"Your guess is as good as mine. I thought I'd dreamed her, but then there was the baby. Obviously, I questioned the other men, but no one had seen or heard anything."

"Did she come back? The woman?" Wendy asked, intrigued by Hook's tale, but confused as to how useful it could be.

"No, I never saw her again."

"What happened next?"

Hook cleared his throat. "There was no rhyme or reason to what happened next. The only thing stopping me from questioning my own sanity was the fact my crew saw the same things I did. The boy grew at an alarming rate—it was inhuman, but there was no escaping that. By the end of that first day, he

231

looked to be a year old. The second day he was a toddler. The third day he was a young boy of about five—it was then he told me his name was Pan. The fourth day he was ten, the fifth day he became a teen, the sixth day he turned eighteen, and the seventh day he was a young adult. If that wasn't hard enough to comprehend, with each day that passed, I had to watch my crew die, one by one, painfully and inexplicably. I never entertained the idea that it was a coincidence—we all knew it was Pan, but there was nowhere to go, nowhere to hide. Fear and tension grew among the crew, and they would have mutinied if they'd thought for a second they could fix the ship and escape. I was certain the only reason they didn't kill me outright was because they called Pan the son of the devil. I, too, was terrified of the child—my child. On more than one occasion, I tried to kill him, yet something always stopped me. I wouldn't call it a fatherly bond, or even a sense of responsibility. It was more like I was physically incapable of hurting him. I still recall holding a blade barely an inch over his chest, intent on driving it through his heart. As much as I wanted him dead, I fought an internal battle when it came to actually killing the monster, my child. So instead, I was forced to watch my men die, and with each death that passed, Pan grew stronger, more vibrant. I know that sounds like a bizarre way to describe a young man, yet that's exactly how he looked. We didn't speak—I was still trying to wrap my head around the fact that I had offspring, let alone a son that had become a man in a matter of days. Then there were his eyes… well, no description needed, I'm sure." Hook paused for a moment, giving a small cough into his fist before continuing. "On the seventh day, I finally spoke—to beg him for the lives of my remaining crew. There were only the three of us left, and we approached him together as he stood on the sand at the water's edge, the waves lapping at his feet as though in supplication. With his hands planted on his hips and his chest thrust forward, he stared out towards the horizon like he was daring the world to challenge him. He didn't move as we approached, not even when we stood behind him in his shadow, three seasoned travellers of the world, diminished in his presence. For the first time in my life, I felt pathetic, forced to clear my throat to get his attention—wise enough to know he was toying with us, but at a loss as to how to seize the upper hand. Only when he was good and ready did he turn his head, his posture never changing. I will never forget the look in his eyes. Smug. Proud. Aware. Oh yes, he knew exactly what he was doing—what he could do—and as he stared at me with those freakish, unnatural eyes, my First Mate started coughing and gasping. All I could do was watch as he doubled over, one hand clutching at his throat and the other at his chest. He fell to his knees, gasping for air as blood trickled from the corners of his eyes and out of his ears. Within a matter of seconds, he'd fallen face down into the sand, dead." Hook paused again and looked to Wendy, with eyebrows raised as though half-questioning her desire for him to continue, and half-pleading with her to stop him. Swallowing thickly, she cast aside the creeping guilt at making him relive the past by reminding herself she needed to know everything about Pan if she was ever to escape.

"Please, go on."

Hook averted his gaze. "All that was left of that ill-fated voyage was me and my Quartermaster, Smee. We were tired, hungry, dehydrated—and in all honesty, quite likely delirious. How else can I explain away the things we saw? Over the course of the next three days, we suffered at the hands of Pan's endless torment. Days of endless visions, never certain if we were awake or asleep as we drifted in and out of the fitful sleep of dying men. He forced horrors upon us, unlike any nightmare you could imagine—my crew, eternally damned, endlessly flayed by invisible sources. Screams after screams, both theirs and ours, as they underwent eviscerations, castrations... the horror, and Pan's infinite talent for it, seemed to have no end. At one point, I opened my eyes to find his face inches from mine, his eyes wide with glee. With all my strength, I gripped the handle of the knife tucked in my belt and stared him straight in the eye as I yanked it out of its leather sheath and rammed it into his side. I was instantly overcome with pain, and in my weakened state, I didn't immediately comprehend what had just happened. Pan knew. He knew, and he laughed like it was the funniest thing in the world, so overjoyed, like someone who had waited patiently for the punchline, or the outcome of a prank to be revealed. The pain seared, but it also pulled me out of the horror I'd endured; however, I quickly realised I was only trading one abhorrence for another. Gingerly, I moved my fingers down to where I could now determine the pain was emanating from—my ribs. I couldn't believe it—the blade was shoved directly between two of my ribs, right down to the hilt. I had to pull my hand away and stare at the warm blood coating my fingers to believe it. At first, I thought I was so out of it that I had stabbed myself by accident, but I knew that wasn't the case. I knew it. And so did he."

"I don't understand?" Wendy cut in, unable to stop herself. Hook let out a long, weary sigh. "I don't either, to be honest with you. All I know is I stabbed him, and I ended up the one with the injury."

"So how are you still here? I mean, if you were stuck on an island, how did you survive an injury like that?"

"Pan. He healed it. Not out of the goodness of his heart, or due to any sensibilities, he may have felt towards the man who was his father—but as a punishment. To prove to me that he was all-powerful, immortal—and I wasn't."

"So, you can't hurt him without hurting yourself?" Wendy asked.

"No. Believe me, over the years, I have tried more than once to kill him. I didn't care if it meant death for me as well. But all that happened is I ended up in excruciating pain for as long as it takes him to decide to put me out of my misery and heal me." He raised his hook and inspected it. "He could have healed me after cutting my hand off—it would have taken nothing for him to make it grow back, such is his power. However, it entertained him more to do this to me instead. A constant reminder, I suppose, of what happens when I betray him."

Wendy was silent for a moment before speaking. "So the three of you, you've been here all this time? And just how much time has passed since this all happened?"

"Yes, … and no. We are where we are—or should I say, we are where Pan thinks we need to be. Once he lost you, Pan refused to give up until he had you again. But how long have we been bound together in this hellish existence? A good three hundred years or so. Most of which passed before he even knew you existed."

Wendy opened and closed her mouth, feeling slightly ridiculous, but her mind felt sluggish and overwhelmed with Hook's tale. It was too much to absorb on top of everything else.

"It's okay," Hook reassured her. "There isn't anything to say to a statement like that, I know."

They remained in silence, Hook giving her the time she needed to work out what she wanted to say. Wendy didn't know how long she sat there, trying to make sense of her own thoughts before she finally spoke, "All I can think about right now is that you helped me escape before. Help me escape again, but this time, come with me. Smee too. Be rid of Pan for good."

"I appreciate the sentiment, but it's not plausible. Firstly, as much as I would love to help you escape again, I can't—at least, not in the same manner as last time. Secondly, I don't know what point there would be if you were to escape. While this is, in a manner of speaking, the same domicile you resided in during your last period of captivity, it's not in the here and now, so to speak."

"I don't understand."

Hook exhaled slowly, as though trying to determine how to best explain it to her. "We aren't in a fixed location—or even in the mortal realm."

"Mortal realm? What...where the hell *are* we then?" Wendy asked, her voice increased in pitch as she felt a surge of anxiety spread through her like rapid fire.

"I'm afraid I can't explain it any better than that. We exist in a realm of Pan's creation, made to look like a place from your world, but not within it. A place where we are beholden to his whims and wishes..."

He was cut off as a sob escaped Wendy and bounced off the concrete walls before hurtling back at her in an echoing taunt. Hook sat on the bed beside her and softly patted her arm while avoiding looking at her directly. Wendy appreciated the awkward sentiment, and the touch of another seemed to be enough to help her regain control of her fear before the sobbing overcame her.

"I'm never going to get out of here, am I?" she whispered.

"I won't lie to you, Wendy. An escape seems impossible this time." Wendy couldn't answer, biting her lip as her chin quivered uncontrollably, yet she refused to let the tears spill over. She feared if she started crying, she wouldn't be able to stop.

"I have to go," Hook declared as he gave her arm a quick squeeze before removing it. "I can't risk Pan finding me here. But listen to me — I will promise you this—if there is a way to set you free from him, once and for all, I will find it. If it's the last thing, I do. And no matter what happens, Pan mustn't know about your child…"

Wendy looked at him, her mouth open.

"Yes, of course, I know. I knew you were with child back then. I was too afraid to tell you myself, for fear that Pan would hear even the smallest of utterances. It was what pushed me to help you escape. I couldn't let him be a part of it."

"Does Pan…?"

"No. To my knowledge, he is oblivious. If he'd known, I imagine he would have used her to get you to return to him sooner—or taken the both of you." Hook went to get up before he hesitated, suddenly seeming shy. "Do you mind if I ask… what you had?"

"A girl. I had a girl," Wendy whispered, her voice quivering. "I named her Jane."

"Ahh…" Hook replied, his moustache twitching as a smile danced beneath it. "Jane. What a lovely name. I have a granddaughter," he said quietly, the pride evident in his voice despite the quiet tone.

Wendy's eyebrows raised in realisation. "Yes, I suppose you do."

He leaned over, so his mouth was close to her ear, "I don't know how, but no matter what, you keep all thoughts of her from him. Do you understand? Don't think of her, even if you think you are alone."

Wendy nodded, biting her lip. Before she could say anything, Hook sprung to his feet and dashed back into the shadows. Unable to hold it back any longer, Wendy burst into sobs so full of heartbreak and fear that they violently wracked her whole body. Letting herself fall to her side, she buried her face into the pillow as she tried to push away the images of Jane and Lilly as they rushed to the forefront of her mind. The pain in her chest was unbearable at the thought that she would likely never see them again, that they'd never know what happened to her. In her effort to not think of them, Wendy found herself confronted with images of Roberts and the side-smile he frequently cast in her direction. It caused her cheeks to warm, and with a frustrated groan, she tried to think of nothing but a blank slate, not trusting her mind to help itself—or her. Feeling more fatigued than she had in her life, she refused to allow herself to fall asleep. Instead, Wendy sat up, and leaning against the cold, concrete wall, she grabbed the pillow from beside her and pulled it to her chest, wrapping her arms tightly around it while she stared into the darkness, tears streaming down her face.

CHAPTER SEVENTEEN

An unfamiliar ringtone sounded, and Roberts almost dropped Wendy's phone in surprise. After a quick fumble, he held the phone firmly and stared at the photo of Jane as her name flashed across the screen. An out-of-character bout of nerves unfolded within him, and clearing his throat, he forced himself to answer the call.

"Jane?"

"Uh... yes... who is this? Where is my mum?"

"Yes, sorry. I'm Detective Rupert Roberts. Your mother and I are working the Fryair case together..."

"What happened? Is she okay?" Jane cut in, the volume of her voice increasing as her panic did.

Roberts ignored the question. "Is there any way you could meet me at the station?"

"What? Where's mum? Put her on the phone," Jane demanded.

"I can't," Roberts conceded. "She's not here."

"Well, where is she? And why do you have her phone? Tell me what the hell is going on!"

Roberts massaged his temple and squeezed his eyes shut as he tried to think of something to tell her when he had no answers himself.

"Look, Jane. It would be best if you met me at the station..."

"Tell me my mum's okay! You have her phone... how do you have her phone?"

"Jane, I don't know where your mother is, or what has happened, but I'm sure she'll be okay..."

"How do you know that? How could you possibly know she'll be okay if you don't even know what's happened? I..."

Roberts took the opportunity to do the cutting in. "I'm doing everything I can to find her, and I'll explain everything I know, I promise. Just meet me at the station, okay?"

There was a brief silence on the other end. "I'm about forty-five minutes away. I'll need to call Lilly on the way. She needs to know too."

"Who?" Roberts queried, momentarily confused as he tried to think if Wendy had told him about a second daughter.

"Lilly? Mum's girlfriend?"

"Uh..." Roberts took a moment to recover from his surprise before answering. "Yes, of course. Both of you are to meet me at the station. I'm about thirty minutes away, but on the off-chance, you get there before I do, the chief will be expecting you." He hung up the phone before Jane could ask any more questions. For the first time in his career, he felt incompetent and incapable of answering any further questions for the moment. Shoving Wendy's phone into his pocket alongside his own, Roberts purposefully strode out of the hospital.

Lilly sat on Wendy's favourite chair by the bedroom window, looking out at the night, but instead of leaning back with her legs up on the small table as she preferred, she sat on the edge of the seat, her knees pressed together as her feet tapped impatiently on the floor. Her gaze frequented towards where her phone rested on the arm of the chair as she willed it to ring, or at the very least buzz with a message. From the moment Wendy left, Lilly felt agitated and on edge—and no matter how she tried to rationalise it, she couldn't shake the feeling that something was wrong. It wasn't the first time Wendy had left her in the middle of the night, and yet this was the first time she'd suffered such strong foreboding. Forcing herself to inhale slowly as she stared out at the stars, she held her breath and sang a little mantra in her head. It did little to quieten the negative thoughts, but it was enough to allow her to send safe vibes out to her love, wherever she was. Lilly was so focused on the task at hand that she jumped when her mobile rang, the music sounding startlingly loud after the never-ending silence. Her positive thoughts fell away at seeing Jane's name on the screen, and her mouth felt dry as she swiped the screen and picked up the phone.

"Jane? What's happened?"

"I don't know, Lilly, but something has."

Lilly closed her eyes, her anxiety intensifying at the sound of Jane's shaky voice. "Just tell me she's alive."

"I don't know," Jane replied, and Lilly could hear the tears in her voice. "I spoke to her partner, Rupert

Roberts. All he would say is she's missing, and he doesn't know what's happened."

"What do you mean, missing? How can he not know where she is when he was the one that picked her up?"

"I know it doesn't make sense. All I know is they were at the hospital together, and then she wasn't."

"Okay, okay..." Lilly stood, her free hand on her hip as she walked up to the window. "Well, that's not that big of a deal, right? Maybe she got called away or something?"

"Her phone was left behind. I called Mum, and he answered."

Lilly was silent as she paced up and down the room, her mind trying to make sense of what she was hearing, trying to find some sliver of hope to grasp, but unable to. "Wait, why did you call your mother at this hour? Is everything okay?"

"Yeah, well, no. I just had this overwhelming feeling that something bad was going to happen, and I just wanted to hear her voice."

Lilly lowered the phone, pressing it to her chest as she swore aloud. She knew with both of them experiencing the same sense of foreboding, something horrible must have happened.

"Lilly? Are you there?" Jane's voice echoed from the speakers, and Lilly quickly raised the phone back to her ear. "Yes. Did he say anything else? Anything at all?"

"He asked us to meet him at the station so he can tell us what he *does* know, but I thought it might make sense if you stayed at Mum's in case she shows up there."

Lilly ran a hand through her hair as she chewed on her lower lip. "Yeah, okay, I guess. But the minute you have any kind of update, I want to hear about it, okay?"

"Of course," Jane confirmed. "And if mum comes home…"

"Calling you will be the first thing I do," Lilly reassured her.

Staving off sleep as best as she could, Wendy's eyes felt heavy as an onslaught of memories caused her head to ache. It was as though Hook's visit had triggered something—like his visit had been the key to unlocking the deeply hidden box. Wendy felt like she was hallucinating, the memories were so vivid, and they spilled forth, one after the other, forcing her to recall details of her prior captivity. They were too disjointed to make much sense visually, but the emotions were there—she could feel the anxiety and fear grow with every image. Yet there seemed to be a cloud hovering over each recollection, a confusion of sorts like she couldn't quite think clearly, and Wendy wasn't sure if this feeling was current or recalled.

I'm sitting at the end of a bed. This bed. I'm hugging a pillow to my chest while Pan sits beside me. He's brushing my hair, and it feels… pleasant… yet the proximity to Pan has me feeling on edge. Lifting my hand to touch my cheek, I'm certain I can feel the cool trail left behind from tears.

Now I see only the concrete wall as I press myself against it. It feels cool against my forehead, and I try to focus on that, pressing my hands over my ears to drown out another of Pan's tirades.

The memories faded as Wendy became distracted by a whimpering sound, and it took her a moment to realise she was making the sound. Leaping off the bed like it was suddenly on fire, Wendy paced furiously around the room. Panic was taking hold of her faster than she could get on top of it. She pulled at her hair, yanking at it with her fists while her breaths came in short, sharp bursts. What little hope she had melted away like ice next to the fire that was her raging panic. She was unable to stop the sobs that wracked her body, causing her to double over—she was torn between wanting to hold on to the images of Jane and Lilly as they flooded her mind while also feeling the need to banish them to ensure their protection. The loneliness that ensued took her right back to when she was fifteen again, helpless and terrified. The realisation angered her, but the anger felt good, tangible, something she could use. Bracing her hands against her knees, Wendy took deep breaths, and her detective mindset returned to her with each exhalation.

Think, think.

Other memories of her past crept back towards her, but this time she was prepared. Emotions cast aside, Wendy forced herself to pay attention—to see past the fear and panic they elicited in her and look for any clues that would help her escape.

While there didn't seem to be anything in her memories to indicate Pan ever laid a hand on her as an act of violence, she did remember what it was like when he lost his temper—how the sound of his anger-filled roars caused her to tremble with fear, wishing a hole would open up and swallow her. But Wendy wasn't a little girl anymore. She was a grown-ass woman capable of taking care of herself. She told herself she would find a way to get out of this nightmare—she was a detective after all.

Wendy stood up straight, her head high as the last of her anxiety retreated back into the darkness, and she gave a little smile of satisfaction. It was short-lived as the sound of jovial whistling drifted towards her, but as she turned in circles, she was unable to pinpoint the direction it came from. She jumped as suddenly a voice greeted her from behind. Wendy spun around to see Mr. Smee standing before her, a tray of food in his hands. "Good day, Mistress Wendy. What an absolute pleasure it is to see you again. I don't doubt that you're starving after your ordeal, but don't you worry your pretty little head, Uncle Smee will take care of you."

Wendy could only stare, open-mouthed, as the rotund man, no taller than her waist, waddled past her, a tarnished silver tray in his hands. He had the same strange light encapsulating him, and after years of being unable to recall Smee's face, Wendy was surprised at how warm and welcoming it was. He wore a red scarf around his head and finely rimmed round glasses that balanced precariously on the tip of his bulbous nose. His white eyebrows were bushy and wild, matching the small goatee that jiggled from his chin as he talked. His smile was wide, yet as Wendy peered closer, trying to get a better look, she could see the discreet glances Smee flicked towards her from under his long, white eyelashes, and the nervous twitch of his goatee as his brows knitted together slightly.

Remaining silent, Wendy watched Smee place the tray on the edge of her bed. Atop the tray sat a squat wooden cup and a chipped plate with a piece of bread and four pieces of sliced apple on it. The sight of the cup triggered an intense thirst in her, and Wendy lunged towards the cup. Picking it up, she gulped the cool liquid down in three large gulps. She was fairly certain it was water, but there was a funny aftertaste to it—slightly metallic. Smee cleared his throat as he fussed about, straightening up her bedding. "How long has it been? Obviously, you have grown quite substantially since we last saw you, but it's so hard to keep track of time, it passes by so quickly, you know..."

"Uhhh..." was all Wendy could muster. His friendliness seemed so out of place in her dark and dank surroundings. Smee seemed undeterred by her lack of response as he continued his babbling.

"Why, it seems like only yesterday, you were a young little thing, perched on this very bed. Oh, what fun we had!"

"Fun?" Wendy couldn't believe the way he was talking—it was as though he'd undergone an entirely different experience than her—either that or he was bat-shit crazy.

"Well," he paused, stepping back from the bed and pausing to look at her. "Perhaps it's much further in the recesses of your memory than mine," he stated, with his hands behind his back as he rocked on his heels, and again Wendy noted the way the smile plastered across his face didn't reach his eyes. When he finally looked her squarely in the eyes, she was taken aback by the intensity of his stare. Despite the poor light, she could swear there was fear in his eyes. He appeared to pointedly look past her, as though in warning, and it was all Wendy could do to keep from turning around and looking over her shoulder.

"Aren't you hungry? It must have been hours since you last ate."

Wendy went to open her mouth but found herself at a loss for words. She saw the faint sparks of green from the corner of her eye. "Tink?" she murmured.

Smee stopped rocking and peered up at her. It seemed to Wendy like his lively expression had gone blank—though she was finding it hard to focus on his features, which now seemed blurry and blended into each other.

"Mind yourself there, Mistress Wendy. Best you sit down, I think."

Wendy meant to nod in compliance but couldn't be certain as she stumbled onto the bed. The shooting sparks increased, now accompanied by a faint tingling in her ears. Clutching at the bedding, she knew she was sitting, yet also felt as though she was still in the process of sitting down. Everything felt like it was just out of reach. Wendy didn't notice as Smee reached out and moved the tray before she could topple it. Despite the fog that now swamped her mind, her adult logic questioned the cause for the green sparks she saw and the tingling sound ringing in her ears—while her childhood memories welcomed back an old friend.

Smee continued to talk to her, his voice taking on a sing-song quality as it drifted away. Wendy peered at him, frowning as she lay on her side, wondering how he could sound so far away when he was standing right there.

"Don't go." Wendy meant to speak firmly, with command, but her voice came out barely louder than a whisper. A bright spark of green flashed again. *Tink?* A tingling response sounded, and Wendy attempted to nod as her heavy eyelids closed.

Jane slid into the front seat of her small, blue hatchback; her phone held to her ear as she pulled her seatbelt across with her free hand. She'd only just dialled Robert's number, but before it had the chance to connect, she heard the beeping sound of another call coming through. Pulling the phone away from her ear to look at the screen, she saw her Uncle's name flash before her. Jane quickly swore beneath her breath—she hoped whatever happened to her mother would be resolved before she had to speak to her Uncles. She debated ignoring the call, but given the time, either they also shared the unknown concern, or something else had happened. Regardless, if she didn't answer, it would only give them further cause to worry.

"Uncle Mike, hey."

"Hi, sweetheart. Do you know if your mother got called into work? I've been trying to reach her, but she's not answering. I also sent a message saying it was urgent, and I figured even if she were working, she'd reply. It's not like her not to get back to me."

Jane took a deep breath. "Honestly, Uncle Mike, I don't know myself. She's missing. I'm actually on my way to the station to speak to her partner. He called me not long ago."

"What do you mean, missing?" Mike asked, his voice suddenly sounding strange, almost deadpan. Jane had never heard him use that tone before, and it did little to calm her as she frowned.

\"They were called back to the hospital a couple of hours ago—something went down with Rosalie Fryair, and then she was just gone. That's all I know right now."

There was only silence in response.

"Uncle Mike?"

"What makes him think she's missing?"

"Well, her phone was left at the hospital, which would be why none of us can get through to her, and secondly, it's just not like her to leave without telling her partner. If it were something urgent, she would have left word for him. Someone would have known about it."

"Hmm..."

Jane sighed. "I was going to call you..."

"You don't have to explain," Michael cut in, "the priority right now is to find your mum. I'll let you go so you can get to the station. Just give me a call as soon as you know what's going on. Do you want your uncle and me to come to town?"

Jane thought for a second. She appreciated the offer, but the tone of his voice just didn't sound right. She didn't know if it was concern about Wendy causing her to be paranoid, but she felt that something wasn't right. "Before you go, what was so urgent?"

"Sorry?"

"Uh, you said you'd asked mum to get back to you urgently. Is something wrong?"

Michael cleared his throat. "Nanna passed away at three o'clock this morning. She went peacefully in her sleep."

"Oh, no! Uncle Mike, I am so sorry. You both must be devastated. Don't worry about coming into town. You have enough going on."

"Carole is here with us. Just keep us posted."

"So, you got a hold of her?" John asked as we walked into the lounge room with a steaming cup of coffee in each hand.

"No, I didn't. However, I did speak to Jane. Looks like there might be more to Nanna's passing after all."

"Can't say I like the sound of that," John replied as he handed one of the mugs to his brother before sitting on the couch opposite him.

"Wendy's missing."

John slowly lowered his mug to the coffee table between them, and the brother's exchanged a long look, neither wanting to be the one to say aloud what they were both thinking. Finally, Michael stood up and started pacing around the room.

"When did she go missing?" John asked, leaning forward with his head in his hands.

"A couple of hours, give or take."

"So, what are the chances of it being a simple coincidence that our sister went missing approximately the same time that Nanna passed away?"

"I don't even want to consider it," Michael sighed, taking a huge gulp of his coffee, wincing as the hot liquid scalded his throat.

"We'd been warned this could happen. Dad tried to tell us more than once..."

"Dad was so unwell towards the end, you know he probably didn't know what he was saying."

"Really?" John raised his head. "You don't believe that any more than I do. We might have been little when she was abducted, but we were old enough to know there was something strange about it all. No one would answer our questions..."

"Because we were children, John. They were trying to protect us from something truly terrible. The things Dad told us later, they have nothing to do with what's happening now." Michael tried to argue, but his voice lacked conviction.

"Why don't you try that again, only this time make it sound a little more believable," John stated.

"Now's not the time to be a smart arse," his brother retorted.

"Then stop pretending. Wendy goes and disappears the same night that Nanna passes away? Come on. If we have any hope of helping our sister, then you need to be honest with yourself."

Michael didn't respond as he stopped his pacing and leaned against the window ledge, unable to see anything other than his reflection looking back at him. He suddenly felt older than his years.

"What are the chances of getting her back a second time?" John asked softly.

Michael looked at him through the window. "They can't be good."

CHAPTER EIGHTEEN

"Good. You're awake," Roberts said gruffly as he strode into Rosalie's room to find the girl with her arm outstretched as a nurse checked her blood pressure and temperature.

"Excuse me. You can't just barge in here. Visiting hours don't start for a few hours, yet," the nurse stated, equally gruff.

"Actually, I can," Roberts replied, flashing his badge as he continued, "I need to have a word with Rosalie."

"Well, I haven't finished here," the nurse replied stubbornly.

"Look, I don't mean any disrespect, but I honestly don't care if you need to stay or go, but I need to talk to her right now."

"Who is this man?" Rosalie asked, her eyes wide as she pushed herself back against the pillows, pulling her knees to her chest.

"I don't have time for games, Rosalie. You know exactly who I am."

Roberts watched as the girl looked from him to the nurse and back again, shrinking further into herself with each glance.

"You spoke to my partner, Detective Darling, only a few hours ago. At your request, I might add. I left the room so you could speak to my partner alone—again as requested—and when I came back, she was gone, and you were asleep."

The girl opened her mouth and half shook her head.

"You're upsetting her. I think you should leave," the nurse stated, deflating the cuff of the blood pressure machine to try and take a second reading. She raised her arm in a wave to get the attention of a security guard as he passed the door.

Roberts ignored her and leaned on Rosalie's bed. "What happened to Detective Darling?" he asked slowly and purposefully, doing his best to keep a hold on his anger and frustration.

"I...I don't know who you're talking about. I swear. I don't remember anything other than waking up and finding myself here."

Roberts gaped at her before turning his attention to the nurse. "Is she on drugs?"

The nurse scowled at him, her distaste evident. "She has been sedated, yes. Obviously, a loss of memory is quite frightening at any age. But she's been through a lot." She looked down at Rosalie as she undid the blood pressure cuff. "We just have to take it one day at a time, don't we, dear?" Without waiting for a reply, she turned and packed up her machine, giving a pointed look over Roberts' shoulder as she did. He looked behind him to see the guard standing in the doorway, his arms folded across his chest, his strong, square chin subtly moving from one side to the other as though he was chewing gum.

"Is there a problem?"

"Not at all. I'm a detective," Roberts gave his best, charismatic smile. The security guard gave nothing away but looked over to the nurse for further instruction.

"I've instructed the detective that visiting hours are later and that this patient has been sedated. She needs to sleep."

Roberts stared at the girl as her eyes fluttered closed on cue, and he tried to determine whether she was legitimate or just a very good actress. Either way, he wasn't getting any answers from her.

"I'll be back," he stated, turning on his heel and pushing past the security guard as he stormed past.

Wendy forced herself to her feet, hoping the movement would help clear the fogginess that hung heavily over her. She stood, swaying slightly as she tried to regain some kind of equilibrium, and it took all her concentration to put one foot in front of the other as she stumbled around the room, helplessly trying to find a way out. She tapped on the walls, listening intently for any hollow sounds, she crawled across the floor, feeling for a hidden trapdoor, something—anything—to get her out of there.

When her search turned up nothing, Wendy sat back on her haunches and let out a frustrated scream, not caring if she attracted the attention of Pan. Green sparks flew in her peripheral vision, and Wendy pounded at the side of her head with the palms of her hands, trying to make them stop, feeling like she was going to topple over as everything seemed to spin around her.

"Where are you? You bastard!" she screamed as she spun around. "You can't keep me here! I will escape, no matter what you do, I will never be yours! Come out and face me, you green-eyed freak!"

The green flashes intensified and closing her eyes, she almost wished a little green fairy caused them like she'd convinced herself all those years ago. A sharp, tingling sensation moved slowly up her back and then her neck, and Wendy didn't have to open her eyes to know Pan had appeared—she could feel the ferocity of his stare boring into her through the darkness. Remaining still, Wendy took a deep breath, gathering all the courage and determination she could muster, before looking up to face him. Once again, all she could see were his eyes, bulbous in anger, the inhuman green amplified by the angry rim of redness that lined them. Wendy felt like the intensity of his fury was sapping her strength, but rather than worrying about getting to her feet, she used what energy she did have to focus on keeping her mind blank of all thoughts—a mirror only of what she presently saw. Pan let out a low, guttural growl, and Wendy wondered if he was angered by his inability to penetrate her thoughts, or if he simply didn't like what he saw of himself through her eyes.

He moved towards her, his footsteps loud against the concrete floor, each one representing the confident and predatory steps of a creature who knows he can take his time. She was trapped—they both knew it, yet she didn't want to give him the satisfaction of showing fear.

"Let. Me. Go," she demanded, the sudden loudness of her voice startling her, though she tried to hide it.

Moving closer, Wendy could see the sneer on his face as he growled again, "Is that any way to speak to your old friend?"

"Friend? *Friend?* You're out of your mind," she hissed in reply.

Pan took a few steps to the side, as though trying to get a better look at her. "You know, I think earlier I was just so pleased to see you return, that I didn't fully appreciate how kind the years have been to you, Wendy. Certainly, you were angelic in your youth, but you've still not been touched by the decimation of age."

Though still a few metres away from her, Pan reached his hand out towards her. Wendy watched in horror as the fingers on his hand extended outwards, like gnarled and spindly branches of a barren tree. Wendy turned her face away in repulsion as he touched her, feeling sick to the stomach as his fingers ran down the side of her face, down her neck, hovering for a moment over her chest before sweeping across to her shoulder.

"Get your damn hands off me, or I'll..."

"You'll what, exactly?" Pan growled, retracting his hand as though bitten, and much to Wendy's relief, it returned to its normal size.

"I'll find a way to end you."

Pan laughed. The sound was surprisingly deep, given his slight stature, and it echoed around the room, taunting her. It sent a chill through her that didn't go unnoticed by Pan as he sneered through his amusement.

Unable to ignore him, Wendy's anger intensified as she spoke through clenched teeth. "I'm not a child anymore. I'm a detective. I guarantee you officers are looking for me as we speak. They'll get the answers they need from Rosalie, and then they'll find me."

Once again, Pan erupted in laughter. "Ahh, the delicate Rosalie. What a little blossom she is, just ripe for the picking. My dear Wendy, surely as a detective, you'd have already deduced that the poor child was just a pawn. Rosalie's recollection was only what I needed in order to lure you in. I wasn't sure it would work, or if it did, I doubted it would be so easy to have you in my grasp once again when it's not been possible before now. But who am I to question our destiny? Besides, by now, all Rosalie's memories of me and this place will have drifted away into nothingness, like spider webs in the wind..." He lifted his hands and dramatically splayed his fingers in demonstration. Wendy swallowed thickly as she recalled how her own memories were cloaked and feared he was telling the truth.

"I searched for you for years, though admittedly, that's hardly anytime at all in my lifetime." Pan continued, "It became my life's purpose, you could say. But it was like you were veiled from me—and it pained me more than you could ever know. From time to time, I would hear of you, like a faint whisper from the mortal realm, but still, I couldn't see you. Then about a year ago, word came to me that you had grown up and become a detective—my how time flies. I knew then the perfect way to get your attention, and while I didn't know if you'd become visible to me, it was still the closest I'd been since you first left me. The plan was perfect, though, mind you, nothing good comes from rushed plans. I made sure I took my time to find the right girl, the right family. See, it wouldn't be just enough to abduct a girl— there was no guarantee that in itself would get your attention.

The girl had to come from a well-known family—there had to be pressure to find her so I could ensure you would be on the case. The real clincher, though, would be in the details. I needed you to commit one hundred percent, so the girl had to be like you—like you were—in enough ways that your own memories would come back to you in full. I needed your mind to reopen to me if it was to work…"

"Wow, I forgot how much you loved the sound of your own voice," Wendy cut in, feigning a yawn.

"How *dare* you interrupt me with such insolence!" Pan roared, his jaw distending, revealing triple rows of sharp, uneven teeth. In repulsion, Wendy realised the teeth were mismatched—they looked to be children's teeth—hundreds of them. A rush of burning bile rose up into Wendy's throat, but she didn't back down. She wanted Pan angry in the hopes he would unintentionally give away some vital clue she could use against him, or better still, she could escape. As quickly as the thought entered her mind, Pan backed down, his mouth returning to normal, and she clenched her jaw in frustration at her carelessness.

"Yes, you certainly have changed since the last time we were together, haven't you, Wendy?"

This time Wendy remained silent as she stared at him, doing her best to look fierce despite the fear that permeated every part of her being.

"I'm afraid my father won't be as forthcoming in his assistance this time around, Wendy. He knows the consequences of such a betrayal."

"My partner will find me…"

"Detective Rupert Roberts?" Pan scoffed, clearly not intimidated.

"Yes, Detective Rupert Roberts. He's more of a man than you could ever be, and I know he won't stop until he finds me."

In two inhuman strides, Pan stood right in front of her, his face contorted in a manic rage as his mouth fell open again, revealing the teeth, this time, the accompanying smell of his breath instantly caused her stomach to knot. It was a metallic smell that reminded her of the smell of blood, yet there was something else to it as well. Wendy looked away from the repulsive rows of teeth and instantly regretted it as she saw the bulging green eyes of her nightmares, rimmed in red that dripped down his cheeks, which puffed in and out with rage-induced exertion. He was so close that Wendy feared he would actually capture her head with his monstrous mouth, and she felt as though her heart momentarily stopped at the thought.

Pan raised his hand to her throat, the youthful size of his hand no concern as his fingers extended, wrapping themselves around her until she felt like she was in an iron vice. Wendy tried to steady her breathing and not let the sensation of his fingers cause her to panic. As he squeezed, she glared at him in defiance, refusing to show any fear despite her heart thundering against her ribcage or the burning of her lungs. Forcing herself to look him in the eyes, the ground felt as though it was opening up beneath her. Doubt of her own escape entered her mind, and she shoved it aside, not wanting to give him the satisfaction of seeing it.

Yet he seemed to sense the split-second of doubt, and Pan retracted his fingers and removed his hand from her neck. Wendy was unable to stop the instinctual gasp for air, all too aware that Pan's hand hovered before her, should she give him any further cause to restrain her again. Seemingly content that she would behave, the red tracks on his cheeks sucked back up into his eyes as they shrank back to their normal, albeit freakish state. Wendy watched as his rage melted away, and the sneer was again replaced with his boyish smile.

"Wendy, Wendy, Wendy. You're a smart woman from all reports. I'm sure it won't take you long to realise it does neither of us any good to make me angry. I don't enjoy it when you make me hurt you. In fact, it saddens me. We lived together quite peacefully the first time around, and it's my hope we can have that again. I do understand; however, you've since built a life for yourself in the outside world. It would require an incentive to accept a new life here with me."

He stepped aside and waved his arm with a flourish at the nothingness behind him. "It doesn't have to be a dark and dank existence—not now." The shadows shrunk away, framing a scene of absolute beauty that caused her to gape in awe. Wendy was so entranced that she forgot herself as she rose to her feet and moved towards it. Before her, on either side, stood two enormous trees. Their sturdy trunks were so wide she could only see one edge and so tall that only their delicate, low-lying foliage was visible to her, as they sheltered an array of flowers that spawned across the luscious green grass. Wendy questioned her senses as the scents of jasmine and lavender wafted towards her. She knew, somehow, it wasn't her imagination.

She startled as she heard a *whoop!* A group of young boys burst onto the scene, gallivanting and playfully jabbing at each other with their wooden swords. Wendy's breath caught in her throat as she recognised them from her nightmares, and she questioned if Pan had somehow seen the remnants of them in her mind.

Part of Wendy told her to turn and confront Pan. Still, another part of her felt strange, like a combination of tranquillity and docility, and her angry questions fell away, leaving only a faint question hovering just beyond her grasp. Abandoning it, Wendy stepped closer still and felt the touch of a breeze as the leaves of the trees danced in a delicate wind, as though beckoning her closer. Despite the boisterous sounds of the boys as they ran ahead in the distance, there was something peaceful and serene about the place before her. The light seemed different—softer—somehow, and golden, as though it wasn't quite penetrating. There was no denying her desire for the place. She longed to leave the cold isolation of her concrete cell and walk barefoot on the lush, cool grass—to rest her back against the trunk of one of the magnificent trees and look up at the sky through the foliage-laden branches.

As though sensing he was winning her over, Pan finally spoke, the enthusiasm in his voice evident as he all but hovered from one foot to the other. "I can offer you a world free of the ugliness of the mortal realm, a world where there is only beauty. Peace. Happiness. It's what I have wanted for you—for us— since the moment I first laid eyes on you, all those years ago…" Pan's voice wafted over her in hypnotic waves, and her eyelids felt heavy as she shuffled closer.

"It can all be yours," Pan whispered suddenly in her ear. Wendy yelped, the spell broken, and she lashed out, but he was too quick. The shadows swiftly engulfed the oasis, and the sudden departure made the reality of her captivity appear that much colder and depressing.

"Leave me the hell alone!" Wendy yelled, scanning the shadows for her oppressor. She spun around as she heard his voice from the shadows behind her.

"You can't deny me forever, Wendy," he stated, his arms folded across his chest, and his mouth turned down in a sulk. "I saw your reaction—you wanted to join them on the other side."

"The other side of what?" Wendy asked, before holding up her hand with a quick shake of her head. "Actually, I don't want to know. Whatever it was, it was just another one of your mind games, and I'm not interested in being your pawn."

"That's where you're wrong, my love. Firstly, you're not a pawn. Secondly, you don't actually get a choice in the matter. You're in my realm now—I'm in control. The sooner you learn to succumb, to relinquish your need for your old life, the easier this will be for you. What I showed you was just the smallest glimpse of Neverland. There is so much more for you to see—a world so magnificent in its beauty it would take you a life without end to see it all. Something which I long to give you."

"Ugh…" Wendy rubbed her eyes with the heels of her hands as he continued.

"Neverland—is my creation. A place for those chosen few to experience life unburdened by suffering or the ugliness of the mortal realm. There is no death, no illness—no growing old. I suppose it could be likened to a mortal perception of heaven, so to speak. I want this for you."

"You're delusional! Nothing you can ever say or do will make me want to do anything other than escape!"

Pan roared, the sound reverberating off the cement walls, causing Wendy to cover her ears. She braced herself to witness the horror of his anger once again, but Pan kept his back to her. His fingers lengthened until they brushed the floor, his fingertips curling towards her as though with a life of their own, longing to wrap themselves around her. Wendy braced herself, waiting for the attack that didn't come. Instead, Pan kept his back to her, hunched over and heaving with exertion like he was trying to regain control. Slowly, he straightened and set his shoulders. He turned to the side, enough for Wendy to see the edge of the sneer on his face.

"Don't be a fool, detective. You belong to me. You always have and always will—you'll never be free of me. But I'm giving you a choice. I want you to join me of your own free will in Neverland. Be a mother to those boys who are in such need of maternal love. Remain youthful for all eternity, never want for anything, never again feel pain. If you don't, I will leave you to rot in this concrete cage until you are nothing but dust and bones which I will gather up, take with me to Neverland, and keep by my side for eternity. Either way, you're mine."

"You're insane!" Wendy screamed at him, feeling the truth of his words.

"Sanity is just perspective." He turned away and started walking back into the shadows until she could no longer see him, but his voice came back for her. "Make your choice—you have until the flame of this candle burns out to decide." A candle wafted out of the shadows towards her. Its dancing flame seemed as bright as the sun after the darkness.

As the oppressive air of the room faded, Wendy knew Pan was gone. Letting out a shaky exhalation, Wendy retreated to the bed, the candle hovering after her like an obedient servant. Lying on her side, she stared towards the space where Neverland was revealed to her. There was something about it that was like nothing she'd seen before—she couldn't say how or why. It just was. Wendy didn't know if it was because of the boys, but she felt tethered to them, to Neverland, now that she'd seen it.

Pushing herself upright, Wendy shook her head fiercely against the thought. She wouldn't give in. She couldn't give up. Wendy knew she would do everything in her power to free herself of him, one way or another. It occurred to her that he hadn't mentioned Jane in his plans for her relocation, and Wendy wondered if it was really possible that he didn't know about her. If so, she needed to make sure it stayed that way. As Wendy watched the candle burn, the droplets of wax dripped onto the ground in front of her. She was grateful to find it appeared to be a slow burn—she would need all the time she could get if she was ever going to escape.

CHAPTER NINETEEN

Roberts strode through the station, ignoring the stares shot in his direction, both concerned and accusatory, and he knew the word about Darling's disappearance had already spread. He walked into the chief's office without knocking and found the chief with his back to Roberts. He looked over his shoulder as Roberts entered.

"Close the door," he instructed, and Roberts obeyed, refusing to meet the eyes of those in the station and pretending they weren't watching on.

"Take a seat," the chief demanded as he turned to face him, a file open in his hand. Roberts looked at it with curiosity as he sat down in the chair on the other side of his boss's desk. The chief didn't sit but placed a surprisingly thick file on his desk and leaned on his hands, which he placed on either side of the menacing file.

"I'm assuming you still haven't heard from Detective Darling?"

Roberts shook his head. "I still have her phone. I spoke to her daughter, Jane, and she hadn't heard from her either. Speaking of, she should be here already."

"She is," the chief confirmed. "I have her waiting in one of the interview rooms. I thought it might be less daunting for her, considering everyone here knows her mother."

"You notified them without speaking to me first?" Robert's asked.

"No—Jane called her mother's phone, and I answered it. How could I not tell her why her mother didn't answer the phone?"

The chief sighed while staring at the file before him. Roberts shifted in his seat as his boss remained silent, finally clearing his throat and asking, "What's that?"

The chief let out a noisy sigh and swore under his breath. He spun the file around and shoved it across the desk to Roberts. Roberts reached for it and pulled it towards him, flicking his boss a quick look, one eyebrow raised before he opened it. The first page was the beginning of a standard case report with a photo of a girl who appeared to be in her teens clipped to the top left corner. Judging from the pose, Roberts assumed it was an old school photo. He found himself drawn to the girl and distracted from the notes before him as he witnessed something familiar in her delicate, almost elfin, features. Especially her eyes. They pulled him in, and he shifted again, uncomfortable with his intrigue given the age. Frowning, he lifted it up and focused on the paperwork beneath it.

"What the fuck…"

The profanity escaped him before he could check himself as he read the victim's name. He quickly looked up at his boss, who was watching him, a deep observational frown etched across his forehead.

"I apologise, Sir…"

"No need, Roberts. The sentiment is justified."

Roberts gave a small nod, feeling absolutely speechless as he quietly read the name to himself again—Wendy Moira Darling, Age 15. Not trusting himself to have anything more eloquent to say than what had already come out of his mouth, he buried himself in the notes, intently reading one page after the other.

"Darling was abducted," he stated softly, leaning back in the chair while finally looking at his boss.

The chief nodded and grabbed the chair back, pulling it out from under the desk so he could sit.

"Okay…" Roberts tried to sort through the myriad of thoughts that ran through his mind. "So you're showing me this because either you think the Rosalie Fryair case was too much for her, and Darling's had some kind of trauma-induced breakdown or something… or… surely you don't think her disappearance has anything to with her previous abduction? There couldn't possibly be a connection— an eerie coincidence perhaps…" he trailed off, realising even he didn't believe the argument he put forward, but not wanting to allow the possibility to take hold.

"Between you and me, I don't know what I think just yet. We can't jump to conclusions, but we can't rule anything out either."

"You knew about this before assigning Darling to the case? You let her go ahead knowing all of this? I mean, she wasn't just abducted for crying out loud—

she ended up pregnant! Why didn't either of you tell me?" Roberts demanded, unable to keep the edge out of his voice.

"Don't forget who you are talking to, Roberts. Firstly, Darling's personal file is of no business to you, and secondly, any risk I thought might be present was mitigated before she joined you on the case. This isn't the first abduction case Darling has worked, as I'm sure you're aware."

"Yeah, but Sir, I mean these notes…there are so many similarities between her abduction and the Fryair case…I don't mean any disrespect, but…"

"All you need to know is Darling did what was asked of her to ensure she was fit to take this case, and if I'd thought there was any risk to assigning her, I wouldn't have done so."

"Well, obviously, there was a risk because she's *missing.*" Roberts banged his hand on the desk before he could stop himself. The chief leaned forward, his steely glare enough for Roberts to retract his hand from the desk.

"You need to pull your head in, Roberts, and focus on the task at hand. Your…concern…at your partner's disappearance is noted. So use it to find out what's happened to Detective Darling. I don't think you need to be told this is now our highest priority."

"Yes, Sir." Roberts closed the case file and tucked it under his arm as he stood up. He saw his boss glance at the file, and he hoped he wasn't going to ask for it back.

"That file is for your eyes only, understood?"

"Of course, Sir." Roberts stepped aside and pushed the chair in. "I should go and speak to Jane Darling. I don't want to keep her waiting any longer." With a nod of dismissal from his boss, Roberts turned to leave the room.

"And Roberts?"

He stopped, turning back to his boss. "Yes, Sir?"

"I would recommend you take a moment to compose yourself before you enter the interview room. I understand you feel a responsibility to your partner, but we also require professionalism."

Roberts opened his mouth to argue, but quickly closed it again, deciding he didn't need another battle on his hands. "Of course, Sir." Roberts matched his boss's intense gaze, knowing he would have to be the one to back down and not quite able to bring himself to relent. He felt the click in his jaw as it clenched and slowly sat back in his seat without diverting his gaze. The chief remained leaning on his hands that rested on the desk.

"Is there anything else, Sir?"

The chief stood, rising to his full intimidating height. "Actually, yes. Once you've spoken to Jane, call Detective Darling's brothers in as well. Given she's spent most of her time with them in recent weeks, they might be able to shine some more light on anything unusual in Darling's life of late."

Roberts nodded.

"Then, I want you to run a quick debrief with a team of your choosing—everyone is at your disposal and obviously eager to help."

"Thank you, Sir," Roberts replied, rising from his chair, feeling his anger mould into a fixated determination.

"One last thing, Roberts," the chief stated as the detective froze, his hand fixed firmly on the door handle. Looking over his shoulder, he looked at his boss inquisitively.

"I want her found. Quickly."

"So do I." Roberts yanked open the door and strode out into the station, not oblivious to the quick movements of his colleagues as they all swept into sudden action in an attempt to look like they were busy and hadn't been waiting for him to come out.

"I want everyone in the conference room in half an hour. Notify any incoming crews to join us as well," he demanded, refusing to meet any of their questioning stares as he stormed past them towards the interview room.

"Miss Darling. I'm Detective Rupert Roberts," he introduced himself as he opened the door.

"Hello." Jane gave him a half-smile of greeting from where she sat at a small table in the middle of the room, her hands clasped in her lap. Roberts noted the way she was picking at the quick of one thumb with the other and felt a stab of guilt that he was somehow responsible for the pain she was inflicting on herself.

"Can I get you a coffee or some water or something before we start?"

"No, thank you."

Roberts nodded and walked over to the table, taking the seat opposite her as he carefully made sure her mother's file was tucked and hidden under his notepad.

"You mentioned you were going to contact your mother's, uh, partner. Lilly, was it?"

"I did. She was at mum's already, and I suggested it might be best that she stay there in case Mum comes home."

Roberts frowned, and Jane was quick to apologise. "I'm so sorry, detective. I didn't mean to undermine you. Bloody hell, what was I thinking? It just made sense at the time," Jane rambled, placing her hands on either side of her head.

"It's fine, Jane—can I call you Jane?"

She nodded without looking up at him.

"Now, it's not a bad idea, Jane, for Lilly to wait at your mother's, but I need to speak to her sooner rather than later."

"Yes, of course. I apologise." Jane lowered her hands and returned to picking at her fingers. "Can you tell me what's happened to my mum?"

Roberts looked at her properly for the first time and was annoyed at the pang he felt at the resemblances she bore to her mother. They looked more like sisters than mother and daughter, and the notion reminded him of how young Wendy was when she'd had Jane.

"Detective?" Jane prompted.

"Yes, sorry. As you know, we started working the Rosalie Fryair case, and it was during a follow-up visit to the hospital in the early hours of this morning that your mother went missing. I had left her alone in the room with Miss Fryair as the girl was more comfortable speaking one-on-one with Darh... with your mum. I went to get us a couple of coffees, and somehow during the brief time it took me to do that, she vanished. All I was able to find was her phone, which was left in the waiting area."

"Not in the girl's room?" Jane asked, and Roberts couldn't help the small smile that tugged at the corner of his mouth—Wendy's daughter clearly had her tenacity as well as her looks.

"No. Now, I'm sure I don't need to tell you anything we discuss here is to stay in this room."

Jane nodded, her eyes wide with both anticipation and anxiety.

"I examined the footage from the security cameras while at the hospital, and there seemed to be a glitch in the system during the short window of time that Wendy disappeared. There was no sign of her leaving the room or the hospital for that matter." He paused, letting the information sink in. Jane frowned as she looked from one side of the room to the other.

"How can that be possible?" she finally asked.

"I don't know yet, but I promise you, I will get to the bottom of it."

"And what about the girl? What did she say?"

Roberts leaned back in his seat. His arm stretched out as he lightly tapped his forefinger on the table. "She doesn't seem to have any recollection of us even being there."

Jane's mouth fell open. "What the hell is going on, Detective? None of this makes any sense. Where the hell is my mother? What's happened to her?"

Roberts leaned forward again and reached out to grasp Jane's clenched hands in his. "I know this is confusing and upsetting, but I assure you, I will find her." Roberts gave her hands a quick squeeze before releasing them. Jane wiped away the dewy tears that had started to trickle down her cheeks with the back of her hands and nodded.

"What can I do?"

"As you know, I don't know your mother well. She was on leave when I first came to the station. I understand her mother was ill and then passed?"

Jane nodded, lowering her gaze as she wiped another tear from her cheek. "Yes. My grandmother passed away last week."

"I'm truly sorry for your family's loss," Roberts stated with as much sincerity as he could muster, but the reality was, he didn't want to dwell on their family loss. He just wanted to get to the information that would help him find his partner.

"In the lead up to your grandmother's passing, your mum was staying at the family estate. Is that correct?"

"Yes. When they found out Grandmother didn't have much time, Mum went and stayed with her brothers at the house so they could spend as much time as they could with her. I stayed there more often than not, depending on my work schedule."

"Do you live with your mother normally?"

"No. I mean, I do have a room at her place for whenever I want to stay over there, like if we decide to have a few wines over dinner. But no, I have my own place."

"Okay, so going back to the past few weeks spent at the estate, had you noticed anything… different… going on with your mother?"

Jane chewed on her bottom lip while staring down at the table, as though debating on what to say.

"Even a seemingly irrelevant piece of information could prove useful, Jane."

"Well, I'm sure you can understand it wasn't exactly a pleasant time for the family. I mean, my grandmother was dying."

"Of course I do, and I'm sorry to have to make you talk about it so soon, but time really is of the essence here."

Jane took a deep breath. "Mum loves seeing my uncles and my grandmother, but she's never really been comfortable at the manor. We rarely spent time there when I was growing up. I could never understand why, it's such a beautiful, peaceful estate, but…" Jane trailed off as she looked up at Roberts. He could see she was battling with wanting to help him, but also concerned with revealing personal information about her mum. The question was, how much did Wendy's daughter know? He wanted her to trust him, but he also didn't want to add any more weight to the girl by adding any further trauma by revealing unknown information to her.

"If it's any help, Jane, I've recently learned of your mother's… troubled… teenage years." He held the girl's gaze, trying to determine how much she knew when she finally gave a slow nod.

"She only recently told me. Like, very recently."

"That must have been extremely hard for you to hear," Roberts said carefully.

"What, that your father wasn't actually a random teenage one-night-stand, but in fact was an abducting rapist? Yeah, it wasn't the best of news. Certainly not what I'd hoped for all those years when I'd privately longed to find out who my father was. Be careful what you wish for, right?"

"I can't imagine. Does anyone else know about it?"

Jane shrugged. "Well, my grandparents would have known, and I'm assuming my uncles. I don't know if she's ever told Lilly. Nanna would have also known, but for all I know it could have been long forgotten."

"Wait, Nanna? As in your grandmother?"

"No, sorry. Nanna's my grandfather's nanny and became part of the family. She's lived in that house since he was a boy."

"She must be quite elderly?" he queried as he jotted the information on his notepad.

"Yes. Well, she was. She's just passed away."

Roberts looked up in surprise. "What do you mean by 'just'?"

"As in she only passed away this morning. Around 3 am apparently."

"I am so sorry, Jane," Roberts stated, trying to stop himself from staring at her in surprise. He discreetly noted 3 am on the notepad, knowing it was also the same time Wendy disappeared.

"Let me go and get you something to drink." He quickly left the room to fetch a clean glass to fill with cold water from the water cooler.

3 am. That can't be a coincidence. But how could the two events be connected?

With the glass in one hand and a box of tissues tucked under his arm, he entered the interview room and placed both on the table in front of Jane.

"Thank you," she sniffled, reaching for a tissue. "I don't even know why I'm so upset. Nanna and I never got along. We were never close."

"You've had a lot to deal with this evening, Jane. It's understandable that you would be upset. We can pick this up later if you need to."

Jane shook her head, scrunching up the damp tissue and tucking it into her balled fist as she took a sip of water with her free hand. "No, I'll be fine. We need to do this now so you can get back out there and find my mum."

"Okay," Roberts replied, taking his seat and picking up the pen off the notepad. "So your mother and Nanna, were they close? Or were they estranged also?"

"Oh, they were very close. In fact, Nanna's closest relationship in the family after my grandfather was with my mum."

"Am I right in assuming your mother wasn't aware of Nanna's passing?"

"No. That's what I was calling her for when you answered the phone. My uncle called me as he'd been unable to reach her."

Roberts jotted another brief note on the pad. "Is there anything else you can think of that stood out in recent weeks?"

"Not really. She was eager to get on the Rosalie Fryair case, which was causing some friction between her and my Uncle Mike."

"Oh? How so?"

"Well, Mum's always been super driven when it comes to her work, which we all know. It was really eating at her that there was such a big case, and she wasn't working it. My uncle thought she was being insensitive or something that she should have been more focused on our family than someone else's."

"How about you? How did you feel about it?" Roberts prompted.

Jane shrugged. "I've always supported Mum and her job, though I did think she seemed a little more fixated on the Fryair case than she normally would be on any case. At the time, I put it down to simply being her way of dealing with her grief—you know, by throwing herself into her work. Though in hindsight, knowing what I now know about Mum's past, I understand there was much more to it. It would probably sound crazy to anyone other than you, but she was so relieved when she finally was assigned to the case."

Roberts gave Jane a small smile. "You're right; we're a rare breed. What about your other uncle? What did he think of it?"

"He didn't seem phased either way. I think he just didn't want any sibling fighting with everything else they had to deal with. Though he's probably the most chill of the three of them."

"So, your uncles are aware of the situation?"

Jane nodded. "Only that Mum seems to have gone AWOL."

"That's fine. I'll ask them to come in and have a chat with them as well. Is there anything else you can think of? Anything at all?"

He looked at her just in time to catch an odd expression flash across her face, but it was gone as quickly as it had appeared. Either way, he knew she was sitting on something.

"No. Nothing I can think of at the moment."

Roberts nodded, deciding not to push it further for now, but making a note to follow his suspicions later. "Right, well, I appreciate you coming in. For now, go home, try and get some rest and I will call you as soon as I have something new to report."

"Okay. Thank you, detective," Jane said as she stood up. "I'm going to stay at Mum's place for now. I feel like that's where I need to be."

"Speaking of, could I get a contact number for Lilly? You're listed as your mum's primary next of kin on her file, with your uncles as secondary, but those are the only contact numbers I have."

"Yes, of course." Jane provided the number and left the interview room. Roberts stared after her, tapping his pen on the notepad as he wondered what she was withholding.

With a sigh, he took his phone out of his pocket and dialled the first number on his notepad. Lilly answered on the first ring and readily agreed to come straight in. Next, he called Michael Darling.

"Hello?" The voice sounded exhausted, and it dawned on Roberts for the first time just how much the Darling family had been through in recent weeks.

"Yes, hello. This is Detective Rupert Roberts..."

"We have been waiting for your call. I take it you haven't found our sister yet?"

Roberts paused, slightly taken about by his tone. "Uh, no, not yet, but I'm working on it."

He could hear someone talking in the background.

"One moment, detective, my brother is here with me, so I'll just put you on speakerphone."

Roberts waited impatiently despite it taking a matter of seconds.

"Yes, detective, hello?"

"Yes, I'm here."

"So Jane told us that our sister has somehow vanished from the hospital you two were visiting earlier this morning?"

"That is correct. We're in the process of trying to piece together what happened, and finding her is our highest priority. I was hoping you both could come into the station so we can have a chat."

There was a muffled pause, and Roberts could have sworn the brothers had covered the phone while they conversed. He stared at the phone, confused by their strange reaction, and was more than a little bit annoyed when they finally decided to rejoin him.

"We can be there in a couple of hours." The call was terminated before Roberts had the chance to respond.

What the fuck is going on with this family?

He suddenly felt overwhelmingly tired, and he allowed himself a brief moment to stretch and yawn, only because he didn't want to risk yawning before everyone in the conference room—he knew there would be judgement in the minds of his colleagues. Despite his spotless reputation, he was now the new detective who had lost his partner. He didn't want there to be any further doubt regarding his ability to find her safely.

Pushing himself up out of his chair, he grabbed his pad and Wendy's file and strode out of the interview room. He was pleased to find the station quiet, hoping it meant everyone had congregated in the conference room as requested—he didn't want any indication that finding Detective Darling was anything less than everyone's top priority.

CHAPTER TWENTY

Jane took the stairs leading to her mother's front door two at a time and almost dropped her keys in her hurry to get inside. Firmly locking the door behind her, she stepped over to the staircase and peered upwards. "Lilly?" When there was no answer, she walked through the living room and into the kitchen to find it empty, but the stove light on. There was a note on the bench, and Jane swore under her breath as she saw it was from Lilly, letting Jane know she hadn't heard from her mother and had left for the station.

Sitting down on a stool, Jane pulled out her phone and started to text Lilly, but thinking better of it, she deleted the text and put her phone down. She'd wanted to tell Lilly she hadn't mentioned the box from the past but worried if he happened to see the text message, it would make everything seem like something it wasn't. Placing her head on her hands, she closed her eyes and groaned. She wasn't even sure why she'd kept it to herself—in fact, in hindsight, it sounded downright stupid. With a yawn, she told herself that it wouldn't make any difference in finding her mother—if anything, she was certain it would only slow the search by bogging the police down with a twisted and mysterious family history that had nothing to do with anything now.

As much as she didn't like the idea of snooping, it occurred to Jane that if she was going to look for any clues about her mother's disappearance, then now was the time to do it, before Lilly returned. Pushing herself up off the stool, she walked back through the living room and upstairs to her mother's room. Fortunately, her mother wasn't a hoarder, so it wouldn't take long to conduct a fairly thorough search. Pulling the stool out from under the dressing table, Jane stood atop it to scan the length of the single shelf in the room. Aside from some haphazardly stacked books, some old folders, and a significant amount of dust, there was nothing of any interest. Jane moved to the drawers, carefully opening them, not wanting to disrupt her mother's belongings any more than she had to. Still, she uncovered nothing. Despite it feeling like too childish a hiding place for a detective, Jane even checked under the bed and under the mattress itself. Sitting on the floor, her back against the bed, she sighed. It made it hard to search when she wasn't sure exactly what she was looking for. Her eyes stung as tears tried to break through, but Jane pinched herself to make them stop. It was then she looked over at the large dresser of drawers against the other side of the room. Yes, she'd already gone through them, but something about sitting on the floor and looking at them from that angle reminded Jane of a childhood memory. It was faint, but there was enough of it there for Jane to recall her 'Harriet the Spy' phase and playing with her mother. Scrambling to her hands and knees, she scurried over to them, gripped both handles, and yanked the drawer right out of the dresser. Carefully sliding it along the carpet beside her, she reached into the shallow cavity left between where the base of the drawer would have sat, and the carpet beneath it. Her eyes widened as she felt something. Pulling it out, she saw that it was a small sketchbook. Jane hesitated for a moment, torn between needing to see what was inside and betraying her mother's privacy when she clearly hadn't intended anyone to see it. Taking a deep breath, Jane lifted the cover, letting it fall open. She frowned as a blank page stared back at her, but as she turned it over, Jane found herself staring at a pair of hideously terrifying green eyes, rimmed in red.

Bloody hell, Mum...

Page after page, in one variation or another, her mother had drawn these eyes. The thought of her mother sitting there, scratching away with those dark, angry lines of charcoal, perfecting the eerie shade of green, sent a shiver along her spine. Jane wondered what had possessed her mother to draw them in the first place. Closing the book, she slipped it back into the recess and replaced the drawer, deciding to keep it to herself for now. Admittedly, she was no detective, but she couldn't see how a series of tortured drawings would aid in her mother's search. Jane sat there, looking over her shoulder and out the enormous glass window as dawn broke across the sky, feeling lost and alone for the first time in her life.

"Thank you for your patience, Miss... uh," Roberts paused, frowning as he realised he hadn't made a note of her surname.

"Piccani. But please, call me Lilly."

Roberts gave her a small nod, barely acknowledging her as he strode into the interview room for a second time and took a seat.

"I'm Detective Rupert Roberts, and I was working with your, uh, with Wendy prior to her disappearance. Her daughter, Jane, said you were already at Wendy's home when she called you. Do you live there?"

Lilly shook her head. "I was spending the night when Wendy received the call from you to say you had to return to the hospital."

Roberts made a small note on his pad as he tried to unclench his jaw. He felt ridiculous, but he'd been overwhelmed by jealousy from the minute he stepped foot in the room. It made no sense to him whatsoever, and if anything, it angered him. Forcing himself to look up, he found Lilly's chocolate brown, almond-shaped eyes staring at him, a slight frown on her brow. "You look exhausted, detective," she stated.

Roberts raised his eyebrows. "Well, it's been a long twenty-four hours or more..." He quickly took in her olive skin, her long dark hair that fell in effortless waves over her shoulders, and her high, exotic cheekbones and lowered his gaze back to his notepad as he suddenly felt inadequate for the first time in his adult life. Clearing his throat, he forced himself to focus on the task at hand. "Was there anything about Wendy or her behaviour prior to my call that seemed off? Even slightly?"

"Well, the whole box thing certainly was different, but aside from that, Wendy seemed fine—happy to be back in her own home. I cooked dinner for the three of us, and we hung out in the kitchen, talking and drinking wine."

"Then what?"

"Then we went to bed. Admittedly, not straight to sleep," Lilly stated with a hint of a smile. Roberts frowned, keeping his stare focused on his notepad as he shifted in his seat.

"What's this box you mentioned?"

When Lilly didn't answer right away, Roberts looked up to find her staring at him, wide-eyed.

"Uh, Jane didn't mention that?"

"No, she didn't." Roberts sat forward, waiting for her to continue.

"Shit. I'm sure it just escaped her mind. Obviously she's in shock with Wendy missing…"

"I don't need you to make an excuse for her," Roberts stated softly, but firmly. "However, I do need you to tell me about his box."

He jotted down notes rapidly as Lilly spoke of the contents of the box, his frown deepening the more she went on.

"And Wendy absolutely had no prior knowledge of this mysterious aunt?" he finally asked.

"No, I mean, how could she?"

"I'd like to see the contents of this box myself if you or Jane would mind bringing it into the station."

"Sure, I guess. But what could it possibly have to do with Wendy disappearing?"

"Lilly, it seems all too much of a coincidence that this new genealogical evidence becomes apparent the same night she goes missing. It could be nothing at all, but I don't plan on leaving any stone unturned until Wendy is found."

Lilly gave a nod. "I appreciate that detective, as I'm sure we all do."

"Is there anything else you can think of?"

Lilly was quiet, and Roberts waited patiently as she went over her own thoughts.

"She was a little on edge about something Nanna had said to her. I don't know what it was exactly, but Wendy was given a locket and told never to open it and never take it off. When I tried to prompt her further, she just said she didn't want to talk about it."

Frowning, Roberts tried to recall if Wendy had been wearing a locket in the car or at the hospital. He felt himself flush a little as he recalled looking at the graceful curve of her neck, at the shallow indentation between the base of her neck and her collarbone; he fought to block out the thoughts he had. He cleared his throat again. "I don't recall seeing any jewellery on Wendy. Is it possible she ignored Nanna's warning and took it off?"

"No. She'd said Nanna was very specific about… "

"What is it?"

"Shit. Wendy had a soak in the bath before bed. She probably took it off so that it didn't get wet."

"I'd like you to see if you can find it and bring it in as well."

Lilly nodded.

"Is there anything else you'd like to add?" Roberts asked. Lilly shook her head. He rose from his chair and saw her out of the room. He gestured to the nearest officer to escort her out of the station before re-entering the interview room and closing the door behind him. Spreading his notes out before him, he drew a question mark next to Jane's name. He honestly didn't think she had anything to do with her mother's disappearance, but he was concerned that she had withheld the information about the box. Given the nature of the discovery, he doubted it would slip her mind, despite the shock of her mother vanishing. As he scrawled further notes, his writing became faint as the ink ran out of his pen. With an inward groan, Roberts let it fall to the table and patted the pockets of his pants, hoping he wouldn't have to leave the room to get another pen. When he found nothing, he reached into the inner pockets of his jacket. Retrieving his small notepad, he saw a small piece of paper fall to the ground. He quickly swooped down to pick it up, unfolding it deftly. His heart started pounding in his chest as he read the words scrawled across the page, with Wendy's name in large print at the bottom like she wanted to ensure there would be no doubt as to who wrote it. With his mouth agape, he tried to process the words—tried to wrap his head around how the notes ended up in his pocket in the first place. There'd been no indication Wendy had been anywhere near him in the security footage. The only thing he was certain of was that Wendy had written it—and she needed his help.

Wendy's throat felt like it was nothing but sandpaper as she tried to swallow. There was some liquid left in the cup she'd drunk from earlier, but there was no way she was touching it—she was old enough now to recognise it didn't contain just water. Against her will, her eyes refused to be drawn from it as her body's longing for hydration took over. Wendy found herself reaching for the cup, but at the last minute, she reached out and shoved it away, sending it clattering across the concrete, it's precious liquid spreading out in a dark, ominous puddle. She watched as the cup rolled away, coming to a stop at the corner to the entryway to the bathroom. Wendy's eyes widened; her eyebrows raised as she mentally chastised herself for not thinking of it sooner. Staggering to her feet, she stumbled towards the bathroom, semi-acknowledging the way the hovering candle followed her like a loyal pet. She bent down, grasping the doorway to keep herself from toppling over, and picked up the cup. As she slowly stood, she inspected the cup for the first time. Wendy hadn't realised until now that it was wooden and well-aged from what she could make out in the candlelight. There were markings around it, which she couldn't quite decipher. Wendy tried to move closer to the candle to get a better look, but as she moved, so too did the candle. Groaning in frustration, she decided to let it go for the moment and walked into the bathroom. Turning on the single tap over the basin, Wendy felt her heart sink as nothing happened. Her throat seemed to tighten in disappointment, the constriction making her feel as though she couldn't breathe. Just as she was about to give up, the pipes banged and groaned, and water erupted in small bursts from the tap before the flow evened out. Forgetting the cup in her hand, Wendy leaned down, trying to get her mouth close to the faucet. When that didn't work, she cupped her free hand under the water, using it to gather the water, which she lapped up as quickly as it pooled. Once she'd had her fill, Wendy pulled back and held the cup under the tap until it was full. Turning the tap off, she left the bathroom, finding herself steadier on her feet after the huge drink.

She yelped, dropping the cup to the floor and sending a splash of water over her feet and up her legs.

"Oh, my dear. I'm so sorry. I didn't mean to startle you," Smee said as he smiled from where he stood in the centre of the room, holding another tray in his hands.

"You drugged me," she accused, glaring at the little man, finding it difficult to be cross when he was so overly cheerful.

"I've brought you some soup," Smee continued as though she hadn't spoken. "I made it, and if I do say so myself, it's rather delicious." When Wendy made no move to take the tray, Smee waddled over to the bed and put the tray down carefully. She watched on with a frown, confused by his continued ramblings as he avoided her gaze.

"Oh, my!" Smee stated as he stood up and looked her squarely in the eyes. "I seem to have dripped soup all the way to your room. I don't know how I managed that."

Wendy's confusion deepened as Smee stood there watching her.

"I hope I haven't spilled it all the way from the kitchen!" His voice remained comically upbeat, and Wendy's brows unstitched from their frown, raising in surprise as she determined Smee's error wasn't an accident. "Eat your soup while it's hot," he stated, and with a quick bow, Smee turned and hurried from the room, leaving Wendy gaping into the shadows after him.

Making her way over to where Smee had stood by the bed, she looked down at the bowl of soup on its tray before letting her gaze fall to the floor. She felt her heart skip as she saw there was, in fact, large drops of soup leading away from the bed and into the shadows beyond the reach of the candlelight. She took a moment to consider if it was some kind of trap, but upon the realisation that she didn't care either way, she carefully followed the trail. A slight smirk fluttered across her face at the irony; it was Pan's slowly diminishing candle that enabled her to see at all.

Wendy followed the drops, but they only led her to the cement edge of the room. Leaning her head against the coolness of the wall, she felt too exhausted to cry as she pondered Smee's cruel joke.

This doesn't make any sense. Pan's the only cruel one. Smee wouldn't set me up...

Lifting her head, Wendy scanned the wall for any signs of a crack or indication of an exit and found nothing. Her foot brushed against something on the floor, and as she looked down, she noticed the prongs of a broken fork lying on the ground at her feet. She bent to pick it up. As she gripped it, she found it wasn't broken but that the remaining section was concealed by the wall, as though it'd been hidden within it somehow. Wendy placed her palm against the wall, running her hand slowly over it and scowled when she only felt the solid concrete beneath her palms. With a yell, she bunched her hand into a fist and banged it against the wall. Her hand moved through the concrete, and Wendy yanked it back against her chest in surprise, rubbing her knuckles, as though ensuring her hand was still intact.

What kind of Harry Potter magic is this?

Wendy placed both her hands against the wall and raised her right leg slightly, her toes pushing against the cement. She gave a gentle push and was met with slight resistance. Leaning into the wall with a little more force, Wendy felt the wall give and squeezing her eyes shut in anticipation, she went through, almost falling over in the process. The first thing she noticed was the cool air sweeping over her, and she opened her eyes to find she was standing in a narrow corridor. She looked over her shoulder and saw only the concrete — no door. The only indication that there was anything on the other side of the wall was the number 1, which sat against the wall, twenty centimetres or so from the ceiling.

NEVER, NEVER

Wendy realised the candle had stayed behind, and she feared that the separation might somehow trigger Pan's attention. She knew she had to hurry. Pressing her back to the wall, she felt exposed in the openness of the corridor, which was lit with a cool, blue light. Yet as Wendy scanned the walls and ceiling, she couldn't see any light fixtures. She looked to the left, then her right, unsure of which way to go until she remembered herself and looked to her feet. Almost dry now, she had to crouch down to see any trace of Smee's soup trail. Faintly, she could see it trailing off to her left. Wendy frantically scurried down the hall for what felt like ages, all the while concerned about her precarious position should she run into someone—that someone being Pan. There seemed to be nothing but endless walls, and she began to panic at her inability to detect any sign of escape. The corridor had started to arc, and Wendy feared she was walking in a giant circle and would end up exactly where she started.

As Wendy followed the corridor around a bend, she stopped dead in her tracks. Her hand flew to her mouth to silence the panicked yelp that escaped her. The opposite wall was set up like a maniacal shrine, covered with photos of her. With slow steps, she reached out to touch the images, her mouth agape. She shook her head, unable to make sense of them. The fact they were all of her was scary enough—but in every single one of them, she was asleep.

How? When? I thought he couldn't find me.

She clutched at her chest as she felt herself hyperventilate, thinking of all the times she'd woken from her nightmares, fearful she was being watched. She wondered how many hours she'd spent in the middle of the night trying to convince herself that she imagined it, that the tingling that ran up and down her spine *wasn't* a warning that he was there in the shadows, watching her. Forcing herself to face the evidence of Pan's obsession, she inspected every single image before her. Wendy was oblivious to the tears that streamed down her face as she moved from one photo to the other. In one, she wasn't long since home after her abduction, a teenage girl grabbing her pillow fiercely in her sleep, her bedside lamp on to keep the shadows at bay. There she was through her late teens with blonde hair, black hair, blue hair, short hair, long hair. The worst was to come as she saw images of her sleeping, her pregnant belly evident beneath the sheets. Her hands trembled as she raised them to her face, clamping her head tightly as though she could somehow evict the images out of her mind.

He knows.

Wendy felt the terror seep through her entire body, and she started to shiver as though her blood had slowly turned to ice.

Jane. Oh my god, please let my daughter be safe.

She didn't waste another second as she darted off down the corridor, knowing she had to find a way out of there. Now. With every step came a soundless plea: to Lilly, to her brothers, to Roberts - keep her daughter safe. Yet with every step she took, she couldn't shake the sinking feeling that she was already too late.

CHAPTER TWENTY-ONE

Roberts fixed himself a fresh cup of coffee in the largest mug he could find in the station's tearoom. He yawned, feeling the strange but not uncommon sensation of feeling both extremely wired and fatigued right through to his bones. Twice, the chief had attempted to persuade him to go home and grab a shower, even get a few hours of sleep, but he seemed to have given up. Roberts was determined to keep working the case until they brought Darling safely home. He didn't allow himself to consider that it would take time to find her or that they wouldn't find her at all. In his mind, those scenarios just weren't an option.

"Detective?"

He turned to find one of the officers peeking their head into the tearoom. "Detective Darling's brothers are here. I put Michael in interview room one and John in interview room two."

"Thanks. I'll be right there." He gave the officer a tired smile—or at least, he thought he smiled but couldn't be sure. He finished making his coffee, holding it in one hand as he meticulously wiped the counter, then stifled a yawn as he left the tearoom and wove his way through the bustling station towards interview room one. He paused for a moment at the door, mentally preparing himself for what he expected to be a complete barrage of abuse from his partner's brothers. Honestly, he was looking forward to it—he felt it was the least he deserved. Roberts gripped the doorknob tightly, hoping he was conveying competence rather than just fatigue as he stepped purposefully into the room.

"Mr. Darling, thank you for coming in. I hope it wasn't too long a trip for you."

"Traffic into town is fairly cooperative at this time of the evening. And please, call me John."

Roberts nodded and took his seat on the other side of the table, placing his cup of coffee on the table. John's eyes flickered quickly towards it.

"Can I get you a coffee? Something else to drink?"

John held up his hand. "I'm fine. Thank you. It just smells like a strong cup of coffee."

"That it is," Roberts stated, distracted by his urge to rub his tired eyes.

"So, how can I help you, Detective?" John asked, his relaxed and friendly disposition causing Roberts to stare at him with a mixture of surprise and suspicion.

"Well, as you are aware, your sister is missing…"

"Yes, my niece Jane called us earlier. Obviously, we're concerned…"

"Really? You seem fairly relaxed to me. Especially given this isn't the first time this has happened, is it?"

"And as you recall, Wendy came back to us then. I have full faith she will come home to us again this time."

Roberts leaned back in his seat, staring at the man in front of him. There were only a few times he'd been surprised during his career, but this was certainly ranking.

"So let me get this straight," he started, tapping his forefinger on the table edge. "Your sister, who was abducted as a teen and was missing for a number of months before she showed up pregnant, has once again gone missing—only this time she appears to have disappeared into thin air—and you're content with 'having faith' that she'll just show up in good time?"

John took a moment, pushing his black-rimmed, rectangular glasses further up his nose. "How exactly did she vanish into thin air?" he asked, ignoring the rest of Roberts' question.

"Well, if we knew that, then we would be all the closer to finding her, wouldn't we?" Roberts could hear the annoyance in his voice, his ability to remain neutral significantly diminished by his fatigue. However, he was fairly certain he'd still be pissed off by John's attitude regardless. "One minute, she was at the hospital with a victim, and the next, she was gone. Yet, what I'm finding equally as disturbing is the fact that none of what's happened seems to come as a surprise to you. That leads me to believe that perhaps you had something to do with it, or at the very least, know far more than you're letting on."

"Are you saying I should call my lawyer?"

"I'm saying you should bloody tell me what the hell is going on!" Roberts banged his fist on the table, not caring that he was losing his cool.

John cleared his throat and leaned forward on his arms. "Isn't that your job, Detective?"

Roberts stared at him, his eyes narrowed in equal parts anger and surprise. Without a word, he grabbed his things and stood up with such force he sent his chair stumbling backwards. He left the room without another glance, closing the door behind him with a slam. Taking a moment to compose himself as he leaned against the wall, he shook his head.

What the fuck is going on?

An image of Darling came to mind, of the little side smirk she did when he'd said something that had amused her, but she didn't want to give him the satisfaction of knowing it. The thought of her caused a sense of calm to fall over him, pushing the anger aside. He rubbed his chest with the heel of his palm to ease the unfamiliar pang that radiated from within. Roberts didn't know if it was her aloofness or the way she rolled her eyes at him one second and stole a sideways glance at him the next, but he knew he'd never met anyone like her. Nor had he ever felt so captivated by someone. If she'd stood there beside him, he would have ignored the thoughts and feelings that flooded him whenever she was near and tell himself it was ridiculous. They'd only just met. In fact, he was well aware he'd likely distract himself with a harmless flirt with one of the numerous officers that seemed to gravitate to him as he walked through the station.

But she's not here, is she...

Roberts groaned loudly, causing a couple of officers to look at him in alarm from the other end of the hall. He gave them a quick nod and pushed himself off the wall before walking to the second interview room.

You're going to find her. There's no other option.

As he opened the door, he decided on the spot he'd try a different tactic with Darling's other brother in the hopes it'd prove more fruitful.

"Mr. Darling, I'm Detective Roberts. Thank you for coming in on such short notice." He strode over to the table, identical to the one he'd just sat at and sat down.

"Not at all. Anything we can do to help—and you can call me Michael."

"That's good to know. I'd like to start with the box of keepsakes your sister had at her house."

"Keepsakes? Mum's? I hadn't realised she'd taken anything with her yet."

"I believe the box was found in your mother's room, but it seems as though it actually belonged to your father."

"Okay..." Michael said slowly, lifting his hands and clasping them together as he rested them on the table in front of him. "I'm not sure what this has to do with my sister's disappearance?"

"That's what I'm here to find out. Were you aware your father had a younger sister?" Roberts stated bluntly, waiting to gauge Michael's reaction.

"What? No, he didn't. He was an only child."

"Apparently not. Jane found the box at the manor with Wendy's name written on it and took it back to her mum's house, unaware of the contents. When they opened the box, they found it filled with the belongings of what appeared to be your aunt."

Michael remained silent, slowly shaking his head, his mouth open. Roberts continued, "What I find particularly interesting is the belongings only appear to date up until she was in her mid-teens." He watched intently as a frown darkened Michael's brow.

"Why? What happened?"

"I'm still looking into the details, but I assure you it's no coincidence that your sister wasn't the first female in your family to go missing as a teen."

Michael's mouth opened, closed, and opened again. "But Wendy came back. I don't understand..."

"So, you're saying you had no knowledge of this family history?"

Michael shook his head, opening his mouth again before quickly closing it, but not before Roberts saw his reaction. "Now's not the time to withhold anything. Your sister's missing again, Michael, and I'm beginning to think there is a hell of a lot more going on here that you and your brother aren't telling me."

Michael slowly unclasped his hands and stretched them out before him. "You should probably speak to John..."

"See, that's the thing," Roberts interjected. "I have spoken to your brother, and he was less than forthcoming. In fact, I would even go so far as to say he was hostile—and even more interesting; he didn't appear in the least bit surprised by your sister's disappearance."

"Hostile? No, that doesn't sound..."

"Someone else might think you and your brother don't want your sister found."

"Now, that's ridiculous!" Michael exclaimed, and Roberts almost felt relieved by the emotional display.

"Is it? Then why can't I get a straight answer out of either of you? Regardless of whether you knew about your aunt or not, both you and your brother are holding back, and while you insist on doing so, the chances of finding Wendy start slipping away."

Michael lowered his head, once again clasping his hands. Roberts said nothing, allowing the silence to hang heavily between them. Finally, Michael lifted his head. "Look, the news of an aunt comes as a surprise, and I want to see the proof myself before I accept that, but as far as my sister is concerned, you're right in thinking her disappearance hasn't come as a surprise. At least, not exactly."

Roberts leaned forward, hoping Michael would continue. Michael flicked a quick look towards the closed door, as though hoping to see his brother standing there and turned back to Roberts. "I'm assuming you heard Nanna passed away earlier."

Roberts nodded.

Michael sighed. "It's going to sound ridiculous, saying it aloud…" he looked up briefly, but Roberts just gave him a nod.

"As you probably know already, Nanna isn't our blood relation. Instead, she was my father's nanny when he was a child. Over time she just became part of the family and became our nanny when we were little. Well, when Wendy was abducted, obviously John and I were terrified. I had nightmares about monsters climbing through the bedroom window and dragging me out into the night by the ankles, kicking and screaming. Nanna would calm my brother and me with stories. Almost like fairytales she'd created just for us. At least, that's how I've always thought of them. I was only a young boy when Wendy was abducted, and it was during the period of her disappearance that Nanna's stories started, but they continued even after Wendy returned. To my knowledge, she only ever told them to John and me— probably because we were younger, or she thought she was helping us make sense of what happened to our sister. Who knows. As we got older, she still insisted on ensuring we hadn't forgotten the stories, and John and I humoured her—but they were just stories after all. Even once Nanna's mind started to go, she'd have moments of panicked lucidity where she'd want us to recite the story to her, to prove we still remembered." He paused, looking up at the detective, but Roberts wasn't going to interrupt him with questions now.

Michael repeated the story from his childhood, about the youth who never aged and his magical land. As the words swept over him, Roberts found himself overcome with fatigue. At the same time, the tension and anxiety he'd carried from the moment Wendy disappeared slipped away, and he felt himself relaxing. Opening his mouth to interrupt, Roberts quickly forgot what he was going to say and closed it again as his heavy eyelids drooped closed. Without realising what he was doing, he folded his arms on the table and rested his head upon them, the sound of Michael's voice encapsulating him in a haze.

A loud bang on the table caused Roberts to start, and he sat upright, looking around him in wide-eyed disorientation. His eyes fell on a uniformed officer standing before him, a concerned frown on her face. Roberts blinked rapidly as he both tried to shake off the fog and recall the officer's name.

"Detective Roberts, are you okay? Can I get you a coffee or something?"

"Uh, yes, that would be appreciated. Thank you, Sargent."

The officer nodded and turned to leave the room. "And Sargent?"

She paused, looking back over her shoulder.

"Let's keep this between the two of us, right?"

"Of course, Detective."

"Thank you. I'll be at my desk." He made a show of gathering his folders while he waited for her to leave the room. Once he was alone, he leaned back in his chair, clasping his hands behind his head.

What the fuck was that?

He didn't need to search the station to know the brothers had left. He deliberated, sending a couple of officers out to pick them up but questioned to what end. Roberts didn't think either brother had anything to do with Wendy's abduction per se, but there sure as hell was a lot more to the Darling family than they let on. Lowering his arms, he glanced at the watch on his wrist, groaning as he realised he'd been out for at least an hour. Roberts stood up, unable to resist the urge to stretch after his mystical nap and found himself drawn to a piece of paper sticking out of the folder before him at an odd angle. Flicking the folder open, he saw an elegant handwritten note on the reverse side of one of the forms, and he picked it up as he read it.

"We appreciate your dedication to our sister's disappearance. I didn't want to wake you when you're clearly exhausted. Please know my brother, and I are at your disposal."

Roberts swore as he shoved the papers off the table and across the room. He huffed, leaning on his fists as he tried to think beyond his anger. He needed more information before he approached the brothers again, that much was clear, and he decided he wanted to inspect the contents of Wendy's mysterious box for himself. Fishing his phone out of his pocket, he gathered up the papers from the floor and dumped them on the desk, searching for where he'd written the contact details for Jane.

Roberts pulled his car alongside the curb and turned off the engine. As he got out of the car, he took a moment, staring up at the front door to Wendy's home. It felt surreal. It was now daylight, causing it to feel like much longer than the few hours it had been since he was in this very spot, picking Wendy up to take her to the hospital. Thinking of his partner renewed his resolve, he closed the car door before striding up onto the footpath and up the stairs to the front door. He raised his hand to knock, but the door opened before he had the chance.

"Detective. Please, come in." Jane stood aside to let him in, and Roberts noted her red-rimmed eyes, amplified by the dark bags beneath them, but said nothing. He waited for her to close the door before wordlessly following her across the lounge room and into the kitchen, where a cardboard box sat on the island bench in the middle of the room.

"Good morning."

Roberts started as Lilly suddenly appeared beside him. He stammered a quick hello that came off gruffer than he'd intended, but her presence riled a jealousy in him like he'd never experienced. As Lilly gestured for him to join them at the bench, he noted her puffy eyes, still red from crying—yet it didn't diminish her exotic beauty, which only pissed him off.

"Are you alright, detective?" Jane asked, peering at him as she walked around to the other side of the bench. He cleared his throat.

"Yes, of course. Though could I trouble you for some coffee?"

Jane nodded and turned to the coffee machine that sat beside her on the kitchen bench.

Roberts stepped up to the box and peered inside, acutely aware of Lilly's stare. He told himself the accusation he felt under her gaze was merely transference, but it did little to calm him.

Focus, you bloody idiot.

Roberts concentrated on pulling out everything from the box and spreading the items out across the bench. "Okay. So this boy here, this is Wendy's father—your grandfather, Jane?" he asked, his finger pointing to a photograph.

"Yes, that's what Mum said. Plus, his name is on the back."

Roberts picked it up and turned it over. "So, this girl beside him is his sister, yet your mother had no knowledge of her?"

Jane nodded, placing a steaming cup of coffee on a small free space of bench. "None of us did."

"Is there a chance that she knew more than she let on?"

"No way," Lilly interjected. "Wendy was genuinely shocked and upset by all this stuff. Wouldn't you be if you found out you'd been lied to your whole life?"

Roberts remained silent as he studied each item: the keepsakes and memories that made up the short life of the Darling child. "Do you mind if I photograph some of these? I want to look into it a bit further."

"Of course," Jane said. "But it can't possibly be connected to what's happened to Mum, can it?"

"At this stage, I'm not counting anything out. Besides, there's just too much going on here for it to be mere coincidence." He pulled his phone out and opened the camera, carefully lining up shots and checking them for clarity before taking the next one.

"Is there anything else you can think of that might help?" he asked, as he reached over and picked up the coffee mug, enjoying the scalding sensation as the liquid ran down his throat.

"Uh..." Jane started, looking sideways as Lilly looked at her in surprise. "One sec."

Jane jogged out of the kitchen. Roberts and Lilly stared after her as they listened to her head up the stairs.

"Do you really think any of this will help you find her?" Lilly asked softly, fingering the edge of one of the photographs.

"Honestly, I'm not ruling anything out—but at the moment, I seem to be accruing questions faster than I can answer any of them." He flicked a discrete glance

301

in her direction in time to see her wipe a tear from the corner of her eye.

"Did she ever talk to you about what happened to her?"

Lilly lowered her hand and looked at him squarely. The sadness in her eyes caused him to shift his footing—it made him feel like a prick for feeling jealous.

"A little. I mean, it's no secret she was abducted. But she's never gone into any great detail."

"Do you think it's because she doesn't remember much?"

Lilly scrunched her face up as though trying to decide either way. "I used to think so, but as I got to know her better, I realised she's still haunted by it... I mean, who wouldn't be?"

"What makes you say that?"

"She's a terrible insomniac. Like a high-functioning insomniac. Is that a thing?" Roberts opened his mouth to answer, but Lilly rambled on before he had the chance. "When she does manage to sleep, it usually results in nightmares. I used to try and talk to her about them, you know. I thought it might help if she brought them out into the light of day. It was like trying to squeeze blood out of a stone. She'd pretend like she couldn't recall them, but I could tell from the look in her eyes that she did. It was like she was trying to protect me or something. So, I stopped asking about them. I let her know I'm here, and then I leave her to her thoughts. It's a huge part of her that I'll never know about."

Roberts let a silence fall between them, tapping his fingers on the bench as he looked at the display before him. "What about her family? Did they ever mention it or maybe pull you aside at any stage?"

"No, never. The Darlings are a lovely family—very close-knit—but they keep everything close to their chests. I guess I still haven't broken through their circle of trust or something. If Wendy had never told me what happened to her all those years ago, I'd never suspect they'd undergone something that traumatic. Honestly, if you didn't know it had happened, you'd never guess by the way they are when they're together."

They were interrupted as Jane rushed back into the kitchen and held out a small book towards Roberts.

"What's that?" Lilly asked, peering over at it.

"I found it in Mum's room when I was... well, looking for clues, I guess."

Roberts took it from her and stared at the nondescript cover, frowning at the thought he'd just been handed his partner's personal journal, but when he opened it up, he was confronted by horrific drawings.

"Your mother drew these?" he asked quietly, flicking from one page to the next.

"I'm assuming so," Jane replied, keeping her gaze averted, but Lilly approached.

"Can I see?"

Roberts held up the current page, displaying a horrific sketch across both pages—large green eyes rimmed in red, bulbous and fierce with such an intensity that they almost seemed aware. Below the eyes was a mouth opened wide in a silent scream, the rest of its form made up of dark shadows of angry strokes of charcoal. Lilly said nothing as her mouth fell open, and Roberts took that as his cue to close it.

"Do either of you mind if I take all this back to the station as part of the investigation?"

Lilly looked to Jane for approval. "We'll get it back, won't we? I'd like to learn more," Jane said as she started to pack the items back into the box.

"You and me both," Roberts replied.

CHAPTER TWENTY-TWO

Wendy picked up the pace, focusing on putting one foot in front of the other as she stumbled rapidly along the curved corridor, trying to find a way out. She didn't know how far she'd gone before she finally registered the low, mechanical hum echoing off the walls, and Wendy slowed her pace, straining her ears, curious as to its cause. As she kept walking, the curve of the wall seemed more apparent, and after a few more metres, Wendy found herself in front of a floor-to-ceiling window along the inner wall of the corridor. There was little visibility, as the glass seemed to be covered in fog from within the room. Raising her hands, she pressed them against the glass and was surprised to find it felt as cold as ice. Cupping her hands against it, she tried to peer in. She blinked a couple of times, as though that would somehow clear the fog so she could see. When that didn't work, she stared impatiently, hoping her eyes would adjust enough that she would be able to make out what was on the other side of the glass. Slowly, her eyes started deciphering the scene before her, but her mind couldn't. As her mouth fell open, Wendy struggled to comprehend what she was seeing. She pushed herself away from the glass, overwhelmed with the nauseating sensation that she was going to be sick. Turning her back to the glass, she braced herself against her knees and took deep breaths, willing the sensation to pass. She began to pace with her hands clasped behind her head. Her eyes were firmly closed. Wendy wished she could wipe the vision from her mind. It was etched there, like the afterglow of a flash or having looked too closely towards the sun.

With a shaky breath, she forced herself to step up to the window and peer through the fog once more. Suspended from the ceiling, equally spaced, hung young boys. A quick count came to at least twenty, but she couldn't see far enough into the fog to count any further. The longer she stared, Wendy realised she was looking at the children she'd watched playing in Pan's Neverland—and in her nightmares. Her hands started to shake uncontrollably, and she wiped away the tears that threatened.

Is this a punishment for denying him? For escaping in the first place?

Wendy forced the thoughts from her mind and instead focused on trying to extract as much information as she could. She had enough visibility to see the faces of the boys closest to her were a deathly hue of blue-grey, further offset by blue lips. They looked dead, and she said a quick prayer to herself and hoped that wasn't the case. It saddened her deeply to see how peaceful they looked—like they were sleeping, despite the horror of their surroundings. Forcing herself to absorb the details, she noted the boys were suspended by a metal brace that cinched around their chests, allowing the rest of their bodies to dangle freely with their heads lulled to one side. Their arms hung limply, and each boy had an IV from his left arm filled with a vibrant green concoction.

Okay... so that must mean they're still alive.

Wendy felt as though a fuse lit within her, and her energy was renewed as she frantically ran her hands over the glass, trying to find a way in. She scurried to her right until the glass pane ended and the wall began, but there was no way in. She ran to the other end, but it was the same. Swearing under her breath, she ran back to the centre of the glass pane and placed her hands firmly against it. Squeezing her hands shut, she pushed, willing herself to transport through it like the exit to her own cell. When nothing happened, she swore aloud and banged her fist against the glass.

A ticking sound wafted along the corridor towards her, and Wendy turned her head as her mouth fell open. Each rapid breath caught in her throat, making her feel as though she was going to gag. The ticking quickened, but what frightened her more was the sound of a long dragging and scraping.

Drag. Pause. Scrape. Pause. Drag.

Wendy knew the crocodile was approaching, and that she couldn't be there when its evil snout came around the bend.

"I promise I'll come back," she whispered to the boys before she turned and fled back to her room.

Roberts stood before the new lot of evidence boards he'd set up. They were laden with items from Wendy's family box. He'd received both curious and confused looks from officers as they came and went, but his gut was telling him it was all connected. He just had to work out how.

It astounded him that there was nothing in any of the police or government databases about another Darling child—as a last resort, he'd even tried Google, but again, nothing showed up. Yet the girl obviously had existed—he had the photographs before him to prove it. Grabbing a marker, he stepped up to a blank space on the board and wrote the names of those Jane had confirmed were present in the photographs—Mr. and Mrs. Darling, their son, the woman Jane called Nanna, and the mysterious sibling. Roberts had done his best to try and arrange everything in chronological order. With an educated guess, he determined the line stopped when their daughter was approximately fifteen years of age.

What happened to you? Where did you go?

He drew two lines under her name and wrote 'abducted?' before writing the same under Wendy's name. There was no way his mind would let him try and explain away the similarities between the two girls as coincidence. Never had he ever encountered repeated generational abductions.

The family must have been involved somehow. But why? Why was Dawn never seen again but Wendy was? Was Wendy just lucky that she was able to escape and Dawn couldn't? Or was it more a case of Dawn was murdered not long after her abduction, but there was something the perp saw in Wendy that made him want to keep her alive?

He massaged his temples, frustrated by his ever-increasing list of questions and total lack of answers. A knock on the open door pulled him from his thoughts. He looked up to see an officer standing there. "Sir, you asked to be notified once Rosalie Fryair was discharged."

"Yes. Thank you."

The officer's gaze flickered across the new boards.

"Was there anything else?" he asked. The officer lowered his gaze.

"No, that's all, Sir."

Roberts gave him a nod of dismissal, and the officer turned and walked away. Roberts took one last look at the boards before conceding. Maybe stepping away for a while might help him see more clearly. He picked up his half-cold cup of coffee and raised it to his lips before lowering it back to the table. Roberts already felt on edge, unable to shake the fear that he was running out of time. He didn't think caffeine was going to help him any. Picking up his jacket, he left the evidence room. It was time to pay another visit to Rosalie Fryair.

Roberts knocked on the door of the Fryair's residence and wasn't surprised to find Malcolm Fryair was less than enthused by his unannounced visitor.

"Look, Detective. I appreciate you have a case to work on, but my daughter just got home and needs her rest.

"I appreciate that, Mayor, but time is of the essence, and I really need to have a quick word with Rosalie."

Malcolm Fryair straightened his shoulders and lifted his chin. "I'm sure you're aware all I need to do is make one call to the commissioner…"

"And I'm sure you're aware," Roberts cut in, "we can either do this here or at the station. It's your choice."

Roberts stood patiently, refusing to divert his gaze or shift his stance as he watched an angry vein pulsate across the Mayor's forehead. Finally, he pushed the door open the rest of the way and stood aside. "Make it quick," he threatened as Roberts stepped past him into the foyer.

"Hi, Detective!" Jessica said with a goofy smile as she walked out of the kitchen carrying two plates with enormous slices of cake.

"Hello, Jessica. How are you today?"

"Same, same," she replied as she walked into the living room.

"Oh! Hello, Detective! I didn't know we were expecting you," called Anne Fryair as she stepped through the archway of the kitchen, wiping her hands on her apron.

"I know it was a last-minute thing." He gave her a smile and a little wave.

"Rosalie's in the living room. I'll bring you a coffee and some cake."

"That would be lovely, thank you," he replied, but Anne had already retreated back into the kitchen. Roberts walked up the hallway, feeling Malcolm's stare boring into the back of his head. He was relieved for the reprieve as he walked into the living room. Rosalie was settled in a huge recliner, her feet up and a blanket draped over her lap. The cake her sister had delivered sat in front of her, but she didn't appear interested in it. Jessica sat on the couch beside her, legs curled up beneath her as she held her plate in one hand and a fork in the other.

"You can sit next to me, if you like, Detective," Jessica offered, and Roberts did his best to hold back his amusement.

"Thank you, Jessica." He walked over and perched on the edge of the cushion as Anne scurried in and placed a steaming mug of coffee and a plate of cake on the coffee table in front of him.

"Thank you, Anne, that looks amazing." He looked up to find her hovering, waiting for him to taste it. Clearing his throat, he leaned forward and picked up the fork, burying it deep into the cake before pulling off a generous portion and putting it in his mouth. There was no need to feign delight—the cake was sensational. Anne clasped her hands together, beaming from ear to ear before turning to leave as Malcolm appeared in the doorway.

"Oh! Would you like coffee and cake too, love?"

"That would be lovely, dear," he replied without looking at her, his focus fixed intently on Roberts. Roberts washed his mouthful of cake down with the coffee before he turned towards Rosalie.

"How are you feeling, Rosalie? You must be relieved to be home," he said, doing his best to withhold his impatience at wanting to question her.

Rosalie shrugged but said nothing. Roberts flicked a quick look at Jessica. "My sister hasn't really said much since she's been home…"

"Because she's tired, is all. She's had quite the ordeal, which I'm sure we can all agree on," Malcolm piped up from the doorway. Roberts refused to look at him, instead looking back to Rosalie.

"Rosalie, I know this is the last thing you feel like doing, but I really need your help with something important."

Rosalie looked up at him, her eyebrows raised high. "Me?"

Roberts nodded. "That's right. Now I know you said you don't remember anything, but I just wanted to ask you some questions to see what we can gain from them—you might remember something without even realising it."

Rosalie's face fell. "Sure, I guess. But I really don't remember much at all."

"That's okay, just do your best."

Rosalie nodded.

"Alright. Now you may have already been asked some of these questions by my partner, Detective Darling, so just bear with me and answer them as best you can." He waited for Rosalie to nod again before he continued, ever conscious of her father still standing in the doorway.

"Firstly, do you recall how you were found?"

Rosalie poked at her piece of cake with her fork. "No. At least, not really. It kind of seems like a dream."

"That's okay. Just tell me anything that you recall."

"There was fog; I was surrounded by it. That's all I remember. It was like I was moving through clouds, but at the same time, it didn't feel like I was moving. But I must have been, I guess."

Roberts remained silent for a moment before carefully phrasing his next question. "Do you have any recollection of the hospital? How you got there? What happened while you were there?"

Rosalie chewed on her bottom lip as she looked up at the detective. "No. I don't remember getting there. I don't remember anything except waking up in the hospital bed, and you were angry."

Roberts cleared his throat, trying not to twitch under the heat of Malcolm's stare from the doorway. "So you don't remember chatting to my partner, Detective Darling?"

Rosalie shook her head. "I'm sorry, but I have no idea who you're talking about."

Roberts did his best to hide his frustration, but he feared by the tears welling in Rosalie's eyes that he wasn't doing a very good job of it. "It's fine. You're doing fine. You've been through an ordeal. It's not surprising that you can't remember. What about before your... abduction? Was there anything strange in the weeks leading up to it?"

Rosalie shrugged. "I was having trouble sleeping, but that's got nothing to do with anything."

"What was causing the sleeping issues?"

"I…" Her eyes flickered up past Roberts' head to her father, before lowering back to her piece of cake. "I was having weird dreams. Bad dreams. Like, every time I fell asleep. So I just tried to stay awake as much as I could."

"Would you feel comfortable telling me about them?"

"It was just the one dream, over and over. A pair of green eyes, really bright, almost like they were glowing. They were rimmed in red, like blood. They would move towards me in the dark, and it was like someone was talking to me. Even though I don't recall hearing any words, I somehow knew what they were saying. I guess just from the vibe, you know?"

"The vibe?"

"Yeah, like the way it made me feel."

"And how was that?"

"Scared. Powerless. The dreams made me feel like whoever the eyes belonged to, knew who I was. Where I was. It was as though they were trying to convince me to do something, but I didn't want to. But at the same time, I didn't seem to have a choice."

"What did they want you to do?"

"I think that's enough, detective. It was a bad dream, that's all."

Roberts ignored Malcolm and nodded towards Rosalie to continue. "I…I don't know. I just know I didn't want to do it. I wanted them to leave me alone."

"And have you had these dreams since you've been back?"

Rosalie shook her head. "No. They've stopped." She looked up at Roberts and wiped away a stray tear from her cheek. "Do you think those eyes...whoever was behind them...was who took me? Do you think they made me do something horrible?"

"That's it. This is getting ridiculous. It's time to leave, Detective, before I call your superior."

Roberts heard Malcolm stride into the lounge room, and he reluctantly rose to his feet. "You don't need to worry, Rosalie. You're safe now."

He walked around Malcolm, refusing to meet his stare, and walked to the doorway before turning around. "Rosalie, if you do happen to remember anything, you know how to reach me, right?" The girl nodded, and Roberts turned and left the house.

Wendy overestimated the force she required to enter back through the wall into her room and stumbled forward, falling heavily onto her knees. She howled in pain, rolling onto her back and hugging her knees to her chest.

"My dear child, what on earth are you doing?" Smee asked jovially, causing Wendy to yelp in surprise as she pushed herself up off the ground.

"Where the hell did you come from?"

Smee shuffled from one foot to the other, and despite the cheerful smile plastered across his face, his eyes darted around the room. "I came to bring you some more food, but you were gone. Well, you can imagine the thoughts that went through my mind. We're just lucky Pan didn't decide to visit you during your absence. Things would have become quite unpleasant, indeed."

Wendy kept her eyes on him as she carefully stood up, her knees almost buckling beneath her. Smee stood aside as she hobbled over to the bed and sat down. Hearing a clatter, she looked down to see a tray beside her, with a cup of liquid and a plate of food atop it. She ignored it.

"What the hell is that out in the corridor?" she hissed.

"I've made you a lovely lunch. I'm sure you'll be most pleased. It used to be one of your favourites if I recall correctly—though the old noggin isn't what it once was."

Wendy stared at him, her mouth open as he rambled on. "I asked you a question."

He paused and looked directly at her. His grin was wider than ever, but there was a distinct apologetic look in his eyes. "You really should eat up. You need your strength. And don't forget to drink all your juice—it's important to keep hydrated, you know."

"I'm not hungry. Or thirsty. Even if I was, I wouldn't touch that after what happened before."

"Before? I don't know what you're talking about." He hopped from one foot to the other while wringing his hands, and Wendy noted that he looked comical, if it wasn't for the look of sheer terror in his eyes, despite the smile. It dawned on her—and she didn't know why it hadn't sooner—that Smee was just as much a prisoner of Pan as she was. But that didn't mean she was going to let him off the hook.

"You're drugging my food. Why? Is it to keep me here? So I can't escape again?"

Smee looked over each shoulder before shuffling closer to her. "Please, Wendy," he whispered. "You must drink it. I promise no harm will come to you, but you have to trust me."

"No!"

A whimper escaped him as he glanced over his shoulder once again. Wendy almost felt bad for him.

Waddling closer, Smee reached out and placed a hand on her shoulder. "I know you don't have any

315

reason to trust me," his whispered voice rushed at her like he was running out of time. He was in such close proximity that his breath smelled like cotton candy. "But if you drink that, I promise you will get at least some of the answers you seek."

He turned on his heel and scurried back into the shadows, leaving Wendy to frown after him. Smee had said the one thing that would almost certainly ensure she would drink his concoction. Her curiosity always won over, and the thought of getting some answers, something she could use to either escape Pan—or kill him—was hard to pass up. She stared down at the tray beside her, oblivious to anything on it other than the mug. Watching the candlelight reflecting off the surface of the liquid, Wendy battled with what was left of her logical side as it tried to convince her not to drink what was in the mug. Her gaze flickered back towards the shadow and the invisible door. She could see beyond it to all those boys, hanging there, their lives in the balance. Holding her thoughts with them, she grabbed the mug and raised it to her lips. Wendy took a deep breath and sculled the contents before letting the mug fall to the ground. The sound of it smashing against the concrete sounded dramatic as it echoed off the walls.

"Good girl, good girl," Smee's voice floated around her—she was already so dizzy that she couldn't determine from which direction his voice came. It sounded like it came from all around. From the corner of her eye, she could see the bed approaching her head, but she could swear she wasn't moving. The pillow felt soft and welcoming as the side of her head came into contact with it, and as her eyes fluttered shut, she saw three Smee's backing away.

Unable to determine how much time had passed, Wendy tried to open her eyes, but they felt weighed down. There was something, a noise, she couldn't quite put her finger on it, and she rolled on her back.

316

The slight movement made her feel like she was falling through the mattress with no end in sight. A voice broke through her delirium.

"Wendy. Wendy, can you hear me?"

She tried to answer, but it sounded incoherent to her ears.

"All I can do is show you what I know. Hopefully, it will help." Wendy felt a hand grasp hers and squeeze it tightly. The voice continued to whisper, but she could no longer make any sense of the words. She felt the slight tilt to the side of her bed as though someone sat down on the edge. Wendy gasped as her eyes widened, and a flood of images forced their way into the forefront of her mind. A roaring filled her ears, and she wanted to raise her hands up over her ears, but they didn't seem to respond. The roaring intensified, and Wendy realised it was coming from the imagery, and she tried to focus on what she was being shown. It was as though she was looking through someone else's eyes, peering through a narrow gap like she was in hiding. She pressed her face up against the crack, trying to see where the noise was coming from. Pan stormed around on the other side, and instinctively, Wendy wanted to pull away, but she couldn't—it wasn't her memory to pull away from. Instead, she was forced to watch on in horror. Pan was in a furious rage. His eyes bulged larger than she'd ever seen, rimmed in so much red that it ran down his cheeks like he was crying bloody tears. His fingers were lengthened like gnarled claws as he tore at his clothes, seemingly unaware of the long cuts across his skin as his pointed nails ripped across his body. Pan raised his head and let out a roar, unlike anything Wendy had heard before, his head flipping back as his mouth opened wide, revealing the horrific rows of razor-sharp baby teeth.

Wendy's heart pounded so fiercely she could feel it in her throat, threatening to choke her.

"Wendy!" A chill ran along her spine and up the back of her neck as he howled her name.

His head snapped back into focus, and he swung his arms in swirling fury at the wall leaving long, ferocious scratches in his wake.

"Reveal to me your escape!" Pan roared again, and the walls started to shake. Wendy took a step back, trying to find somewhere else to hide. Before she could, the wall crumbled before her, leaving her standing in the midst of a pile of rubble. She stared at Pan's back as he suddenly became still, hoping that there was some way he wouldn't see her. Wendy couldn't breathe as Pan's head slowly turned to the side and looked at her over his shoulder.

"You," he sneered and turned to face her. Wendy took a step to run, but Pan raised his arm, and his hand shot out and grasped her by the throat.

"Betrayed by my own father," he hissed, and Wendy stared at him, confused.

"Why?" His arm shortened with every step of his approach. "Why now? Why her? Did you do this specifically to hurt me?" Pan's voice increased in volume with every step, causing her head to pound, and she felt something warm trickle from her ears.

"Do you have any idea what you've done?" His hands cinched tighter around her throat, and she tried to swallow but couldn't.

"I did what I had to." Wendy felt her mouth move, but the voice wasn't her own.

Pan squeezed tighter, and Wendy started to see sparks of white before her eyes. Just as she thought she would pass out, he released her and backed away, gasping for air. Wendy did the same, thinking the worst was over. Pan raised his head and stared at her with a gaze so full of anger and hatred that Wendy felt like she could quite possibly turn to stone.

"I might not be able to kill you, *Father*, but I can make you pay." He took slow, deliberate steps to the side, his eyes not moving from Wendy's. She frowned slightly, wondering what he was up to, but then she heard the ticking.

"No!" she shouted, trying to move her feet, but she was firmly cemented to her spot.

"Yes..." Pan sneered as the lines of red on his face drew back up into his eyes.

Wendy wanted to put on a brave face, not to show any weakness in front of him, but as the slow scraping sound filled her ears, she was unable to stifle a whimper. The ticking clock ticked faster, and Pan started chuckling as the crocodile's snout protruded from the opposite wall. Its enormous head followed, and Wendy willed her eyes to close, but again she was powerless. Ticking filled her ears, and as the crocodile neared, it raised its head and opened its mouth, revealing its knife-like teeth. The ticking stopped, leaving an eerie silence in its wake as Wendy's head turned away. She held her arm out as though it would somehow stop the inevitable. The ensuing pain was blinding, taking her breath away as the crocodile retreated. She turned slightly, only semi-registering the torn material protruding from its snout, and the trail of blood it left in its wake. Wendy tried to piece together what had just happened—she didn't need to look down to know that her hand was no longer there. Pan's laughter echoed around her, and once the crocodile disappeared, he strode over and looked into Wendy's eyes.

"Consider this your warning, Father. One I won't let you forget." He rammed something sharp into what remained of Wendy's arm, and she gasped, engulfed in a searing, white-hot pain. Her breaths came in short, gasping bursts as Pan reached up and grabbed her by the back of the head, pulling her down so he could whisper in her ear. "We may not be able to kill each other, Father, but betray me again, and rest assured I will find a way. You'd better hope we find her again because I'm going to make your existence a living hell until we do." He planted a hard kiss on Wendy's cheek and released her, turning away and walking through the wall after the crocodile.

At his departure, it was as though the spell was broken. Wendy fell to her knees, oblivious to the chunks of concrete wall digging into her knees. Raising her shaking arm up before her, she saw the gleaming, silver hook that was now embedded where her hand once was. She tried to get to her feet, but the pain was too much. Wendy tumbled sideways, unconscious before her head hit the rubble.

CHAPTER TWENTY-THREE

R oberts rubbed his eyes with the heels of his hands. The insides of his eyelids felt like sandpaper and made his eyes water with the friction. Picking up his phone from where it sat beside him on the table, he checked the time and groaned inwardly—he'd been at it for hours. And for what? The growing number of unanswered questions had started to eat at him, making his insides churn. Wendy may have only been his partner a short while, but she'd had a profound impact on him like no one he'd ever met before. There was chemistry between them. He was sure of it.

You're an idiot. She has a girlfriend.

"How's it going over here?"

Roberts jumped as he heard his boss's voice, and he turned and looked over his shoulder. "It's a shit-show if I'm going to be honest."

If his boss was surprised by the update, he didn't show it. Instead, he grabbed a chair from a neighbouring desk and pulled it up opposite Roberts. "Start from the top."

"It's evident to me that this case is far bigger than Rosalie Fryair. Call me crazy, but I don't think this was about her at all." He paused, trying to gauge his boss's reaction, but his expression was neutral.

"Go on."

Roberts got up from the desk and walked over to the evidence board he'd set up with the items from Wendy's mystery box and pointed to the photo of her father and his sister. "This is Mr. Darling as a boy. This girl beside him is his younger sister, and from what I can gather, she disappeared around the age of fifteen."

His boss shifted in his seat, and Roberts knew he'd piqued his interest. "There's no record of her death in any of the archives; in fact, there's no record of her at all. Not even in the Births and Deaths Registry."

"While that's unusual, that doesn't necessarily mean that she didn't pass away. The Darling family was notoriously private back in the day—they could have kept it quiet."

Roberts shook his head. "No, there's more to it than that. I mean, why go to all the effort of erasing her? According to Jane Darling, neither she nor her mother had any knowledge of the aunt's existence. I think she was abducted."

His boss sat quietly, inspecting Roberts' handiwork while Roberts stood back, trying to contain his impatience.

"Now, I'm not saying I don't agree with you— there is definitely something off about this family. But what evidence is there that she was abducted?"

Roberts scowled. "Honestly, there is no evidence of anything other than the fact that one minute there was a Dawn Darling, and then there wasn't. My gut says she was either abducted or disappeared, and I think her parents—or at least one of them—knew exactly what happened."

"What would drive a parent to erase their child from existence?" the boss said, more to himself than to Roberts.

"There's more. I think there's a connection between the disappearance of Dawn and the abduction of Wendy when she was fifteen. The similarities between the two can't be ignored." He paused, expecting a protest from his boss, but received none. "Boss, what it comes down to is this... I think the Rosalie Fryair case was really about Wendy from the start."

Wendy staggered across the room, trying to push through the waves of dizziness. While it eased slightly with each step she took, her nausea grew in its place. Yet, she'd worked up the courage to get back to the boys, crocodile or no crocodile. She reached the wall where she'd exited earlier but was only met with the resistance of the cold cement. Stepping back, she peered at the wall as a wave of panic washed over her at the thought of once again being trapped.

No. No. This can't be right!

Placing her hands back on the wall, she walked slowly to the right, gently pushing against the concrete every few steps. Her breathing came in sharp gasps as she shifted back to the left, her dizziness and nausea forgotten. As her hands shifted into the wall, Wendy let out a sob of relief. Not caring how the exit had come to shift, she was just grateful that it was still there at all.

Stepping out into the corridor once more, Wendy took a moment and leaned with her head back against the wall, closing her eyes against the harsh white light. She listened intently for any sound approaching from either side of the corridor and was further relieved to be met with silence. Slowly opening her eyes, she blinked a few times and pushed herself off the wall. Wendy felt strengthened with each step she took, as though having a sense of purpose pushed aside the lingering symptoms of Smee's concoction. Forcing herself to walk past the shrine of photos, she slowed her pace as she neared the room. Wendy could feel the cold coming through the glass without having to touch it, and a chill ran through her as she placed both hands against it and peered in. The fog within the room seemed denser than before, and she struggled to see through it.

Wendy could just make out the outlines of the row of boys hanging closest to her, and she squinted, trying to get a better look. Pan's bulbous, iridescent green eyes glowed through the fog, and Wendy darted away from the window, pressing herself against the wall. Her rapid breathing filled her ears, and she tried to slow it down, fearful the sound would prevent her from hearing Pan approaching. When nothing happened, Wendy took a deep breath, pushing her fear down as she focused her thoughts on the boys. She needed to know what Pan was doing with them. With her hands pressed against the wall, she shuffled back towards the window, pausing as her fingertips touched the cold glass. Wendy hesitated, just for a moment, and then closed the gap between her hand and the rest of her body. Carefully, she turned her head and leaned around just enough to see through the glass. She hoped that the fog within the room would hide her from Pan's gaze as much as it hid the boys from her.

All she could hear was the pounding of her heart echoing in her ears as she waited for any sign of movement—any sign of Pan. Just as Wendy was starting to doubt that she'd seen anything in the first place, the fog swirled, and she got a glimpse of Pan, this time with his back to her. He stood before one of the boys in the first row and appeared to be either turning off or disconnecting him from the green-filled tube. Wendy's neck started to hurt from the angle, and she shifted as slowly and as carefully as she could, not wanting to draw any attention to herself. As she looked on, Pan grew in height, and he reached up, gripping the boy's shoulders with his lengthened and gnarled fingers. A shudder ran down Wendy's back as she watched on, not wanting to see what happened next but knowing that she needed to. Pan's head now came up to the boy's chest, and he slowly moved his hands away from the child's shoulders, up his neck, before cupping his face with his hands. Wendy watched as Pan tilted his head back, and for a moment, she thought he was just staring up at the boy. But then the child's mouth fell open, only slightly, but enough that she could see green smoke waft out of his mouth. Pan's head dropped further into an impossible angle, and she pulled back, worried he would see her. She panted, torn between her fear of getting caught and needing to see what was happening. Carefully she looked back through the glass, relieved to find that while Pan's head was still tilted back, his eyes were tightly closed. His mouth was wide and enormous, revealing the rows of teeth as they rose up out of his jaw. The green smoke drifted down towards Pan's mouth, slowly at first, but then it looked as though he was sucking it in, and it spilled out of the boy's mouth in thicker and faster torrents.

Wendy barely registered the way her body now shook or the warmth of the tears that trickled down her cheeks. After what felt like an eternity, an ear-piercing howl erupted from the room, causing Wendy to jump in wide-eyed panic. Pan's head flipped forward, and there was a flash of white light that was so bright, Wendy pulled back from the window, covering her eyes with her arm. When she recovered, she leaned back to peer through the glass once more. Her mouth fell open as she saw the boy alone, his drip once more in place. With a gasp, Wendy turned and ran back to her room. Fearful of encountering Pan— or worse—that he'd be waiting for her when she got there.

She stumbled through the concrete wall, the darkness almost comforting after the exposure of the brightly lit corridor. Wendy flicked a quick look at the hovering candle, barely registering how little there seemed to be left of it as she dashed to the bathroom. Gripping the edges of the basin with both hands, she heaved and gagged on the hot, acidic bile as it rose up her throat and into her mouth in violent spurts. When it finally ceased, Wendy raised her head, her arms shaking, and looked at her reflection in the mirror. Frowning, she leaned forward, peering at herself in the candlelight. She could swear she looked different somehow, but she couldn't quite put her finger on what it was. Turning her face one way, then the other, she inspected her face. Then it dawned on her—she looked younger. The heavy frown line that had been a permanent fixture across her forehead for as long as she could recall was no longer there. Nor were the fine laugh lines that had graced the corners of her eyes and mouth. Releasing the basin, Wendy stood up, frowning at herself.

What the hell is going on?

NEVER, NEVER

Wendy opened her eyes, blinking away the disorientation as she tried to place where she was. She saw the hovering of the candle at the foot of the bed, and the nightmare of her location flooded back to her. Turning her head to the right, she screamed when met with Pan's intense stare. She scrambled to sit up, turning and pushing her back up against the wall. Thick bile rose up into her throat, and she forced herself to swallow it down as she waited for him to say something.

He knows. He saw me. He must have.

Pan smiled at her, rocking back and forth on his heels, his hands clasped behind his back. He remained silent, but the smile spread further across his face causing his eyes to twinkle malevolently. Wendy felt the ice-cold fingers of terror rising up along her spine. He glanced slightly to his right, to where the candle still hovered at the foot of the bed. It was less than an inch high now, smaller than the fiercely burning flame atop it. Her thundering heart picked up the pace upon the realization she'd slept far longer than she thought. Her acknowledgement seemed to be the reaction he needed, and Wendy watched on in perplexed silence as Pan turned and disappeared back into the shadows. She sat there, gasping for air, wondering if he was toying with her like a cat allowing a mouse to believe it was safe, right before striking.

He mustn't have seen me...he'd be angry if he knew...

Slowly stretching her legs out over the side of the bed, Wendy's thoughts were on the wall of photos and the horrible churning in the pit of her stomach at the thought that he could get anywhere near Jane.

Roberts paced the length of the room, his hands clasped behind his head. The only pieces of the case that fit together seemed ridiculous and created more questions than answers. There was something off about the entire case, and he cursed his cocky former self from only a day ago, so eager and proud to be the lead on such a high-profile case—a defining moment in his career without a doubt with a grateful Mayor on his side once Roberts found his daughter. Now he was torn between wishing he'd never taken the case and wanting to find Wendy. The way she'd made him feel after such a short time together frustrated the hell out of him, more so for the fact that he didn't want the inconvenience of an emotional connection to the case. It was only a weakness.

Clearing his throat, Roberts lowered his hands and turned to the evidence boards, forcing himself to focus. He looked at the images of Dawn Darling, a girl wiped from existence except for some keepsakes. The fact that someone had gone to the trouble of keeping her belongings while so much effort had been invested in pretending she'd never been born, only heightened Roberts' instinct that the family knew what happened to her—and were likely complicit in her disappearance. Then there was the fact that Dawn was fifteen at the time of her disappearance, as was Wendy and Rosalie. He struggled to find a logical answer as it seemed unlikely that the same person was the culprit in all three cases—the time frame alone would make him too old if he was even still alive.

He moved along to the board with what he'd gathered on Wendy's past and stared at a photo of her beloved Nanna. Frowning, he looked from Dawn to Wendy. This Nanna, no relation, was a direct link between the two girls in so far as she was present in the house when both girls went missing, but again, she wasn't in any condition to orchestrate the abduction of Rosalie.

Unless she had someone's help? But what could the possible motive be?

A memory triggered, and he turned from the board to the table behind him, picking up his notepad and flipping furiously through the pages. Roberts stopped as he found what he was looking for. Nanna reportedly passed away in the Darling home at 3 AM. Lowering the notepad, he shook his head. The footage from the hospital put Wendy's disappearance at 3 AM.

Fuck fucking fuck!

He grabbed his jacket and stormed out of the room.

Squinting against the brightness of the sunshine, he cursed himself for leaving his sunglasses behind. He'd been so focused on his work that he'd lost all track of time, but he could tell from the height of the sun that it had to be around noon, possibly later. Roberts hadn't bothered to call ahead. Something about the entire Darling family didn't sit right with him, and the last thing he wanted to do was give them a head's up that he was coming.

Driving along the road to the house surrounded on either side by grapevines stretching out in the sun, he wondered if Wendy would have been content here had it not been for her trauma. He'd seen enough in his career to understand that a peaceful exterior was no reflection of what was happening behind closed doors. He pulled up in front of the house, the tyres crunching along the gravel and signalling his arrival. Sliding out of the car, he stepped back, his hand shielding his eyes as he thought he saw movement at one of the above windows. When all he saw was the closed curtain, he dismissed it as paranoia and strode up to the front door and pressed the doorbell. When there was no sound, he wondered if it was broken and raised his hand to knock just as the door was opened before him, revealing a woman of about fifty, dressed in a crisp black dress buttoned severely to her throat and falling demurely below her knees. Her hair was pulled back into an impeccable bun that was so tight it seemed to tug at the corners of her eyes. Roberts recovered from his surprise while flicking a glance over the woman's shoulder, trying to see into the house.

"Hello, I'm Detective Roberts. I'm sorry. I was under the impression the Darling family didn't have staff and hadn't for quite some time."

The woman smiled tersely. "This is my first week, Sir. I imagine with so many recent passing's, the dear Darling brothers felt they needed the assistance. Why, they spend all their time out in the vineyard, after all."

Roberts nodded slowly, not impressed by their ability to be so practical while their sister was missing. "Is that where they are now?" He turned and looked over his shoulder towards the vines but couldn't see them.

"They're likely taking their lunch in the barn. They've been hard at work all morning."

Roberts frowned—there was something about the slight edge to her voice, the steely glint in her eyes like she was daring him to question her honesty. He found it an odd disposition given she was only recently hired. He made a mental note of it but remained focused on the task at hand.

"I would actually like to speak to Carole. I wasn't sure if she was still here, or whether she had moved on now that Nanna had passed away."

"Yes, she is still here. To my knowledge, she will reside here until the funeral. I'll take you to her, and then I'll let the brothers know you're here."

"Really, there's no need to disturb them..."

"I hardly think it appropriate to let a detective wander the manor without notifying the occupants." She cut him off as she stepped aside to allow him in. Roberts stepped over the threshold and admired the spacious foyer for a brief moment before he realised the maid was already off and briskly walking away.

He hurriedly caught up. "I didn't get your name."

"I didn't give it."

Roberts said nothing as he followed her through the manor. As beautiful as the home was, the more he saw of it, the less he could see Wendy there. It just didn't seem like her at all. He pulled up alongside the maid as she rapped twice on a closed door. The sound of heavy footsteps approached the door from the other side before it was cast open.

"Yes?"

"Sorry to intrude, but the detective here was hoping to speak to you." The maid left the way she'd come, leaving Roberts and Carole staring at each other.

"Uh, a detective? What is this about?"

"May I come in?" he asked, and Carole nodded as she led the way to the couch where she sat in Nanna's favourite spot in front of the television. Roberts took a seat on a lounge chair to the side and cleared his throat. "Have you spoken to Michael or John today?"

Carole shook her head, a frown weighing down her tired-looking face, puffy and blotchy from crying. "No, why? Please tell me nothing else has happened...I don't think I could take any more bad news." Her eyes started to well, and Roberts looked down at his hands clasped over his knees, trying to contain his discomfort.

"I'm working a case with Wendy. Earlier this morning, during the investigation, she went missing."

Carole's frown deepened; her mouth opened before she closed it again. Roberts sat quietly, observing, but it was evident the woman was both confused and surprised, and he waited until she was ready to ask her questions.

"How? I mean, where? What happened?"

He gave her a brief run down, not wanting to reveal too much while also keen to get to the reason behind his visit. "I'm here because I need to discuss Nanna's behaviour in the lead up to her passing."

"What? Why? What has Nanna got to do with Wendy disappearing?"

"That's what I'm trying to determine. There are some connections which I can't discuss with you, but suffice to say, they can't be ignored. I was hoping you would answer some questions for me."

Carole nodded as she wrung her hands together. "Uh, of course. I don't know what help I can be, but I will do what I can."

Roberts pulled his notebook from his pocket and clicked his pen. "Firstly, how was Nanna's behaviour prior to her passing? Were there any notable changes?"

Carole looked down at her hands as she answered. "She did seem to deteriorate rapidly."

"How so?"

"Well, she became restless and agitated, which was unusual as she'd been relatively unresponsive for quite some time," Carole paused, looking up at Roberts in hesitation.

"Any detail could be of use," he reassured her.

"Well, she started speaking, which was a rare occurrence at the best of times, yet she was suddenly uttering whole sentences. Only, none of them made sense. It was just the ramblings of her dementia-riddled mind. Whatever it was she thought she was talking about, it upset her."

"What kind of things was she saying? Do you recall?"

"There was something about a necklace—I think she was talking about the pendant that she wore around her neck. I noticed when she started talking about it that it was no longer around her neck, and I've hunted high and low for it but can't find it anywhere. She never took it off, not even to bathe."

"So it was just the fact that it was missing that upset her?"

"Yes and no. She kept saying it was the only way she would still be protected, that she was too tired and couldn't fight it anymore."

Roberts scribbled the words on his notepad as he formulated his next questions. "When Nanna said 'she', do you think she was talking about herself, or could she have been referring to someone else? Wendy, perhaps?"

Carole looked at him, her eyebrows raised. "I...I don't know, I hadn't considered that. I just assumed she was talking about herself, but, yes, it could be possible. Nanna and Wendy were very close."

Roberts rose from his seat and walked over to the wall of photographs on display. He found a black-and-white photo of a very beautiful woman sitting on a rug outside with a little boy he recognized from Dawn's belongings. "This is Nanna?" he pointed at it and looked over his shoulder.

Carole nodded as she got up from the lounge and joined him. "Yes, it is. I haven't really looked at these for so long. She loved being surrounded by her photos."

"This painting is interesting." He pointed to where it hung in the centre, approximately 40cm by 50cm, painted in vibrant oil colours. It depicted a garden of Eden-like scene, though in the centre was a group of blissfully smiling children in various stages of play. Roberts leaned in for a better look, and while he couldn't be one hundred percent certain, they all appeared to be boys. He suddenly reached into his pockets and pulled out his phone. He opened the camera app and used it to zoom in to a small section of the painting. There was a tree trunk partially hidden by the low-hanging branches, heavy with abundant foliage, not unlike a weeping willow. Yet it wasn't the tree so much that intrigued him. It was the woman sitting at its base, her back resting against it as though she was watching over the boys as they played.

"Take a look at this," he instructed, stepping aside to allow Carole a good look. He watched on as her mouth fell open, knowing his suspicions were confirmed.

"That's Nanna! But like when she was young…"

"That's what I thought. How long has she had the painting?"

"It's been here for as long as I've cared for her. I found it fascinating when I first saw it—it looks like such a happy place. Only this isn't the same."

Roberts started. "How so?"

"Well, that woman, Nanna, sitting under the tree. She wasn't there before."

"Are you sure? You could've just overlooked her before. She's partially obscured by the branches after all."

"No. I'm not mistaken. I know she wasn't there before, because I remember looking at this painting and thinking how perfect that very spot would be to curl up with a good book. Nanna definitely wasn't in this painting before. I don't understand—how is that possible?"

"That's what I'm trying to find out."

CHAPTER TWENTY-FOUR

"Smee!" Wendy hissed towards the shadows as she watched another drop of wax drip down the dwindling candle and onto the floor. "Smee! Please, I need more. I need to see more." When she was only met with silence, she lay back down on the bed and groaned. As much as she hated the way Smee's liquid concoction made her feel, it seemed to be the only way to get any information to use against Pan, as obscure and as nonsensical as it came to her.

She jumped as Smee's jovial voice ruptured the silence, and she turned to see him bustling towards her. "Hello, my dear. I thought it was high time you had some sustenance."

Wendy sat up, swinging her legs over the edge of the bed as she watched him approach. She wanted to thank him for coming, but he wouldn't meet her gaze. As he placed the tray beside her, she quickly reached out and gave his arm a gentle squeeze. He froze, and she squeezed again before removing her hand. He gave a discrete nod. "That should be enough to keep you satiated for a while. I recalled you used to love my special apple tea cake, so I whipped one up—doesn't get any fresher than that." He turned and shuffled away, whistling to himself, and Wendy felt like he was doing so to ensure she wouldn't speak any further. Once she could no longer hear him, she glanced down at the tray and was momentarily distracted by the delicious looking slice of cake as her stomach growled in response. Ignoring it, she reached for the cup, and without hesitation, she held it up to her lips and drank copiously. Wendy was instantly hit with intense nausea, and she lay back down, pushing the tray aside, oblivious to its clatter as it fell to the floor. Squeezing her eyes shut, she forced herself to breathe through it, willing herself to keep it down long enough to see what she needed to see.

In a matter of seconds, she saw the familiar haze sweeping across her closed eyelids, and she tried to peer through it.

Laughter. I can hear children laughing. Two. A boy and a girl.

On cue, they were revealed to her, and she instantly recognised the boy as her father from the photographs of him in the family home. But the girl she was certain she hadn't seen before. As she watched them play, she tried to work out what was going on when they suddenly aged before her very eyes until both were in their teens.

The two of them are sitting on the porch, watching the sun set over the vineyard. The girl covers her mouth to stifle the lengthy yawn, and the boy nudges her gently. "Still not sleeping?" he asked. The girl shook her head. "Still having the nightmares?" he prompted, and she nodded. He sighed. "I really think we need to tell Mum and Dad…"

"No. It will only worry them, and what for? They're just nightmares. I'm sure they'll pass."

"Well, what about Nanna then? She might know a way to help."

The girl shrugged and yawned again, and the boy sighed. "Why don't I crash in your room tonight?"

"You don't have to do that."

"What kind of brother would I be if I didn't? Honestly, I don't mind if you think it will help."

She turned and smiled at him. "Thank you, but I'll be fine. Besides, I think you're too tall to find any comfort on the trundle bed these days."

Her brother chuckled and placed his arm around her shoulders.

Wendy gasped, unaware she'd been holding her breath, and she inhaled deeply, not wanting to lose the momentum of the vision.

The girl sat on the edge of her bed. Something had woken her, but she wasn't sure what. There was no need to turn on the lamp. The light of the full moon flooded through the window. The open window. The girl frowned, certain she'd closed it before she went to bed. Slowly rising to her feet, the girl blinked as sparks of green flashed at the edges of her vision. With a quick shake of her head, she tried to rid herself of the tingling that accompanied the green sparks, but it did no good. She seemed to be aware that she was walking towards the window, but her movements made it seem like she was sleepwalking. The window opened wider at her approach, and as she stepped up onto the window ledge, her nightgown billowed out around her. She stood there a moment; her head tilted to the side as though she was listening to something—or someone. The girl nodded slowly and stepped off the ledge.

NEVER, NEVER

Wendy sat upright, gasping for breath as she tried to process what she'd seen. It appeared that she wasn't the only member of the family abducted by Pan—and almost as disturbing was the fact that she was certain the bedroom was her own.

Overcome with a sudden thirst, Wendy tentatively slid off the bed and almost collapsed under the wave of nausea that swept over her. Stumbling past the bed, she fell against the wall, shuffling against it until she reached the bathroom. She braced herself, gripping the basin tightly as she tried to judge whether she could keep her balance if she tried to bend over. As the pang of thirst came again, she knew she had to risk it. She leaned heavily on her left arm as she reached out for the tap with her right. The sound of the water running down the pipe was like music to her ears, and she cupped her free hand beneath the flow. Lowering her head, she carefully drank from her makeshift cup, gulping thirstily until she'd had her fill. The worst of the side-effects felt like they'd passed, and she shakily straightened. Wetting both her hands, she patted the cool water against her face and the back of her neck before finally turning off the faucet.

Still rubbing her hand against the back of her neck, Wendy walked towards the exit and yelped as she saw Pan once again waiting for her.

"Cake not to your liking?" He pushed at it with one foot before squashing it, watching her expression as he did so.

She stepped out of the bathroom and to the side, pressing her back against the wall. "I had an aunt." Wendy tried to maintain a steely resolve, but even she could hear the tremble in her voice.

His expression didn't change as he lifted his foot from the cake and wiped the bottom of his shoe clean on the concrete.

"You abducted her, didn't you?"

Pan made a *tsk* sound. "Abduction is such a horrid word. It conjures too much negative imagery, in my opinion."

Wendy tried to respond but only managed a choking noise at his answer. He continued on, seemingly oblivious to her repulsion. "Her name was Dawn—a pretty name that suited her perfectly, and I freed her. Just like I did with her aunt. And her aunt before her..." he clasped his hands behind his back and started to pace, letting the magnitude of what he'd said sink in. Wendy's mouth fell open, her eyes darting as she tried to make sense of it.

I'm not the first. Did they know? Did my family know?

"Though as lovely as Dawn was, or any of your ancestors for that matter, none of them could give me what I needed most."

Wendy frowned, the pang in her heart telling her she knew the answer even though her mind refused to acknowledge it. She could feel her body start to tremble, and despite her efforts to control it, it only worsened.

"What happened to Dawn?" the question came out in a hoarse whisper.

"She made the same choice you will inevitably make once the candle flame flickers out. Dearest Dawn leads a wonderful existence in Neverland. Happy, carefree, and still as youthful and beautiful as the day she first came to me."

"She didn't come to you—you abducted her! Just like you abducted me!"

"You know how I feel about that word..." He stopped in his tracks, his voice taking on a hint of a growl. Wendy stared back at him, her brain trying to fight off the last of whatever drugs she'd ingested while trying to make sense of everything. She felt a hot tear trickle down her cheek but felt incapable of raising her hand to wipe it away. Pan raised his arm, and Wendy whimpered as his hand outstretched to its inhuman length, his fingers gnarling as they reached for her. She tried to pull away, wondering if she could slip back into the bathroom and close herself in before he could grab her, but as she felt the sharp points of his fingernails scrape down the side of her face, she knew she was already too late.

"Tears. Just think, Wendy, if you accept my offer, you will never cry again. Never experience a moment of sadness for the rest of your life." His fingers trailed down her neck and across her collarbone, hesitating above her left breast before they retracted.

"Why do you need me if you have Dawn here already?"

"You know, for a detective, you're not a very good listener, are you?" he mocked. Wendy's attention darted toward the hovering candle as the flame flickered dangerously low.

Pan started his pacing again. His head tilted up towards the ceiling as he spoke, "You would be pleasantly surprised how many of your ancestors there are for you to meet in Neverland—and I love each one of them. They're all wonderful maternal influences on my precious boys. My poor Lost Boys. But, as I already told you, none of them can give me what you can. You're the one, Wendy, I've spent all eternity searching for."

Jane...

Wendy felt like she was going to choke on the sob that rose up her throat as her trembling intensified. She felt terror more intense than anything she'd ever felt before—the terror of a parent fearful for their child's safety. More than ever, she knew she had to get out, to free herself, and get to her daughter. Yet she now knew, simply escaping wouldn't be enough this time. It would never stop. *He* would never stop. The only way to ensure Jane would be safe, that her daughter, and her daughter's daughter would be safe, was to find a way to kill Pan.

Pan watched her for a moment, as though trying to determine whether to say anything further. "You look a right mess, Wendy. It will not do. I need to... attend to something... so I will leave you to rest, and when I return, I hope you will look much improved." He turned on his heel, his hands still clasped behind his back, and strode off back into the shadows that inched further forward as the candle dwindled. When she was certain he was gone, Wendy ran over to the bed, buried her face into the pillow, and screamed as loud as she could. She screamed again and again until she had nothing left, and she passed out from exhaustion.

Roberts hurtled through the station, bumping into colleagues and knocking things off desks as he navigated his way to the boss's office. The door was open, and he walked straight in, but the office was empty. He turned back. "Anyone seen the chief?"

The officer at the desk closest to him pointed toward the investigation room, and Roberts gave him a nod as he walked towards it.

"Tell me we're getting close," the chief said without turning around.

Roberts let his eyes run over the evidence boards for a moment before he answered, "Honestly, this is proving to be about so much more than Detective Darling. Wendy."

The chief nodded slowly, his stare fixed on the board with the evidence about Dawn Darling. "Did the visit to the house prove useful?"

NEVER, NEVER

Roberts walked into the room and stood beside his boss, crossing his arms against his chest. "I'm not sure yet. This Nanna woman passed away at the exact same time that Wendy was taken. Rationally it has to be a coincidence, but looking at all of this, I can only feel that it's connected. I spoke to Carole, the carer, and she said Nanna was agitated toward the end— she kept saying how she couldn't stop it anymore, she wasn't strong enough…"

"So she knew the abductor? Or she knew who abducted Wendy when she was a teen and what? Was she fearful it would happen again, or did she actually play a role in the prevention of its recurrence?"

Roberts shook his head slowly. "That would seem to be the logical conclusion, but she was an elderly woman suffering from advanced dementia, completely reliant on her carer for everything. Firstly, I can't see how she'd be capable of having influence over anything. Secondly, who's to say her words weren't just the paranoid delusions of her illness?"

His boss didn't answer but paced along the boards as though trying to commit everything to memory. Roberts knew better than to interrupt. Finally, his boss turned around. "Let's entertain the theory that despite the old woman's condition, what she said has some truth to it. But what if she wasn't responsible for protecting Wendy—what if she was actually complicit in her abduction—in both of them?"

"What?" Roberts asked, stepping forward, wanting to see what his boss could see.

"Look." He pointed at the photo of Dawn and her brother, the much younger Nanna standing behind them with a hand on each of their shoulders. "She was there before Dawn's abduction. She was their nanny as well. That's two girls abducted under her care."

"She would have been questioned after both abductions..."

"But you and I know just because nothing was proven doesn't mean she didn't at least know something about it."

"If that was the case, then why would the family have kept her on? From what I can gather, she was adored by the entire family."

"Okay—maybe it's the fatigue talking, but what if the parents knew about it also?"

"What are you saying? That Wendy's grandparents knew what happened to Dawn? And Wendy's parents knew what happened to her—or worse still, knew it was *going* to happen?"

His boss turned and looked at him. "Perhaps not the wives. But the Darling men... worst-case scenario—what would it mean for the case if they did?"

"It means we're running out of time."

"Excuse me, Detective?" They both turned to see one of the sergeants at the door. "Jane Darling is here asking to speak with you."

Roberts raised his eyebrows at his boss before answering, "Thank you. Please show her through to interview room one, and I will meet her there."

"Did you call her in?"

Roberts shook his head. "No, but let's hope she's got something to help us unlock this bloody mess of a case."

He considered grabbing another cup of coffee first, but after inspecting the shake in his hands, he determined it probably wasn't the best idea and tried to recall the last time he ate anything. He couldn't.

"Miss Darling, what can I do for you?" he asked as he stepped into the interview room and took a seat opposite the girl, instantly noticing the notebook that rested on the table beneath her clasped hands, knowing she would mention it when she was ready.

"Jane, please."

Roberts nodded. "Okay, Jane."

She cleared her throat; his eyes fixed on her hands so tightly clasped he could see her knuckles turning white, but he waited for her to speak first. "Do you remember Mum's notebook I showed you? With her drawings in it?"

"They're a little hard to forget…"

Jane took a deep breath and pushed the notebook towards him, and he stared at it, suddenly awash with trepidation. "I don't really think I need to see them again?"

"Trust me. You need to open it."

He reached out and moved it closer, inspecting the cover, trying to ignore the nerves that came from left field at the thought of opening it. He could feel Jane staring at him, and Roberts bit the bullet and opened the cover. The nerves were forgotten, and a frown took over as he flicked from one page to another.

"Bloody hell…" It came out barely louder than a whisper, but he didn't look up as he flicked the pages faster and faster. What was once the dark and horrific images with the green eyes that seemed to peer straight into his soul, were now mere shadows. All except the eyes which appeared brighter and more ferocious than ever. Leaning forward, Roberts peered at the images before him. "Is it… are they… "

Jane nodded. "Fading away. The images are fading away—except the eyes."

Roberts came to the end of the journal and closed it before he looked up at Jane and sighed, "I appreciate you bringing this to me. But I don't know what this means—or how this is possible."

"I thought nothing could scare me more than knowing mum drew those images, but this… I don't know what to think, but it terrifies me. Please tell me you're closer to finding her?"

Roberts looked at her, hoping he conveyed more confidence and positivity than he felt. "We will find her, Jane. I promise you."

CHAPTER TWENTY-FIVE

Wendy paced back and forth, the remnants of the candle hovering behind her, barely still holding together as the last of the wax warmed and softened. Banging on her forehead with the heel of her hand—she knew she was running out of time. Smee had tried to help her in his own way, but the past was the past. The glimpses into it had only served to confuse her more about who she was, who her family was, and her own past. There was only one person left she could turn to, but he'd already told her there was nothing he could do. Wendy closed her eyes. It was almost painful. They were so dry from tears, fatigue, and dim lighting.

347

"Captain!" she hissed into the shadows, biting her lip as she waited for him to come—hopefully before Pan did. "Captain!" she hissed again, raising her voice only slightly. She gripped at her hair with her hands, tasting the blood in her mouth from her lip as her anxiety took siege.

Why isn't he coming? Where is he?

Her hands fell to her sides as it dawned on her. "Hook!" she called. She was about to call a second time when the toe of a black boot protruded from the increasing shadows. Wendy felt a wave of hope swell within her as she watched Hook step towards her. His dark curls obscured his face as he bowed his head.

"I... Thank you for coming," she said quietly.

Hook only responded with a curt nod as he approached her, his eyes only on the remnants of the candle. He raised his hook, and Wendy watched the fading light glint off its silver, fearful that the slightest touch would destroy it. Hook lowered his arm, finally turning his eyes to her. They widened, scanning her face before his bushy brows cast down. "What did he do to you?"

"What? Nothing. Not yet, anyway. Though I think he might once this candle runs out if I refuse him. I don't know what to do—he knows about Jane."

Hook's eyebrows shot up again at the mention of his granddaughter's name.

"I need to keep her safe—to keep him away from her, and the only way I can think of is to go to Neverland with him. I can't stand the thought of never seeing her, or Lilly, or my brothers again. They'd never know what happened to me—I don't want to do that to them. I don't even know if that would guarantee Jane's safety." Wendy could hear the tremble in her own voice as the gravity of the situation increased with every unstable flicker of the candle flame.

Hook stepped closer and gently placed his hook under Wendy's chin and tilted her face upwards. She quieted as he seemed to inspect her face intently before removing his hook and stepping back again. "You found a way to leave the room." It was a statement rather than a question, and Wendy didn't answer, unable to determine if his expression darkened in reaction or from the dwindling light. He turned on his heel and marched away. Wendy feared he would leave her, but at the last minute, he turned back around. "What did you see beyond these walls?"

"What do you mean?"

"What did you see on the other side? Did it take you outside? Was it day or night? Were you back in your own bedroom? What did you see?"

"I have no idea what you're talking about. On the other side is just a sterile-looking corridor slightly curved with doors. Each one has a number placed above it, close to the ceiling. There is an alcove that is covered in photographs of me—I'm sleeping in all of them. That's how I know he knows about Jane. There are photos of me pregnant." She paused, confused by the way Hook was looking at her, as though he had no idea what she was talking about.

"Where did you go from there? What did you see?"

She told him about the glass room, the boys, and what she'd witnessed before the flash of light. Hook nodded slowly, as though some kind of realisation dawned on him.

"Why do you look surprised?" Wendy asked, unable to make sense of his questions and wondering if he was as sane as she'd first assumed.

Hook looked down at his feet, and Wendy tapped her own, clenching her jaw as she willed him to answer. He finally looked up, and for a moment, he looked every bit as old as he really was. The candle flickered, and the image passed. "Pan was right all along. You truly are different." Wendy shivered as she felt the ice-cold fingers of fear rush up her spine, but she kept her mouth shut, not wanting him to stop talking. Hook stroked his moustache with his long fingers. "I don't know how, but you can see this place as it really is. The magic of his illusions doesn't seem to work on you. Interesting..." Wendy watched as his eyes lit up, and a hint of a smile caused his moustache to twitch. She felt her own hope increase as she watched him.

"You can see something no one else can—my son when he's at his weakest."

"What are you talking about?"

Hook suddenly strode forward and grabbed her by the shoulders and lifted her to her feet. "Those boys you saw, Pan calls them his 'Lost Boys'."

"Lost, as in he abducted them too?"

"Some, yes. Others went with him willingly— orphans and children from horrible home lives, for the most part, as sad as it is, young boys that wouldn't be missed. He brings them here, to this place, a place that cannot be found by any mortal. He keeps them here."

"But why? Why like that, just hanging there? Are they in pain?"

"The only small mercy he affords them is a pain-free existence. You've seen them when you have glimpses of Neverland, haven't you?"

Wendy nodded.

"That's their reality. In their minds, they're happy and free in Neverland, not wanting for anything, never feeling pain, never feeling unloved, never growing old."

"You sound like you think he's doing them some kind of favour," Wendy stated, the thought making her angry.

Hook gave a shrug. "I suppose he is, given their backgrounds. But I'm no more naïve than you are, my dear. He gives them Neverland only because it keeps them docile, easy to manage. I don't even know how many he has under his wing, but I know he has enough to live a thousand lifetimes."

"So, he's…feeding off them?"

"Well, I've never seen him with them myself, but from your description, yes. I think that's exactly what he's doing."

"We have to stop him. There has to be a way…"

"…and I think we may have just found one."

"Really?"

Hook nodded. "Pan would be his most vulnerable when he feeds—which is why he does it in secret. If there was ever going to be an opportunity for you to kill him, it would be then."

"But how? We have no weapons to speak of. He's not even human, so how do I kill him?"

"I have a plan, but you're going to have to trust me."

Wendy watched as a third of the candle base broke away and fell to the floor. "I don't think there's any other option."

Hook gave a quick nod, his expression serious. "I need you to lead the way. We need to go out in the corridor, back to where you were before. There's no guarantee you'll be lucky a second time, but it's our only shot."

Wendy nodded and walked over to the far wall. She pressed at the wall, but couldn't find the exit. She felt nervous, and her stomach churned.

"Just take a deep breath and try again," Hook instructed quietly from over her shoulder. Doing as she was instructed, she moved her hands along the wall and tried again. Finally, her hand went through the wall. She looked back at Hook, not wanting to stay where she was, but anxious about walking back through the wall. His attempt at a reassuring smile came out more like a grimace, and Wendy realised he was just as nervous as she was—he'd waited for this opportunity far longer than she had.

Hook placed his hand on her shoulder, and Wendy turned back towards the wall. Closing her eyes, she led them through to the other side. Relief washed over her once she opened her eyes and found herself back in the corridor. She felt Hook's hand fall from her shoulder, and she turned to see him looking around, his eyebrows arched high, and his mouth slightly open.

"You've really never seen this before?" she asked.

"No. This must be the true core of this place— what it looks like under all Pan's illusions." He looked her squarely in the eyes. "We must hurry. There's no way to know how much time we have."

Wendy led them down the corridor, refusing to look at the wall of photographs as she hurried past. She followed the curve of the wall that seemed to go on further than before. Just as she began to fear she wouldn't find it again, she felt the shift in the air, the coldness, and she surged forward. Within a matter of steps, she saw the glass and slowed her pace, hearing Hook's pace echoing her own. She gestured for Hook to continue, to have a look for himself. Stepping past her, he walked along the glass staring into the swirling fog. Wendy remained silent, knowing the myriad of expressions that flashed across his face had been mirrored on her own when she'd first stumbled upon it. Finally, he looked over at her, his shoulders slightly shrugging. Wendy understood—there were no words to explain what he saw. As much as she didn't want to witness the countless boys in their suspended states, she knew there was only one way forward if she was going to save any of them. She walked over to where he stood, forcing herself to look through the glass, her eyes only taking a matter of seconds to once again locate the boys amidst the fog.

"Do you think you could get us in there? The way you brought us here?" Hook asked. Wendy didn't reply but placed her hands on the glass, willing them to move through it. It took more focus and a little more force, but she finally felt the shift. Wendy felt Hook's hand clasp her shoulder once again, and she led them through to the room. The chill caused her to start shivering the moment they were inside. She rubbed her arms briskly, but to no avail.

The boys looked so helpless, so cold and alone. Wendy wanted to reach up and wrench the tubes out of their arms, cutting them off from Pan's insidious concoction. It took all her will power to hold off. She understood the only way to really save them all was to wait. Pan had to die.

"What now?" she whispered.

"We wait," he replied and gestured towards a large metal trunk on wheels. Atop it sat plastic tubing, needles, and tape, the sight of which made Wendy feel ill as they ducked down behind it. Without thinking, they shuffled in close together against the cold, both listening intently for any sign of Pan entering the room.

A melodic whistling drifted through the fog, and Wendy opened her eyes, feeling groggy. They widened at the realisation that not only had she fallen asleep in the frigid cold, but so had Hook. His head rested back against the wall, his mouth slightly open, his breathing was deep and louder than she would have liked. She worried if she woke him, she would startle him and draw attention to them. Yet as the whistling neared, she felt fear at Pan's nearing proximity and gently nudged Hook with her elbow while covering his mouth with her other hand. His eyes flew open, and he looked set to lash out.

Fortunately for Wendy, he recovered quickly, and she removed her hand from his mouth, moving it to her own and placing a finger over her lips. Hook nodded that he understood. The whistling came again, and they stared at each other. "What's the plan?" Wendy mouthed.

Hook looked up, trying to peer over the cabinet they still hid behind, but he couldn't see his son without giving away their location. The whistling stopped, and they kept perfectly still, hunched together as they listened for any further movement from Pan. When there wasn't, Wendy slid along to the end of the cabinet. Hook reached out and grabbed her arm, but she shook him off. Peering around the edge, her heart started pounding before her head had the chance to process what she was seeing. She hardly registered Hook scooting to the other end of the cabinet to look for himself.

Pan stood along the second row of boys, gazing up at a youth no older than six or seven. The boy's ebony hair was short, slightly curling around his hairline, especially over his ears and at his temples. His expression was peaceful, like he was merely sleeping. His shirt was plaid, green, and buttoned up to the collar. A pair of black suspenders crossed over his shoulders and gripped the boy's brown corduroy pants. His shirt was tucked in, except for a small section over one hip that had come free. The boy's feet hung bare, slightly crossed at the toes. Pan reached up, his fingers gnarling and stretching to three times their normal length as they travelled up the boy's torso. The sight of it sent a shudder through Wendy, and she had to lower her gaze momentarily. At the sound of a strange hum, she looked up again to find Pan's head tilted back, and a green-tinged essence trailed out from the boy's nose, his mouth, and his ears. She recoiled in horror, and the acidic burn of bile rushed up her throat and into her mouth.

Wendy forced herself to swallow it back down. Slowly, she slipped her hands up to the top of the cabinet, blindly feeling for something she could use. Her fingers touched something slim and cold—a scalpel. Carefully, she dragged it off the top of the cabinet and into her hands. She inspected it, doubting it would be enough to kill him—not unless she could either get a series of quick blows in, which she doubted or get a single, lethal shot. But where? With his back to her, the only option she could think of was to go for the brainstem. She squeezed her eyes shut as she allowed herself only a brief thought of Jane and of Lilly before she cast the images aside and mustered up all the courage she could.

Wendy launched herself to her feet and ran towards Pan. The fog appeared to part, clearing the path for her. For one horrific moment, she could have sworn the lost boys' eyes were all open, staring down at her. She gripped the knife firmly in her hand as Pan continued to feed, and for a moment, Wendy allowed herself to hope she was actually going to do it. She was only a matter of steps away when she pulled her hand back past her hip, planning to drive it upwards into the back of his tilted neck.

Five steps...

Four steps...

Three...

Pan's mouth snapped shut, and he spun his head around and glared. Wendy staggered in surprise and almost fell to her knees as an eerie hiss escaped him. As his eyes bulged in his anger, he released the boy and swayed towards her as though drunk and Wendy took the opportunity to lunge. She knew it was now or never. But she'd already lost the element of surprise, and he gripped her tightly by the wrist, forcing her to her knees as the scalpel clattered to the concrete. She screamed as he pushed her onto her back, and he lunged at her. Pan's mouth opened wider and wider, revealing row after row of horrid teeth as he roared at her. Wendy turned her face away, fearing he'd engulf her face in one bite. He pulled back, panting heavily. "Wendy! How dare you betray me! After everything I have offered you, after everything we could have had together. *Why?*"

Wendy took the opportunity to strike, pulling her knees upwards before pushing them with all her might at his heaving chest. She hit him squarely, and he fell backwards. "Hook!" she cried out as she scrambled onto her stomach, pulling herself across the floor to where she could see the scalpel glinting. Just as she went to grab it, she felt a rough tug and looked over her shoulder to see Pan's arm extending across the floor towards her, his repulsive fingers gripping her ankle.

"No!" she yelled, kicking and bucking while trying to free herself, but his grip was as strong as a vice. He flipped her onto her back, moving his other hand to her neck and wrapping his fingers around it.

"We could have had everything. I would have given it all to you," Pan growled, squeezing tighter. Wendy tried to fight, but he had her pinned. She started to see spots of white light flashing before her eyes as the panic set in.

This is it… he's going to kill me.

Her lungs burned as she struggled to breathe, but it was impossible. Her vision started closing in until there was more darkness surrounding her than light. Suddenly she saw a glint of metal flash before her. She struggled to focus, trying to piece together what was happening, but her oxygen-restricted brain was failing her. Pan's fingers fell away from her neck, and she gasped for air while pushing herself back along the floor and away from his reach. As her lungs swelled, she gaped at the scene before her.

NEVER, NEVER

Pan was still on the floor, on his knees, his arms now lay limp across the floor. His eyes, though always wide and bulbous, now had a look about them she hadn't seen before—one of surprise. Hook stood behind him with his unseeing eyes fixed on her. His sharp hook wedged so deeply into Pan's neck that it protruded from the front. The pair, father and son, appeared frozen. Wendy slowly reached over and picked up the scalpel, not taking her eyes off them for fear Pan would somehow break free and lunge towards her again. She got to her feet and walked closer to them—they didn't move. Reaching out, she gently touched Hook on the shoulder, uncertain what else to do. There came a strange burning smell followed by a brilliant flash of lights so fierce, Wendy was forced to throw her arm up over her eyes. Once it had faded away, she lowered her arm and took a step back, horrified to find Hook and Pan now reduced to ash. They retained their form for a few fleeting seconds before collapsing into a pile on the floor, bound together for all eternity.

CHAPTER TWENTY-SIX

The table between them started to shake violently, and both Roberts and Jane jumped to their feet, their expressions mirror images of each other's surprise. The journal vibrated across the table before falling to the floor. Roberts left it there, dashing towards the door and yanking it open, Jane right behind him. He led her into the heart of the station, where officers tried to save their computers and personal effects from crashing to the ground.

"Is it an earthquake?" Jane shouted.

"Here?" was Roberts' reply. He ran over to the windows and looked out, Jane and a number of other officers joining him. A brilliant beam of green light shot up into the sky. Roberts estimated it was at least half a dozen blocks away. The light disappeared almost as quickly as it had appeared, and the shaking stopped.

"What the hell was that?" Jane whispered.

The surrounding room started to rumble, the vibration causing the ashes to disperse across the concrete. Looking up, Wendy saw the boys swaying from their suspension, and she feared they'd all come crashing down to their deaths. As she watched, the ceiling peeled back, and the walls cracked and shook before fading away as well. The fog intensified, and Wendy struggled to keep her balance, but a dizziness took over her while the ground shook beneath her feet. She collapsed as unconsciousness swept over her.

"You wait here until we know what's going on," Roberts instructed Jane, and she merely nodded, feeling no desire to go running outside. The detective barked orders at neighbouring officers, and they ran out en masse to the waiting squad cars before driving off in a rush of lights and sirens.

Wendy heard the sirens and thought she was dreaming. Yet the pain in her head and the hard surface of the ground beneath her told her otherwise. Carefully she sat up, checking herself over for injury, unable to recall what had just happened or how she'd come to be there. She felt strange like something wasn't right, but her thoughts were directed outwards as she realised she was surrounded by the Lost Boys, all of them in varying degrees of consciousness. Some looked teary, some looked scared, and her maternal instinct took over. "It's okay! You're all going to be okay. Help is coming!" She had no idea where they were. The fog surrounded them, but she could see the flashing blue and red lights as they neared. The car doors opened and shut, and Wendy jumped to her feet as she saw Roberts peering into the fog. Tears stung her eyes—she didn't think she had ever felt so relieved to see anyone in her life.

"Roberts!" she called. She could see him scanning the scene before him as he jogged forward, but he didn't seem to be able to see her. She didn't care as she ran up to him and threw her arms around his waist, squeezing him tight. "You did it! You found us…"

Roberts reached behind him and gently pulled her arms from around him and gave her hands a reassuring squeeze before releasing her. "Everything will be okay—you're safe now. Just stand here, and one of these officers will take your name and details. Tell them whatever you can, and we'll get you away from here as soon as possible." He started to walk away.

"Roberts?" she called out, and he froze in his tracks before turning around. He stared at her, as though seeing her for the first time, and she didn't like his expression. Her eyes locked on his. She moved backwards until she reached his car, breaking their stare only to take a look at herself in the side mirror. Wendy clamped a hand over her mouth as she tried to take in her reflection. Her breathing came in hot gasps as she ran her hands over her face as though hoping it was all just another illusion. Despite her efforts, the reflection didn't change. She was looking at herself... at fifteen.

"How is she?" Jane asked as Roberts returned with a fresh box of tissues. She grabbed two and dabbed at her eyes.

"How can she be?" He sat down opposite her and placed his head in his hands, suddenly feeling like he could sleep for a hundred years.

"I still don't understand," Jane said softly, her chin quivering as she fought to hold back a fresh torrent of tears. "It's all crazy, yet looking at her, I know she's my Mum. Not just because I've seen photos of her from when she was that age—the first time around. It's in her eyes, the way she looks at me. My heart knows it's her, and yet my head can't come to terms with it."

"I know exactly what you mean," he replied, raising his head and leaning back in the seat. The station was relatively quiet—most of the on-duty squad had accompanied the group of boys to the hospital to gather details while they were checked over. He closed his eyes and instantly regretted it, as he again saw the expression on his boss's face when he'd told him they found a group of missing boys, some, as it turned out, had been missing for decades. There was at least one he'd spoken to who last remembered walking to school in 1920. He was still in his office, the door shut, on the phone to the police commissioner trying to determine what the hell to tell the media. It was going to be a shit storm. One Roberts wished he could avoid.

Jane's sniffing pulled him back. "I want to try and keep your mother out of the spotlight as much as I can. In fact, I can't see why anyone beyond this station and your family even need to know."

"I agree. I think the best thing is to take her back to the vineyard. She'll have more privacy there. I think returning to her own flat would be..." She couldn't talk as she pressed the tissue to her mouth.

Roberts swallowed thickly. "I think that's the best idea. At least for now." He looked up as he saw one of the officers lead John, Michael, and Lilly into the station, and he felt a rare moment of panic as he tried to think of how to tell them.

But it was Jane who surprised him by getting to her feet and meeting them half-way. "She's going to be okay. She's still ours." She hugged each of them in turn. Michael looked over to where the detective now stood and gave him a nod. Again, Roberts felt taken aback by how... calm... the brothers seemed. Lilly, on the other hand, was wide-eyed and bewildered, seemingly uncertain where to look as her eyes darted from one object to another.

"Can we see her?" John asked, and Jane looked over her shoulder at Roberts. He nodded and held out his hand, gesturing for them to follow him. He hadn't wanted to leave Wendy in one of the interrogation rooms—it seemed too cold, and she'd already been through so much. Instead, he'd offered her the privacy of the investigation room. He'd wanted to clear the boards of the evidence first, not wanting to upset her any further, but she'd insisted on leaving it up.

He paused at the door for a moment, gathering himself, feeling the eyes of her loved ones staring intently at the back of her head. He knocked, waited a few seconds, and opened the door.

"Wendy? Your family is here to see you," he announced gently, and she turned from where she sat cross-legged on a table in front of the boards. She responded with a kind smile—her smile—that made his heart flutter, and his face flushed as his brain reminded him she was now a teenage girl. He stepped aside to make room for them to enter. Jane stood against the wall beside him and watched. Michael and John walked in first, and Wendy slid off the table to greet them. The three of them hugged for a long time, without a word. What was there to say? Finally, her brothers took a step back, revealing Wendy to Lilly.

"Hey," Wendy said, and Lilly tried to smile through her tears, her trembling hands clasped under her chin.

"I'm sorry. I can't." She turned and fled from the room.

Roberts watched through the doorway as she ran through the station like the devil himself was chasing her. He turned back to Wendy and felt a fierce pang in his chest at the sadness that weighed down her delicate features. "I know you just got here, but I need to have a quick word with Wendy before you take her home," Roberts announced, pushing himself away from the wall.

"We'll be waiting just out there, okay?" John stated.

"We aren't going anywhere," Michael reiterated, and Wendy gave her best reassuring smile.

"I need to use the ladies' room and freshen up a little," Jane added, and the three of them left the room.

Roberts walked toward Wendy, his eyes on the carpet as he approached.

"You can look at me, you know."

He couldn't help but smile as he lifted his eyes to meet her rueful gaze. They stared at each other for a moment, as though each of them was thinking of all the things that might have once been spoken between them. Without realising what he was doing, he reached out and tucked a stray strand of hair behind her ear. She grabbed his hand before he could pull away and pressed it against her face.

"I don't know how, but I *will* find a way to fix this. I'll do whatever it takes. Anything you need, night or day, I am here for you."

She gave him a sad smile, pulled his hand from her face, and kissed the palm of his hand before returning it to him. "I know you will."

Jane splashed water on her face, and the coldness stung her eyes, red and dry from crying. She wiped her hands and zipped up her black hoodie. Gazing up at the air-conditioner vent, she wondered if it was cold in the bathroom or if it was just her. A searing pain pierced through the centre of her forehead, and she clutched at her head with one hand while fumbling for the basin with the other. The pain was so intense that even though her mouth was open wide, not a sound could escape. Slowly, it subsided, and she raised her head to check herself in the mirror. Jane leaned over the basin for a closer look. It was her own reflection, but it felt different somehow. There was a gleam of light that appeared to pass over her eyes, and as she squinted at her reflection, she watched them turn a vibrant, iridescent green. As they started glowing, she smirked at her reflection, lifting the hoodie up over her head. Jane turned, walked out of the bathroom, and left the station, ignoring the voices of her uncles calling out to her. She had work to do.

NEVER, NEVER

ABOUT THE AUTHOR

Liz Butcher resides in Australia, with her husband, daughter, and their three cats. She's a self-confessed nerd with a BA in psychology and an insatiable fascination for learning. Liz has published a number of short stories in anthologies and has released her own collection, After Dark, in 2018. Her debut novel, Fates' Fury released September 2019, soon followed with LeRoux Manor in September 2020.

You can follow her at any of the below links:

Website: https://lizbutcherauthor.com.au
Twitter: https://twitter.com/lunaloveliz
Instagram: https://www.instagram.com/lunaloveliz/
___Tiktok: @lunaloveliz
Facebook:https://www.facebook.com/Liz-Butcher-1394868604152823/
Goodreads: https://www.goodreads.com/author/show/13845425.Liz_Butcher
Pinterest: https://www.pinterest.com.au/lizbutcherauthor/
Amazon: http://www.amazon.com/-/e/B00X6XN5O6

FATES' FURY

The last thing Jonah Sands expected on his thirtieth birthday was to have his life thrust into the hands of a dangerous, red-haired woman—or to be the only person in the world to survive an encounter with her. As the death toll skyrockets, Jonah and his two best friends, the siblings Tristan and Ava Carter, find themselves at the epicentre of inexplicable phenomena—a stranded ferry transforms into a barge headed for the Underworld; young girls levitate to whisper ancient riddles; technology across the globe is controlled by some unseen hand. And it all seems to lead back to the woman with red hair. When a stranger finds them in the midst of a thunder storm and offers his otherworldly assistance, Jonah finally unravels the truth about who he really is. And what it means for the rest of humanity.

REVIEWS FOR FATES' FURY

"...This novel is an impressive and ambitious undertaking in the "Modern Myth" genre. The author has woven together many threads from ancient mythology-the heroic journey, diverse pantheons of gods, prophecy, and fate-into a tale of world domination in the present time. Overall, the writing is excellent with lively descriptions and crisp action. Definitely a highly recommended book for lovers of mythology and fantasy in general." A. Wang.

"...The Fates have come to town, and they are pissed. Jonah Sands finds his life turned upside down as he and his friends become entangled in the battle to save humanity from the rage of the Fates. Fates' Fury is an action-packed tale that weaves modern-day Brisbane Australia with ancient mythologies from around the world and will keep you turning pages furiously as the truth of who Jonah truly is unfolds before him and changes his life, and the world, forever." C. Milton.

"...Fate's Fury is a gripping, 'edge of your seat' fantasy, filled with intrigue, mystery & a touch of romance. Throw in 3 young friends, gods from Greek mythology, ancient Egypt, Hades and Indian culture and you have a modern-day apocalyptic situation where the very survival of mankind is threatened by the beautiful but deadly trio of Fates. Strap yourself in for a wild ride that will take you on a journey that gets more and more addictive as you turn each page towards the nail-biting climax. 10 out of 10 for author Liz Butcher, a fantastic read!" A. Lewis.

LEROUX MANOR

Camille's father just inherited the family manor from his estranged uncle, forcing her to leave her friends and city life just before her senior year of high school for the small town of Woodville, England. After seeing a strange old woman lurking on the estate grounds, she embarks on a mission to uncover the history of her new home. What she finds is wilder than she could have imagined—the murder of her ancestor, Caleb LeRoux, on the same day his six-year-old daughter vanished without a trace. And an unforeseen connection to Camille herself, as the only female LeRoux born to the family in over two hundred years. With the help of her new school friends, Camille delves into the secrets of the manor, uncovering an all-encompassing truth that will change the entire course of her life—past, present, and future.

REVIEWS FOR LEROUX MANOR

"...A powerful, gripping YA Horror novel like no other, author Liz Butcher has established a wonderful tale in "LeRoux Manor". Blending the great atmospheric nature of a good Gothic horror novel with the modern-day mystery and suspense element made this story shine, and the shocking final chapter will leave readers reeling as the story concludes." A. Avina.

"...Absolute page turner! Liz has done it again with this beautifully written tale. She sets the eerie tone beautifully; you can almost hear the creaking hinges. This book had me saying 'just one more chapter' repeatedly before bed, to find out what twist Camille will stumble upon next." C. Milton

"...Liz manages to grasp the reader's attention with a telling Prologue that offers the nidus for the strange tale. Liz paces this novel very well indeed. As with her other stories Liz impresses as an obviously gifted artist who knows how to blend human drama with horror. Very highly recommended." G. Harp.